ARCHER'S IRISH JIG

*To my long-time friend, Audrey – a constructive critic
and, through marriage, a confirmed Hibernophile!*

Also by Colin Eston

Saint and Czinner mysteries

Dying for Love
The Dusk Messenger
The Pepys Memorandum
The Seed of Osiris

Will Archer mysteries

Archer Bows In

COLIN ESTON

Archer's Irish Jig

The second *Will Archer* mystery

1

...the land of the shadow of death...

'There - over to the middle. Keep her out, Patrick, the tide runs strong here.'

The moonlight path across the brown river is momentarily fractured. For a slow second a dark shape rolls across it, shivering splinters of light across the sluggish swell. Then it is gone and the silver path glitters whole once more on the dark waters.

A boat, dirty and disreputable, floats on the Liffey. In it, two figures. One squat and ragged, the other slight and youthful, pulling on the oars.

'Steady now, or we'll lose him.'

It is the older man who speaks, his body twisted as he peers through the darkness, searching for the shape to roll once more on the swell.

Slowly, the skiff skirts the silvered path, an oar occasionally catching the moonlight, sending glittering shards skittering over the surface. The older man holds aloft a lantern by whose feeble light he scans the dark river.

Marked by the steady dip of oars, seconds stretch into minutes. The silence of night, broken only by the slap of water against the bow, the faint distant screech of a night bird, wraps itself about them.

Then, suddenly, all is action. The older man lunges for a boat-hook and reaches over the side, fishing for a solid shadow in the

5

darkness. With much grunting, he drags his catch alongside. Patrick ships oars and jams his feet against the side thwarts, straddling the precariously rocking boat, steadying it against his father's hauling.

Both have done this before. Their actions have the efficiency of habit as they heave their catch over the stern.

A few minutes and they have the reclaimed object lashed tight.

Then, 'Pull for the shore, boyo,' growls the older man hoarsely.

The youngster needs no second bidding. Unshipping his oars he sets out with a will.

'A fresh-un, da?' he asks once he has got into his stroke.

His father holds his lantern aloft. 'Fresh enough. A few scrapes where the tide's took 'im, but he's not been in the water long. No more'n a dozen hours I'd reckon.'

'Pickings?'

'I doubt it. He looks no more'n a middling sort. We'll see as soon as we gets him ashore.'

With one hand laid proprietorially upon the corpse and the other upon the rudder, the older man settles back into his seat at the stern while Patrick pulls strongly for the shore and the buildings of Dublin loom from the darkness.

2

...full of heaviness...

'Done a'puking yet?

Charlie's face hovers over me. Scant sympathy – just a grin from ear to ear.

'My, but you look green still.'

He's munching on a pie. Crumbs of pastry fall on my cheeks and the rich aroma of gravy makes my gorge rise. I push him away, feeling my guts rebel. They rumble but, with nothing left to spew, all I manage is a dry retching.

'Careful!' He jumps back. 'This pie's the business – prime Irish beef.'

My voice comes faint. 'Well keep it out of range, then.'

With an effort, I raise myself on one elbow. Through the ache which holds my head in a vice, I dimly recall a journey.

A bright spring morning in London, Mr Garrick handing Mrs Woffington into the coach whilst Charlie and I clamber up atop. Two days of incessant rumble of iron-clad wheels, the clatter of hooves and cold air scorching our numbed faces as the Stage bumps along the turnpike road to Holyhead.

New territory to Charlie and myself.

I travelled from Yorkshire to London when I was not much older than he is now – though to a far less certain destination - and it is only a matter of weeks since I rode pell-mell in pursuit of a murderer to Gravesend. But westwards is new to me – and Charlie has never left the streets of London till now.

I hardly forbear smiling at his wide eyes and mouth agape at all the sights betwixt London and Birmingham, nor his bewilderment on hearing the mumbled, mangled vowels of the speech native to those parts when we arrive at the Hen and Chickens in High Town where we lodge overnight to change horses after our first day's travel.

Next day I, too, am equally amazed as we climb and snake our way amongst the Welsh mountains. Such natural grandeur, with snow still on the peaks!

But of our sea passage from England I recall little. Only the sight of flying spume over the rail and the heaving of the contents of my stomach into the churning water.

Blearily, I look around me. I am on a chaise in a strange room. Of course, this must be our new Irish lodgings!

We are in Dublin where Mr Garrick has been asked by Mr Tom Sheridan to appear at the Smock Alley Theatre.

Mrs Peg Woffington accompanies him. Being Irish born and bred, she is no stranger to this country, having made her name on the stage here in Dublin before coming to London. She is both Mr Garrick's fellow actor and, of late, companion of a more intimate nature.

My own presence here is not so much as a member of his company (though I may perhaps be called to play an occasional minor role) but as Mr Garrick's servant-cum-valet.

I am also here, less willingly, at the behest of Sir William Hervey, head of Mr Walpole's secret service. He hinted, before we left London, that he might require some service of me, the nature of which has not yet been revealed – and which, now I am recovered from my present indisposition, I am not over-eager to discover.

And Charlie? He is here because Mrs Wiggins, our cook-housekeeper back in London, refused to have him under her feet while she and Susan (maid of all work – and my frequent companion in amorous dalliance) pack up Mr Garrick's belongings at his present London lodgings and move, during our absence, to the house he has taken in Bow Street for our return.

Besides, the young wretch has become like a little brother to me and would pine in my absence so I, too, prevailed upon Mr Garrick to bring him along, citing his usefulness at errands and the cheapness of his keep.

Now, judging by the way he's scoffing this malodorous pie, young Charlie Stubbs, twelve going on thirteen, seems to have suffered none of the ill effects of the sea voyage that have laid me so low!

Slowly I put my feet to the floor and unsteadily ease myself into sitting position.

Charlie, in between mouthfuls, grins encouragement.

'Steady as you go, Will. You look no better'n a dead'un.'

I catch sight of myself in a mirror on the wall and see the truth of his observation.

I am a spectre, my face the colour of old porridge, my eyes like smudged thumb-prints.

'Here,' says Charlie, 'put your arm around my shoulders and lean on me. Mr Garrick says to bring you to him as soon as you're *compos mentis* again.'

Much as I'd welcome his support, I decline the offer, reluctant to show a weakness which the scamp is hardly likely to let me forget.

Instead, gathering all my resources, I totter towards the door.

Charlie clicks his tongue and, with a dismissive hoist of eyebrow, trots before me down two flights of stairs while I stagger after.

As I tread gingerly, I take note of my new surroundings. As with the attic room I woke up in, the rest of the house is both like and yet unlike our lodgings back in London. Similar in layout and decoration, but here every surface is bedecked with some ornament or gewgaw, with no curtain or hanging lacking a frill or furbelow.

Arriving at a door in the lower hallway, Charlie cocks a thumb and mutters greasily, 'In 'ere.' Then, applying himself to the remnant of his pie, he disappears along the corridor, leaving me to knock and enter.

I find Mr Garrick in conversation with a lady of middling years, dressed in black.

'Ah, Will, my boy. You are up and about.'

He jumps to his feet, beaming, and the lady turns also. She is older than I first thought, perhaps in her fifties. Under her neat cap, her hair, once auburn is now bleaching to pale gold. Her expression is polite, but her eyes are attentive as she allows a questioning smile to play about her lips.

Garrick brings me forward. 'Allow me to introduce our landlady, Will. Mrs Fitzgerald, this is my young friend Will Archer.'

I bow as far as my light-headedness permits. 'Ma'am.'

The lady inclines her head. 'Master Archer. You are, I hope, recovered from your indisposition?' Her accent bears no trace of Irish, merely over-refined English gentility.

'Indeed, ma'am, my spirits are much restored, I thank you.'

'The sea-crossing can be a sore trial for those of a delicate disposition. I have essayed it but twice or thrice. My late husband's business, however, required frequent journeys and I never knew his temper to be improved by the ordeal.'

'Mrs Fitzgerald is but recently widowed, Will,' says Mr Garrick, 'and, sensible of the loss of company, has graciously offered the use of her house for the duration of our stay in Dublin.'

Her black attire is now explained. I express my condolences for her loss. 'Your late husband was in business, ma'am?'

'A haberdasher, sir, to ladies of quality. A position of some repute which, you must appreciate, gave us a certain *cachet* amongst people of note. We had attained, I may say, a position in society, but the nature of his recent and importunate demise...' Unable to continue, she dabs a black lace handkerchief to her nose.

'Please, madam,' says Garrick, 'do not distress yourself.'

But the lady is not to be distracted. Crumpling the flimsy lace in her fist, she continues, her voice quivering with righteous indignation. 'He was cruelly cut down, sir, while defending our property against Irish ruffians who seek only destruction and riot! Trampled by a mob of factional apprentice boys, he was. We English try to civilise them, but it would seem the ignorant bog-dwellers do not wish to be civilised. They run amok like savages at every week's end...'

Perhaps sensing her lady-like refinement slipping, she blows her nose and continues in gentler manner, 'As I was saying, gentlemen, my late husband and I maintained a position in society, but opportunities for such polite discourse in my widowed state are, alas, sadly limited.'

'A deficiency,' says my master somewhat over-heartily, 'which I am sure we may hope to rectify, I'm sure, during the coming months. Now, if you would excuse us, ma'am?'

Mrs Fitzgerald curtseys low to Mr Garrick and, with nice distinction for my humbler status, condescends a mere inclination of her head in my direction as she graciously departs.

Garrick utters a sigh of exasperation. 'That woman! How are we to bear it, Will? We are here for two months or more!'

'She is but newly widowed, sir,' I try in mitigation.

'And with little regret, other than his passing robs her of her position in society! I cannot but think him in a better place, away from her simpering affectation.'

'For one who lives in Dublin, she seems to hold her fellow countrymen in low regard?'

'That is because she is not Irish, Will.'

'Not Irish? I thought her refinement of speech was merely put on for our benefit?'

'Doubtless it was, Will, but her origins, I would hazard, are more Cockney than Celt. In common with most of the merchant and ruling class in this country, she is as English as you or I... and so damnably pretentious!'

12

I cannot help but laugh at my master's irritation. 'We will not be much in her company, surely? Our days will be spent at the theatre ...'

'To be sure. Mistress Peg is even now at Smock Alley, renewing old acquaintance.'

'And Ned and Kitty, are they arrived?'

'A week ago.'

Members of our company at the ill fated Goodmans Fields theatre, Ned Phillimore and Kitty Blair were the first to tell me they had been invited to Ireland for the season.

It is but three months since our company was obliged to disperse due to the jealousy of Mr Fleetwood at Drury Lane and Mr Rich at Covent Garden who, seeing their own receipts suffering from the success of my master's performances at Goodmans Fields contrived to have the Lord Chamberlain shut us down.

But now, by good fortune, Ned, Kitty, Mr Garrick and Mrs Woffington are reunited for a season at the Smock Alley Theatre, here in Dublin, at the request of Mr Thomas Sheridan where one of the highlights of the season is to be Mr Garrick's *Hamlet*.

'We shall be much occupied, sir,' I say, hoping still to take his mind off our importunate landlady.

'Indeed we shall.' Suddenly his face clouds and he takes me by the shoulder. 'But are you sure, Will, that you are fully recovered? You look pale still.'

I essay a smile. 'Nothing that a visit to Mrs Wiggins's kitchen would not cure, sir.'

So much recovered are my spirits after talking with my master that even the remembered smell of Charlie's pie which nauseated me only minutes ago now stirs only hunger. Not to mention a faint stirring adjacent to my belly at the alternative delights offered by Susan in that same kitchen... my appetites, I am grateful to note, have not been totally vanquished by the sea voyage!

Mr Garrick claps me upon the shoulder. 'Alas, the redoubtable Mrs W is still in London. We must see what Mrs Fitzgerald's cook can do! But then you must needs consume it on the hoof for I have arranged to meet Mr Sheridan at Aungier Street and it would not do to be late.'

Thus it is that, a few minutes later, having collected both Charlie and another slice of beef pie for myself, we all three set out into the crisp Spring air of Dublin.

Already I feel the colour returning to my cheeks.

There is a hint of rain in the air as Mr Garrick, Charlie and myself set out for the Smock Alley Theatre. No-one, says Mr Garrick, comes to Dublin with the expectation of fine weather. But this morning the sun is doing its best in a watery blue sky as we turn from Mrs Fitzgerald's lodgings in Lamb Alley and head towards the River Liffey, whose stink is thankfully masked by the aroma of the pie in my fist.

But there is another smell here on the southern side of the river - the smell of money. Wherever you turn, demolition and construction is all around as the haphazard streets of the mediaeval city are being flattened to make way for fine, wide new thoroughfares.

Ahead is Dame Street, Mr Garrick tells us, which is to link the Castle with the new City Hall. 'Wealthy merchants having an eye to their security, are creating a swift pathway for the soldiery in case of riot,' says he as we pass by the Castle.

If this edifice acts as a barracks it has certainly seen better days. One glance at its towers shows them to be crumbling and in a sad state of disrepair.

The imposing new facades of Dame Street, in contrast, bear witness to the burgeoning power of commerce.

But our route does not take us far into Dame Street. After only a few hundred yards, we turn off once more towards the river.

The Smock Alley Theatre is newer than I expected and as soon as we enter, Mrs Woffington descends upon us. 'Davey, where have you been? Mr Sheridan and I had almost given up hope of your arrival.'

Mr Garrick brings me forward. 'Will, allow me to introduce Tom Sheridan. His reputation here in Dublin eclipses mine in London. His *Richard III* puts mine to shame.'

A pleasant young man, no more than three and twenty, proffers his hand. A high forehead and prominent nose and a mouth whose habitual expression seems set in a smile. He is soberly dressed in black, with a plain white cravat. His hair, like mine, is this morning tied in a simple queue.

'Take no heed of my friend Garrick's exaggerations, Master Archer,' he says with a laugh. 'None, least of all myself, would claim such eminence as he. And you, too, I hear, have a talent as a solver of mysteries?'

I feel myself blushing. 'No talent, sir,' I stammer. 'More stubborn curiosity.'

'Well, then,' says he, clasping my hand with great good

humour, 'I hope that our fair city provides you with ample scope for the satisfaction of that curiosity!'

Certainly it will, if Sir William Hervey has any say in the matter. But that is a subject I do not care to dwell on.

Instead I ask him about the newness of the theatre.

'Indeed,' he informs me, 'there has been a theatre here since good King Charles's time. The acoustics were reputed excellent, but the same could not be said of the ground on which it is built! It has collapsed no less than three times, most recently in 1734.'

'And you rebuilt it?'

'Not I, Master Archer,' he replies. 'I have not the means. No, it was the city authorities, seven years ago. It is bigger – they are men of business and want value for their money! But essentially the original form was preserved.'

I glance around - the proscenium stage, the pit, boxes and upper and lower galleries with a loft for the orchestra – much the same as Goodmans Fields back in London, but larger.

'So, yes,' continues Mr Sheridan, 'the theatre you stand in today is relatively new. But it has a venerable history nonetheless. And I can vouch, from my own experience, that its acoustics are still excellent! Now, by your leave, I have surprise in store for you all.'

'A pleasant one I hope,' says Mrs Peg with a coy smile.

'I trust so. We have been invited to sit in on a rehearsal for Mr Handel's new work at the Great Music Hall, round the corner in Fishamble Street.'

'A new work?' says Garrick with interest.

'A grand oratorio, by all accounts, never before performed.

'Tis a great honour for Dublin, that its first performance should be here. Mrs Cibber is to sing the contralto role.'

'Susannah?' exclaims Mrs Peg. 'She is here, in Dublin?'

'Indeed, she sang in the second series of concerts of Mr Handel's works this last winter,' confirms Sheridan. 'She and Mrs Avoglio, the soprano, were the talk of the town. Their performance in this new work is a source of much speculation and anticipation. But come, we must make haste. Mr Handel, by all accounts, is unforgiving to latecomers.'

Throughout all this, Charlie has been a model of reticence. But now, as we emerge once more into the fresh morning air, he mutters peevishly, 'Powdered ladies a-wailing! Lawks, the mornin' just gets better!'

Fortunately it is only I who hears him.

3

...nations so furiously rage together...

As we walk, Mr Sheridan acquaints us with the history of the Music Hall.

'Built only last year through Mr Neal's kind offices...'

Mr Neal, it transpires, is the landlord of the *Bull's Head* next door to the new hall.

One of the most popular and well-known establishments in Dublin, the *Bull's Head* is much in demand for anniversary and celebratory dinners by the various city guilds and bodies. The Bull's Head Musical Society has undertaken the building of the Music Hall to provide a more congenial and spacious resort for events of this nature.

Mr Handel's new work, Sheridan tells us, has caused so much interest that gentlemen have been asked to attend without their swords and ladies without hoops in their dresses in order that the maximum number may be accommodated.

And, indeed, the approach to the building does seem somewhat restricted. All but hidden behind the towering four storey iron works of Kennan and Son it is accessed through a small fenced yard leading to an arched double door within a plain white facade, the main feature of which is a large square window of sixteen glass panes.

Already, from inside come stray fragments of sound, lowings and trills of woodwind, shivers of strings as the orchestra tunes

18

up. A group of choirboys pushes giggling past us as we enter.

'The choirs from St Patrick's and Christ Church Cathedrals,' says Mr Sheridan, flattening himself against the wall and waving them along. 'Sixteen men and sixteen boy choristers. The largest ensemble of voices ever seen. 'Twill be a magnificent sound indeed!'

Inside the hall, all seems chaos. Choirboys mill and chatter as they are herded ineffectually by a lean young man in black.

At the far end of the hall a scattering of musicians shuffle sheets of music and test their instruments. Strings are plucked, pegs tightened, trumpets and recorders poked with cloths wound about sticks. Then sawing and blowing snatches of tune and shaking of heads followed by more tweaking of pegs and prodding.

'What an infernal row!' mutters Charlie.

'Infernal now, lad,' laughs Mr Garrick, 'but once brought to order, trust me 'twill be a heavenly harmony.'

Charlie is unconvinced as we take unobtrusive seats near the back of the hall where several clusters of spectators already sit, for this is one of several public rehearsals designed to whet interest in and spread the word about the forthcoming event. Mrs Peg sits between Sheridan and Mr Garrick, Charlie and myself at a little distance.

As we await the arrival of Mr Handel, I count the number of musicians. Here, too is a fine assemblage, no less than twenty. Only the harpsichord stands empty, awaiting the maestro.

And that deficiency is soon remedied, for Mr Handel himself, elegant and portly in full bottomed wig makes his appearance accompanied by various similarly grandiose individuals.

His companions sit in chairs reserved for them near the front. To my left, I hear Mr Sheridan whispering names to Mr Garrick. These are evidently representatives of the charitable institutions for the sick and the society for prisoner's debt relief that are to benefit from the performance.

Soon Mr Handel has brought the unruly masses to order. But all is apparently not well.

'Mr Acres, my second violin,' he growls irritably, 'where is he?' His voice still bears traces of his German origin.

A meek man rises, clutching his violin, 'I regret, sir, he is not here. Noting his absence, I sent to his lodgings to enquire of him.'

'Is he unwell?'

'Alas, sir, I am unable to say. It appears that no-one has seen him since two nights ago when he left rehearsal.'

Mr Handel's face turns puce. 'Verdammt! But a week before the performance and he deserts us! Scheissekopf!'

The first violinist, already pale, goes ghostly white. His violin visibly trembles. 'Herr Handel, sir... please, language - there are ladies present.' Then, as the great man seems on the point of exploding again, 'I shall see to it that if Mr Acres cannot be found, a replacement will be sought for tomorrow...'

'*Tomorrow!* And what of *today*?'

Mr Handel glowers in anticipation. I sense the embarrassment of those around me. The violin player, at a loss for words, mouths helpless as a stranded fish into the growing silence.

Then, like a stone dropping into water, the silence is suddenly broken.

'Perhaps I can be of assistance?' The voice, broad Irish, comes from the back of the hall, to our right. 'I happen to have my instrument with me.'

All heads swivel to regard the speaker who raises aloft a battered violin case.

Handel, too, peers in the direction of the interruption. 'You are a violinist, sir?'

'A fiddler, to be sure, and some would say of no mean competence.'

'Are you able to con musical notation?'

'That I am. As easy as a babby sucks milk.'

'Then come forward, sir.'

Amongst the audience there is a buzz of chatter as all eyes follow the fresh faced young man with a shock of bright red hair as he rises jauntily from the back of the hall and strides towards the front. The other members of the orchestra show equal consternation.

'But, sir - Herr Handel...' The first violinist reaches out and almost has the temerity to touch the great man's sleeve. 'This cannot be - the man is - *Irish!*'

Handel turns a stony gaze upon him. 'Ja, dummkopf and we are in Ireland, are we not? Why should an Irishman not play as well as an Englishman - or even,' he continued with a malicious glint in his eye, 'a *German*? Perhaps, Mr Russell, you think I should not be here either, ist das so?'

Russell, mortified, slinks meekly to his chair.

'Sit there, Mr...?'

'Kelly, sir,' replies the red head.

'Gut, Mr Kelly - there beside Mr Russell. You will show us how you can play today and if I find you satisfactory, the job is yours.' The great man grins wolfishly at Russell, whose face is thunderous, but who utters not a word.

The newcomer sits cheerily beside a simmering Mr Russell. 'Thank you, sir. I'll not disappoint.' Then, without more ado, he unpacks his violin and sets to studying the sheets of music before him.

This unexpected drama has cheered Charlie. 'Sandy pate's a rum duke, eh Will? Cheek of old Nick on him. D'you think he'll do it?'

'Who knows? But at least Mr Handel is prepared to give him the chance.'

Mr Handel himself now addresses his audience, telling us that we are yet in the early stages of rehearsal, that there may be halts and repetitions during the day and we must not expect a fully formed work to come springing forth.

It strikes me that music is not unlike a play in this respect. I have seen how hard Mr Garrick strives to achieve his much-vaunted 'natural' style. I now realise that notes, like lines, must be conned, different phrasing tried out before, in the end, both melody and character emerge in a form which is seemingly effortless.

I don't hear all Mr Handel says, however, for Mr Sheridan leans across to me. 'Here, Master Archer, in the strange disappearance of this unfortunate musician, may be the first test of your skills.'

'How mean you, sir?'

'Does it not pique your curiosity? This mystery of the missing violinist. I know the fellow slightly. He has played on occasions for productions at Smock Alley. And now it seems he has vanished without trace. As far as I know, he is reserved and of good character, not at all the sort to absent himself deliberately in this manner. I fear some harm may have befallen him and would be glad to have the matter resolved.'

What can I say? I have been in Ireland but a day and a half. My head is still light from sea-sickness, my stomach empty of all but the thin slice of pie grudgingly given by Mrs Fitzgerald's cook. I hardly have either the physical or mental resources for investigation. Nor any knowledge of the country, the people or their ways.

Yet Mr Sheridan is right. My curiosity is roused. Perhaps after the rehearsal is concluded, with Mr Sheridan to smooth the way, I may mingle with the musicians and find out more.

But now, as Mr Handel seats himself at the keyboard and raises his arm, an expectant hush falls. The string players raise their instruments and, at a sign from the maestro, the air is filled with a stately series of chords. Like someone thoughtfully pacing it proceeds before brightening into an almost joyful march rhythm.

Beside me, Charlie sits open mouthed in wonder that such sound can come from the chaos of instruments which filled the hall with clamour only a few minutes ago.

Then one of the men from the choir stands, the music pauses and he begins to sing in a clear tenor voice, 'Comfort ye, comfort ye my people...'

I recognise the text from the Bible. It is Isaiah 40, verses 1-3, one of the many passages that the Rev Purselove had me learn by heart back in Yorkshire when I was but a boy.

The thought of Rev Purselove sends a cold shiver down my spine. I have no reason to remember him with any degree of kindness. It was he who under the guise of charity to my poor mother undertook to educate me after my father lost all in the South Sea calamity and took his own life.

But the education he gave me went further than the study of books and numbers. In my innocence I thought nothing of it when he first touched me. The friendly arm about my shoulders as we knelt together in prayer. Even his hand caressing my neck then wandering as if by chance over my buttock, my thigh... these engendered only puzzled surprise. I was, after all, only a seven year old boy - and he a man of the cloth.

But then came the inevitable unlacing of my breeches, the laboured breathing, the almost apologetic imploring smile as he fondled and took me in his mouth... I was still a child and, though I felt unease, had no understanding. Each time I endured it obediently as his face grew more rubicund, his hand in his own breeches more frantic until, with a final gasp, he deflated like a stuck bladder.

At every week's end, prior to his composing his sermon for the coming sabbath, this regular ritual concluded with us kneeling together to ask forgiveness for our sins. Mildly bewildered, I put it down to the idiosyncrasy of adults in general and of clergymen in particular.

The real shock only came as I approached fourteen and grew too old for his tastes. He persuaded my unsuspecting mother that I should seek my fortune in London, where he knew a lady who would take me in. The 'lady' turned out to be Mother Ransom, keeper of a molly house where she made me the plaything of sodomites until fortune engineered my release.

Passages from the Bible, therefore, bring me little solace. Rather memories that I would fain forget. Yet the majesty of Mr Handel's music is such that by the time another of the choir, a bass this time, sings 'The people that walked in darkness have seen a great light; and they that dwell in the land of the shadow of death, upon them hath the light shined,' I cannot but think that it is of me he sings. I have walked in darkness and Mr Garrick has been my light.

Thus affected, I brush an unwonted dampness from my eye, glancing aside at Charlie in the hope that he has not noticed. But he is rapt in the music and when, several minutes later, Mr Handel calls for a pause, he turns to me. 'I know this story,' he babbles excitedly, 'the baby in the stable, the shepherds - 'tis the baby Jesus.'

How Charlie, who was abandoned as an infant to fend for himself on the streets of London, has heard the gospel story I know not but his eyes are aglow.

'Aye, lad,' say I, ruffling his hair affectionately, 'and thinking on a child born in a humble stable should make us count our own blessings.'

Beside me, Mr Garrick, Mrs Peg and Mr Sheridan have risen.

'Here,' says Mr Sheridan, 'may be an opportunity to start your inquiries, Master Archer. Mr Handel has called a pause to proceedings that the musicians might take some refreshment. Now might be an opportune moment to engage one or two in conversation.'

As we speak, Mr Garrick and Mrs Peg make their way across to Mr Handel who greets them warmly and begins to introduce them to the representatives of the charities who will benefit from the forthcoming performance.

Choirboys are being shepherded by their choirmaster towards a formidable woman in black bombazine. She marshals two timid looking servant girls bearing what appears to be a soup tureen.

The senior choristers and musicians, meanwhile, are dispersing.

'They will be going to the *Bull's Head* next door,' says Mr Sheridan. 'Shall we join them?'

But my eye has been caught by the red-haired Irishman with the violin.

'I shall join you in a moment, sir, if I may. First, I would offer my congratulations to the young man over there.'

Mr Sheridan raises a sceptical eyebrow. 'Be not surprised if he scorns your compliments, Master Archer. He may not take kindly to your accent.'

'I shall rely then upon the proximity of our ages as proof that I intend no condescension.'

'Very well,' says Mr Sheridan. 'I see that Mr Garrick and Mrs Woffington are engaged with Mr Handel for the present.' He glances at Charlie. 'By your leave, I shall take the lad across to Sister Mary Catherine and see if her charity extends to feeding yet another young heathen! I shall see you anon at the *Bull's Head*.'

The red-haired young man is in conversation with another

whose coat, like his, though faded and worn at elbow, is neat. His hair, of a slightly darker shade than the violinist, is tied in a simple queue. They are, I guess, apprentices or journeymen and, from a certain similarity in their features, perhaps brothers.

At my approach they fall silent, their eyes wary.

I incline my head. 'Will Archer, newly arrived in Dublin with Mr David Garrick who is to perform with Mr Sheridan's company at the Smock Alley Theatre.'

The names provoke recognition and a flicker of interest but little thawing of hostility.

'An Englishman,' sneers the companion. 'What business may you have with us, sir?'

I address myself to the violinist. 'I would offer my congratulations, sir.'

A half smile curves his lip. 'Congratulations upon what, Mr Will Archer - my playing? Or my impudence?'

'The skill of your performance was ample justification for your boldness.'

'Oh-ho, Mr Will Archer! Such silver-tongued flattery from one so young!'

'No flattery, and not so much younger than yourself, sir. I am near twenty years old and you, I hazard, are not much older?'

He regards me narrowly. 'Indeed, twenty-two this last month.' He extends his hand which I take. 'Finn Kelly. I thank you for your kind words. For all you be English, I believe them to be genuine.'

'I am a Yorkshireman and used to speaking my mind, Mr Kelly. I cannot see how Mr Handel will refuse to employ you.'

'Then you know little of Ireland,' grumbles his companion.

'Forgive my brother's surliness, Master Archer. Come, Sean, Will here has been open in his praise. It is only fitting that we respond in kind.'

Sean offers grudging acknowledgement. 'Kind words are welcome, Englishman, but they butter no parsnips. His preferment lies not in your approval.'

'True, sir. It lies with Mr Handel. And he is neither Irish nor English, but German. Should he be satisfied I doubt not he will have his way, 'spite of all Mr Russell's tutting.'

'Master Archer is right, Sean,' says Finn Kelly. 'It is up to me to impress, which, if my luck hold, shall not be so difficult.'

'Luck has served you well so far,' say I. 'Fortune herself must have decreed you be here - and your violin with you - on the very day Mr Handel finds himself in need of a violinist! An uncommon stroke of luck for all concerned.'

'All?' says Sean. 'You include the poor devil whose place Finn may take? An Englishman replaced by this rascally bog-trotter...' he laughs, ruffling his brother's hair. 'Long may he continue absent, eh brother?'

Finn looks grave. 'My brother's youth must excuse his levity, Master Archer. That any supposed fortune of mine should depend upon another's misfortune is not an agreeable situation, but if it be God's will...'

'Nay, brother, do not bring God into it. We make our own fortune, you and I. You can fiddle as well as those English popinjays - and to be sure you have as much right to be up there with them in this, our own country. They are the usurpers, are they not?'

'Peace, Sean!' says Finn urgently. He looks around the hall. 'Such talk is folly. Pay no heed to my brother, Master Archer. Though he is of an age with you, he lacks your discretion.'

'I own I am yet green in the ways of this country,' say I. 'Yet though I have not been here above a day or so, I already sense a disquiet that exists between our two peoples...'

Sean lets out a bark of a laugh. 'Ha! Nicely put, Will Archer! That's discretion indeed! *Disquiet!* A fine word for the centuries of oppression we have suffered to become a mere colony of you English! You steal our land and rent it back to us. You appropriate all profit from our labour. Stop us observing the true religion and deny us to power to govern ourselves. Is it, then, any wonder that there is *disquiet* between us?'

His raised voice has drawn enquiring looks from those few who remain in the hall. Finn attempts to quiet him, but Sean's ire is not to be quenched. He pushes aside his brother's arm and turns on the onlookers. 'Aye, look, why don't you! Gach tú damanta Béarla! Take your fill of the wild Irishman!'

Finn abandons all attempts at polite restraint. He thrusts the violin case at me and seizes his brother's arm, hissing at him as he bundles out of the hall, 'You fool, Sean. Would you mar all?'

Even out in the open air, Sean continues to struggle.

Finn cuffs him violently several times, berating him in Irish. 'Tá tú bastaird dúr! Fós do theanga!'

Under the rain of blows, Sean eventually subsides, cowering.

White-faced, Finn grips his brother's shoulders. Fighting to control his own anger he brings his face close to Sean's and says

29

through gritted teeth. 'Enough! Now I have got this far, you would have me go no further? Is that it? You would prove our uncouthness to all those who accuse us of it?' He pushes him away and turns to me. 'What sort of brother is this, Will, who aborts with his unruly tongue my little success ere it be half-formed?'

'Had I a brother, I would look for kinder usage certainly,' I reply. 'But we may be thankful that no-one of influence witnessed the outburst. Your reputation with Mr Handel, I think, is safe.'

Finn clasps my hand. 'I thank you, Will - I may call you Will, may I not? You cannot know what comfort I have from your words. Would my brother was more like you - with less passion and more reason!'

I hand him back his violin. 'That reason, sir, is hard-won. I do not lack passion - it is an admirable quality, Finn, as your playing proves. But I have found that, like a skittish horse, it needs a tight rein.'

His eyes look deep into mine. 'Not yet twenty and such wisdom...?'

I lower my gaze, nonplussed. I have neither time nor inclination to tell of the events of the last few months which have made that wisdom so hard-won - my infatuation for Agnes Mayer who so very nearly proved my nemesis.

Instead I take my leave, pleading my appointment with Mr Sheridan in the *Bull's Head.*

4

...a man of sorrows...

The *Bull's Head* next door to the Music Hall in Fishamble Street is, like most of the neighbouring properties, a building of several storeys.

The entrance is unprepossessing enough - no more than a doorway that might belong to any domestic dwelling. It opens into a dim room, the air thick with the warm, sweaty reek of bodies, pipe smoke and the smell of spirits. Like many of the rougher London establishments there is no furniture. Real men drink standing - when they cannot stand, they reason, it is time to stop drinking. With the hands of the clock hardly past two in the afternoon, most here are still upright though a few are already leaning upon the bar at the far side of the room or, failing that, an accommodating neighbour's shoulder.

All eyes turn upon me as I enter and the hum of conversation is stilled. Foreigners, it seems, are instantly recognisable - by what secret instinct I know not, for there is nothing outlandish in my dress or appearance as far as I can tell - and I have not yet opened my mouth to speak.

Behind the bar, a stout, ruddy faced fellow, clad in a long apron looks up, alerted by the sudden hush. Squinting through the fume, he sees me hesitating at the entrance and jerks his thumb in the direction of an inner door at the left side of the room.

Can this be the landlord, Mr Neal? His stony expression and

curt manner hardly accord with the beneficent patron of the *Bull's Head* Musical Society who has built the Music Hall and of whom Tom Sheridan spoke so respectfully.

Seeing me waver still, he growls, 'Upstairs, the function room.' Then mutters something in Irish that elicits a guffaw from the assembled throng. I redden, feeling myself literally the butt of some joke as I am propelled through the room with hearty slaps on the back and not altogether friendly verbal encouragement.

I am relieved to reach the sanctuary of the stairs and take my time ascending them, allowing time for my thudding heart to steady.

The upper room seems bigger. A window stretches almost the whole width of one wall, the assembled company is more civil and no pall of smoke and sweat clouds the air. The centre of the room is occupied by a table on which are the remains of several platters of food whilst lesser tables and numerous chairs and stools are dispersed about the margins.

At one of these sits Mr Handel, together with my master and Mrs Peg and two other ladies whom I recognise as the soloists, Mrs Susannah Cibber and Signora Avoglio. Tom Sheridan stands with them, but of the charitable beneficiaries there is no sign. They are, perhaps, not returning for the afternoon rehearsal.

As soon as he sees me, Mr Sheridan excuses himself from the ladies and comes over. 'Ah, Will, there you are.' He leads me to the central table. 'You must be ready for this. Come, eat your fill.'

Indeed, at sight of the repast, depleted as it is, my stomach sets up a low growling of anticipation. This morning's thin slice of beef pie has only served to whet my recovering appetite.

No sooner have I loaded my plate with a variety of meats and pastries than Mr Sheridan places a tankard of porter in my hand and escorts me across to a table where a group of young men are animatedly chatting.

I recognise several of them from the orchestra. Mr Russell, the stubbornly timid first violinist is not of their number. Glancing about the room I see him and another man deep in conversation in the far corner. Asserting their status, perhaps - or, from their clouded looks, commiserating upon the maestro's capriciousness?

But Mr Sheridan is introducing me. 'Gentlemen, this is Will Archer who, as I told you, is a distant relative of the missing man...'

I narrowly avoid choking upon a mouthful of veal pie at this falsehood and the brazenness with which Sheridan utters it. A swig of porter saves my face as Mr Sheridan continues, 'Please feel free to repeat what you have told me of Mr Acres as a friend and colleague - and I am sure,' he adds in a respectful hushed tone, 'that any observations of a more personal nature at this time of uncertainty for his family will be of great comfort.'

With a comradely squeeze of my shoulder and a condoling look, he leaves. There is such sympathetic gravity in his demeanour that any earlier modesty about his acting ability is now completely exploded - I only hope my own will equal it in the role he has now assigned me!

As they clear a space for me, I become the object of curious looks and polite sympathy for my supposed distress.

In the role Mr Sheridan has assigned me I immediately establish that I am so distant a cousin of the missing man that in truth I know him less than they. My interest in his disappearance is, I tell them, more a matter of family duty than of genuine concern.

This loosens their tongues. Freed of any deference to my finer feelings they are happy to inform me of every aspect of his character.

Thus I learn a great deal about Tobias Acres. In appearance, they tell me, he is unlike me in almost every respect - short, fair-haired and with an unevenness of feature which might by some be deemed ugly. 'No-one seeing the two of you together,' says one with no suspicion of irony, 'would take you as being related.'

He is twenty-five years old, unmarried and with no prospect of being so as he has little success with the ladies, being of a retiring and studious disposition. 'Aye,' says one, 'studious at keeping his distance.'

'Aloof,' adds another, only to by contradicted by a third who maintains that he is a good fellow once you get to know him. Civil enough in conversation, rarely speaking ill of others and ever ready to enter into discourse upon practically any topic.

'A sociable fellow?' I suggest with a nod towards the tankards scattered about the table. 'You drink together of an evening?'

'Oh, no, not Tobias,' says the one who called him studious, pulling a long face. 'Dead against drink is Tobias. The talk is that his father fell prey to strong spirits and beat him when he was young. This is not from Tobias himself, you understand - he never talks of his family...'

'Save his sister,' interjects another.

'Ah, yes - the fair Eugenie, with whom he lodges in Great

Boater Lane...'

'Nay, 'tis no lodging, it was their parents house.'

'You say it *was* their parents' house... where are the parents now?' I ask.

'Nay, do you not know they both died a twelvemonth gone? Truly you must be a distant cousin indeed!' says one with a curious look.

To forestall further inquiry about our supposed relationship, I stammer platitudes of losing touch, of historic rifts - I know not what - and then, 'They left Tobias and his sister well provided for, though?' Adding, by way of authenticity, 'My mother occasionally talked, with some bitterness, of our estranged wealthy Irish relations.'

'That's as may be. Mayhap there is some inheritance, for a second violinist's stipend does not run to a house in Great Boater Lane. Without his sister plies some trade more lucrative...'

He sniggers and digs his elbows in his companions' sides. They laugh briefly but then, embarrassed, recall to whom they are speaking.

'Forgive us, Master Archer, we mean no offence...'

'None taken, sir,' I reply with what I judge to be suitable magnanimity. 'But I am curious to know about the last time you saw him. Was there anything in his manner to suggest why he would disappear so unexpectedly?'

They ponder awhile. The last time they saw Tobias Acres was no different from any other time. They rehearsed, they packed away their instruments and took their leave of each other as they had done every rehearsal day for the past weeks.

'Nay, there was one singular thing,' pipes up one. 'Ned and I and a couple of others came here to the *Bull's Head* before going home. We had but one drink, yet it was dark when we left.' He turns to the others. 'You remember, Ned, 'twas but half an hour at most, yet when we came out, Tobias was just leaving the Hall?'

'Aye, I recall it now. He said he would stay behind to practise a certain passage where he had found some difficulty in phrasing.'

'And earned sour looks from old Russell for his diligence...'

'So,' say I, 'he was later than usual - and it was already dark? He was alone, though?'

'That was not unusual. His way lies in the opposite direction to most of us and whilst he may not spurn company, he does not invite it. Early or late, 'twould have been the same.'

Any further questions are thwarted by the appearance of Mr Russell at our table. He coughs, sotto-voce, and announces in a prim tone, 'Mr Handel is about to move, gentlemen. We had best reassemble so as to be ready.'

In the general upheaval I manage to catch the arm of the musician called Ned. 'The sister, Eugenie - she lives in Great Boater Lane, you say? I have forgot the number and I would pay my respects...'

He provides the information I seek without so much as a backward glance. I memorise it - No 56 - resolving to visit my presumably distraught 'cousin' at the first opportunity.

Back at the Hall, Charlie slides in beside me as I take my seat once more at the back. Finn, the red-haired Irish fiddle-player, is at the front, standing to one side as the musicians reassemble. He is alone, and a glance about the Hall shows no sign of his brother. No doubt Finn has sent him packing, the comfort of brotherly support outweighed by his volatility. Even at this distance, I sense his unease. Catching his eye, I raise my hand and receive a nod of acknowledgement in return.

I turn to Charlie and ask how he has got on with the soup lady and the boys in the choir. The soup was to his taste - the choristers not.

'They weren't your sort, then?'

'Be blowed if I'd get up at six in the morning to warble at matins! And when I asks them if that's a Roman Catholic thing, they gets huffy, saying they're not Church of Rome but Church of Ireland. Sorry, says I, I thought you Irish was all Catholic. We're not Irish, says they, mighty offended. They sounds Irish to me, but they calls 'em bogtrotters and culchies. My pate's fair addled with it all!'

'Mine, too, lad. 'Tis a strange country and no mistake!'

But opportunity to further ponder upon the vagaries of the land we find ourselves in is curtailed by the arrival of Mr Handel and his party and the rehearsal re-commences.

Signora Avoglio's sweet voice tells of the shepherds abiding in the fields keeping watch over their sheep, and gradually the familiar story unwinds. From time to time in the choral pieces, Mr Handel has cause to stop and give instruction. The choirboys, it seems, need more guidance than the soloists.

Thus, with the sweet strings and the tinkling harpsichord, I find my mind wandering, returning to what I have learned of Tobias Acres, the missing man.

A competent musician, conscientious enough to remain behind to perfect his performance. A man of sober and unexceptional habits. What reason would he have to disappear?

I can think of none. I shake my head, letting my mind be drawn back to the music as Mrs Susannah Cibber rises.

'He was despised and rejected, a man of sorrows and acquainted with grief,' she sings, and there is something so compelling about the low pitch of her voice that the words worm themselves into my brain.

Was Tobias Acres one such? Not despised, according to his colleagues, nor yet rejected, though by all accounts he kept himself to himself. But could he have been a man of sorrows? His fellow musicians had hinted at his father's violence towards him as a child - was his self-imposed solitude a cover for secret griefs? Griefs so great that he could bear them no longer...

Might they cause him to make away with himself? Should I be looking not for a living man, but a dead one?

Beside me, Charlie has fallen asleep, lulled by the music and a stomach full of broth. Gradually he has subsided and his head now rests on my arm which is slowly going numb. But I am loth to disturb him. The oratorio is at the moment going through a depressing phase, all sorrow and suffering.

It accords well with my trepidation at the thought of meeting the missing man's sister. How am I to accomplish it? I doubt she will countenance the fiction of a distant cousin. Yet I have no other credible reason for visiting her...

I make an effort to concentrate on the music and look about the Hall to see how others are responding. Most seem rapt, and indeed the tempo is now becoming more inspiring, almost jaunty as the choir sings of the King of Glory. I find my foot tapping along with the rhythm.

This is followed by a lilting solo from Signora Avoglio after which the orchestra launches into a stirring, galloping piece in which the bass soloist asks why nations so furiously rage together.

The words are very apt in view of Sean's earlier outburst against the English oppressors. The Irish certainly rage against the English - and the chief violinist, Russell's, opposition to Finn suggests the English have little regard for the Irish.

And, according to Charlie, even the choirboys who have lived all their lives in Ireland seem to scorn the native Irish. Are there any in this country who do not hate each other?

In England, there is division between rich and poor, town and country - but the intricate hostilities of Ireland baffle me.

And where does Tobias Acres fit in all this? Living in a house inherited from his family, it would seem Dublin is his home. And yet he is not, like Finn, his replacement, of true Irish descent...

As I wrestle with this conundrum, the orchestra and chorus burst into a magnificent chorus of Hallelujahs! Charlie wakes with a start and starts bouncing to the rhythm. And indeed the glorious surge of sound resonates not only through the hall but through one's very body, awaking such a sensation of well-being that I can hardly forbear shouting with joy.

At its conclusion, the audience erupts. They leap to their feet shouting, 'Huzzah! Encore! Bravo Maestro!' Charlie and I among them. The clapping and stamping of feet persists for several minutes as Mr Handel rises from the keyboard, mopping his brow with a kerchief, and acknowledges their acclamation.

Then, raising his arm to still the hubbub, he announces a brief pause to proceedings. The audience falls to murmuring enthusiastically.

'Spanking fine tune, eh Will?' Charlie enthuses.

As I agree wholeheartedly, my attention is caught by a movement in the orchestra. A man from the audience has approached one of the young men with whom I dined - the sceptic who questioned my family relationship - and, after a brief exchange, I see him pointing towards where we sit at the back of the Hall.

The stranger looks directly at me. Our eyes meet and he averts his gaze.There is nothing shifty in the action, rather an acknowledgment that I am the one he seeks.

I half rise to follow him as he strides from the Hall, but at this moment Mr Handel calls all to order for the final part, and I am shushed back into my seat.

Throughout the final half hour, the stirring trumpets and choruses fail to move me.

I cannot shake off the cold unease occasioned by the unequivocal summons of the stranger's gaze.

5

...dash them in pieces...

The concert over and farewells taken, Mr Garrick, Mrs Peg and Mr Sheridan will go to one of Dublin's many coffee houses for refreshment. There is much discussion. Mr Garrick has heard good reports of *Dick's* in Skinner Row. But Mr Sheridan, whilst attesting to its popularity, believes it may be too crowded at this time of day. So, too with the numerous establishments in Essex Street near the Custom House; *Dempster's, Bacon's, Norris's, Walsh's* - all are like to be awash with businessmen and merchants.

'The *Anne* at Essex Bridge?' suggests Mrs Peg.

Mr Sheridan regrets it has seen better days. 'No,' says he, 'the fashionable place to be seen is at *Lucas's*. 'Tis at Cork House, hard by the castle and but a short walk. At this hour, young beaux, newly risen, often peacock there. They've even been known to duel upon a whim in the yard behind!'

Mrs Peg rises to the bait, clapping her hands in delight. 'Indeed, let us go there!'

My master, I can see, has reservations, but will not gainsay the lady, so it is to *Lucas's* we all repair.

I am included in the party, for Mr Sheridan wishes to know the outcome of my inquiries into Acres's disappearance but Charlie is sent on home to Mrs Fitzgerald's, a Coffee House being no suitable place for a child.

Cork House has seen better days. It is near on an hundred and fifty years old I guess, judging by the style of its architecture which is of the time of the old Queen Elizabeth, all small-paned windows and sugar-stick chimneys. No longer in use by the Boyle family, the Earls of County Cork and Orrery, it was leased, says Mr Sheridan, by a Mr Lucas some ten or twenty years since and its downstairs rooms converted into the present coffee-house.

Those same rooms, well-proportioned but dark with wooden panelling, lead off an entrance hall that acts as a general meeting area. Here several of Mr Sheridan's promised beaux hold centre stage, preening and shrill as cockatoos. Eyes swivel as we enter, alighting mainly upon Mrs Peg who acknowledges their attention with demure gratification.

A young waiter asks if we would prefer a quiet room or one with food and entertainment - they have a Mrs Shaughnessy, newly arrived from Connemara, whose vocal talents, highly praised, will be on show in the music room within the half-hour.

Having had our fill of vocal accomplishments for today, Mr Garrick requests, 'A coffee and quiet company with perhaps one or two newspapers, if you please?'

We are ushered into a side room to a cluster of comfortable chairs around a table in the window. Half a dozen other occupants are reading or conversing quietly.

Dishes of coffee are ordered, though Mrs Peg will have chocolate and Mr Sheridan requests a dram of Irish whiskey in his. The waiter brings a newspaper and whilst Mr Garrick becomes engrossed in it and Mrs Peg, nodding and smiling, peruses the others in the room, Mr Sheridan takes me aside to apologise for his 'distant cousin' subterfuge and sound me out on my findings so far.

When I have told all, he nods reflectively. 'As I thought, my opinion of him from the few times he has played at the theatre accords with that of his colleagues in the orchestra. A man of sober and unremarkable habit. There is no reason why he should absent himself.'

'His sister may know more,' say I. 'But if, like her brother, she is of a mild and modest disposition, I do not wish to alarm her. She must already be in a state of some distress at his unexplained absence.'

'Indeed, you are right, Will. The lady's testimony will be invaluable - but how to get it...? We must further think on how best to accomplish it.'

It is at this moment that Mr Garrick, who has not been party to our discussion, lets out a triumphant 'Ha!' and thrusts the paper towards Sheridan. 'See, Tom, our persecutor has met his nemesis at last!'

Faced with Sheridan's look of puzzlement, he explains. 'Walpole has fallen. It is confirmed beyond doubt. Cartagena has done for him.'

'Cartagena?'

'Aye, in the Caribbean. 'Twas rumoured Admiral Vernon had blundered against the Spanish, but now we know it all. Fifty ships lost, eighteen thousand men dead. The Spanish outmanoeuvred us, pretending to retreat but keeping up skirmishes until the onset of the rainy season when tropical downpours sent the English scurrying back to their ships. Most are dead not from action but from sickness and disease through having to remain at sea off the coast for two months. Vernon has retreated to Jamaica to recoup and gather reinforcements.'

Sheridan looks bewildered. 'I had heard that we were victorious at Cartagena?'

'That was Vernon jumping the gun!' My master waves the news-sheet triumphantly. 'Early on in the battle, seeing the Spanish apparently retreating to the fort of San Lazaro, he dispatched Captain Laws to Britain to inform King George of their victory. There were even medals struck in celebration. But they've been withdrawn from circulation in short order now the truth is out!'

'So how came such a reversal? The Caribbean campaign was going so well...'

'Aye, so it was - under the command of General Cathcart. But he died of dysentery en route to Cartagena and 'tis common knowledge that General Wentworth, his successor, and Admiral Vernon detest each other. This correspondent attributes the disaster to that antipathy.'

Excited as Mr Garrick and Mr Sheridan are about battles in far off lands, it is the news that Walpole has fallen that arouses my interest - and my anxiety.

That glance from the stranger in the music hall reminded me that my presence here in Ireland is not solely as part of Mr Garrick's household, for my recent adventure with Agnes Mayer led me into the path of Sir William Hervey, the head of Walpole's security service.

Prior to my departure for Ireland, he gave me covert orders to keep my eyes and ears open. For what, I know not. Only that with Spain occupying the government's attention, Hervey would not have simmering discontent in Ireland erupt and cause trouble by the back door, as he put it.

I recall Hervey mentioning Mr Walpole's reluctance to enter into a war with Spain. Now that the expedition has come to grief, it seems the right time to mention it.

'It seems unfair that the Prime Minister should suffer for something that was not of his choosing?'

Garrick gives a brief bark of laughter. 'How little you know of politics, Will! 'Tis true Walpole resisted war with Spain, but mercantile interests forced him into it. Too many of our merchants' ships have fallen prey to Spanish privateers of late. They seem to think they may attack us with impunity. And Walpole could not afford to ignore those business interests any longer - he saw he was losing votes.'

'King George, too, may have exerted some pressure,' adds Sheridan, 'for Spain supports the cause of Frederick of Prussia against Maria Teresa of Austria in the matter of the Austrian throne. And it is no secret that King George has pledged our army's aid to Maria Teresa.'

'Aye,' say I, drawing further upon knowledge gleaned from my discussions with Hervey, 'in the hope he can prevent Prussia's allies marching through his homeland of Hanover.'

My master nods in approbation. 'Exactly, Will. A policy in which he had his Prime Minister's full support. And which, in turn, earned Mr Walpole his monarch's protection against those

45

who would seek to topple him. But now, with such a loss of manpower at Cartagena, there are not enough troops to back up our pledge. King George will be forced to withdraw his support for Maria Teresa, and doubtless see his beloved Hanover overrun by Prussian, French and Spanish soldiers. The bond that held Prime Minister and King together is now meaningless. Neither can hold out against their enemies - so Walpole has had his day.'

And if Walpole has lost power, can Sir William Hervey retain his position as head of the Secret Service? I would like to think I am now free of him - if it were not for a stranger's glance across a crowded concert hall...

But all this talk of politics is not to Mrs Peg's taste. 'Fie, gentlemen, this is dry stuff indeed for a social occasion! Tell me, Mr Sheridan, what have you in mind for Davey and me this season?'

Sheridan, all too ready to outline his plans, beams an apology. 'My pardon, Mrs Woffington.' Then, in confidential tone, he continues, 'I hear that Quin and Delane have been booked to appear at the Theatre Royal in Aungier Street. The management there intend to put up a fight against the attraction of yourself and Davey here at Smock Alley. Rumour also has it that Mrs Cibber, after the final performance of Mr Handel's oratorio, will join them.'

'No matter,' says Mrs Peg. 'You have me. And sweet as dear Susannah is, she is not as great a draw as I.'

'Immodest as ever,' tuts Mr Garrick with a twinkle in his eye.

'Now, Davey, do not be severe,' pouts the lady. 'You know it to be true.'

'I am counting on it, Mrs Peg,' says Mr Sheridan. 'Which is why, as our first production at Smock Alley, I would have you reprise your Sir Harry Wildair.'

'With pleasure. The breeches role always brings in the crowds.'

It is part in which Mrs Woffington made her name back in London. Which is hardly surprising. I, for one, can understand the appeal of the dramatic device which calls for a woman to dress as a man in tight knee-breeches and stockings. One may cite the necessity of the drama, but I'll wager most of the gentlemen in the audience, who in the daily round of polite society only ever glimpse the occasional flash of a lady's ankle, are there for the pleasure of ogling a shapely female leg.

'Then,' continues Tom Sheridan, 'Davey has agreed to *Lear* and *The Alchemist*. A fine contrast of roles to demonstrate his breadth of talent. And to end the season I have a mind for *The Fair Penitent* if the two of you are agreeable? An unadventurous choice, perhaps, but always a crowd pleaser.'

As the three of them fall to discussing plans, I excuse myself. I tell my master I would put my mind at rest that Charlie has returned safe home to Mrs Fitzgerald's in Lamb Alley. The byways of London may be as familiar to him as his own hand but Dublin, for all its Englishness is an unknown city and he is but a twelve-year-old boy.

So I take my leave. Daylight is already fading for it is as yet April and the days are still short. Also the damp Dublin air, further thickened by the mists from the river, lends a grey miasma to the encroaching evening.

The main streets still throng with walkers like myself, intent on their business. Hawkers add their cries to the rumble of carriage wheels and clop of horses' hooves. Sedans carried by panting chair-men thread their way among the traffic. I could be in London, the life of the city streets is so familiar.

But in one respect, I cannot help but notice a difference. In London, I have learnt to ignore the beggars. They may be ragged and dirty but in general they are sturdy and often with the light of insolence in their eyes. Also it is not unknown for the 'blind' to miraculously regain their sight or 'cripples' to walk as night falls. But here in Ireland I cannot see that happening for these poor wretches are like barely animated corpses, hollow eyed, with hardly rags enough to cover their nakedness or strength enough to hold out stick-thin arms to passers-by.

Those same passers-by seem immune to these victims of poverty who lie slumped at almost every wall, but they inspire in me a guilt that I have nothing to give.

And it is because I am thus distracted that I am almost half way to my destination before I sense I am not alone. At the edge of my vision I become aware of a shadow - one who turns when I turn, stops when I stop.

It is only a little over two months ago that I was attacked and left for dead by just such a follower in London, one whose presence I did not suspect. My instincts since then have been sharpened.

Twice, as if in thought, I stop, then spin on my heel and scan the street behind me. Nothing seems amiss. But the feeling of pursuit persists.

Soon it is time for me to quit the main thoroughfare and take to less frequented side roads. Here the encroaching shadows of evening are my ally. Turning a corner into a street empty of other pedestrians, I slip into a doorway.

Sure enough, a few moments later, a man rounds the corner and, seeing no one before him, makes to retrace his steps. In turning, he comes face to face with me as I step from my hiding place.

He is of slight build and a head shorter than myself. There is no contest between us. I seize him by the collar and push him to the wall.

'So, sir,' say I, lacing my tone with aggression, 'you follow me, do you? Your business, if you please?'

His reaction to my sudden assault is not what I expect. After the initial surprise his lips twist into a mocking smile.

'Well done,' he says with a calm surprising in one whose cravat is bunched in my fist. 'I saw you had descried me and expected something of this sort. You may release me now.'

I tighten my grip upon his throat. 'Not till I know your business, sir.'

'Not my business, Master Archer, but Sir William's.'

My heart sinks at the conjunction of my own name with that of Sir William Hervey, The head of Walpole's secret service has not, it seems, suffered the same fate as his master. But, before I release my hold, I must be sure.

'Sir William is Walpole's man, and Walpole is no more.'

The stranger laughs. 'Sir William is his own man, Master Archer. Prime Ministers may come and go, but all require Sir

49

William's services, whether they know it or not.' His eyes flick down to my hand about his throat. 'Think you, will he take kindly to your mistreating a colleague thus?'

I release him.

He adjusts his neckerchief. 'You have a sudden temper, Master Archer, and a firm grip. I hope I shall have no occasion to taste either again!'

'You would not have tasted them now if you had not been skulking after me.'

'A drawback of our profession, wouldn't you say?' He holds out his hand. 'Richard Semple.'

I give his hand a curt shake. 'Your business with me, Mr Semple?'

'Shall we walk, Master Archer? I see that the road is no longer ours alone - and whilst no-one has noticed us so far, I would not give any cause to do so now.'

As Semple knows my name, I can only presume he also knows my lodging. There is little point in altering my route, so we continue to stroll in the direction of Lamb Alley.

As we walk I am able to observe him more closely. Thin and dark-haired, he has the sallow complexion of a clerk, more used to toiling by candlelight than in the open air. His manner is easy and animated, yet I feel he gives away nothing more than is necessary. His gaze, which appears candid, is nevertheless watchful. And it is the same gaze that I have already seen earlier today - in the music hall in Fishamble Street.

'Are you a lover of Mr Handel's music, sir?' I ask, letting him know that I have recognised him. 'Did you find the performance enjoyable?'

He parries the taunt with an easy laugh. 'Informative, let us say. It allowed me to put a face to a name.'

'My name?'

'Indeed so. And, if I may say so, Sir William's description of that same face does not do it justice.'

'He had you seek me out merely to flatter me, Mr Semple?' I say acidly. 'Pray, get to the business in hand, if you please.'

'Oh dear - touchy indeed!' says Semple, making me wonder just how much of my past history Hervey has imparted to him. 'Very well, Master Archer. To business. Our mutual friend believes that the change of government at Westminster necessitates we be more alert than usual here in Ireland. Sir William believes there are those who would use the uncertainty of the time as an opportunity to cause trouble. Indeed, he believes it may already have begun.'

'Already begun? In what way?'

'That he does not yet know. But he now thinks it time to enlist your help.'

'My help?'

'Yes. A body was recovered last night from the river. In itself, that is not unusual - drownings are common enough here in Dublin. Normally Sir William would not concern himself with such matters. But in this instance he would know the cadaver's identity. And he asks you, Master Archer, to make inquiries.'

I am at a loss. 'But how? I am a stranger here in Dublin. What possible reason can I give to examine a corpse dragged from the river? Why, I don't even know where such a body may be kept...!'

'That is the easy part,' says Semple. 'There is a house for the dead hard by the Charitable Infirmary at King's Inns Quay on the north bank of the river. Bodies retrieved from the water are taken there. The newly gentrified on this side of the Liffey prefer not to be troubled by such things!'

'Would it not be easier for you to identify the body, Mr Semple? You are resident here - you know the country...'

'Exactly - and that is the very reason why Sir William would have me unremarked. My post in the Custom House is at once lowly and useful. It would not do for me to show too much curiosity.'

'Whereas I, being but a foreigner, may show as much as I want, I suppose!'

'Tut tut, Master Archer - such petulance! Sir William said you could be peevish...'

'And with reason, sir, considering he asks the impossible of me!'

'Come, Master Archer, we are nearly at your lodging. I will be brief.' He puts a hand upon my arm, staying me at the corner of Lamb Alley. His tone becomes business-like. 'I appreciate your apprehension in this matter, but I have already paved your way. Whilst I may not be seen to act officially in this matter, I have many, shall we say, *unofficial* contacts. I have arranged for a young man to meet you outside the west door of Christ Church Cathedral at eight this evening. He will show you the way to King's Inns Quay and the body, no questions asked. As far as he knows, you are a medical student - you have some skill in acting, I believe? - who, instruction at the university being of a largely theoretical nature, would examine the body as a way of furthering your practical studies. A coin or two might leaven the deceit.' Here, he pulls a purse from his coat and gives it me. 'Sir William sends you necessary expenses. Good luck.'

He turns to go.

'One moment, sir,' say I. 'How shall I apprise you of aught I discover? Where may I find you?'

'You won't, Master Archer. *I* shall find *you!* Good evening.'

6

...since by man came death...

Prompt at eight I am pacing the cobbles outside Christ Church.

I am not the only night-walker. Occasionally others, clerks and legal gentlemen by their sober dress and packets of documents clutched to their chest, hurry by intent on their own business, affording me never a glance before being swallowed up in the night. Only I, restlessly pacing, am unsure of what I am doing here.

There are few lamps in the environs of the cathedral to light the dark shapes of buildings which cluster round the central edifice like mangy dogs about their master's feet. The great churches of London are not so beset and enclosed.

As the evening thickens and passers-by become even fewer, shadows seem to shift and solidify.

I have almost given up hope, the clocks of the city beginning to chime the quarter hour, when a ragged figure takes shape from the darkness and slinks towards me.

In the dimness I descry a face, dirty under an unruly mop of ginger hair. Its owner cannot be above sixteen or so and his manner is furtive, his accent near impenetrable. 'Youse'll be the medical gent, I'm thinking?'

Taking my silence as consent, he grasps my elbow. 'Come,' says he, 'let's get out of here 'tis not a place to my liking.'

'The church?'

'No, not the church - the Four Courts. 'Tis the nests of lawmen, to be sure, that infest most of the buildings around here.'

I follow him through dismal lanes towards the river which rolls sluggish, dark under a deepening fog. Not without a sense of trepidation, for someone with so little love for the law must surely live his life on the edges of it. And to trust myself to such a one at night in an unknown place...

I push the thought from my mind.

I am not yet conversant enough with the city to know by which bridge we cross the Liffey - the Essex, the Ormond? Wrapped in night, even the little I know of the city is unfamiliar. And the far bank to which we are headed is totally unknown, for I have not yet ventured over the river in my short stay in the city. All I have gleaned so far is that, whereas the wide roads of the South bank are home to the better-off, the merchants and nobility, the narrow lanes of the Old Town on the North bank harbour the poorer sort, apprentices and labourers.

As we cross the bridge and the far bank emerges from the dusk, I become aware of a multitude of small boats and vessels rolling on the swell, for all the world as if sections of the banks of the river are breaking free. It is hard to see where the shore ends and the boats begin.

King's Inns Quay is not so well maintained as the quays upon the side of the river we have just left. Hardly more than a bank of tumbled stones and mud on which all the refuse of the river accumulates. I cover my nose as we reach the end of the bridge, but the boy seems not to notice the stink.

A few more dark alleys, then, 'Here's my father's, sir - where

55

the light is.'

A feeble glimmer of candlelight issues from a low building, hardly more than a wooden hut that crouches in the obscurity of the night.

'Your father's?' say I, alarm beginning to stir. 'I thought you were taking me to the house of the dead?'

He barks scornfully. 'House of the dead! That's a grand description, to be sure, for the old cold-barn! But don't fret yerself, I ain't about to kidnap youse. I has to take youse to the auld feller becos 'tis he has the key.'

He lifts the latch and we pass into a low-ceilinged room. A man, grizzled and squat but muscular still about his arms, is sitting beside a meagre fire. On a bare wooden table in the middle of the room a single candle in the neck of a stone bottle flares and smokes in the draught from the door as we enter. The only other furniture in the room consists of a sort of wooden bunk in the corner and a simple dresser with drawers. Beside it, two or three sculls lean up against the wall.

'The gentleman, pa,' says the boy by way of introduction.

The old man's eyes are piercing. 'Paddy Rafferty at your service, sir.' He clasps my hand in a calloused fist. 'And you'll be the medical student, eh? I'd best not be asking your name, I take it?'

Such is the scepticism in his tone I feel my subterfuge already exploded. But then his face breaks into a gap-toothed grin that suggests complicity. It is clear he intends to enquire no further. Instead, he nods towards the mop-haired youth who has squatted beside the embers to warm himself. 'No matter. 'Tis enough that

Patrick brought you safe here. He's a good lad. Willing.'

I hear the implied suggestion and dutifully take a coin from the purse provided by Sir William Hervey. 'Here's for his pains, sir.' Then I turn to the business in hand. 'Is it here?'

'Close by. I does everything reg'lar. I done notified the crowner and had notices printed.'

He shoves a piece of paper across the table. I examine it under the light of the candle.

'BODY FOUND,' it reads, giving the barest details of time place and condition.

'Nothing in the pockets?' I ask.

'A few coins, piece of wax or some such, nothing more.'

'Wax?'

He crosses to the dresser and produces a small cube, perhaps three-quarters of an inch square. It is dun-coloured with a slightly greasy texture, like wax but harder. One side is worn into a groove.

I am as mystified as they. 'May I keep this?'

He shrugs his shoulders. ''Tis all one to me. He has no further need of it.'

'Do you suppose he took his own life?'

'I don't suppose nothin', sir. I get my livin' haulin' bodies from the river. I ain't a supposin' sort. Now, would you see the body - for your *medical studies?*'

Again the sly tone which suggests he doesn't believe a word of my imposture.

But as he rises, there is a commotion immediately outside and the door of the hut is violently thrown open.

All three of us start back in surprise as a hooded figure enters. With a single gesture, the hood is thrown back and we are confronted by a young woman.

She does not wait for us to speak but addresses the old man directly. 'Your name is Rafferty, is it not? You have a body here, sir - a man pulled from the river last night? By your leave, I would see the deceased.'

The old man is momentarily at a loss, overawed by the woman's firmness. She has an air of determined authority which he hesitates to question.

As he wavers, she spies the printed bill, snatches it up and scans it rapidly. 'Is this the man? There are no marks of identity mentioned.'

At last the old man finds his voice. 'None were found, miss. No papers, no timepiece - nothing.' He points towards me. 'This gentleman also is here upon that business.'

The woman turns, noticing me for the first time. Her stare is questioning, imperious but I sense uncertainty behind the bravado. 'And you are, sir?'

Indeed, who am I? And what legitimate reason have I to be here? I call upon my powers of invention.

'A gentleman of my acquaintance has not been seen for some time. His absence is out of character and I would satisfy myself that he has come to no harm.' It is not entirely a lie, but beside me Rafferty stifles a grunt of amusement at my abandonment of the medical pretence. 'And what, if I may enquire, is your interest, ma'am?' I ask.

Her reply is cool, guarded. 'Not so very different from your

58

own, sir. Though the gentleman in question, if it be he, is somewhat more than an acquaintance. Now, sir,' she says, turning back to our host, 'are we to see the deceased or not?'

I cannot help but admire her boldness. Not only has she, a woman of obvious breeding, ventured out alone at night into such a place as this, but her tenacity is such as to brook no dissent. She is clearly a woman of spirit, a force to be reckoned with.

Rafferty is evidently of the same mind, for he takes up a large key and lantern which he lights from the solitary candle and bids us follow him.

A little winding through a muddy yard brings us to another wooden structure, not unlike the one we have just left. The old man plies his key and lights us into a cool room. The boy was right when he called it the 'cold barn' for there is a penetrating chill that strikes up from the stone floor as soon as we enter. By the dim glow of the lantern I see that the walls, too, are partially hewn out of rock onto which the wooden structure has been built.

Beside me I hear a sharp indrawn breath from the lady, whether from the unexpected chill or from sight of the shrouded form that lies on the table before us I cannot tell. I feel her hand on my arm and lay my own over it in reassurance.

The old man makes to draw aside the sheet that covers the face but I stay him, thinking of the lady's feelings. 'There is no - er, disfigurement from being in the water?'

'None, sir,' says the old man. 'He's as fresh almost as when I pulled him out. His face only a little swollen by the natural process...'

On my arm, the lady's grip tightens at this intimation of decay.

I turn to her. 'Would you have me look first, ma'am? To ensure the sight will not be too much for you?'

'That would be kind,' she murmurs.

So I move forward, between her and the body while Rafferty respectfully lifts the cover from the dead man's face.

Death has robbed the face of character. Blank eyelids hide those windows of the soul that can tell so much. The slightly parted lips, pale as the surrounding flesh, are devoid of expression. The skin, bluish in colour and already puffy with the first signs of decomposition, give an almost inhuman look. It might almost be an alabaster statue lying here.

But one thing strikes me as odd. Across the left temple, almost hidden by the straw-coloured hair, is a dark contusion. I bend to observe it more closely. Regular in outline and, as far as I can judge, about four inches in length and an inch broad, it seems too defined to be the result of a chance collision with rocks in the river.

My concentration is interrupted by the lady. 'Have you looked your fill, sir. Is the sight so horrible?'

I straighten up, apologetic. 'Not so distressing, ma'am. You may look without fear of revulsion.'

With remarkable composure, she steps forward to survey the corpse. After the merest shudder of distaste she says quite calmly. 'Mr Rafferty, this man is my brother, Tobias Acres, who has been missing for two days.'

'The violinist!' I exclaim.

She turns to me. 'You know him?'

'Not exactly know him,' I stammer, 'but I have some interest

60

in him...'

'Indeed, sir? You are a colleague, perhaps?' Her tone has become frosty again.

'I, er - no, not a colleague...'

Now she is pure ice. Her face expresses a contempt which I do not feel I merit but she says nothing further to me. Instead she turns to Rafferty, ignoring me as if I have ceased to exist.

'There will be documents to sign, I presume, for me to claim the body?'

'Indeed, 'tis so, ma'am. I have them in my house, if you would care...?'

I brace myself and ask, 'Mr Rafferty, would you leave the lantern? I would examine the deceased further, if I may.'

Tobias Acres's sister looks aghast. '*Examine,* sir! What possible cause can you have to *examine* him further.'

'I believe his death may not have been an accident, Miss Acres...'

'Not an accident?' She regards me closely then turns to Rafferty. 'Kindly leave us the lantern, Mr Rafferty, and prepare the documents for me to sign. I would speak with this gentleman alone.'

Once again I marvel at her assurance, that she is prepared to trust herself in the company of a total stranger. Rafferty, too, seems unsure, until with a disarming smile she says, 'You need not fear on my behalf. This gentleman, I am sure, will do me no harm.'

Reluctantly, and with a warning scowl in my direction, Rafferty departs.

As soon as he is gone, she demands, 'Who are you, sir? If you are not a colleague of my late brother, what are you? Are you of the Watch or the Militia? Or something - less - *official*?'

I decide that only the truth - or at least part of the truth - will suffice. 'No, ma'am. My name is Will Archer and I am in Dublin as a member of Mr Garrick's company, newly arrived from England. Mr Sheridan, the manager of the Smock Alley Theatre, perturbed to hear of your brother's disappearance and fearing some harm had befallen him, asked me to investigate, knowing that I have shown some skill in that line. And here,' I say with a theatrical nod towards the body, 'it appears his worst fears have been realised.'

She nods, apparently satisfied at my explanation. And, in some unaccountable way, relieved. Her manner towards me thaws somewhat, yet her gaze remains level, assessing. 'So, Master Archer, on what evidence do you base this opinion of yours?'

I motion her once more towards the corpse. 'If it will not distress you too much...?'

'No need to cosset me, Master Archer. I will not throw a fit of the vapours at sight of a dead man.'

'But - your brother...?'

'In name alone. I shall mourn him from duty, not love. Now, show me what you have to show me.'

I point out the contusion on the left temple.

'You suspect a blow from behind, or from the side, with some sort of cudgel?'

I am surprised at her perspicacity and the neutrality of her tone.

'Indeed so, ma'am. You will observe that the skin is split in the middle of the bruise, suggesting some force. Now, if you will permit, I would examine his hands for any signs of struggle?'

She bends close as I lift first the left, then the right hand.

Her proximity as I examine them is at once exhilarating and unnerving. She smells of perfume and the cold night. A stray lock of blonde hair brushes my cheek as she leans yet closer to see where the nails of the right hand are broken. I cannot help but notice in the dim glow of the lantern how blue her eyes are...

'He was right-handed,' she says, 'his bowing hand, where the nails were longer for when he played pizzicato. Those of his left hand, which he used upon the frets of the violin, were kept short and have suffered little damage. You think he fought with his attacker?'

'It is possible - see the cuts upon the knuckle here, where they may have caught a button.'

'So he may have been dead before he went into the water?'

'Impossible to say.'

'Nay, not impossible.' Rafferty has returned, alarmed no doubt by our lengthy absence. I suspect he never got as far as his hut, but has been listening outside the door. 'A body as isn't breathing don't take in water so fast. It floats longer. Them as breathes in water sinks faster and we don't get 'em until days later when the putrefying gases brings 'em to the surface. This one's fresh, saving your presence ma'am - which leads me to say we probably got 'im afore he sank. Now, if you're finished here, I'll be after asking you for your signature, ma'am.'

Ten minutes later, with young Patrick's aid, we are back at the

Liffey.

'Would you have me escort you home, Miss Acres?' I ask as Patrick, another sixpence in his pocket scurries back homewards.

'You would be my protector, Master Archer?' she asks wryly.

'I would see you safe, ma'am.'

She laughs. 'Oh, I shall be safe, sir, in Dublin's streets. Safer perhaps than you. No, get you home, Master Archer, back to your English friends. But tomorrow, should your duties with Mr Garrick allow, I would have you visit me that we may discuss the matter of my brother's death more fully.'

'I shall be honoured, ma'am.'

'You do not ask where you should call.'

'Great Boater Lane, is it not?'

'So, your skill in investigation is not exaggerated I see! Yes, number 56. I look forward to your company in more propitious circumstances, Master Archer. Goodnight.'

For several moments after she has gone I stand in the stillness of the night lulled by the gentle lapping of water. Looking out over the river, I notice for the first time that the fog has lifted and that high in the dark sky clouds like carded wool drift silver across a cold moon.

7

...he was cut off...

Next morning we assemble at the Smock Alley Theatre to be assigned our parts. Like any other theatre in the daytime, it is a dreary place without the glamour of candlelight and the buzz of fashionable society, though being fairly newly restored it has not the tired and tawdry air of Goodmans Fields which we have so recently vacated back in London.

Mr Garrick and Mrs Woffington, their parts being already settled, are not here when I arrive. I remain awhile in the shadows at the back of the auditorium, for most of those here are unfamiliar and Mr Sheridan is not yet arrived.

After a moment, someone taps me on the shoulder and I turn to see Ned Phillimore. Flinging wide his arms, he enfolds me in a delighted embrace. 'Will, my boy!'

He clasps me to his bosom almost depriving me of breath. Over his shoulder I see Kitty Blair giggling indulgently at this extravagant greeting.

Releasing me at last, he holds me at arms length, hands on shoulders and peruses me with fondness. 'Will - and looking so well! Recovered from that business in London? Indeed, it is good to see you again.' I step back as he threatens to hug me once more. Instead, he puts an arm about my shoulders. 'Since Kitty and I came over two weeks since, we have longed for a familiar face.'

Very prettily, Kitty leans in to him upon the other side as if re-

65

establish her claim upon his affection. He puts his hand on hers with such casual intimacy that it seems the most natural thing in the world. It is only two months since he first told me Kitty had allowed him to pay his addresses to her. It seems that much has transpired since then!

This doesn't surprise me. Kitty has always been a flirt, fluttering her eyes at most of the men in the company. Even I, despite my lack of years, wealth or talent, might have merited her attention had she not discovered a mutual attraction in Ned.

All the same, I worry for Ned. I can see he is besotted, Good-hearted, straightforward, he doesn't deserve to have his heart broken.

Even as I coolly return her effusive greeting I notice her eyes straying towards the plush seats in the front row where a handsome young man of Mr Sheridan's company is nonchalantly chatting.

As if at some silent signal he looks in our direction. and I cannot fail to observe how his slow smile and briefest of nods brings a blush to Kitty's cheeks.

Ned, however, has noticed nothing. He is eager to share his opinion of our future colleagues. 'Members of Mr Sheridan's company, resident here in Ireland. To them we are interlopers.'

'They have spurned your company?'

'Nothing so direct. The few we have talked to appear convivial enough. Yet there is something - I know not what - below the surface.'

'Oh that!' I laugh. 'I have been in Ireland but two days and already I know it for a characteristic of all hereabout. A sort of unwilling civility covering a simmering resentment.'

'You have hit it, Will!' He gives me an anxious look. 'And Mr Sheridan, is he the same? For if so, I cannot see our time in Dublin being a happy one.'

'Rest easy on that score, Ned. From my small acquaintance with him he seems a fellow of wit and pleasant disposition.'

Kitty pricks up her ears at this. 'You have met him, Will? Say, does he have looks to match his wit?'

I tell them of our visit to Mr Handel's rehearsal, of the missing violinist and of Mr Sheridan's request that I find out as much as I can about his disappearance.

Ned hangs upon my account with interest. 'So you are to play detective once again, eh Will?'

'It seems I cannot avoid it. After hearing what I learned from his fellow musicians, Mr Sheridan suggests I visit his sister this very afternoon to offer his condolence and support.'

I do not tell them of my discovery that Acres is not just disappeared but dead, I suspect murdered, or that the lady herself has invited me. Knowing how my life was imperilled in such similar circumstances such a short time ago, Ned is sure to warn me off.

His concern, however proves to be more about social impropriety than any potential danger.

'Alone?' He raises a quizzical eyebrow. 'Do you not appreciate what a slight that will cast upon the lady's reputation?'

The thought had not entered my mind. After all, did not the lady herself invite me last evening? There was no mention of a chaperone - but then the circumstances of our meeting at the mortuary were not exactly conventional...

'The matter is easily remedied,' says Kitty. 'Ned and I will accompany you. Three may represent Mr Sheridan's good wishes more effectively than one. And in matters of this sort a female presence is more comforting.'

Kitty comforting? I doubt it! Her motive, I am sure, is more curiosity than comfort.

But, just as I open my mouth to protest, Mr Sheridan makes his appearance with Mr Garrick and Mrs Peg, and we are all called to the front of the theatre.

I take care to place myself between Kitty and the young man whom she found so fascinating, and study him covertly.

I reckon him to be in the mid-twenties, his clothes suggesting not only an awareness of style but also the wealth to indulge it. He is handsome enough, with blond, somewhat sandy hair tied back in a queue, and features that, whilst not in themselves perfect, are striking in combination. I can imagine that ladies find him attractive and I sense that he knows it for he bears himself with languid confidence.

Kitty giggles at something Mr Sheridan says. The young man leans forward slightly to glance along to where she sits with Ned on the other side of me. The slightest of smiles plays across his lips as she acknowledges him with a demure lowering of eyes. Leaning back once more, his gaze meets mine and his eye flickers in the merest semblance of a wink. I frown in return. It is a complicity I have no wish to share.

But now Mr Sheridan is announcing parts for the first production. Mrs Peg is, as I already know, to play Sir Harry

Wildair, whilst Mr Garrick will be Colonel Standard. Ned is to be Monsieur Marquis, the main comedy role. Kitty is to take on the role of Parley, maid to Lady Lurewell, who will be played by Mrs Poynter, a rather regal looking lady of Mr Sheridan's company.

Mr Sheridan assigns the part of Dicky, Sir Harry's servant, to the young man beside me. I feel a stab of unease, for it is more than likely that the two servants, he and Kitty, will have several scenes together.

After distributing other speaking parts, Mr Sheridan comes to the minor roles. I fully expect either to be overlooked altogether or to be cast as some footman or other. But, with a twinkle in his eye, Mr Sheridan assigns me the part of Remnant, a tailor who has a dozen or so lines in a scene with the formidable Lady Lurewell in Act 2 Scene 1. Near enough the beginning to get it over and done with, but late enough in the action to store up nerves!

My trepidation is in no way relieved when the young man next to me whispers, 'A gem of a role! Tiny, but a laugh every line, unless you foul it up badly.' I remember how I tripped over lines in the straightforward part Mr Garrick gave me in the ill-fated *Changeling* back in London, and my heart sinks.

When Mr Sheridan is finished, the young man next to me proffers his hand. 'Richard O'Sullivan - and you are?'

'Will - Will Archer.'

'Good to meet you, Will Archer. I trust we'll become firm friends during your stay in our lovely city.'

His voice is gently Irish, but the smile on his lips does not reach to his eyes, and I cannot help thinking his little speech more of a challenge than an invitation.

The clock of St Patrick's cathedral is chiming half past one when I set out for my appointment with Miss Acres.

Unlike Christ Church which is hemmed about by buildings for the judiciary, St Patrick's stands proud within its own grounds. Even so, with its sole tower, it does not compare with the majesty of Westminster Abbey or St Paul's back home. It bears much evidence of restoration, for the roof and buttresses are barely weathered in comparison with the rest of the fabric. Mayhap, like other Catholic churches, it suffered damage and neglect in the time of Protector Cromwell.

At the end of this morning's casting meeting I took the opportunity of Kitty being busy with the other actors to slip away. Nothing further was said about her and Ned accompanying me to see Miss Acres.

But my hopes of visiting the lady alone are dashed when I come face to face with the pair of them as I round the corner into the cathedral close.

'Why, Will, what a happy chance! We thought we'd missed you,' says Ned. There is no hint of suspicion or rebuke. Such things are not in his nature.

Kitty, however, is less trusting. 'One might think you were avoiding us, Will Archer.' She fastens herself about my arm, that I may not escape again. 'See how he blushes, Ned. For sure, we have caught him out!'

I sigh in resignation. 'To be sure, I have not told you the whole story...'

'There!' exclaims Kitty in triumph. 'I knew there was more to it!'

And so I tell them of my visit to the dead house yesterday evening - glossing over the manner in which I came to be there - and of the chance meeting with the dead man's sister.

Ned, learning that Tobias Acres is dead and that I am going upon the sister's invitation, reacts as I expect. Where murder and strange women are concerned, he fears for my safety and is all for abandoning the expedition entirely. But Kitty, devious as ever, argues all the more reason for us to go. 'He can come to no harm if we are with him,' and holds on to my arm even more firmly

'I wonder shall we see the famous Dean,' she wonders as we pass through the cathedral Close.

She is referring to the author of *Gulliver's Travels,* Jonathan Swift who, I learned from Mr Garrick but yesterday, is Tom Sheridan's godfather.

'I very much doubt it,' say I. 'Mr Garrick says he is much indisposed, some say not in his right wits, and keeps to his chambers. His faculties are in severe decline now that he is well stricken in years.'

Her eyes widen. 'Why, surely he cannot be that old?'

Ned laughs at her incredulity. 'The old Dean must be seventy if a day. I truly believe that Kitty thinks authors, like their literary creations, remain perpetually young! Why, she asked me but two days ago if I thought Mr Farquhar might attend our performance of *Sir Harry Wildair...*'

'Ned!' she pouts. 'Be not so cruel. I was not to know the poor fellow's dead.'

'And has been since before we three were born. Though, to tell

71

truth, if he were still alive, he would yet be younger by a decade than the good old Dean. He was but thirty when he died.'

Kitty shivers. 'God grant we be not cut off so.'

As one so recently in danger of meeting such a premature demise, it is not a subject to my liking so, as we set off along Bride Street and the wide spacious streets of the Aungier estate, I comment instead upon the buildings around us. Less than eighty years old, many of the houses have a Dutch look about them, having had stepped or rounded gable ends added. These, I imagine, are due to the influence of old King William and English immigrants.

Most are four storeyed and would, were the streets not so wide, give the impression of walking between oppressive cliffs. Dwellings in the long terraces all follow a similar pattern: a door atop a few steps, usually with a stone surround that contrasts with the warm red brick of the wall. Two windows adjacent to the door of the grander houses, one window in the less opulent. The living quarters upon the *piano nobile* above have, according to this same social division, either two or three high windows, usually with wrought metal balconies. The next storey two or three windows, not so tall, and the top floor but one or two, depending upon the size and shape of the gable.

I am sure there are many streets like this back in London, yet these feel different in some indefinable way - strangely chilly despite the warm brick.

It takes me a while to realise why - there are hardly any but we three walking. Coaches and chairs a-plenty, carrying fine gentlemen and ladies whithersoever, but none of the hubbub or usual human clutter of hawkers, vagrants and beggars that so characterises the London streets.

Now and then a maid or footman hurries by intent on some errand for their employer but, other than these, it could be midnight instead of midday, so profound is the silence that settles once the sound of steps or carriage wheels recedes.

Number fifty-six Great Boater Lane is one of the more modest residences. Nonetheless the door is answered by a footman. But such a footman as would not be brooked by any London establishment. Young, not much older than myself, his attire is remarkably disheveled - shoe buckles dull, coat almost out at elbow and cravat grubby.

'Master William Archer to see your mistress,' I inform him.

His eye fixes on my companions. 'And who might these be?' he enquires, his manner as uncouth as he himself is unkempt.

Beside me, I sense Kitty bristle. 'Mistress Caitlin Blair and Mr Edward Phillimore of Mr David Garrick's company,' she says haughtily, invoking the dignity of full names. 'Be so kind as to inform your mistress of our arrival.'

Her hauteur impresses him not a jot. 'This one,' he says with a nod in my direction, 'she's expectin', but she's not said anyt'ing about youse two.'

The casual insolence brings out Kitty's Irish roots. 'Now look you here...'

But her ire is cut short by a voice calling from within, 'Who is it, Liam?'

The next moment Miss Acres herself appears in the passageway behind him. She wears a plain day dress, sober of hue but not black as one might expect of a household in mourning. Her eye lights with recognition. 'Master Archer - do come in. And your companions...' she adds, almost as an afterthought. Then, turning to the footman, 'Liam,we will use the withdrawing room. Ask Bridget to prepare a dish of tea, and bring it up if you will - and pray do not scowl so!'

The footman stalks off, leaving his mistress to usher us upstairs.

'You must forgive Liam. He has only been in my service a twelvemonth. His manners are rough, but he has a good heart and is intensely protective - perhaps too much so at this present time.'

The room she shows us into has a neglected air. Its aspect, I guess north-facing, imparts a gloomy chill which speaks of infrequent occupation.The furniture is old-fashioned, the legacy perhaps of her dead parents, the colours faded. Indeed the whole room seems colourless, misted by a layer of grey dust. Miss Acres directs Ned and Kitty to an upright settle and myself to a chair facing her own. She herself seems stiff and ill at ease, as uncomfortable in this room as we are.

Once squashed in at Ned's side, Kitty adopts her most sympathetic expression and offers condolences upon the loss of the lady's brother. They are accepted with brief, almost curt, civility before Miss Acres changes the subject.

She enquires upon how Kitty and Ned find Ireland and what might be expected of Mr Garrick's season in Dublin. The conversation runs along with unexceptionable politeness until interrupted by a peremptory thump on the door. The footman, Liam, enters, followed by a kitchen-maid carrying a tray.

The next few minutes are occupied with the pouring and serving of tea while the four of us sit in awkward silence. For all she is our hostess, Miss Acres takes no part in the business. It is Liam who takes charge and she seems content to let him.

Kitty's eyes widen in disbelief at such social maladroitness. I lower my eyes, feeling inexplicably embarrassed for our hostess.

Once Liam has thrust cups and plates at us all, he and the maid remain in the room as we sip tea and nibble cake. Desperate attempts at conversation flicker into life before expiring altogether. Even Kitty, normally the fount of incessant chatter, admits defeat, retreating into sulky contemplation of her cup and saucer.

As soon as the last of the tea is drunk and the maid has carried out the tray, our hostess stands, straightens her dress and, all awkwardness gone, firmly announces, 'Miss Blair, Mr Phillimore, it has been a pleasure to make your acquaintance. Please feel free to call upon me again during your stay in Dublin and, if circumstances allow, I look forward to enjoying one or more of your performances during the forthcoming season. Now, if you will be so good as to excuse me, I would deprive you of Master Archer's company for a time. There are some matters pertaining to my poor dead brother that I would speak of to him alone. Liam will show you out and, if you wish to wait for Master Archer, he will advise you of one or two places of interest which may entertain you in the meantime.'

The dismissal, though courteous, is unmistakable. 'Whether or not you decide to wait,' she adds drily, 'I promise that you shall have him back unharmed within the hour.'

I can see Kitty is piqued by the dismissal and would demur. But Ned takes her hand saying, 'We thank you, Miss Acres. The pleasure has been ours entirely. Once again, Kitty and I offer you our condolences upon your loss. We look forward to seeing you again in happier circumstances and for now bid you good-day. As for Will,' he says with a sly grin, 'I am sure he is well able to find his own way home!'

As soon as the door closes behind them, I turn to the lady. 'I am sorry, Miss Acres, they insisted on accompanying me. Miss Blair impressed upon me the impropriety of my visiting a single lady alone...'

She gives a wry smile. 'A sentiment my late brother would doubtless have endorsed, Master Archer.'

'Indeed, ma'am, I apologise. You must miss him.'

'Why must I? I can assure you there was little love lost between us. Twins we may have been but, like the two faces of a coin, despite being always joined we were forever opposed. We had nothing in common but the date of our birth. Consequently the only emotion I feel at his passing is one of relief. I am sorry if that shocks you, Master Archer, but that is the way it is.'

Her candour is such that I cannot think of a suitable response. Instead, I say lamely, 'I did not know you were twins.'

'Aye, few would. For I was the better man of the two,' she laughs bitterly. She looks about the room and shivers. 'But come, Will - I may call you Will, mayn't I? And you must call me Jeannie - let us leave this dismal room and retire to more congenial surroundings.'

She hurries me to the stairs, where Liam is on his way up from

76

showing out Ned and Kitty.

The look of concern upon his face makes her break into laughter. 'Oh, and here is my faithful hound come to see no harm betides his mistress!' Gaily she turns him about and we all descend to the room adjacent to the front door. This is obviously the retreat for the servants Liam and Bridget who, it appears, comprise the whole domestic staff. It is as homely and comfortable as the reception room upstairs was bleak.

Bridget, eating a remnant of cake with her feet up on a stool, rises hurriedly at our entrance, brushing crumbs from her skirts.

'Come in, Will,' says my hostess. 'Pray excuse the slatternly ways of my housemaid,' she laughs.

Eugenie - or Jeannie as I must now call her - a familiarity that at once unsettles and delights me - is entirely different from the formal creature of a few minutes ago. Clearly she is more at ease in the company of Liam and Bridget than she was with Kitty and Ned though, heaven knows, few would call them intimidating!

'Liam, some beer for Master Archer. And bring yourself a mug, too.' Hitching up her skirts in a most un-genteel manner, she perches on a stool next to the table and signals for me to do the same. After a moment, Liam puts down three tankards of ale and, having given a fourth one to Bridget who lolls in her seat by the hearth, pulls up a stool and, much to my consternation, joins us. Elbows on table, he takes a large gulp of ale and wipes the foam off his lip with the back of his hand.

I have spent enough time in Mrs Wiggins's kitchen with Susan back home in London to be at ease the company of servants. But I have never known the master, much less the lady, of the house to join us.

I am not exactly uncomfortable, for my own position is such that I am neither servant nor gentleman. Brought up in Yorkshire of a good family, fortune brought me to London, where circumstances have brought me into contact with the highest lords in the land as well as the lowest of the city's underworld. One thing my chequered history has taught me - a person's rank is no guide to character. There are as many villains amongst the nobility as there are fine fellows among humble folk.

So, whilst I can converse as easily with servants like Liam and Bridget as with fine ladies like Eugenie, it is disconcerting to be doing so simultaneously.

So easy are they with each other, however, and so accepting of me that it takes but a few moments for my initial reserve to disappear.

'Now, Will,' Jeannie begins, 'tell Liam what we found last night at the dead house.'

Liam leans forward, chin supported on steepled hands, attentive to my every word as I recount details of the state of the body, the bruise on the left temple with the split skin at its centre, the broken nails upon the right hand.

'And there was this,' I add, taking the small cube of waxy substance from my pocket.

Jeannie takes it, fingers it distastefully for a moment then tosses it disdainfully upon the table. 'That is no mystery,' she says. 'Rosin - to rub along the horsehair of the bow that it may glide more easily across the strings. Its fellow may be found in every jacket he possessed.'

'There was nothing else in his pockets?' asks Liam.

'A few coins, Rafferty said. He was the boatman who found him.'

'Rafferty? Would that be Paddy Rafferty, now? Has a tow-haired lad name of Patrick?'

'Yes. You know him?'

'I know *of* him.'

'An abrupt fellow, but I took him to be honest.'

Liam gives a sly grin. 'To be sure, he's honest - with his fellow Irishmen. Though he'd be a mite warier with an Englishman like yourself, no doubt. Did he not inquire into your interest in the affair?'

I look down at the table, uncertain whether to reveal my medical student fiction. I do not know how well this Liam may know Rafferty, and I don't want to be found out in a lie.

So I kill two birds with one stone. I repeat the explanation about Mr Tom Sheridan's concern over Tobias Acres's disappearance that I gave to Eugenie last night at the deadhouse, then add, 'Not wishing to mention Mr Sheridan's name or our suspicion as to the identity of the dead man, I presented myself as a medical student in search of practical experience.'

'And Rafferty accepted that?'

'He accepted the coins I gave him.'

Liam utters a short bark of laughter, then gives me a shrewd look. 'But it was Mr Sheridan's interest took you there? He told you where you might find the body, did he so?'

'Aye - he, er - he sent word to have the son, Patrick, meet me and take me there...'

79

It sounds lame, but there is no way I can reveal the real source of the imposture - Sir William Hervey and his agent, Richard Semple.

I can see Liam is not convinced. For a servant, his dress may be shabby, but his wits are sharp. He gives me a keen look and a sly grin twitches his lips. 'Well, to think a respectable man like Tom Sheridan would have such low connections!'

'Come, Liam,' says Eugenie, 'Mr Sheridan is a gentleman. His concern for Tobias is commendable.'

'Aye, though misguided...'

My astonishment at his effrontery in speaking so ill of his dead master obviously shows, for Eugenie breaks in, 'Be not offended by Liam's boldness, Will. As I told you, there was little love lost between my brother and myself. The animosity I felt was no secret from Liam and Bridget here.'

'A right bastard, he was,' mutters Bridget from her chair by the hearth.

'Had he wronged you in some way?' say I to Eugenie.

'He wronged everyone by his very existence!'

The vehemence of this outburst seems to deprive her of breath for a moment. But then she resumes more calmly, 'This must be very shocking for you, Will. Have you a brother or a sister?'

'Neither,' I reply, seeking to divert her from the emotion that is still evident in her flushed cheeks. 'My father was a farmer who had the good fortune to marry into money. Wishing to do right by his new wife, he took advice and invested that money in the South Sea Project.'

'The South Sea Bubble?'

'The very same. The biggest Stock Market collapse in history.He lost everything. For a while he attempted to remedy the disaster - used what little money he had left to make a new start. He sold his farm. He and my mother   moved into a cottage that had once belonged to one of his own workers and they lived as frugally as was possible He did everything, in short, as they say in my native Yorkshire, to 'cut his coat according to his cloth'. At first, so my mother says, things began to improve. But he never shook off the feeling he had failed her and when, as a sign of her love she presented him with a child - me - he saw not a blessing but an added burden. He hanged himself in our neighbour's barn when I was but six months old.'

I pause for moment. 'So, no - I have neither brother nor sister.'

But I do not tell them that my mother, too, is lost to me. I do not tell them how, thinking it was for my advancement, she allowed Rev Purselove to take me to London when I was fourteen years old. Nor how there he handed me over to Mother Ransome to serve gentlemen in her molly house from which degradation I was eventually rescued by Mr Garrick. I have never seen my mother since.

Thinking these things, I fall silent. Yet even the little that I have just confided in these three strangers I have never told anyone else. Is it Jeannie's raw emotion about her brother that has provoked this revelation? Or the singular situation?   Whatever, I must present a forlorn aspect for Jeannie reaches over the table and gently takes my hand in hers, her touch sending a thrill skittering to my very core.

'Oh, Will,' she says, her eyes glistening.

81

Out of the corner of my eye, I see Liam's face cloud. 'An affecting tale, right enough. But then we all of us have our own tragedies, to be sure. And at least you're here to tell the tale. There's thousands that aren't that lucky. The loss of a farm is one thing, but the loss of your country - why that's something else altogether.'

Jeannie's hand tightens momentarily around my fingers, before relinquishing them altogether. 'Tut, Liam,' she says. 'Will is not interested in your factional views - keep your apprentice-boy cant till another time. Time has overtaken us. Will's friends will think we do not keep our word. Within the hour, I said.'

'Pray, ma'am,' say I, 'do not discompose yourself. I assure you, they will not have given me another thought. You were about to tell me about your brother...?'

But it is not to be. She rises swiftly. 'It is a tale that will keep for another day. His ignominy will keep. Meantime, his body must be attended to.'

'If there is aught I may do to help...?'

'Thank you, Will, but Mr Callaghan, our family lawyer, will make all necessary funeral arrangements - and Liam will do what is necessary else.' She escorts me to the front door. 'One thing more, Will? What will you tell Mr Sheridan to put his mind at ease?'

'Why, the truth, what else? That, going home from rehearsal, your brother must have been set upon by unknown assailants intent upon robbery. Finding nothing of value, they clubbed him and he either fell, or they pitched him, into the river.'

'Indeed, that is what must have happened.' On the threshold, she pauses. 'I am glad to have met you, Will Archer. You must visit me again - we have unfinished business, you and I.'

And with that, the door of 56 Great Boater Lane closes behind me.

8

...every one to his own way...

'Good day, Master Archer.'

Hardly have I walked a mile than I become aware of Richard Semple at my side. My head is so full of my meeting with Eugenie Acres and the promise implicit in her parting words that I have no idea where or when he joined me.

I acknowledge his presence with little enthusiasm. 'Mr Semple.'

'Your trip across the river was profitable, I trust?'

'The body now has a name, if that is profit enough for you.'

'Mr Rafferty proved co-operative, I take it? He accepted your, er - *medical* credentials?'

'I do not know about *accepted.* Leastways, he did not question the deceit.'

'Good. He is a man who values his own skin, I see. The less he knows, the less he can tell. A sound dictum in our line of work, wouldn't you say, Master Archer?'

We might simply be passing the time of day, so casual is his tone. But his reference to 'our line of work' irritates me. He may be content to live as one of Hervey's spies, but I am only so against my will

'You managed to see the body?' he asks.

'I did. A young man - twenty-five - of medium build. Fair hair, only passing handsome but with the singular characteristic of having one hand with nails cut short whilst the other had nails somewhat grown.'

'And the manner of death - drowning?'

'Possibly - if he was conscious when he entered the water... The boatman seemed to think he may have been dead beforehand.'

I detect the smallest flicker of interest. 'His reason?'

'The body was not putrefied, as one submerged for some time would be. A body that takes in water sinks quickly, whereas one that has already stopped breathing stays longer on the surface. This one was still fresh and floating. Rafferty surmised they'd fished him out before he sank.'

'A pretty theory - already dead, eh? No accident, then?'

'There was a bruise upon the skull and torn nails upon the right hand which suggest a violent struggle. I'd guess a robbery. There was nothing of value in the pockets.'

Semple taps his lips with his forefinger. 'Aye, a robbery, very like. A blow to the head and a body thrown into the river... Common enough in this city. No suggestion of a more - er, *particular* motive?'

I give him a withering look. 'How would I deduce that from a dead body, Mr Semple?'

If he is stung by my sarcasm, he doesn't show it.

'Yet you say you have managed to deduce a name, Master Archer.'

'And a profession. He was called Tobias Acres and he was a violinist, lately engaged to play for Mr Handel's forthcoming oratorio at the Music Hall in Fishamble Lane.'

This time he shows a greater interest, nodding admiringly. 'Well, well, Master Archer. You amaze me. May one enquire how you came by this information? Not from Rafferty, I think - I hardly see him as being conversant with cultural life...'

I tell him of Tobias Acres's disappearance, of Mr Sheridan's request that I look into the matter and of how, putting together the description given by his colleagues, the time of his going missing and the finding of the body in the river, I conclude that he can be no other.

'Also,' say I, 'his sister happened to be there at the dead house, and identified the body.'

He glances up sharply. 'A sister, say you?'

'Aye - a sister,' I say, surprised by his sudden attention. 'That is not so unusual, surely? Anyone may have a sister.'

'Indeed, Master Archer. But identifying a drowned corpse is hardly a young lady's duty.'

'Their parents are dead. So his colleagues in the orchestra told me.'

'And the name is Acres, you say?'

'Yes, he lived in Great Boater Lane - where the sister still lives.'

'Hmm, thank-you, Will. The trust Sir William reposes in you is not misplaced, I see. You have been very informative.'

'I am sure I have not told you anything you could not have discovered for yourself.'

'Oh, but you have, young man.'

'Is that my task fulfilled, then?' I ask.

'Perhaps - though there are still matters which need further elucidation.'

'You have the identity of the dead man and the means by which he died. What more can there be?'

'Think about it, Will. What facts do we have? He was last seen two or three evenings ago, you say, yet his body was taken from the river only last night - and still fresh? A poor musician - why would anyone want to rob him?'

He looks at me, eyebrows raised in question. For all I would be done with the affair, my curiosity is piqued.

He gives me a knowing look. 'If I mistake not, you are but now on your way back from Great Boater Lane - and the deceased man has a sister...?'

I feel the blood rise to my cheeks.

He smiles, satisfied. 'Handsome, is she? And young? Grateful, in her sad loss, for the kind thoughts of a presentable young man such as yourself...?'

I bridle at his implication. 'If you are ordering me to intrude further upon the grief of a bereaved lady, sir, just to satisfy your curiosity, I tell you now, I will not do it!'

He raises a placatory hand. 'Peace, Will, neither I nor Sir William is ordering you to do anything. Report this bungled robbery of a penniless musician and its unfortunate consequences to Mr Sheridan if you wish. As long as your own mind is easy as to the circumstances of Tobias Acres's death...'

It is as if he can read my thoughts, but before I can summon a reply, he is gone as swiftly and silently as he first appeared.

At the same moment, a small fist punches my thigh. 'Wotcher, mate!'

Out of habit, I aim a cuff at Charlie's head, which he adroitly dodges.

'Oo was that cove, then?' he enquires. 'The skinny lizard?'

His casual irreverence makes me laugh - his description exactly catches Semple's lank pallor. And it gives me an idea. He, it seems, knows much about me, but I know little enough of him.

I draw Charlie close. 'Did you see which way he went? Can you follow him - without being seen?'

Charlie snorts in contempt. 'Easy!' His eye lights up, 'You at it again, Will, detectin'? What is it this time?'

'No time now - be about it or you'll lose him!'

Charlie takes no further telling. He is away like a ferret after a rabbit.

Looking about me, I see I am nearer home than I thought. Lamb Alley is but a few yards away.

Just as I near it, I see Ned Phillimore approaching from the opposite direction.

'Will, my boy,' he hails me, 'you have escaped the clutches of the frosty Miss Acres, I see!'

I notice he is alone.'Where's Kitty?' I ask.

'Ah,' sighs Ned, 'you know what women are like - entranced by the sight of ribbons and gew-gaws. 'Twas fortunate we met the young man who is to play Dicky...'

'O'Sullivan?' I say sharply.

'Is that his name? Whatever, he seems as enamoured of trinkets as she. I left them to it. I have no taste for frippery.'

'Was that wise, Ned? You know nothing of him.'

Ned gives a knowing smile. 'A popinjay who finds shopping

to his taste? I don't think I have much to fear there, do you? Besides,' he adds self-mockingly, 'why would Kitty look at another man when she's got me?'

'All the same Ned...'

'Come,' says he, laughing, 'we are nearly at your lodging - might we prevail upon your landlady for a glass of porter? I long to hear how went your tete-a-tete with Miss Acres. If I am not mistaken,' says he digging me in the ribs, 'you were not over sad to bid adieu to Kitty and myself. I'll wager there was more that her brother's business in your converse...!'

We arrive at my lodgings, where Mrs Fitzgerald proves more than willing to provide us with beverage - in the form of tea rather than porter - but also insists on keeping us company, that she may hear all the theatre gossip. Ned gallantly obliges, with the result that, by the time he takes his leave, I have, to my relief, imparted no more than is necessary of the conversation between Eugenie Acres and myself.

9

...bruised for our iniquities...

On Sunday morning, the ladies express a desire to go to church.

'More to preen, I suspect, than to pray,' opines Mr Garrick mischievously.

Indeed, never having known Mrs Peg or Kitty attend church in London, I cannot help but agree.

Which is more than the two ladies themselves can.

Seeking advice from our landlady, Mrs Fitzgerald, they are now debating which particular place of worship to grace with their presence. Mistress Peg, being of Irish descent and ingrained Catholic sensibility, is all for the tradition of St Patrick's Cathedral, whilst Kitty, of a more dissenting cast of mind, would venture to the Protestant St Mary's. She is dissuaded from this by Mrs Fitzgerald, however, on account of distance, St Mary's being some considerable way north of the river. And, with the weather threatening rain, such a long walk might prove unwise.

A compromise is reached in the form of St Werburgh's. 'It has a most venerable tradition which will, I am sure, be most agreeable to you. Though the present building is scarce thirty years old, the original foundation dates back to Celtic times,' Mrs Fitzgerald informs them. 'Dr Wells was a regular visitor here when my late husband was alive - a man of impeccable orthodoxy who eschews the extremes of both papistry and presbyterianism.'

Then, with hushed confidentiality 'It is much favoured by those of influence. The Lord Lieutenant himself is known to attend...'

This proves the clincher. Traditional enough for Mistress Peg, Anglican enough for Kitty and with the added attraction of celebrity, how could it fail to please?

Mr Garrick heaves a sigh of relief and, as the ladies busy themselves with capes and boots, he gallantly invites our landlady to be one of our party.

She accepts with such fulsome expressions of gratitude that, in order to escape, I make haste to search out Charlie and prepare him for enforced devotions.

He is, to say the least, unenthusiastic. 'Church! I never bin inside a church in my life...!'

'Time you started then, you heathen.'

Taking a firm grip of his shoulder I set to on his tangled mop.

'Ow, watch wot yer doin'!' he yells. 'Anyway, you're a fine one to talk - when wus you last in a house of God?'

'Last year, as it happens - twice,' say I, smugly, tugging the last unruly strands into submission.

To be fair, I have no cause for smugness - both occasions were funerals for men I'd been accused of killing. One, the father of a woman I thought I was in love with. The other a man who would have killed me.

I wet the corner of my muffler and wipe away an errant smudge from his cheek.

'There,' say I, holding him at arm's length, 'you'll pass. Now, best foot forward - Mr Garrick and the others are waiting.'

Mr Sheridan has arrived in our absence and is in the clutches of Mrs Fitzgerald, pursuing a one-sided discourse in which he is cast as listener.

We set off towards Werburgh Street - my master arm in arm with Mrs Peg at the front, Ned and Kitty chatting animatedly, and myself keeping Charlie in check at the rear. Poor Mr Sheridan is trapped with our landlady. But as Dublin Castle looms in view, he makes his excuses and falls in by my side.

Charlie skips ahead leaving Mr Sheridan and myself out of earshot of the others.

'Well, what have you found out about Tobias Acres?'

I opt for the simplest course. 'It seems he fell victim to a footpad. He suffered a blow to the head. Mayhap his attacker mistook his violin case for something of more value. Then, discovering his mistake, pitched Tobias Acres - and his violin for aught we know - into the river.'

Mr Sheridan sighs, 'Poor Tobias - an unfortunate end, to be sure. Such a waste! Not only of talent, but of life itself.' He turns to me. 'And what of his sister? She must be distraught. Should I, perhaps, call upon to lady to express my condolences? Although I knew her brother but slightly...?'

Thinking back to Jeannie's passionate dislike of her brother, I doubt the reception he might get. 'That is generous of you, Mr Sheridan, but I have already met the lady and conveyed our sympathy for her loss. I fancy, at this trying time, your visit, though well-meant, may prove too much for her.'

'You're a good man, Will,' says Tom Sheridan with a squeeze of my shoulder. 'But tell me, is she now in straitened circumstances - would she, perhaps, accept some token of our esteem? I would not wish to offend, of course...'

'The lady has, I believe, sufficient means, sir. She may consider a monetary donation perhaps, er - inelegant?'

He colours. 'Of course, of course - it was crass of me even to suggest...'

'She is, however, a cultured young woman,' I say to spare his embarrassment. 'Mayhap, when her grief is somewhat abated, her spirits might be raised by a night at the theatre?'

He seizes upon my proposal gratefully. 'An excellent suggestion, Will. I shall write a note as soon as I get back, offering her own private box for the season. And you shall convey the missive for me, if you would be so good?'

The matter thus satisfactorily concluded, I am left feeling guiltily pleased. I have not been wholly honest with Mr Sheridan, yet his opinion of me is improved. And I have the perfect excuse to visit her again.

We catch up with others and soon arrive at St Werburgh's church where the congregation is all that Mrs Fitzgerald promised. I recognise several of the charitable gentlemen who were with Mr Handel at the rehearsal and, judging from the dress of many in the gathering - together with the multiplicity of coaches waiting outside - we are amongst the cream of Dublin society. There is hardly a noticeable Irish accent among them.

The incumbent, Dr Wells, our landlady's frequent guest in more prosperous times, is a round, colourless man who would pass unnoticed in any gathering. Unlike Richard Semple whose deliberately cultivated anonymity exudes a sort of menace, the reverend gentleman's is totally innocuous. So bland that he seems nebulous, so devoid of doctrinal extreme as to exhibit no discernible belief. His sermon is tedious, pointless and mind-numbingly dull. Against my arm, Charlie soon falls sound asleep, snuffling at dreams that are more interesting.

By the time the service ends, I feel a need to stretch my limbs in the fresh air. As we file from the church, I excuse myself from the rest of the company on the pretext of taking Charlie to see some of the town while the weather holds.

Mr Garrick, deep in conversation with admirers from the congregation, waves absent-minded assent.

The sky to the west is already looking bruised and heavy with impending rain. So Charlie and I put our best foot forward.

It's clear he's itching to say something. At last, with an offended air, he says, 'You ain't asked me yet about that cove as you told me to follow yesterday. Don't you want to know what I found out?'

To tell truth, meeting with Ned straight after and concern for his credulity over Richard O'Sullivan's intentions, has driven my spur-of-the-moment instruction to Charlie from my mind.

'Well,' say I, 'you're clearly wanting to tell me...'

'Never mind tellin' - I can show yer. We're goin' towards the river, ain't we?'

Short of winking and tapping his nose, he's determined to make a mystery of it, so I humour him. 'Yes - alright, if you like.'

I point out Dublin Castle as we pass. Charlie seems unimpressed. 'It's not used by the soldiery, you know,' he says dismissively.

'Oh, really?' I respond, 'and how, pray, do you know?'

'One of the choirboys told me the other day - his pa's in the town guard. Over the river at Oxmantown - that's where the Barracks is. And the stables and 'orses - wot I can vouch for, 'aving seen 'em with my own eyes...'

'You've been near the Barracks?'

'Aye - a-follering the skinny lizard...'

He relays this information with such jaunty smugness that my hand rises to clip his ear.

But before it makes contact, we are stayed in our tracks by a sudden cry of fear, followed by an almighty shouting.

Suddenly the street empties. Our few fellow walkers melt into air.

Charlie and I exchange bewildered glances.

But hardly have our mouths dropped in astonishment than a figure shoots from a side street behind us. He charges pell-mell at us, all but tipping us over in his headlong flight. His face is a picture of terror, blood-soaked. His clothes torn and shredded.

The next second, we see the cause of his panic. A baying mob careers around the corner. Whistling and hallooing as if in chase of a fox, coat tails flying, they brandish clubs and knives aloft. Mouths twisted in maniacal fury yelling obscenities, Irish and incomprehensible.

I haul Charlie aside and we flatten ourselves against the wall as they descend upon us.

But we cannot escape the crush of bodies.

Like straws whirled in the torrent, Charlie and I are sucked up and carried along in a maelstrom of pounding feet and jerking elbows. Borne helpless upon a reeking surge of sweat and drink and foul breath.

I make a grab for his hand but only succeed in grasping his finger ends. His nails dig into my flesh as he tries frantically to hold on. For he, much lighter than myself, is tossed about like a cork in the onrush.

Out of the hubbub occasional phrases leap out. '...Liberty boy...get the bastard...string him up...'

Inexorably Charlie's finger-ends are sliding from my grasp.

'Charlie!' I yell. 'Keep hold!'

But it is too late. He is gone.

In desperation I elbow aside jostling limbs, dodge flailing clubs and heave myself onto the shoulders of my unwelcome companions, earning curses and bruises for my pains. But I am rewarded by a glimpse of Charlie's tousled pate a few yards ahead.

'Charlie!' I yell again.

He squirms around and the sight of his terrified face makes me redouble my efforts. I jab my elbows more sharply, I push and pull my way through the bodies, tripping and toppling many in my frenzy.

Hands claw at me. Cudgels thud against my bones. A blade rips my coat. But I neither feel nor heed the pain.

A voice is shouting in my very ear.

It is me, urging Charlie to hold on, I'm coming...

Then, suddenly, mine is the only voice shouting. The din has moved on, fading in the distance.

But six or seven of the louts have slowed to a trot. Now, as their companions swirl away into the distance, they, like grounded flotsam, come to a halt, standing in a circle about me, panting, glowering.

Two of them have Charlie pinned between them.

He struggles, kicking at their shins and scratching the beefy hand that holds him. With a curse they hoist him from the ground. His legs kick nothing but air. They wrench his arms so hard he screams in pain.

'Let him alone!' I roar, lurching forward. 'He is but a child!'

A fist makes contact with my face and I stagger back, blood pouring from my nose. Strong arms pinion me from behind.

A hand grabs my hair and jerks my head back. Through a veil of blood, a face thrusts itself near to mine.

'A choild he may be, but a bloody vicious one. Shut his squalling, Seamus!'

From the muffled splutterings I can tell that one of the ruffians has clapped a hand over Charlie's mouth. Then the face floats into my vision again.

'And you - what may you be, eh?' he growls.

The back of my throat is clogged with blood and snot, any attempt at speech a mere gurgle.

'Come, speak up!' Another jerk of my hair cracks my neck.

'He's a fucking Englishman,' rasps another voice. 'Didn't youse hear him just before you belted him one?'

'English, is it? We knows what the Ormond boys does to the fecking English!'

'Hough him, lads. String him up to the nearest lamp-post - and his bawling brat!'

They close in on me menacingly, prodding, jeering.

Suddenly, there is a cry from where the men are holding Charlie. 'Sod beag fuilteacha! He's bit me!'

Those goading me turn. Through my tangle of blood-soaked hair I see the man snatch his hand away. Even as he does so, Charlie twists in his loosened grip and clamps his teeth on the man's nose, shaking his head to inflict more pain.

Howling in agony, off balance, the man staggers back, releasing his hold to clasp his ruined face. Charlie, now held only on one side, swings round as he drops and delivers a double-footed kick to his other captor's groin. The second man doubles up in pain.

All happens so quickly that the drunken louts around me are slow to react.

As they gather their addled wits, I plant my feet firm and fling my arms wide, breaking the grip of the man who pinions me. Balling my hands together in front on me, I drive both elbows back into his midriff, winding him.

Meanwhile, Charlie is among them like a fireball punching out in all directions.

But it is no aimless punching. Every blow lands squarely in a pair of testicles.

The pain is immediate and intense but, delivered by a twelve year old punch, it will not last above a few seconds.

'Come on, Will, get 'em in their bellies,' shrills Charlie.

I follow up, driven by anger and revenge, slamming my fist with all my might into as many bellies as I can. Hands still clutching their injured privates, they deflate with a grunt, expelling air like stuck bladders.

Then the two of us take to our heels.

But our effort has taken it out of us and, with blood clogging my breath and blinding my sight, we cannot hope to get far.

Staggering to their feet, the gang pursue us with a roar and within seconds they are gaining on us.

Desperately, we search around for some means of escape, some door or road-end. But this street seems to go on forever...

Then, just as I must fall or choke to death on the bloody mucus that clogs my throat, salvation comes. Turning a corner, we are confronted by another mob.

They halt, uncertain, seeing us.

For a brief second, we stare at each other.

But in that second our pursuers charge round the corner behind us.

They skid to a halt and immediately from those in front the shout goes up, 'Ormond boys! Get the scum!'

Our pursuers turn tail.

Most of our saviours rush past us in their wake, but three loiter behind. In concern, I hope, for our bedraggled state.

One approaches us. But he shows no interest in our wounds. Instead he asks, 'Youse be Liberty boys, is it?'

Blankly, I shake my head. I have no idea what these youths are talking about - Liberty boys? Ormond boys? - and I am now too exhausted and angry to care.

Lost in a strange city and surrounded by people who care nothing for our injuries...

And, to make matters worse, it is getting darker by the minute.

None too gently, one of the youths takes me by the shoulder

and hustles me forward.

'Come on, now,' says he, 'there be more o' they Ormond bastards about - 'tis their territory we're in.'

Irritated, I shrug him off and croak. 'Let us be, for God's sake. We can find our own way.'

They stop dead.

'Hear that, Dermot?' says his companion. Then turning to me, 'Are youse English?' he asks menacingly.

Oh, not again! I think. At least this time, there's only three of them.

But even as the thought forms in my head, there is renewed yelling and a further rabble appears.

The three around us take to their heels.

Wearily I sink to the ground, pulling Charlie down with me against the wall. 'Keep your head down and your mouth shut,' I mutter. 'Whatever side they're on, they don't like us English. With luck we can feign beggars and just point them the right way.'

By now, the sky is black as night with the oncoming storm. I can only hope the gloom will prove our ally.

As the mob closes in, however, my heart sinks. In its midst I see a couple of our first tormentors.

And they have seen us. Their faces split into evil grins.

There can be no hope of escape this time.

But just as they break away from the crowd and start towards us, an almighty crash sounds directly above us and the darkening sky is riven with brilliant light. At the same time the heavens open. Rain sluices down like buckshot, soaking us in the instant.

Cursing, the mob disperses.

Staggering up from our seat by the wall, Charlie and I cling on to each other under the heavens' onslaught.

We have not gone more than a few steps, however, than something thuds into my back, sending me staggering.

Beside me Charlie struggles. His yelp of protest is cut off at half cock.

Strong arms seize me.

A heavy blow to the back of my head.

Consciousness deserts me, and I sink into a yet deeper blackness.

10

...they were sore afraid...

I open my eyes to such pain and impenetrable blackness that I think I must be dead and suffering the torments of Hell.

I am racked with cramps and blows, every bruise aches, every cut stings. I taste the salt of crusted blood upon my lips...

But if this is Hell, why is it so cold? And damp? Where are the everlasting flames and reek of sulphur? The only smell here is of damp and dirt. An underground smell not of fire and brimstone but of rooms long shut up, of rain-soaked clothes and sweat - and fear. The smell of myself and my prison.

I am lying on a hard surface. I run my fingers stiffly over it - not stone, but packed earth. A few inches further reveals a wall of rough bricks coated with mouldy smelling slime.   My limbs, numb with cold, are a patchwork of sudden jolts of pain, as I ease myself, wincing, into a sitting position. Reaching up, I feel no roof to this dark hole.

In response to my shifting, something, somewhere in the blackness, stirs. I listen, alert. A rat? But rats do not whimper - my fellow prisoner is human...

Of course! Memory trickles back - the storm, rival gangs - I was not alone...

I try my voice. It comes out in a hoarse whisper. 'Charlie, is that you?'

'Will?'

The reply comes weak, pathetic hope trembling beneath the terror. Tentatively I reach out in the direction of his voice. He hiccups with dread and instinctively recoils as my fingers make contact. Then seizes my hand. He uses my outstretched arm to haul himself to my side.

'Oh Will, thank God...'

His fingers, like those of a blind man, search out my face. He hugs me, sobbing without inhibition like the child that he is. The fervour of his embrace makes all my injuries cry out. But the pain is nothing to the joy of relief that he is safe. Stroking his head, brushing the tears from his cheeks I draw him to me, the uncontrolled heaving of his thin body prompting my own tears of gratitude for our deliverance.

So for several seconds, we cleave to each other in this dank underground hole, knowing naught of where we are or what is to happen to us - except that, whatever may chance, we will face it together.

At length, childish weakness passed, Charlie will be once more the man. With an embarrassed grunt, he recoils from the hug. Yet he is unwilling to relinquish our proximity altogether. He sits a hand's distance from me on the cold hard earth and says gruffly. 'I wasn't mewling, mind - don't think it! Just perishin' cold- 's all. What is this place, Will? It's bloody dark...'

'Then our hands had best do the seeing for us,' say I. 'Keep close.'

Knees bent, one hand on the floor, the other testing the darkness before me, I begin to explore our prison. Charlie crawls behind me holding on to my foot as we assess the perimeter of our domain.

A room about ten foot square, empty of furniture beyond a couple of wooden chairs, but with empty bottles and clay pipes strewn about, the smell of drink and tobacco still on them. It may not be lived-in but the place has obviously been used recently.

At the side furthest from where we started we come upon rough-hewn steps leading up to a wooden hatch or door. Dim light shows in a thin sliver along the bottom. I creep up the steps and put my ear against the rough wood. If there are people upon the other side, they are very quiet.

Our foray completed, we sit once more with our backs against the wall opposite the door.

And wait.

After a few minutes, Charlie says, 'Is it them roaring boys as put us in 'ere, Will?'

'Your guess is as good as mine.'

'They goin' ter bump us off, d'yer think?'

'Don't be daft,' say I making light of it, 'why take the trouble to bring us here when they could have finished us off on the street?'

'Fair point,' admits Charlie. Then, as if it clinches the matter, 'But they're Irish, ain't they?'

We lapse into a silence broken only by the sound of our breathing. I strain to hear if the storm still rages outside, but there is nothing. After a few minutes Charlie's shifting beside me becomes a shuffling, then a fidgeting.

'Cripes, Will, I be bustin' for a piss - if they bog-trotters don't come soon, I'm goin' ter burst...'

'Do it in the corner over there if you're that desperate...'

But the necessity is cut short by the sound of boots and voices beyond the hatch. Our captors have returned.

Charlie huddles closer, clutching my arm.

'We're a match for them, Will,' he whispers. 'We've shown 'em once, ain't we? We can do it again.'

My aching bones don't share his optimism.

In the opposite wall, the sound of bolts being drawn.We shield our eyes as a square of light appears, momentarily blinding us.

A dark silhouette peers in at us.

'A touching picture, to be sure!' says an Irish voice. 'Well, come on out, the pair of youse, for sure as bejasus, I'm not a-coming in to get youse.'

Getting to my feet sets every ache a-jangling. Putting a protective arm about Charlie's shoulder, I shuffle slowly to the doorway.

We emerge into a cramped chamber, no bigger than the cellar that has been our prison. We come out under a staircase that leads to an upper floor.

The light which seemed so blinding now proves feeble enough - a guttering oil-lamp set upon a bare wooden table in the middle of the room.

The rest of the furniture, sparse as it is, is no better. A decrepit wooden dresser, a wash-tub beside a crude hearth in which smoulder a few feeble embers. Beneath the grime-encrusted window next to an outer door, a stone sink and wooden board on which stands a water pitcher. In one alcove beside the chimney breast a patched curtain half-hides a pallet bed. The other is fronted by rough wooden doors, one of which hangs askew, its top hinge roughly repaired with wire, revealing shelves on which sit motley pots and jars. The neatness of their arrangement, the smell of soap and scrubbed wood, together with a tattered knitted shawl or blanket draped over the arm of a wooden rocking chair next to the hearth suggest a woman's influence, but no woman is present in this wretched room.

The man gestures us towards some stools around the central table as he seats himself in the rocking-chair.

Charlie's grip upon my tattered coat tail tightens. Looking towards the table, I see why.

On a couple of the stools sit two of the men who attacked us.

I squeeze the lad's shoulder reassuringly and, with slow deliberation, I pull out one of the stools for Charlie and sit on another. My eyes meantime do not budge from the two faces on the opposite side of the table.

They, in turn, follow the stiffness of my movements and take in my battered face.

One of them bares rotten teeth in an evil grin to his companion. 'Been in the wars this one, eh Dermot? Now where could he have got bruises the like of that from, d'ye think? Surely not from a stroll of a Sunday afternoon.'

Their laughter is cut short by the third man. The sound of his voice wrests my attention from the two ruffians opposite me and I know we have met before. I turn in surprise to where he lolls in the rocking chair.

'Enough, you daft gobshites! Pray, take a seat, Master Archer - Will. Pay no heed to these eejits. They have shit for brains.'

106

'Watch who you're calling an eejit, Sean Kelly,' growls one, half rising, his fist bunched.

The threat does not perturb the man in the rocking chair, whom I now recognise as the obstreperous brother of Finn Kelly, the fortuitous violinist of two days ago.

'Give o'er with your bluster, Ciaran O'Dowd. It's you I'm calling an eejit, for it is an eejit you are. Do you not know a gentleman when you sees one?'

'I knows a fecking Englishman when I hears one.'

'To be sure, and that blinds you to all else!' Sean rises and comes across to me. 'My apologies once more, Will.' Resting a hand upon my shoulder, he turns to his two companions. 'Listen here, you arse-bollocks, this is Will Archer, friend of David Garrick, the famous actor, and Mr Tom Sheridan, godson of Dean Swift.'

Mention of the good Dean's name wipes the scowls off the faces of O'Dowd and his crony. But they are reluctant yet to accept Sean Kelly's recommendation.

'So how comes it that you know him, Kelly? You have as much gentility as a turd! What the bugger have you to do with men of refinement?'

'It is Will, here, and not myself as mixes with them theatrical sort,' retorts Sean, not in the least affronted by the insult. 'And I call Will a gentleman, not on account of the company he keeps, but because of the great favour he has done our family.'

I cannot hide my surprise. 'A favour - how so? I have exchanged but a dozen words with you and your brother...?'

'Indeed, but they were words of approbation from an

Englishman to an Irishman - words spoken in friendship and in the presence and the company of other influential Englishman. You have no idea how rare a thing that is, Will Archer. It is what has saved your hide and that of your young companion this day, after being foolish enough to venture forth when the Boys are abroad.'

I cannot hide my mystification. '*Boys?*' say I.

'Aye, the Liberty and Ormond boys - sure you must have heard of them?'

'Indeed, I have not. Not till today.'

'And how long have you been in Dublin?'

'Under a week.'

'Then it is time you were better informed , mi bucko, if you want to survive here another week!'

Settling himself once more in the rocking chair, he proceeds to tell us of the territorial gangs that roam the streets of Dublin. The weavers from the Earl of Meath's Liberty to the north of the river, known as the Liberty Boys, and the butchers of Ormond Market south of the river.

Their rivalry is long-standing. O'Dowd, the more vocal of the two ruffians, interrupts to speak nostalgically of a gang called the Kevan Bail, also mainly butchers, who regularly skirmished with the Watch and City authorities during his childhood. 'We protects our own areas, so,' he says, 'and our own people. Those damned weavers had no right to muscle in on the bull baiting.'

This, I gather, is a reference to an incident a dozen years ago when some weavers of the Liberty faction took cattle from Smithfield Market for the purpose of baiting with dogs. The Butchers, not taking kindly to this intrusion into their territory and into an activity they regarded as their domain, violence ensued. Since then, it's become a regular occurrence. 'Nigh on every Sabbath,' says O'Dowd's hitherto taciturn companion with grim satisfaction, 'we gives the bastards a drubbing. One or two smart skirmishes wi' stones and clubs, nothing serious. 'Tis only their pride we're after injuring.'

'And me,' say I indignantly, recalling the fist in my face, the threat to hang me from the nearest lamp-post, 'was it just my pride you intended to hurt? What did the fellow mean by *hough him?*'

'Away wit' you, we'd never have done it!' scoffs O'Dowd with a coarse, nervous, laugh.

'It is the butcher's signature punishment,' says Sean quietly. 'Hamstringing. Seldom done, except in extreme cases.'

'But beating up innocent strangers going about their lawful business is acceptable,is it?' I say bitterly. 'Not only for you but for your opponents as well?'

Sean endeavours to placate me. 'You must remember, Will, you are in Ireland. However much the Ormond and Liberty Boys hate each other, they hate you English more. You are the common enemy.' He holds up a hand as I begin to protest. 'Fine fellow that you are, the history of our benighted country does not allow for fine distinctions. Just count yourself fortunate that I came along when I did, or God knows what further hurt these two might have done youse.'

It seems Sean came upon O'Dowd and his companion at the very moment the ruffian felled me. Recognising me and Charlie from the rehearsal at the Music Hall in Fishamble Street, he stayed their hands.

The house we're currently in is his and its fortunate proximity allowed him to persuade our attackers to carry us here and dump us in the cellar - they, doubtless, in hope of further private retribution when we regained consciousness, he mindful of our safety. During the short time we've been locked below, a couple of tankards of ale have helped cool their ire.

'Now,' he concludes, rising in business-like manner from the rocking chair, 'Ciaran and Dermot are leaving.'

The two scoundrels open their mouths to protest, but one look at Sean make them think better of it. Grudgingly, they get to their feet and shuffle surlily towards the door. They leave in silence, their disappointment hanging like a cloud about them.

'Are you one of them?' asks Charlie, echoing my own thought. He is hard put to keep the awe out of his voice.

'The Ormond Boys?' replies Sean with a lopsided grin. 'It's more sense I have than to be risking my pate cracked every Sabbath!'

'Yet they obey you,' say I.

'They recognise me as one of their persuasion even though I do not choose to be of their company.'

'You are not a butcher by trade, then?'

He holds out his hands. 'Do they look like a butcher's ham fists?' he scoffs. 'No, I am a clerk at the Custom House - an errand-boy, more like, for, being Irish, I am not trusted with the business side of things.'

'Mayhap you know a Mr Richard Semple there?' It is out before I can stop myself.

'Semple? No - no - I cannot say I do. A merchant, is he - or one of the brokers?' There is just enough hesitation for me to know he is lying. 'A friend of yours, is he?'

'An acquaintance merely.' I shift uncomfortably upon my stool. 'Your pardon, sir, but my bruises begin to stiffen.'

'My apologies, Will.' He goes to the water pitcher beside the stone sink, dips a rag into it, wrings it out and brings it to me. 'Here, a cold compress will help soothe the worst of the ache.'

Then, going to the cupboard, he begins searching among the jars and bottles. 'My sister Biddy will have some salve or other, I am sure. She's a great one for dosing herself.'

It is as Charlie is helping me unlace my shirt to get at the most painful of my hurts that the door opens and the lady herself appears.

I look up as Sean says, 'Bridget, this is Will Archer. He's fallen foul of the Ormond mob - have you any salve for cuts and bruises?'

But her only reply is to stand there open-mouthed, staring with an astonishment that surely reflects my own.

For Sean Kelly's sister Bridget is none other than Eugenie Acres's housemaid.

11

...break their bonds asunder...

The afternoon is well advanced as we leave Kelly's house. The storm has passed, leaving the sky pale and translucent, the colour of alabaster, lending an eerie glow to unfamiliar surroundings.

It is not as late as I thought. Clearly Charlie and I were unconscious for less time than I imagined. The strange light, the fractured sense of time makes me light-headed. It is like stepping into another world. I touch my fingers to the abrasions on my cheek to convince myself that this morning's events have not been all a dream.

But no, the cuts and bruises are real enough. As are the cramped houses huddled in the narrow street, now a foul quagmire of dark puddles and slimy rubbish from the dungheaps loosened by the rain. Rats, lured by the spoils, skitter boldly through the muck paying little heed to us in their search for booty. It reminds me of the noisome lanes in the East End of London, down by the docks.

And here, too, the river stench is undeniable. We must be very close to the Liffey, in one of the older parts of the city that still cling to its banks, not yet demolished to make way for development like that along Dame Street and the newer Quays.

It is a far cry from the Aungier Estate where Eugenie lives - and where Bridget is the housemaid. Like Susan back at home in London, Sunday must be Bridget's day off, which is why she is able to visit her brother. Hers must be the woman's touch in that wretched place.

After her initial surprise at seeing me, Bridget asserted her practicality. Brushing aside Sean, she went straight to the remedies he was at a loss to find. She applied tincture of arnica to our bruises, rubbed salve into my cuts then set to stitching up the worst rents in our coats and breeches.   We are now more or less presentable again. All the same, Sean has insisted on accompanying us.

'Now you're mended, I'd not have you broken again!' he jests. 'There may yet be some of the Boys about the streets.'

On the way, I enquire about his brother, Finn, and learn that he does not live with them, but lodges with his employer for he is a lawyer's clerk.

'Our father was a dealer in shoddy,' Sean tells me, 'but he determined that Finn and I should have every opportunity to better ourselves. We were given the best schooling available, though Finn was always more adept than I. Nevertheless, his advancement came not through his brain, but through Bridget.'

'Your sister? But she is a maidservant...'

'Aye - and an incorrigible chatterbox. Her employers, the Acress, hearing Finn's accomplishments so lauded, asked to see the prodigy in person. You have seen how natural and amiable a man is my brother, have you not? 'Twas that same amiability that led them to recommend him to their family lawyer.'

We have come to the edge of the river, and my suppositions are proved correct. We are on the north bank. Only here would such a noxious area survive. We cannot be far from Rafferty's

113

shack and the dead house, where only two nights ago I viewed Tobias Acres's corpse.

Yet this morning's encounter with the mob took place on the southern shore. I ask Sean about this.

'Did you pay no heed to what I told you?' he says. 'Though, to be sure, with them two bollox a-staring at youse over the table, 'tis not surprising. The Liberty Boys is from the north side of the Liffey, whilst the Ormond Boys is from the south. A few years back, they'd venture into each others' territory and there'd be pitched battles at Oxmantown Green, Kilmainham Common and the like. The city authorities came down hard on the ringleaders - public floggings, transportation - which subdued it for a while. But you can't kill an Irishman's love for a brawl. So, as long as there's no one gets killed, there's a blind eye turned nowadays. So at the week's end, the good citizens keep to their houses, and the boys keep mainly to the quays and bridges of the Liffey. Who holds a bridge claims the victory. And everyone's had the pleasure of a good fight!'

Charlie and I made the mistake of venturing too close to the river on a weekend. It is not one we will make again!

A mist hangs over the Liffey and coils ghostly about our feet as the air turns cool in the aftermath of the storm. Crossing the bridge, I hear Charlie shivering by my side, wheezing with sharp indrawn breaths, and draw him close. I would not have him catch a fever from the foul miasma of the river.

Meantime, Sean keeps sharp-eyed watch. Though the streets are quiet, we hear occasional bursts of shouting in the distance. The rival mobs are clearly still at large.

'So this Semple who you say works at the Custom House,' says Sean, as the building itself looms up through the mist, 'what does he look like?'

'A shrimp of a man, unremarkable...'

At my side, Charlie stirs. 'Say, wasn't that the cove that you...' I nip his arm to stay his tongue. He takes the hint, for he continues, barely missing a beat, into a fiction that amazes me. '...that you was knocked arsey-yarsey by when those chair-men was a-frighted by that bolting horse?'

I take up his story gratefully. 'Indeed,' I explain to Kelly, 'a mishap in the street. As I helped him up the gentleman inquired my name and gave me his. We assured each other that we were no worse for the tumble, and he said he had only to walk a little way further to the Custom House.'

Kelly seems satisfied with the explanation.

But as we approach Lamb Lane, his mood changes. 'Where exactly do you lodge?' he asks.

'At the house of a widow, Mrs Fitzgerald. Do you know her?'

'I know no good of her,' he says bitterly. 'And lucky it is that Ciaran and Dermot do not know of your association with her. You would not escape harm a second time.'

'Why so?' I ask, bewildered.

'She is a widow, you say?' continues Sean. 'Do you know what trade her husband followed, and how he came by his death?'

'A draper, she said, purveyor of fine silks to the gentry. And he fell prey, like Charlie and me, to a band of rioters.'

'Aye, but his was no accidental encounter.' The bitterness of his tone is laced with suppressed anger. 'It was retribution for

115

sending five fine lads to the gallows - upon his wife's false evidence.' He utters a heartfelt sigh. 'Oh, Will Archer, you know not the half of what we Irish must endure!'

I cannot contain my incredulity. 'Mrs Fitzgerald caused five men to be hanged?'

We have stopped within sight of the door. Sean stares with such intense hatred that I wonder the wood does not smoulder and burst into flame.

I rest a hand upon his shoulder. 'Tell me,' I say.

And so I learn of yet another cause of Irish unrest against their English masters. How Parliament back in London, many years since, passed the Woolen Act forbidding Irish journeyman weavers from selling their goods to any country but England, and at such a low rate that as a result thousands emigrated and the rest fell into penury or starved, their wage being less than half that of an English day labourer.

They formed combinations and tried to sell their wares within Ireland itself but, when these measures failed, they resorted in desperation to attacking shops that stocked textiles manufactured in England.

'And after one such attack on her husband's shop,' Sean tells me, 'the Fitzgerald woman gave the city authorities descriptions of five young men. No matter that there was evidence of their being elsewhere - the word of a respectable woman, allied with a belief that an example must be set, led to a public hanging in Weaver's Square.'

Sean ends his tale with the weariness of resignation. 'You will forgive me if I do not see you to your door.'

Thus we part and, in the few steps to Mrs Fitzgerald's house, I have time to ponder on what I have learned this day of the simmering hatreds in this fair city, and how deceptive our first opinion of people can be.

12

...a vain thing...

Monday's rehearsal of *Sir Harry Wildair* is to include my scene with the redoubtable Mrs Poynter. I cannot say I am looking forward to it. The lady is imperious and aloof and my feeble efforts are unlikely to impress her.

Also Richard O'Sullivan, the young actor playing Dicky, Kitty Blair's fellow servant, will be there. He who told me only an idiot could fail to raise laughter with every line my character, Remnant, speaks. I fear that idiot will be appearing very shortly!

On waking this morning, my whole body aches from yesterday's encounter. Fortunately, Bridget's salve has worked wonders and my face shows only slight signs of the injuries inflicted. My coat, too, is better in the morning light. It is not nearly so damaged as I first feared, mainly scuffed and muddied. After a good brushing Bridget's needlework is almost unnoticeable.

So it is only my nerves which are in shreds as I stand at the side of the stage awaiting the cue for my entrance.

Like Goodmans Fields theatre back in London, the upstage scenery consists of painted cloths one behind the other which can be raised or lowered according to whether it be an interior or exterior scene. On either side from upstage to downstage are tall 'legs' of canvas painted to match the back-cloths that can be slid in or out on runners in the floor.

Scene shifters are not involved this early in production so there is no uniformity of scene. Some of the wing canvases depict a panelled room while others display sylvan greenery. And the back-cloth shows a tossing sea-scape which does nothing for my churning stomach as I wait in trepidation for my cue.

At last I hear it and in my guise as a tailor am ushered onstage by the girl playing one of Lady Lurewell's maids.

"*Oh, Mr Remnant,*" gushes Mrs Poynter, with even more condescension now she is in character, "*I don't know what ails these stays you have made me; but something is the matter, I don't like them.*"

"*I am very sorry for that, madam...*" I begin.

Mr Sheridan interrupts almost immediately.

'A little more, er - *effeminate* if you please, Master Archer. Flap your hands a little and fuss about - let your fingers flutter about the lady's - ahem - nether regions...'

I pale even more at this direction and my mouth goes dry. But obediently I stoop and let my hands hover at a safe distance from Mrs Poynter's ample rump.

I gulp as I deliver my next line, my nervousness causing me to seize upon words like a drowning man. "*But WHAT FAULT does your LADY ship find?*"

'Very good, Will.' calls Mr Garrick from the pit. 'Invest the emphasised words with the hint of a French accent, perhaps?'

And so I stumble through my dozen lines in a totally unrealistic French accent, prancing and flailing my hands around the lady like a demented gnome.

"*Are they TU WI-IDE MADam? - TU STRITE perhaps? - Your*

LIEdi SHIP, I think is a LEETLE too SLENder for the FASHion.'

To me it sounds hideous, but it seems to meet with the approval of my master and Mr Sheridan who chuckle throughout.

At last, exhausted and sweating, I utter my last line, "*I shall TEK care to PLIZ your LIEdiSHIP for the FEWcher,"* then bow deeply and make my escape.

'Well done,' says a soft Irish voice beside me as I stumble into the wings. 'If you can make the guv'nor laugh now, you'll have no trouble wit' the audience later on.' Richard O'Sullivan puts a comradely arm about my shoulders. 'What, Will, sweating? A cooling tankard of ale is what you need - our parts are done for today. I know an inn down by the river where we may pass a convivial half-hour. What say you?'

Little as I know or like the fellow, I agree to his proposal. My friend Ned will be on stage for much of the morning and I would, for his sake, prevent this man and Kitty spending too much idle time together.

So we step out of the Smock Alley Theatre into streets a-bustle with the daily life of the city - ladies parading in the latest fashion, children hawking trinkets and flowers, gentlemen alighting from chairs and coaches. The crisp Spring morning is alive with noise and activity, so that O'Sullivan and I are hard put to hear each other above the din. Instead we wend our way through the throng, for all the world like easy acquaintances about our accustomed business, exchanging only the odd shouted comment in each other's ear.

Anyone seeing us would take us for master and servant, so drab am I next to his finery. His dress, though not ostentatious, is quality, his coat a rich, deep plum colour in the morning sunlight. It is not his clothes, however, but more his confident gait - a sort of swagger - that marks him out. He is a man at ease, one who knows his place in the world.

Our way once more leads to the river. But today there are no roaring boys cascading through the streets.

Custom House Quay is a hive of commercial activity. Merchants hurry to and fro, conducting their business in small groups. Carters, yelling greetings to one another, trundle crates and bags to the stores along the quay. Strangers with business in the area wander slowly along, peering at name-plates on unfamiliar doors. And on the fast flowing Liffey itself, vessels heave and bob on the swell, figures swarming about their decks, like another city in miniature.

I glance up as we pass the Custom House. Somewhere inside are Richard Semple and Sean Kelly - the one busy scribbling away at his desk, the other running errands.

As if in answer to my thoughts, Kelly himself emerges from an archway with a bundle of papers under his arm.

At the same moment a gentleman turns straight into his path. Papers fly in all directions. Sean swoops with an oath to retrieve them, cursing the hapless man's clumsiness in round terms. Contemptuously, the man wields his cane to sweep him aside and stalks off about his business.

All documents recovered, Kelly dusts himself down and makes to go on his way. Then he sees us.

'Bejasus, if it isn't Will Archer!' he exclaims. Then, with a sardonic glance at the retreating businessman, 'Witness the

121

disdain with which you English treat us.'

He notices my companion for the first time and his gaze clouds.

Perplexed, I turn to catch O'Sullivan curl his lip. 'Kelly - still nursing resentment, I see.'

Kelly ignores him. His face hardens towards me. 'You keep strange company, Archer. First the Fitzgerald bitch - and now this lickspittle. I begin to regret my kindness. Next time you get into trouble, I'll leave you to your fate. Good day to you.'

He turns on his heel and strides angrily away.

Bewildered, I turn to O'Sullivan. 'You know him?'

'We were acquainted at one time - we went our separate ways,' he says curtly. Then he puts a smile upon his face. 'But let us talk of happier things. Here is the inn I told you of. I am ready for that drink - are not you?'

The room he leads me into is nothing like *The Bull's Head*. This is a place as much for eating as for drinking. At the tables merchants and brokers are discussing business and persons of quality are debating the matters of the day. A few seconds is enough to tell me that those same persons of quality and merchants are, or would aspire to be, English. Other than the servants, there is hardly an Irish accent to be heard.

Even O'Sullivan's soft Irish lilt lessens as he orders two tankards of ale and a platter of cold cuts. 'You will share some victuals, Will? I always find I have an appetite at this time of day.'

It is clear that he is well-known in the establishment. The waiter recognises him immediately and hastens to find us seats. As we pass through, a number of customers acknowledge him with smiles and nods.

Once we are settled at a table in the corner, he asks about how I came to be with Mr Garrick's company. I give him the briefest account, saying how I was recommended to him by a nobleman, and that Mr Garrick seems to discern in me some talent of which I confess myself unaware.

I do not tell him of our vicar in Yorkshire, Revd Purselove, who defiled me when I was yet a boy and, when I was grown too old for his tastes, carried me off to London to Mother Ransom's molly-house. Nor of Sir Francis Courtney, a client of that vile place who, moved by my heartfelt pleas against further debauchment, recommended me to Mr Garrick as having the conviction necessary for the stage.

My mother and Mr Garrick do not know my history. The only people who do are those who have participated in it - or those like Sir William Hervey who, I know not how, discovered it and now uses it as a hold over me.

I cannot deny my past, but I do not talk of it. So I give Richard O'Sullivan only the barest outline that courtesy allows.

He takes no offence, however, for he now eagerly launches into an account of his own life. His inquiry about mine, it seems, was merely the necessary precursor to an epic drama with himself as hero.

Born in County Wexford from old Irish farming stock, he came to seek his fortune as a young man in Dublin. 'There was no future in farming, d'you see? We'd lost our land to English landlords in my great granda's time. My da and his continued as tenant farmers, but the landlord back in England took all the income and put nothing back. Being Catholic, we had few enough rights as it was - not allowed to own land, or to practice law or to vote or sit in Parliament - not that the Parliament in Dublin had any say, only the English Parliament could make laws. By the time I was born half the population could barely afford bread, let alone meat. Pigs and cattle in England had a better life than we Irish peasants. And then, when I was ten years of age, we had three years of famine. Twelve members of my family I lost... So, believing that Dublin must have more to offer an ambitious young man than the country, I set off for the big city with little more than the clothes I was wearing.'

So far, so familiar. His story has the resentment against the English colonisers that I have come to expect from nearly everyone I've met in this country. And yet, at the same time, I can relate to the lost boy in the great city, for haven't I myself been there? But if he came with only the clothes he stood, how did he not find himself among the beggars I've seen on Dublin's streets, wretches who make the beggars back in London look prosperous?

He doesn't leave me long in doubt.

'There I was, twelve years old, no possessions, no money - only the determination to succeed. No job was too lowly. A crossing sweeper, begging ha'pence off toffs who didn't want their shoes to get dirty as they crossed the road. Shoveling shit for the night-soil men. Slowly but surely I clawed my way up the ladder, till I got a job as errand boy to a baker, delivering done loaves back to customers who'd left them to be baked that morning. And it was as I was running along, juggling the hot bread from one hand to t'other that I first saw a troupe of travelling players...'

He tells how he was entranced from that moment. The fine words, the gaudy costumes, the world of stories and imagination. Much like his present narration, I think to myself.

'My life was a dreary and dismal struggle,' he continues, 'but theirs was a constant world of wonder in which I could be anything I wanted...'

So he had run away with the players and by the time he was my age had become accomplished enough to audition for Mr Sheridan's company.

He sits back with a smile of expectation - *is he expecting applause?*

'That's certainly some story,' say I in the best tone of congratulation I can muster. But, in truth, I am beginning to wonder if his narrative is not just over-dramatised but actually fabricated. If he is, in truth, so poor, reliant upon the modest earnings of an actor, how is it he can dress so fine?

His tale of adversity overcome might impress credulous young ladies listening in open-mouthed wonder. They might fall under the spell of his honeyed words and handsome features. But I am swayed by neither.

Having cleared his plate and drained a second tankard of ale, O'Sullivan says, 'Your friend Phillimore has bagged himself a beauty in Miss Kitty Blair - she's a fine filly to grace any man's arm, is she not?'

'Aye,' say I, fixing him with a hard stare,'they are very much in love. She has eyes only for him.'

Then I change the subject. I ask about his acquaintance

with Sean Kelly and why there is bad blood between them.

He gives a theatrical sigh. 'There is no harm, I suppose. We met as boys. He was carrying wool for his da, and I was carrying bread for my master. Our ways coincided. So, for a while did our views. We were both young, we both burned with youthful injustice at our lot as Irishmen and would change the world if we could. For three years we both planned how to better our condition - in the end we chose different methods.'

'But you have both met with success, surely? You in the theatre, and he at the Custom House...'

'As a glorified errand boy?' says he with raised eyebrow. 'He has ability and intellect, Will,enough to become a lawyer - but the English law will never allow it. Whereas acting is a profession where nationality counts for little - Mrs Woffington, Kitty, Mr Macklin, they're all Irish by birth, but as highly regarded as any English actor. And one day I hope to rank alongside them. But to Sean I am a traitor to my country. toadying to the English oppressors! He,like so many Irishmen, is blinded by bitterness.'

He rises, pushing back his chair. 'But come, Will Archer, this is heavy talk for a sunny day. Shall we make our way back to Smock Alley?'

I decline his offer, saying I would observe the activity about the quayside for a while.

'Of course,' he says with a lecherous wink, 'you are young man with an appetite. The best ones are to be found in the lanes just beyond the Custom House. Good value and clean.And at this time of day, you will have your pick.'

It takes me a moment to comprehend his misconception, by

which time he is at a sufficient distance not to see me blush scarlet at his effrontery.

Yet as my anger subsides, its place is taken by a deep dejection. Sinking disconsolately onto a wooden crate which, along with numerous other crates and wicker baskets is piled ready for shipment at the edge of the quay, I am overwhelmed by a longing for London. Homesick for its dingy thoroughfares, for its hucksters and tricksters, for its hubbub and smell. And most of all for Susan - for her teasing smile, her greasy kitchen smell, her warm flesh.

What am I doing in this land where everyone resents me for being English? But just as quickly as despair overwhelmed me, the light of reason starts to dispel the clouds of despondency.

I am, after all, here among friends. Friends who are more to me than family - Mr Garrick, Ned, Charlie. And the task I have been given by Mr Sheridan - to investigate Tobias Acres's disappearance and subsequent death - is still not resolved to my satisfaction. Too many questions still remain unanswered.

Why was he killed? The botched robbery explanation does not satisfy me. I am sure his death was no accident. He was deliberately targeted - but why?

To answer that, I must first consider who benefits from his death...

Eugenie, his sister? She admits she had no love for him - yet her bewilderment over his injuries at the dead house seemed genuine.

Then there is Richard Semple. Was his purpose in sending me to the dead house to discover the dead man's identity - *or to*

127

confirm it? Was Tobias Acres simply a musician? Or could he have been one of Hervey's agents - or one of Hervey's victims?

There is a third possibility - Irish unrest. Lord knows I've learned enough about *that* these last few days! Was Acres killed by those who hate England - Liam, the footman in his own household, whose fierce loyalty to his mistress also gives him a personal motive? Or even Sean Kelly, his housemaid's brother?

The more I explore the possibilities, the more possibilities present themselves, becoming ever more fantastical. It is only as I begin to contemplate Finn Kelly doing away with Acres for his own musical advancement that I shake myself from my musings.

Whatever the motive, and whoever the murderer, I need more evidence. And some of that may be forthcoming this afternoon when I deliver Mr Sheridan's offer of a box at the theatre to Eugenie Acres.

13

...borne our griefs...

A carriage stands outside 56 Great Boater Lane. It is a modest affair, faded grey with no crest and but one horse idly tossing its head.

My knock is answered by Liam with less reluctance than last time, but no more ceremony.

'Mistress is with her lawyer, Callaghan. He'll not be long. Will you wait?'

'Here?' I glance along the narrow hallway.

Liam sniffs and grimaces. Then, with some reluctance, 'In the parlour if you want.'

I follow him into the room next to the front door. It is as untidy and homely as before. But this time there is no Bridget with her feet up eating cake.

Liam notices my glance at the empty chair. 'Biddy's in the scullery, black leading. 'Tis my company youse'll be having, or nothing.'

I smile at the gracelessness of the invitation. 'Am I allowed to sit?'

'Please yourself.'

I sit on the same stool I occupied last time. Liam hovers awkwardly.

Before the silence becomes embarrassing, I say, 'I suppose you've heard of yesterday's encounter?'

'She said she had to patch you up. Teach you not to be abroad when the boys are about, so it will.'

'Too right!'

I'm curious to know if he, like Bridget had the day off yesterday. If he, perhaps, was in one of the marauding gangs, casting aside the shackles of service for the pleasures of affray. But I have not the temerity to ask.

'You took no major hurt so?' he asks. Do I detect a hint of disappointment?

'A few scrapes and bruises. They'll heal.' I change the subject. 'And your mistress? How is she?'

He becomes defensive. 'She's grand. Why, what else would you expect?'

'Nothing - just, a woman alone...'

'Sure she's not alone. She has us, me and Bridget, who're more family than her own ever was. She's her own woman now.'

The challenge in his tone is reflected in the unconscious clenching of his fist.

I tread a careful path. 'I'm glad to hear it. I just thought - all the legal arrangements, the funeral... might be a burden?'

'A joy, more like. To be rid of him - to have her freedom at last.'

I would ask more, but a bell rings and Liam jumps to his feet.

'The gobshite lawyer's going.'

I follow him to the door.

Eugenie and Callaghan, the lawyer are coming downstairs.

I don't know what I expect. A white-wigged, venerable old man? But Callaghan can not be more than forty years of age, slim and elegant, his dress and black wig sleek and stylish.

Eugenie catches sight of me in the doorway and a look of pleasure crosses her features.

'Mr Callaghan,' she says, 'allow me to introduce Mister Will Archer.'

The lawyer pauses on his way out. He inclines his head, 'Mister Archer.'

I respond in like manner, 'Your servant, sir.'

His look is at once candid and curious. Open, affable and, at the same time, expectant.

He holds my gaze for just a few seconds longer than comfortable. Then nods politely and turns back to Eugenie.

'I have made all necessary arrangements, Eugenie. I respect your decision not to attend and to have the ceremony private. I shall, of course, be there.'

'I would not expect it to be otherwise, John.'

'I shall send the documents in due course for you to sign. Meanwhile, if there is anything else you require, let Liam be the messenger.'

With a most un-lawyerly gesture, he kisses her outstretched hand and takes his leave. Liam ushers him out.

Meanwhile, Eugenie poses at the foot of the staircase, half smiling, eyebrow raised.

'So, Will, here you are again? It seems you cannot keep away.'

Momentarily flustered by the archness of her tone, I stammer, 'I - I am here as a m-messenger, ma'am, on behalf of Mr Sheridan.'

Slowly she descends the last few steps and, with her hand to

131

her forehead and eyes downcast, she leads me back into the parlour. 'And there I was thinking that it was upon your own account... Ah well!'

Then, hitching up her skirts, she perches upon a stool and brightly asks, 'So, why would the great and famous Mr Sheridan be sending messages to the loikes of me?'

Her skittish changes of mood are quite disconcerting. Seductress, tragedienne and artless colleen all within the space of a minute! I realise she is mocking me.

'Perhaps he would have you join his company!' I reply petulantly.

The vexation in my reply sobers her.

'I am sorry, Will. I have just spent half an hour closeted with Mr Callaghan, going over funeral arrangement and tedious legal affairs. One can only be on one's best behaviour for so long without bursting!'

She leans forward and puts her hand on mine. 'Forgive me. I really am pleased to see you, messenger or no.' Her hand is warm, the pressure of her fingers intimate.

It is at this moment that Liam chooses to return.His eyes go straight to her hand on mine.Quickly she withdraws it, but not before a flash of annoyance clouds his face.

I reach into my pocket for Mr Sheridan's letter and hand it to her.

Excitedly she breaks the seal.

'Why, this is too kind,' she says. 'Mr Sheridan puts a box at my disposal for the coming season - and further invites me to join him at Fishamble Street for the opening performance of Mr

Handel's new oratorio this Thursday.' She looks up. 'Do I detect your hand in this, Will?'

'I knew nothing of the invitation to the Music Hall,' say I, 'but I admit to having suggested the other part of the offer.'

'It is the very thing to raise my spirits. Now that my brother is gone, I intend to be seen more in society. As soon as the funeral is over, I shall erase all memory of him, starting with the drabness of this house. The heavy furniture, the gloomy hangings - all will go. I will have nothing but freshness and light.'

'He has left you well provided for?'

'So Mr Callaghan says.'

I recall the kiss on the hand, the familiar use of first names. 'Mr Callaghan seemed more amiable than most lawyers... More a family friend?'

From where he lounges in the chair by the fire, I hear Liam scoff. 'Sure, you could say that!'

Eugenie cast him a reproving look. 'A true friend to me, at least.'

'You and he...?' I venture. Not, I admit, without a twinge of jealousy.

She gives me an indulgent smile. 'Ever the detective, eh Will? But it is not how you imagine.' She turns to Liam. 'Find Bridget and get us something to eat and drink.'

With a sigh, Liam heaves himself from the chair. 'No good will come of telling him, you know that?'

'Mind your business, cross-patch,' says Eugenie. 'I do not need your leave for what I do. Will here knows my feelings towards Tobias. It is only right that he knows why I feel so.'

Sulkily, Liam goes in search of Bridget.

'You allow him too much licence,' say I when he has gone. 'He is, after all, but a servant.'

'Do not presume to judge me, Will Archer,' retorts Eugenie sharply. 'I owe Liam and Bridget a debt of gratitude that you cannot begin to imagine. Without them I might not be here today. So let me hear no further talk of *servants* - Liam and Bridget are my *friends.*'

'I'm sorry, ma'am. I meant no offence.'

'I'm sure you didn't.' Then, in a softer tone. 'But I shall take offence if you keep calling me 'ma'am' - my name is Eugenie - Jeannie to my friends. And I hope I may count you among them?'

A clatter at the door heralds the return of Liam with tankards of small beer. Bridget, her cheeks smudged with blacking, appears behind him with a tray of assorted victuals - slices of cold meat, pies and sweet pastries.

Once we are all seated around the table, Jeannie begins her story.

'Both my father and mother came from well-to-do families. Unfortunately, my father was the third son with no prospect of inheriting so ,like most third sons, he pursued a career in the military. Well educated and ambitious, he progressed rapidly through the ranks, gaining many influential friends. Then, whilst serving in Ireland, he met and fell in love with my mother, the only child of wealthy Irish wine merchants. With none of the prejudices of the English aristocracy, they raised no objection to their daughter marrying a soldier. They saw that, with his influential English connections, my father was able to offer opportunities that their fellow Irish merchants could only dream of. The native Irish weren't exactly the best customers for fine wines!'

I hear Liam huffing during this talk of English oppression. But his grievances are obviously familiar territory, for Eugenie takes no heed of him.

'As a little girl, I learned all the Irish tales and legends from my mother - of Finn MacCool and his thumb of knowledge, of the Children of Lir being turned into swans, of the hero Cú Chulainn and the ghostly Banshee - until I felt myself to be as Irish as she.'

'And Tobias, your brother - did he listen to these stories, too?'

'When he was not a-mewling, sure. He was a tiresome child, always clinging to mammy's skirts. Little use as a playmate, preferring his own company. I had many friends - he had few or none.'

'Perhaps he lacked a man's influence. As a military man, your father would often be away?'

'Sorry - I did not say - my father gave up the soldiery soon after marrying and joined the family business. Yet, all the same, he was a rare presence in our household, often away on business. So you may be right. At all events, Tobias grew from a whining child into solitary young man, interested only in his books and his music. My father, who had loved him little enough as a milksop child, liked him even less as a studious youth who showed no interest whatsoever in the business.'

'Yet he indulged him in his musical career?'

'Sure, at my mother's behest. Had my father had his way, he would have packed Tobias off to his old regiment in the hope that

135

it would make a man of him. But my mother would have none of it - and daddy, for all his faults, still loved her and would do nothing to hurt her. So, yes, he let Tobias learn the violin.'

'And you, Jeannie - what were his hopes for you?'

'What are any father's hopes for a daughter? That she marry a man of fortune, and over time diminish into a dutiful wife.' She gives a wistful sigh. 'Poor daddy. So many times he tried - and so many times I disappointed him. I think it was what killed him in the end...'

'Sure that's shite and you know it!' exclaims Liam indignantly. ''Twas too much wine and rich food as did for the ould feller.' He turns to me and explains. 'Sure, he was the size of you an' me put together, with a nose that would light you the way to Donegal. Bejasus, didn't he drink as much stock as he sold?'

'And the paddy on him,' adds Bridget reflectively. 'Wouldn't he've walloped me to Kingdom Come many a time if I'd not been so nimble on my pins? Steam come out of his ears, so!'

'He had a heart attack while berating a drayman in the street,' says Eugenie. 'But the previous evening he had all but ordered me to marry John Callaghan.'

'Your family lawyer!'

'Yes, Will, the very same Mr Callaghan who was here when you arrived. A match cooked up by my vile brother...'

'Sorry, you've lost me...'

Eugenie signals to Liam to refill our tankards from the jug on the table. Then, after taking a long mouthful, she continues.

'I turned twenty-one a few months before my father died. In a few years I'd be in danger of being left on the shelf, as they say.

Since I was eighteen several eligible young men had been suggested, but I had rejected them all. They were all of English stock and either namby-pambys or scoundrels. I suppose I had been spoilt by all my mother's stories of dashing Irish heroes...'

'But Mr Callaghan was none of these?'

'No. As you've seen, he is a very amiable gentleman. And, as it proved, both gallant and honest. But I am getting ahead of myself. As I was saying, the night before my father had his attack, he ordered me to marry Mr Callaghan. My brother had recommended him, my father had met him and approved of him. There was no more to be said. And then my father died.'

'So the marriage was postponed?'

'Fortunately, my mother was a stickler for tradition. We must observe a full six months mourning. Of course Tobias objected. Throughout the six months he continually reminded our mother what a fine fellow Callaghan was, how eager he was to marry, how any delay might weaken his resolve... And he sought every opportunity to throw John and myself together that we might learn to like each other. My mother, however, remained adamant, but at the end of the six months, plans were set in motion.'

'What went wrong?'

'Fortunately, nothing,' she says with a bitter laugh. 'On the contrary, most things went right. For the next few months, all talk was of the impending nuptials - where it should take place, who must be invited, how big a wedding banquet. Et cetera. The more certain all the arrangements became, the more reluctance I felt. And I sensed that John was feeling the same. I did not understand why. John was pleasant enough company, attentive, considerate -

always polite. I liked him. You must not consider me unladylike, Will, when I say I would have liked him to be more - how shall I phrase this? - *passionate*. But I ascribed his self-control to the belief that any intimacy must be saved for the actual marriage bed.'

Liam fails to suppress a snigger at this point and is rewarded by sharp glance from his mistress.

'Then, a week before the wedding was due to take place, my mother fell ill. Of course, the ceremony had to be postponed, for it was clear that she was dying. Tobias was near apoplectic. As master of the household, he thought he could simply order me to proceed, but he did not reckon with John. I had sensed his reluctance growing during the past few weeks, and now it was almost with relief that he greeted my mother's collapse. From the side of mother's sickbed I could often hear him and my brother arguing. Tobias by turns angry and pleading with him to go ahead with the marriage. Mr Callaghan reassuring and calmly considerate. It struck me as strange at the time, but of course I did not know the true situation...'

She pauses reflectively. We all three know not to interrupt her reverie. After a moment, she resumes.

'My mother died four months ago. The moment she did, Tobias redoubled his demands. The marriage must take place immediately. The eyes of the world were upon us. We would become a laughing stock if I procrastinated further. Moreover, it would be more suitable if John Callaghan moved into this house, his own apartments being unsuitable for a wife. He, Tobias, would continue to live here, converting the top floor into his own private living rooms. We could all be happy again... And then John told me the truth.'

'Are you ready for this, Master Archer?' grins Liam. 'How old are you? Nineteen - twenty? A babby when it comes to the ways of the world!'

More used to them than you, I think to myself. But even so, the heartlessness of Tobias Acres's plan sickens me.

'One evening when Tobias was at rehearsal, John Callaghan came to see me. Over the last year, he said, he had come to like me very much. Even, in a way, to love me. And because of that, he could not marry me. It would, he said, be a sham concocted by my brother. He and Tobias were lovers and my brother had convinced John that the only way their relationship could continue was by marrying me. I was to be sacrificed - a bride destined to remain forever a virgin - so that they might live unremarked under the same roof. Until now, their affair had of necessity been clandestine and fraught with the danger of discovery. How anyone could love my brother was beyond my comprehension, but John evidently did. At first he had agreed to the deception. I was, after all, just the 'faceless' sister. But having got to know me, he realised he could not condemn me to such ignominy. That is why he and my brother argued.'

For the first time since embarking on this final explanation, she raises her eyes to mine. I see the effort it has taken her to speak of it. She searches my face for signs of shock or disgust, but finds none.

'You are not revolted, Will?'

'No - my only feeling is of gratitude that you have been spared such a fate.'

'You see now why I cannot mourn my brother? And you do not think me lacking in duty by not attending his funeral?'

'There is a point where duty may become hypocrisy. I am sure that Mr Callaghan will represent the family most fittingly. His grief, at least, is genuine.'

'Tobias's death has hit him hard. But his behaviour throughout has been exemplary. He is, indeed, a true and honest gentleman. I do not know what I would have done without him.'

'You'd have us, Miss Jeannie,' says Bridget, tearfully.

'To be sure, and glad I am of it,' her mistress affectionately. 'But even you and Liam, for all your virtues, might find yourselves baffled by legal quibbles and equivocation. I know I do.'

'There's my brother...' says Bridget with pride.

'Finn? A fine fellow, but he is still only a clerk.' Eugenie speaks fondly, as if to a child. Then she turns to me. 'Bridget's older brother, Finn, works for Mr Callaghan, Will.'

'I know - Sean told me.'

'Of course - I was forgetting. How are your injuries? Healing I hope?'

'Very well, thanks to Bridget's salves and potions.'

Liam guffaws, 'Sure, isn't that the way of it - the brother gives you knocks and it's left to his sister to repair them!'

'Actually,' say I, 'Sean saved me from those who would do me harm.'

'Sure, aren't they all of a kind - hotheads and rebels.'

I recall the conversation the last time I was here. 'I thought

140

you shared his sentiments?'

'His sentiments, perhaps - but not his methods. Ireland's freedom will not be won by dunderheads with clubs and cudgels.'

Eugenie rises and puts a restraining hand upon his arm. 'That's enough, Liam. You're upsetting Bridget.'

'Sure she knows it's true. Doesn't she herself say 'tis Finn has all the sense? And he'll need it, working for that gobshite lawyer now the master's dead - the sense to keep his back to the wall, if nothing else!' he adds with a coarse laugh.

Even Bridget joins in his laughter. But Eugenie looks mortified.

'That's quite enough! Master Archer and I do not wish to be subjected to your coarseness. Be off about your business, the pair of you.'

Bridget scuttles back to the scullery looking suitably cowed. Liam follows with contemptuous toss of the head, aimed more, I suspect, at me than at his mistress.

'I'm sorry about that,' says Eugenie when they have gone. 'They are good-hearted, though sometimes inclined to go too far.'

'Their ribaldry does not offend me, Jeannie. It is rather their lack of thought in denigrating a gentleman who has been so considerate of your feelings.'

'As have you. Truly I must be blessed to meet two such when all I have hitherto known is those who would dispose of me for their own advantage.' She sighs and takes my hand. 'Now, it seems, you and I have no pretext to meet again, Will. You have delivered your message - and I have told you all, perhaps more than I should, of the circumstances that have led to my detestation of my dead brother...'

'Don't say that, Jeannie - I'm sure there will be occasions...'

She puts her finger to my lips. 'At Mr Handel's oratorio, perhaps. But, for the meantime, farewell, Will Archer.'

I can think of no suitable reply to express the sudden emptiness that has opened within me. So, in silence, she leads me to the door and I step out into the gathering dusk of Great Boater Lane.

14

...eyes of the blind be opened...

On Tuesday morning the sunlight piercing the threadbare curtains of my attic window wakes me. Mrs Fitzgerald's love of frills and furbelows does not extend to the rooms on this floor. I have not seen the bedrooms allocated to my master and Mistress Peg, but I doubt they are as sparse as this.

Charlie and I have been put in a disused servant's room. Across the narrow landing, there is one other room shared by Mrs O'Shaughnessy, the cook, and Nora, the maid of all work. It is Charlie, of course, who has discovered their names with his usual combination of charm and cheek.

Like most twelve-year-old boys, Charlie can be irritating or invisible, but you ignore him at your peril, for he is a sponge for information. Thus he has learned that Mrs O'Shaughnessy bears little love for her employer. The late Mr Fitzgerald may have had difficulty keeping his hands to himself but at least he was generous, unlike his stuck-up, penny-pinching wife who expects Mrs O'Shaughnessy to provide her guests with food fit for lords though she's only prepared to spend a pauper's pittance.

'And as for poor Nora, it's no wonder she's as thin as a rake, the way Mrs High and Mighty has her running around from dawn till midnight, doing the work of two because she won't pay for anyone else. By rights there should be a footman or butler but Joseph was let go as soon as the master died. 'Not proper,' says

her ladyship, 'in a house of females. As if any man would attempt to board her!'

The source of all this gossip - delivered verbatim, in uncanny imitation of the lady herself - is presently curled up in his truckle bed at the other side of the room sound asleep.

I wish I could blot the world out as easily as he. I've spent a restless night, unable to decide if what Eugenie told me of her brother makes her less, or more, likely to have been instrumental in his demise.

His fellow musicians opinions of him - his lack of success with the ladies, his social aloofness, his reticence to engage in conversation - now make more sense.

To them he appeared reserved. But to his sister he was an ogre.

Eugenie, I am sure, has not the physical strength to have struck him down. But has she the mental strength to persuade another to do it - the over-familiar footman, Liam, perhaps? His loyalty to his mistress is unquestioned and I don't doubt he would have strength enough to deliver a blow from behind and drag the body to the river.

Like so many of the Irishmen I've met, he resents the English oppressor and wouldn't hesitate to kill in the name of patriotism. But would those same fierce principles countenance murder to save his mistress from oppression?

A sudden scuffle from the other side of the room interrupts my thoughts. Charlie has scrambled out of bed, dragged out the chamber pot and is now pissing copiously into it. It seems to go on for ever. How can such a small boy store so much liquid?

At last he is finished. He re-laces, stretches and noisily breaks wind.

'And good morning to you, smelly britches,' say I.

'Mornin', Will. You are awake, then,' he says grinning towards the thin sheet that covers me. 'And there was I thinking it was only your little soldier what was up.'

'Peace, sauce-box!' say I, adjusting myself. 'The little feller has a mind of its own.'

'Needs a good beating, I'd say, teach it who's master!' retorts the impudent wretch. 'Meantime, what's to do today?'

'For a start, you can take that downstairs and empty it,' say I, nodding towards the steaming jordan.

Once he's gone, I consider my plan for the day.

In the clear light of morning, my suspicions of Eugenie seem fantastical. Despite her brother's ill usage of her, I cannot see her as a murderer. She is too honest.

It is less than a year since I had dealings with another woman - Agnes Mayer - who, I now see, set out deliberately to deceive me. But Eugenie is not like her. Her moods are changeable. One moment she rebukes me, then teases - and at other times confides her deepest secrets. Whereas Agnes Mayer was always enigmatic, leading me on to trust her, luring me into her web of deceit.

No, this morning my thoughts lay in another direction.

I want to satisfy my suspicions regarding Richard Semple. As my scene in *Sir Harry Wildair* was rehearsed yesterday morning, I am not needed at the theatre, so it will be a good opportunity to confront him if I can.

It is near noon before I get the opportunity.

Charlie and I spend the morning pleasantly enough observing

the activity of Custom House Quay. His presence opens many a door that would be closed to me alone. If we were in rags, we'd be derided as beggars. If our clothes were too showy, we'd be deferred to as gentility. As it is, respectably dressed, we might pass for brothers out to see the sights. We pose no threat and are treated amiably.

Porters, taken with Charlie's grin, ruffle his hair and let him ride on their barrows. Sweetmeat sellers give him extra portions. His curiosity leads traders to explain their business to willing ears.

And, now we have the opportunity, he tells me of what happened when I directed him to follow Semple two days ago. He trailed him all the way to Dame Street which was busy with people and carriages, and had some ado to keep his quarry in sight. Indeed, at one point he thought he'd lost him, so dense was the crowd. But then, after some injudicious elbowing and narrowly-avoided clips round the ear, he almost stumbled straight into him.

Ducking aside, Charlie saw that Semple was standing at the edge of the road. A hackney carriage was drawn up alongside him. At first, Charlie thought Semple must have hailed it, and that the chase must end there. He'd be hard put to it to follow a carriage on foot. But Semple made no move to get in. Instead a passenger alighted, paid off the driver and sent him on.

'An' you'll never guess who it was.'

'Not unless you tell me.'

'The black beetle - from London.'

'Nathaniel Grey? Are you sure?'

'Once seen, not forgotten, mate. I'd know them spindleshanks

146

anywhere.'

Nathaniel Grey, right-hand man to Sir William Hervey. If he is in Dublin, something serious must be afoot.

Charlie was close enough to hear the first words spoken before the two of them moved off into the crowd. Grey seemed to be imparting urgent information to Semple. What it was, Charlie couldn't hear, for he had to fall back a pace or two, not to attract suspicion. Whatever it was, though, it spurred Semple into an explanation of his own, and here Charlie did catch the odd word, especially the mention of my name and that of Acres.

The two parted at the end of Dame Street, Grey walking back the way he'd come and Semple heading towards the river, doubtless back to his place of work at the Custom House. From where he was on the corner, Charlie heard Grey warn Semple, 'Look to it. Sir William would have you take better care of the boy than you did of your own man.'

'And that was all that was said?'

'They said plenty - but it was all I heard.'

'You've done well, lad.' And as a reward, I buy him a paper poke of cockles from a buxom young woman with a basket full of live shellfish. She flutters her eyes at me as she presses the change into my hand.

With a wink, she whispers, 'I'm here till dark, if you fancy a cockle poke of your own later. Just ask for Molly.'

Fortunately, Charlie is too busy wielding his pin, prising out the little worm-like creatures, to hear. The girl is undeniably pretty and the offer is tempting, but I think of Susan back in London. I give her my most regretful smile and steer Charlie away.

147

Then, almost on the strike of noon, I see a familiar figure emerge from the doorway of the Custom House. It is Semple and he seems in no hurry.

Leaving Charlie by the dockside wall, I urge him to wait until I return. Remembering how, back in London, Grey had once subtly threatened his safety in order to ensure my compliance, I am not about to allow Semple the same chance. I weave my way through the bustle of activity and silently fall in beside him.

He shows no surprise. 'Why Master Archer, you are almost as adept at appearing from thin air as myself.'

'I would crave a moment of your time, sir. Have you the leisure?'

'I have, sir, and I also have an appetite. A dish of smoaked eel would not go amiss. What say you?'

We retire to a small establishment in a narrow street some distance from the quay. It has, says Semple, the twin virtues of cleanliness and discretion. 'The fare is wholesome and the company select. We will not be overheard.'

The dark panelled recess into which we are shown reduces the brightness of noon to a shadowy dusk in which our host flits spectral in his white apron. Semple and I are not the only customers, but we are the most secluded and, after placing a dish of cooked eel and a platter of bread between us, the landlord melts away into the gloom.

'The eels are caught locally,' says Semple, spearing a chunk, 'and you need not fear chalk or lime in the bread. Kennedy bakes it himself and has his reputation to preserve.

I sample a forkful of eel and mop up the juice with a hunk of

148

bread. It is indeed good, and I find I have an appetite.

We eat in silence for a while. Then, summoning my courage, I say, 'You have not been altogether honest with me, Mr Semple.'

He dabs his chin with a napkin, and favours me with a direct stare. 'How so, Master Archer?'

'The corpse from the river - did you know who it was before you sent me to the dead-house?'

His lips purse in a quizzical smile. 'I may have had an inkling... I am sorry if my little deception offended you.'

'I am not offended, Mr Semple. Intrigued, rather. What was Tobias Acres to you?'

'To me? What makes you think he was anything to me?'

His condescending smile begins to irritate me. 'A question countered by another question! Pray, sir, allow me some intelligence - we are, so you tell me, on the same side, serving the same master. If we are to be allies, it is only right that I know the nature of whatever dealings we are allied in!'

My voice has risen and he hushes me with a casually upraised finger.

'Peace, Master Archer. Though we may not be overheard in this alcove, that does not mean there are none who listen! Pray do not make their task the easier with your indignation.'

'Very well, sir,' I reply in a quieter tone. 'But you owe me the respect of telling me the truth. If there is more danger in this matter than merely a drowned man, I need to be aware so that I may be on my guard. And Mr Nathaniel Grey warned you to have a care for my safety, did he not?'

For the first time, I have caught him unawares. The smile

wavers.

'You know that Grey is in Dublin - how come you by this information?'

'How is not important. Suffice it to say, I know. And I know that he would not undertake the journey if there were not some serious work afoot. Now, sir,' I say leaning forward, 'perhaps you will answer my question - *what was Tobias Acres to you?*'

He sits back, folding his arms and surveys me for a moment. Then, as if coming to a decision, he gives a curt nod. 'I see it is unwise to underestimate you, Will Archer. Yes, I admit that I had cause to be interested in Tobias Acres. But before I answer your question, I am curious to know your own view as to why that should be.'

I sigh with impatience. 'Very well, sir, if you insist on playing games... Neither of us believes that Tobias Acres died as the result of a chance robbery. He was killed for a reason. And that reason, I suggest, is that he either knew something which might prove a danger to his killer, or intended to do something that his killer did not want him to do.'

These last words could incriminate Eugenie, so nearly forced into an unwelcome marriage. *Is this the conclusion Semple expected me to reach?* I search his face but it remains impassive as ever.

'Sound reasoning, Will. But still a theory. Have you evidence to flesh the bones of surmise?'

'None, sir. Only my own suspicions which at first pointed me to a more - er, *domestic* explanation of his death... But when I learned of Mr Grey's presence in Dublin...'

'It suggested a more political motive?'

'Sir William would not send his most trusted man to Dublin unless there was real urgency. When you assigned me the task of discovering the identity of the drowned man, were you looking to *discover* his identity or merely to have it *confirmed*? Was Tobias Acres perhaps one of Sir William's agents?'

Semple nods approvingly. Gone is the patronising smile. He now seems willing to treat me as an equal.

'Very nearly right, Will. His death is a cause for concern - but not because he was one of our agents.'

'He was against us, you mean?'

Semple shakes his head. 'I am not sure he was even that.'

'I do not understand.'

'Sir William receives intelligence from many sources, Will. Sometimes these sources are reliable and detailed, sometimes little more than gossip or conjecture. A little while ago, one such rumour hinted at an incident being planned for a public event and Sir William ordered me to investigate. Now Dublin, as you may guess, has many such events - civic ceremonies, military parades and the like. But Sir William drew my attention to two events of an artistic nature - Herr Handel's series of concerts, and Mr Garrick's season at the Smock Alley Theatre. The reason he felt these important was because the rumour made passing mention of a 'fiddler'. This might mean someone who is nervous or restless, or even a cheat, but it's also a common term for someone who plays the violin. So, my attentions being directed that way, they lighted upon our dead friend. His behaviour was a matter of remark among his colleagues - unsociable, prone to staying behind

151

alone - and observation of his domestic life threw up further interesting facts.'

'You are referring to his unusually close relationship with Mr Callaghan, the lawyer?'

Semple raises an eyebrow. 'Upon my life, Will, you are indeed perceptive. You have discovered in two days what it took me as many months to ferret out!'

I acknowledge the praise with a careless shrug. It will do no harm for him to think more highly of my abilities than they deserve. I certainly have no intention of telling him how I came by the information.

Instead, I say, 'You think this knowledge was used to pressure him?'

'It is possible. There is a servant in the household... You have met the fellow, Will?'

'Liam?'

'His views might be considered treasonable by some...'

I surprise myself by leaping to Liam's defence. 'So might those of most true-born Irishmen I have met!. Sir William's instruction to me before I left London was to keep my eyes and ears open for signs of political unrest. But since I have been here, I have had difficulty in avoiding such - near everyone I've met bears some kind of grudge against we English! And I think you mistake if you believe Liam confided in his master in some way. He hated him.'

'If Tobias Acres threatened to reveal Liam's plot to the authorities, he would have signed his own death warrant...'

'That is, if there was a plot in the first place...'

'Oh, I think there is, Will. But I'm damned if I know how Acres's death advances - or retards - it.'

I can clearly see his frustration. And Nathaniel Grey's sudden visit will have done little to alleviate it...

'Sir William thinks you are not doing enough to discover the nature of this supposed plot?'

'Exactly, Will. But I am doing all in my power - yet it is not enough. I must appear no more than a clerk in the Custom House. And the imposture hinders me.' He gives me an almost pleading look. 'That is why I need your help, Will.'

It is an altogether different Semple I am seeing. I came expecting to unmask a schemer, to foil his contemptuous manipulation of me. Instead I see before me a man suffering the disfavour of his masters and desperate to retrieve it. By enlisting a novice like me!

I still do not wholly trust him.

'I think I see,' say I slowly. 'Sir William thinks something is being planned for a public event. Not just the the normal parades and ceremonies, but some artistc endeavour that may attract the highest in the land. I heard Mr Sheridan say that the Lord Lieutenant himself may be at the opening of Mr Garrick's season at Smock Alley, and many persons of quality will attend Mr Handel's concerts...'

'Aye, such events would be the ideal target. In the eyes of the mutinous Irish rebels, audience and performers alike are the English interlopers. This is why you, Will, can be so useful. You are in the midst of these people.' He looks askance at me. 'There are, amongst your troupe some actors of Irish birth, are there not?'

I think at first that he is referring to those of Mr Sheridan's company, resident here in Dublin. *Such as Richard O'Sullivan...? Surely he is no more than a foppish ladies'-man - a danger to Ned, perhaps, but hardly to the state...*

But as Semple's questioning silence persists, I realise he is referring to the two ladies of our company, Mrs Peg and Kitty - both Irish born.

I feel the heat rising to my cheeks. 'You insult them, sir, even to think such a thing. They are   as loyal to Mr Garrick and the company as I am. And they are my friends...'

'Closeness can be a hindrance in our business, Will.'

His calm delivery of the unthinkable only serves to anger me more.

'If we talk of closeness, sir, perhaps you would do well to look to your own colleagues at the Custom House.'

If I think to confuse him, I am disappointed.

'Sean Kelly, you mean? The firebrand apprentice-boy! I have had my eye on him for some time, you may believe me. He and his associates make public mayhem, but I doubt he has the capacity to hatch a plot such as we suspect.'

'And he,' I counter, irritated, 'does he know of you?'

The smug smile returns. 'He knows me as a clerk - and nothing more.'

I have a sudden image of Sean's hesitation when I mentioned Semple's name. I pray that my lapse has not caused curiosity to harden into suspicion in the young Irishman's mind. For all I dislike Semple, I would not wish him harm.

I am startled by a soft voice beside us, 'Was all to your

satisfaction, gentlemen?'

The landlord, Mr Kennedy. It is well that Semple trusts him, for he has the ability to appear silently and move invisibly!

My companion compliments him warmly and then rises. 'My young friend and I are done here, Mr Kennedy. I wish you good day. I look forward to once more enjoying your hospitality - and excellent fare! - before the week is out.'

The brightness as we emerge momentarily dazzles me. I have almost forgot that it is still only two in the afternoon. We seem to have been an age in that gloomy alcove.

And it has given me much to ponder.

The brisk walk back to the Quay is conducted almost in silence. Only as we arrive within sight of the Custom House does Semple say, 'I think it best we part here, Will. But be alert. Our London friend has reason to believe that the event of which we spoke may be imminent. It would not do for either of us to be caught napping!'

15

...gone astray...

I find Charlie chatting away happily to Molly the cockle-seller. He reddens as I approach and looks decidedly shifty.

She, however, looks me up and down in frank appraisal, a half smile hovering about her undeniably pretty red lips. 'Youngster's been a'telling me as you're a man o' parts,' says she. 'Performing. And searching out mysteries...'

Every word is furred with such innuendo that I feel myself blushing.

She comes close, tracing invisible patterns upon my chest. Her tray presses hard across my stomach. 'Don't forget,' she purrs, her breath warm and sweet on my face, 'I'll be here tonight and I've a mystery or two myself I'd like your help to explore.'

'I - er, I'm not sure...' I stutter huskily.

'Give you notes on your performance, too, if you're up for it.'

I swallow, mutter something incomprehensible and retreat hastily, dragging Charlie with me.

'What have you been telling her, you waghalter?' I say, buffeting him on the shoulder.

'Easy with the fists, cross-patch,' he whines, aggrieved. 'She asks, and I tell her no more'n the truth - that you're a fine upstanding fellow. How upstanding, she asks and I tell her, very - cos I shares a room and sees you wiv a bad dose of horn-colic every morning this past week on account of you've left your muff

156

in London.'

He ducks my cuff around his ear and hops to a safe distance.

'Give it a go, Will. I would. She's a flirt-gill, but she's no doxy.'

I can't help but laugh at his effrontery. 'And what would you know of these matters, maggot-pizzle?'

'More'n you, it seems, if you can't see an open door when it's right before you!'

'You're incorrigible,' I say, pulling him close and tousling his hair. 'What am I to do with you!'

'More to the point what you do with *him,*' he grins, tapping me none-too-gently in the privates.

So, in good spirits, we retrace our steps to Mrs Fitzgerald's lodgings.

But we are destined not to complete our journey, for hardly have we turned from the bustle of Dame Street into the quieter byways than someone seizes me by the arm. It is Ned, and he looks worried.

'Will,' he cries, 'have you seen Kitty today? Has she been with you?'

'No,' I say. 'Why, Ned, what's the matter?'

'She's gone,' he says, his face the picture of bafflement. 'The other night, after you'd spoke to me, I charged her, in jest, over her familiarity with O'Sullivan. All day yesterday she was contrary - you know how she can sulk - and sent me off in the afternoon. She was out of sorts and would fain be alone. Then this morning, she was not at rehearsal.'

'Was she needed? I thought it was principals only today...'

157

'It makes no odds - she always attends when I am there.'

'Perhaps she is feeling unwell...'

'No. I thought of that. As soon as rehearsal was over I ran to her lodgings. They said she'd left yesterday evening, in company with a young gentleman...'

'O'Sullivan?'

'No-one knew - but he was not at the theatre this morning either - and since Kitty left her lodgings yestereve, she hasn't returned. Oh, Will, what am I to do?'

He is the picture of desolation.

Have my suspicions of O'Sullivan proved true? I've always thought Kitty a foolish flirt gullible enough to be taken in by O'Sullivan's blandishments.

Or is there some more sinister explanation of her disappearance? Could Semple's insinuations have substance after all?

In either case, it pains me to see my friend Ned so cast down.

'Take heart, Ned,' say I, glancing up to where the sun has just started its descent towards the west. We have over two good hours of daylight left. Charlie will scout about the town to see if he may catch sight of her. Meantime, we shall return to her lodging and you shall contrive some means to gain access to her room. We must find if she has left her things behind or no. Be of good cheer, man, I am sure she cannot have gone far. 'Twill all be something or nothing, you will see.'

I despatch Charlie about his business and take Ned's arm. All the way to Kitty's lodgings, I keep up an encouraging cheerfulness.

Inwardly, however, my thoughts are churning. Richard Semple's hint that there may be dissidents within our company has taken root whether I like it or not. Kitty, I am sure, is too skittish - but O'Sullivan is a different matter. From what he told me of his history, he has every right to bear a grievance. His ingratiating amiability may be a sham- what better place to plot mischief than from within the very society you plan to destroy?

When we arrive at Kitty's lodgings, the landlady is out. Only her son is at home. A comely boy of about eleven or twelve, he regards us narrowly through the half-open door.

We state our business. But he is reluctant to let us in.

Then, as we try to persuade him to let us wait until his mother returns, he cocks his head on one side and says to me, 'I know you, don't I? You was at the Music Hall. With Charlie.'

For a moment I am confused, but then it dawns on me that this must be one of the black-robed choirboys with whom Charlie ate while I was at the *Bull's Head* making my first inquiries about Tobias Acres.

'Charlie pointed you out. Said you was a good'un - so I s'pose it's all right.' He opens the door to let us in. The house is homely and clean, less decorated with frills than Mrs Fitzgerald's.

I make a mental note to reward Charlie later. His recommendation of me, in this instance, is paying dividends.

'Miss Kitty's room, is it?' says the boy, standing guard at the bottom of the stairs. 'I can't let youse up there. mi Mammy would skelp me proper.'

Ned eases his conscience with a sixpence. 'Why don't you come up with us? Then you'll see we mean no harm.'

He considers this a moment, then pockets the coin, nods sagely and beckons us to follow.

He shows us to a bright and airy room on the second floor. The first thing I notice is that the bed has not been slept in. But a dress lies across it as if hurriedly tossed aside.

In a wooden press in the corner of the room hang two or three more dresses. Ned goes to open the drawers, but the boy steps in front of him. 'Hey, mister, them's ladies' things - it's not right.'

I divert Ned by pointing to two pairs of shoes beside an open trunk. 'She cannot be far, Ned. See, her portmanteau is still here. She must only have the clothes she is wearing.'

I turn to the youngster. 'Did you see who called upon Miss Blair the other evening?'

He colours slightly. 'Mammy answered the door. I was in the kitchen blacking my boots ready for next day.'

I recognise the evasion. 'Aye - but you still saw the visitor, didn't you?'

There is a brief mental struggle between admitting curiosity and defying maternal commands. I influence the outcome with another sixpence.

'I heard this unfamiliar voice, see? So I poked my head round the door...'

'As anyone would...'

'And there was this man. About your age, a mite shorter, bit draggletailed - ginger hair worn loose - askin for Miss Kitty. Well, Mammy didn't care for the look of him so she leaves him on the doorstep while she calls Miss Kitty...'

'And...?'

160

'And then I skips back into the kitchen, lest Mammy caught me peeking.'

'But you have ears, lad,' prompts Ned.

'Sure, but the kitchen's at the back of the house - and once Miss Kitty came down to see her visitor, didn't Mammy come to see how I was getting on with mi blacking?'

'All the same - a bright lad like you - you must have heard something?'

'Well, I heard Miss Kitty a-thumping up the stairs and then down again. Mammy went out into the passage to see what all the commotion was...'

'And you just happened to look out as well..?'

'Miss Kitty had her bonnet on and a cape, and was a fiddling with her gloves. She was telling Mammy something, all breathless-like - I didn't hear what. Then she was off.'

'She went off with the fellow, just like that?' Ned is completely bewildered. 'No indication of where she was going? No message left for me?'

But the boy is getting fidgety and is already urging us towards the door. 'That's all I know. Now, gentlemen, you must be gone. Mammy'll be back...'

Ned would stay to question him more but, though I have no experience of maternal wrath, I recall with a shudder the punishments Mother Ransom meted out at the molly house and my sympathies go out to the lad.

'Come, Ned,' say I, 'there is no more to be gained here.'

I thank the boy, and inquire his name that I may send his regards to Charlie, then we take our leave.

161

None too soon, it appears, for as we turn the corner at the end of the road, we come face to face with a formidable matron all in black. Like a frigate in full sail she sweeps past us as we step out of her way.

Ned looks at me. 'Mammy?' he says and we both burst into laughter.

The visit to Kitty's lodgings has eased his mind. Knowing now that her absence cannot be a prolonged one, he considers what we have just learned.

'The boy's description of her visitor does not fit O'Sullivan,' he says.'Who may it have been?'

'How much do you know of her family here in Ireland, Ned?'

Ned slaps me on the shoulder. His face lights up. 'You have hit it, Will! What a dolt am I not to have thought of it! She talked of relations, cousins - now, where was it? One of these confounded Irish names - *Bally*- something...' He pounds his forehead with his fist. '*Bally....Ballycowan? - Ballycoen?* No! I have it! *Ballycullen.*'

'Then our way is clear,' say I. 'We must find out where this Ballycullen is and inquire after her there. Mr Sheridan is bound to know the place if it be anywhere near Dublin.'

We set out at once for the theatre, but after a while, Ned falls silent. His face clouds once more and he stays me.

'Do you think it wise, Will, to pursue her thus? She may take it amiss - you know Kitty, how capricious she is.'

I know exactly what he means. If we find her at Ballycullen, she is as likely to berate Ned as a jealous tyrant intruding on her privacy as to recognise his concern as a lover. *But what if we*

162

don't find her there? What if the   down-at-heel, ginger-haired visitor was not a relative at all..? Damn Semple!

'Might it not be better if I tarry a little?'   says Ned, uncertainly. 'I would not seem too possessive - untrusting... She is, after all, a grown woman...'

I put my hand on Ned's shoulder. 'True, with but the one dress, she can not stay away long. She may even return this evening...'

'You're right, Will. One more night cannot do any harm - can it?'

His eyes plead, unconvinced.

'If she has not returned by tomorrow,' I say reassuringly, 'I shall go with you to Ballycullen.'

16

...we shall all be changed...

I am just passing the Music Hall when I see Mr Sheridan emerge from the doors of that establishment.

A decrepit, white haired old man with a stout cane in his hand leans heavily upon his arm.

As soon as he spies me, Mr Sheridan beckons me over.

'Ah, Will, you come most opportunely. Allow me to introduce you to my god-father, Dr Swift.'

Mr Sheridan's manner, though outwardly hearty, seems anxious. And I can see why, for the old man has a distracted look about him. His wild hair bushes out at either side of his head and his eyes glare from under bushy brows. A lack of teeth has caused his mouth to sink in, giving greater prominence to the gaunt cheekbones and dominating nose.

My outstretched hand is ignored. The old man glowers at me, uncomprehending.

I see I must make the first move. 'It is an honour, sir,' say I, 'to meet the great Dean Swift.'

'Speak up, boy,' he snarls, waving the stout cane perilously close to my head. 'Who're you talking about?'

'Why, yourself, sir. The eminent author of *Gulliver's Travels...*'

'Deaf,' says he, pointing a gnarled finger at his ear. 'Who do you say you are?'

Tom Sheridan leans close to his other ear, articulating his words carefully. 'Will Archer, god-father. He's here with Mr Garrick.'

Dr Swift's mouth sets in a grim line. 'A fiddler, eh? I've told them, I'll not have the cathedral choir singing and fiddling at that club of fiddlers in Fishamble Street...' His voice rises in agitation and the cane is wielded with more vigour than I would credit in one so frail.

'Careful, god-father!' Mr Sheridan offers a restraining hand. 'Master Archer is neither singer nor musician, sir. He is an actor - and a friend.'

The momentary frenzy subsides. Dr Swift looks about, slack-jawed, then leans forward and peers closely at me. 'You're a fine looking boy. What's your name, say you?'

Mr Sheridan told me of the Dean's increasing imbecility and I am now seeing it for myself. Like many aged people, his memory betrays him, causing him to ask the same question many times over. The mind, once sharp, now needs humouring.

I repeat my name. He nods, his toothless mouth champing ruminatively.

Suddenly he prods me with the cane, catching me unawares.

'Your voice - not Irish?'

'No, sir.' I stop myself from rubbing the place on my thigh where he has caught me. 'I'm from England - London. But born in Yorkshire.'

'Yorkshire, say you? Fine county.' He leans close and lowers his voice confidentially. 'I'm of Yorkshire stock, you know. A true Englishman. My misfortune was to be born in Ireland. And

165

now it won't let me go - forces me to live like a rat in a hole!' Then, with another of his irrational leaps, 'Not a Papist are you?'

The light of madness flickers again in his eyes. I choose the simplest response. 'No, sir.'

'Good boy. Religion's the curse of this benighted country. Damned Irish - just enough religion to hate each other, not enough to love each other! You're not Irish, are you?'

'No, sir,' I reply as if he hasn't asked me the very same question not a minute since. 'English born and bred.'

'Be on your guard, boy. Stab you in the back as soon as look at you, these culchies.'

A carriage trundles around the corner and I hear Mr Sheridan breathe a sigh of relief.

'Here's James and George, god-father, come to fetch you home.'

Two burly young men alight from the carriage. Dressed in sober black, they have the garb of clerics, but the air of gaolers.

'Sure, you've had a pleasant outing, Dean Swift?' says one. ''Tis time now to go home, eh? Give me your arm and I'll help you up. There we go.'

The old man looks from one to another as if he should know them but cannot recall the circumstances of the acquaintance.

'Thank you, my man,' says he civilly as they help him into the coach. 'To the cathedral, if you please. I have a sermon to deliver.'

'To be sure, sir. With all despatch.' He tucks a rug about the old man's knees and closes the carriage door. His companion climbs in beside the Dean.

166

'He has not been any trouble?' he asks, turning back to Mr Sheridan.

Mr Sheridan takes his hand. 'None, thank you, James,' he replies. 'Docile as a lamb. He listened to the music and approved of the words. For a while, it was almost as if he were in his right wits.'

'Good,' says James, 'that is a great relief. I was afeard this excursion might bring on his fit again. Two nights ago George and I had to summon help to hold him down to prevent him tearing out his eyes, the pain was so great. Five of us it took to hold him.'

'Can his physician prescribe nothing to allay his distress?'

'You know your godfather's opinion of doctors, sir. Quacks and charlatans, the lot of them,' says James, disparagingly. '*Dr Diet, Dr Quiet and Dr Merryman,* he's always said. *These are the only three doctors you need.* So we do our best to keep him fed and entertained. and make sure he is well-rested. A discreet dose of laudanum in his posset following an attack usually does the trick.'

'You are a loyal servant,' says Mr Sheridan wringing James's hands. 'Keep up the good work.'

James assures Mr Sheridan of their best endeavours, then climbs up onto the seat and, with a flick of the reins and a click of his tongue, sets the horses off at a trot in the direction of St Patrick's.

'It is sad to see a great man brought so low,' say I as the carriage drives off.

'Sad indeed,' agrees Mr Sheridan. 'And sadder still to hear him berate those he has done so much to help. None has been so

167

staunch in defending the native Irish against the injustice and neglect of absentee English landlords as my god-father.'

'It would appear we English have much to answer for in this country. So many Irishmen I've met seem to harbour deep resentments against us. Can not King George and his ministers address the problem?'

'Ah, Will, you have the optimism of youth! The Irish problem is, I fear, intractable. Oliver Cromwell slaughtered so many in a bid to root out Papistry and then successive monarchs gave land to their favourites. Now, as far as Parliament in London is concerned, the English who have lived here for generations are regarded as no different to the Irish natives whose birthright they usurped.'

'Is that why Mrs Fitzgerald is so bitter?'

'Probably. Her late husband was third or fourth generation Anglo Irish. When he brought her over from England as his wife, she doubtless thought she was marrying into a life of deference and respect. Imagine her chagrin on discovering she was regarded as a mere tradesman's wife. And worse, that, for all their airs, they were looked down on by the English Government - just as they looked down on the native Irish.'

'And did Dr Swift suffer the same fate?'

'Not quite the same. When he was younger my godfather held several positions of influence in England and had hopes of even greater preferment. But Queen Anne took against him and then, when the Tory government fell, he had little option but to return to Ireland. It is his writing which has brought him fame. But that has proved a double-edged sword. While he is lauded in England as a writer of mordant wit and invention, in Ireland he is hailed as an Irish patriot! Were he in his right mind, even he would appreciate the irony!'

'Indeed, you told me the Dean was confined to his rooms because his wits were astray - so what brought him here to the Music Hall today?'

'It was upon the advice of Dr Wynne. He suggested my god-father should hear some of Mr Handel's *Messiah* for himself.'

'Dr Wynne? I thought the Dean eschewed physicians?'

Mr Sheridan laughs. 'Dr Wynne is not a medical man, Will, he is Precentor at St Patrick's - a Doctor of Divinity. He acts on behalf of my god-father since his present affliction began. Unfortunately, my god-father, hearing that the Cathedral choir was to assist in Mr Handel's concerts, set adamant against it.'

'Why so?'

Mr Sheridan smiles. 'Ask not for reason where the old man is concerned, Will. That deserted him long ago. But his stubborn intransigence was like to wreck the whole thing, for if the choir have not the Dean's permission, they cannot perform in public.'

'But you would still have the choristers from Christ Church Cathedral.'

'Perhaps - but there are some who sing in both choirs. And if the Dean at St Patrick's withdraws consent, the Dean of Christ Church is like to follow. So Dr Wynne, who is strongly in favour of the concerts - being a member of the Charitable Musical Society and a governor of the Mercer's Hospital which is one of the charities which will benefit - suggested the Dean be brought to hear the work in the hope that it may lessen his opposition. And, to avoid any possible distress that such an excursion might provoke, Wynne suggested that I, his godson - a familiar and trusted face - might accompany him.'

'And has the visit changed his view, do you think?'

'Who can tell, Will? He was impressed by the majesty and serenity of the music, certainly - and he commented most favourably upon the appropriateness of the words. But how much he will remember in a day's time - or even an hour's time! - is open to doubt. However, as Dr Wynne was instrumental in bringing Mr Handel here in the first place, I am sure he will bring the full force of his persuasion to bear! Besides, if the worst comes to the worst, as my god-father's affairs are now legally in the hands of appointed guardians, his opposition may be put down to the vagaries of his condition and over-ridden.'

We have walked but a little way during this discussion when a carrier's cart passes us.

I notice the name on the side: *Thos. Acres & Son, Fine Wines and Spirits.*

Mr Sheridan notices it, too.

'Is that some relation to poor Tobias, do you think?'

'I believe it is,' say I. 'His family were wine merchants.'

We watch as it trundles to a halt outside the *Bull's Head* next to the Music Hall and with a start I recognise one of the two men who start unloading casks and kegs of liquor.

It is Sean Kelly.

I was with Richard O'Sullivan the last time I saw him and remember how the actor's presence caused us to part on bad terms. A need to explain brings the thought of apology briefly into my mind.

But as I step forward, our eyes meet and Kelly pointedly averts his, turning away into the *Bull's Head* as if he has not seen me. The animosity of our last meeting has clearly not been forgotten.

A flush of anger brings a sudden heat to my cheeks. But as it subsides I consider it might be embarrassment rather than contempt that makes him avoid me thus. Perhaps he is feeling as guilty for his hasty words as I am for inadvertently consorting with his enemy.

But the opportunity for us both to apologise has passed.

Since entering the *Bull's Head* with a couple of small kegs Sean has not emerged. His companion has twice gone in and out, rolling casks of liquor. But there is no sign of Sean.

I can only conclude he is avoiding me.

His stubbornness irks me, but it also saddens me. For all his hot-headedness, I like him. And this falling-out is none of my making.

Beside me, Mr Sheridan is becoming curious at my hesitation.

'You seem distracted, Will. Is anything the matter?'

'Nothing,' I reply. 'Just someone I thought I knew.'

With that, I dismiss Sean Kelly from my mind and we resume our progress towards the theatre.

On the way I ask Mr Sheridan if he knows anything of a place called Ballycullen.

It is, he informs me a small hamlet a few miles south west of Dublin. 'No more that a dozen poor dwellings, I imagine. What possible interest can you have in the place, Will?'

Do I tell him of Kitty's absence? I decide against it for the

171

moment. He is, after all, paying her to be part of his company. If she does not fulfil the terms of the agreement, it will go ill with her - and possibly with Ned

For all Mr Sheridan has so far proved friendly and amenable, he is a businessman when all said and done. I do not like deceiving him - but I like betraying my friends less.

'Nothing of any great import,' say I, making light of the matter. 'I overheard the name in conversation and it piqued my curiosity - a curiosity which you now have satisfied, sir. I see the place is worth no further consideration.'

'Indeed not, Will. But here we are at the theatre and I must take my leave. Matters require my attention.' He sighs wearily. 'A theatre manager's life is not all cakes and ale, you know, Will - it is all paperwork and administration! You would do well to remind your master of that if ever he should think of pursuing that course!'

We wish each other good-day and go our separate ways.

17

...take counsel together...

After I leave Mr Sheridan at the theatre I decide to continue towards Dame Street and look for Charlie. There is no point in him scouring the town for Kitty if she is, as we believe, in Ballycullen.

The afternoon is now well-advanced and the streets are busy. Traders eager to clear their wares at the end of the day, merchants sealing final bargains and beaux, only a few hours risen, parading their way to coffee houses to hold court. The *beau-monde* ready to see and be seen, threading its way through the commercial life of the city.

As my eyes are peeled for a skinny boy weaving through the throng, I do not at first take notice of a totally different figure. Or rather a pair of figures in animated conversation coming in my direction.

One is Richard O'Sullivan and the other is the lawyer whom I saw at the house of Eugenie Acres - John Callaghan.

The latter is dressed as soberly as last time, if not more so - in fact his garb is positively funereal.

It dawns on me that he must be just come from Tobias Acres's interment. The strain is still evident in his expression, his cheeks sallow, his eyes dark from recent tears. And he seems but distantly attentive to O'Sullivan's excited exhortations.

I turn aside, hiding my face. So engrossed are they in

conversation that they do not mark me.

But seeing them together disturbs me.

It is as if two separate areas of my existence have collided without reason. O'Sullivan from the life I choose to lead - my friends and the theatre. Callaghan from the life Sir William Hervey forces upon me - one of spies and subterfuge.

For my own peace of mind I know I must follow and discover the topic of their discourse but there is little chance of getting close enough to overhear them as long as they remain in the open. Fortunately, they turn into a coffee house at the next corner.

I wait a few moments, then slide surreptitiously after them.

This establishment lacks the gloom and secrecy of the one chosen by Semple for our lunch of eels. But there are wooden screens between the tables and luck is with me for, as O'Sullivan and Callaghan take a table on the further side of one such screen, the gentleman at the table on this side of it is rising to go. I wait until he has paid his due, then quietly slip into his place.

The room is loud with many conversations, but by putting my ear close to the latticework atop the screen I may, like a priest in a confessional, hear clearly whilst remaining unseen.

A waiter appears at my side and I order a dish of chocolate and today's paper. Under its cover I may hope to hide my interest in the conversation behind me from the other customers.

Thus furnished, I set myself to listen.

The gist of the interchange seems to concern legal matters pertaining to an inheritance due to O'Sullivan. Coming late into the conversation and not understanding many of the legal terms, I initially glean little of its import. But eventually I deduce that

Callaghan must be acting for O'Sullivan in the matter, and it seems O'Sullivan is fretting at the delay in proceedings.

'Your tardiness has already cost you dear,' he says testily. 'I would not have my own expectations similarly dashed.'

This seems to offend Callaghan. 'What mean you?' he demands.

'You know what I mean,' retorts O'Sullivan. He lowers his voice so that I have to strain to hear. 'You would be a wealthy man now if you had not been so squeamish. And now your hope is gone, buried beneath six feet of Irish clay.'

My cup is poised midway to my lips. Are they talking of Tobias Acres? Gently I replace the cup on the table and listen even more intently.

The gibe has taken Callaghan aback for he is silent for a moment. When he speaks, his voice is thick with emotion.

'Unkind, sir, considering from whence I have just come.'

'The interment, to be sure. And suitably moving, I have no doubt. But believe me, John, you are well rid of him.'

'Enough!' Callaghan keeps his voice low, but it vibrates with passion. 'Not content with accosting me in the very churchyard, you now twist the knife in my hour of grief!'

'Come, man,' says O'Sullivan with the bare modicum of apology. 'You were fond of the fellow, I know. But surely now you must know your affection was misplaced?'

Callaghan, however, is not to be mollified. His anger, for all it is repressed, is evident. 'Your very words betray you, Dick. You talk like the profligate you are! Who are you to talk of love - you, who have never truly cared for anyone. To whom women are but idle conquests, to be savoured briefly and then cast aside. How dare you lecture me on what I must or must not feel?'

O'Sullivan, surprisingly, does not rise to the insult. 'Your censure is just. I don't deny I am a mere dabbler in the art of love. But in affairs of the heart it is ofttimes better to swim on the surface than to plunge in deep - it gives you a better view of the world.'

The implication hits home. When Callaghan next speaks, his tone is more of sorrow than of anger. 'I thought I knew him, Dick.' He pauses for a moment, then continues. 'How could he who knew so much of beauty in his music be so insensible to human feelings? He asked too much of me. I could not do it.'

'For the lady's sake - or for your own?'

'I own the thought of lying with a woman repels me. And I failed to understand how Tobias could possibly think of the three of us living under the same roof. We would all have been miserable. No good would have come of it. It would have been a sham - a lie!'

'Oh, come, John, you're a lawyer - lies are your business,' says O'Sullivan mockingly. 'And what of the lady? Does she appreciate your moral stand? Or does she think you as culpable as her late brother?'

'Tobias bears the full brunt of her resentment. Their antipathy is no new thing, but this has turned it into a fierce bitterness. It pains me, but I can understand it. As for me - she seems to consider me as much a victim of his machinations as herself and has dealt with me fairly. I believe I retain her respect and her trust.'

' Respect and trust!' repeats O'Sullivan scathingly. 'Both very well, John - but you have not her hand! Your daintiness in this matter has cost you dear. You could be master now that the brother is gone. But instead, you are her servant. And what future now for the family business that might have been yours? Who will run it if she can not?'

'It is mine in all but name. She takes more interest in it than Tobias ever did - his music was his life - but she is content to leave the day-to-day business in my hands. Even before old Acres died, his increasing incapacity meant that most major decisions were referred to me. By the time the old man died, I had made myself indispensable. And it is no idle boast that I have improved the business. So much so that the lady's future prosperity is assured.'

'And your own pocket handsomely lined as well, no doubt.'

Callaghan utters what might be termed a laugh - a dry, legal sound that refuses to commit itself. But he does not deny the accusation.

'Of course,' says O'Sullivan slyly, 'the whole cosy arrangement might be upset should a suitor appear on the scene...? Why, I might even consider courting the lady myself!'

It is as much as I can do to stifle an incredulous laugh at his presumption. To think Eugenie would consider such a blatant libertine as he! Callaghan is clearly of the same opinion.

'You think Eugenie would not see you for what you are? You underestimate her perception,' says he. 'Besides, your cause is lost already. There was a young man the other day... Archer - that was his name, I think. Open-faced, good looking... He brought a colour

177

to her cheeks I have not seen before.'

'And to yours, by your description,' laughs O'Sullivan. 'Archer? Not Will Archer from Garrick's company, surely? A callow youth - tolerably handsome, I grant you, but priggish. Took offence at my complimenting a certain Miss Kitty Blair... I need have no fear of him, John - a scarce-bearded innocent who has, I'll wager, even less experience with ladies than yourself! Besides, he will be gone back to London in two months.'

My mother always told me that people who eavesdrop hear no good of themselves. It seems now that it was the one good piece of advice she ever gave me!

But now I hear the scrape of chairs as they rise to leave. I hide my burning face behind the newspaper as they pass my table.

Once the heat of mortification has abated, I try to compose myself by piecing together what I have seen and heard.

Callaghan, it seems, is not as noble as Eugenie believes. It was not out of consideration for her feelings that he refused to countenance the sham marriage. Rather, it was his abhorrence of physical contact with a female and shock at his lover's insensitivity.

The refusal to go along with Tobias's plan was also commercially astute. As he already controlled her business interests, and thus her fortune, where was the necessity to tie himself to a wife he could not love?

And with this thought comes another intriguing possibility. If he could do without a wife - could he also do without a lover, especially one who showed such little sensitivity to anyone else's feelings? Could Callaghan have become so disenchanted with

Tobias that he contemplated murder? Love turned to hate...?

But thinking of Callaghan's directing influence over the Acres's wine business leads me back to something else I've seen today.

Did the lawyer hire Sean Kelly as a delivery man? A one-day tenure, perhaps, to supply the place of those at the funeral?

Yet one thing puzzles me. I can see Kelly being grateful for some extra income - but how has he managed to absent himself from his work at the Custom House? And do his employers know?

I resolve to broach the matter with Richard Semple when next we meet.

I drain the dregs of my chocolate, pay my bill and leave the coffee house to resume my search for Charlie.

The evening has closed in and it is now dark enough for lamps to be lit in windows. The Dublin streets, as those in London, rely for their illumination upon occasional lanterns provided by civic-minded citizens upon their house fronts. Here, in the main thoroughfare, they are fairly numerous. But in the side-streets, they are few and far between.

I tell myself that I will spend just a quarter hour longer and if, by that time I have not encountered Charlie, I shall make my way back to Lamb Alley in the hope that he has had the same idea.

My task is made the easier because, now it is dusk, there are fewer people about. The clerks, the traders, the porters and hawkers - all will now be at home in their lonely narrow lodgings, or at board with their wives and children, or carousing in the sweaty inns of the city. The beaux will have completed their progress from chocolate house to salon, to primp and peacock their way late into the night.

In London by this hour, the inhabitants of the night will be starting to emerge. The citizens in search of innocent or forbidden pleasures - and the footpads and whores ready to fleece them.

I push my purse more securely inside my breeches and glance about for darker presences in the shadows.

It is as I am thus looking about me that Charlie trots, unconcerned and whistling, round the corner into my very path.

'Wotcher, mate!' says he with a grin.

It takes but a moment to confirm that he has found no trace of Kitty on his travels.

Together we set off home, but we have not gone far when I spy a familiar figure. Richard O'Sullivan, alone now, having parted company with Callaghan, is striding purposefully towards the river.

My curiosity gets the better of me and I tell Charlie he must make his own way back to our lodging.

'Shall I hail a link-boy for you?' I offer.

'I've eyes in my head, ain't I? And there's a moon, ain't there? I need no stinking urchin with his scrag end of tallow to light my way. Save your pennies, mate.'

All the same, he wants to know why I would stay. Telling him to mind his business, I send him off in the direction of Lamb Alley. I have no fear for his safety - he was brought up on the streets of London and knows how to avoid trouble.

Then I set off in pursuit of the receding figure of O'Sullivan.

It is not hard to remain unobserved under cover of the night. Darkness is more the ally of the hunter than of the prey. The feeble moon, though obscured by filmy clouds, gives enough light to keep a sufficient distance betwixt us.

But as time passes, and the distance between me and the warmth of my lodgings increases, I begin to wonder why I'm doing this. Why should I be interested in O'Sullivan? I have no cause to suspect him of anything. It appears he had naught to do with Kitty's disappearance, and he had no involvement that I can see with Tobias Acres's death.

The fellows he stops to chat with as I lurk, colder by the minute, in the shadows, are rakes like himself. The women with whom he exchanges ribald banter as he passes them are no more than shrill drabs. Isn't it just idle curiosity sparked by dislike that has led me into this?

I am almost on the point of giving up, convincing myself that he is only on his way to some drinking or gambling house, when he stops.

My waning interest stirs.

We are in one of the streets leading to Custom House Quay, not far from the eating house where I lunched with Semple earlier today.

O'Sullivan glances about him, runs a hand through his hair, straightens his waistcoat and coat-tails, then raps upon the door.

It is clear what he is about. A feeble lantern glows red above the door.

It opens, spearing the outside dark with a sliver of warm light. The gaudily dressed girl is all welcoming smiles and piled-up curls as he steps inside. Obviously this is one of the clean establishments he recommended to me the other day.

He enters and the door closes behind him. Darkness shuffles back, leaving me cold and disappointed.

And at that moment a hand rests lightly on my shoulder and gently caressing fingers slide between my legs.

'So you did come back, Will Archer,' whispers a soft voice in my ear. 'I'm sure pleased you did. You'll not regret it, my little bow-man.'

It is Molly, the cockle seller.

My first guilty thought is of Susan, back home in London. But my conscience soon beats retreat at the insistence of her fingers stroking my little soldier. He, it seems, has no qualms about infidelity. Confined to barracks for days now, he rouses himself, straining against the velvet, ready to answer the call to arms.

Molly's nimbly unlaces my breeches to impede his ardour no longer. Her breasts are warm and soft against my shoulder. Her lips are nibbling at my ear.

My virtuous resolve is crumbling under the onslaught. In one last attempt to retain my self-respect. I grasp her wrist to stay the treacherous unlacing.

'I cannot,' say I huskily, 'Susan...'

'Is not here,' she purrs. 'And I sure won't tell, if you won't...Come, mi bucko, your lips say one thing but this...' The last lace is undone. My plucky little soldier springs free. 'Why, he's singing a different tune altogether!'

Then, with a swiftness that I fail to counter, she is on her knees before me.

My willing ensign is engulfed in an all-out assault of warm lips and questing tongue. My resistance takes flight. Hands that were meant to push her away, instead find themselves tangling in her hair, pushing her head in ever more determined forays upon my gallant warrior.

At last, just as he gets within firing distance, she releases him. The cool night air hits him. He wilts a little under the shock. But now her lips are brushing mine. She smells of brine and the sea and her breath is warm and sweet with the tang of my manhood. Our tongues encounter recklessly. I hug her ardently, crushing her yielding breasts. Below decks my man-at-arms is back to full attention.

Suddenly, with a sharp cry, she pushes me away. But it is only to hitch up her skirts. Then, pinning me against the wall, the coarse bricks digging into my back, she loops her arms about my neck and leaps astride me, her legs encircling my waist.

Lingeringly she lowers herself little by little till my battle-hardened champion is fully engaged. Once securely mounted, he is led from a trot to a canter and thence to a full-blooded gallop. I clasp my hands beneath her bouncing buttocks, helping her keep her seat throughout the tempestuous ride.

The race at its height, my breath coming in eager pants, she dismounts within very sight of the goal. My doughty infantryman, abandoned, shoots his volleys into the night.

And then all is tenderness and exhaustion and the fading tattoo of pounding hearts. Her hand caresses my cheek and she whispers soft words. I nuzzle her neck, breathing in her seashore scent. Our two bodies rest gently one against the other, the separate rhythms of our breath and blood blending imperceptibly into one.

How long we stay like this, I do not know. Only that, at some point, we move apart, she whispers, 'You are everything I expected, Will Archer,' and is gone into the night.

18

...thy rebuke hath broken his heart...

Morning creeps slowly into my consciousness. My eyes feel heavy but I awake with a sense of wellbeing I have not experienced since first setting foot in Ireland. I have slept as soundly as a log, untroubled by dreams or thoughts of conspiracy.

Charlie's truckle bed is empty, the cover thrown back. He is doubtless down in the kitchen, charming the graceless Nora and wheedling his way around Mrs O'Shaughnessy for a bite of breakfast.

I roll out of bed and relieve myself in the chamber pot. The stream seems never-ending this morning, steaming slightly in the chill of the attic and coming within a hair's breath of overflowing the lip of the jordan. The last drops shaken off, I cradle my little soldier, his weight and warmth in my palm. Remembering last night and Molly's sweet salt tang... I inhale deeply, eyes closed in contentment.

A drumming of footsteps on the attic stairs heralds Charlie's return. Hastily I scramble into my breeches, stowing the little man back in barracks before the attic door rattles open.

'Oho, you're up, are you?' says Charlie cheekily. 'Mr Garrick and Mistress Peg are already gone to the theatre.'

'Why, what time is it?'

'Past ten o'clock, sleepyhead. The boss says there's linen needs washing, if you're up to it.'

It is the first real reminder of my role in Mr Garrick's household. I am not just an actor - not even an actor, some would say - but am employed as my master's manservant-cum-valet. I am a living example of what my master's detractors see as his parsimony - fulfilling many roles for no salary, but only my keep. It is Sir William Hervey's purse which pays my way. Yet, of the two, it is Mr Garrick who has my first loyalty.

Having not the luxury of basin and ewer in the servants' rooms, I must content myself with a quick sluice at the yard pump before I start on my chores.

I retrieve the soiled linen from my master's room and tap upon Mrs Fitzgerald's door to negotiate the use of a wooden tub, hot water from the cauldron by the fire and some soap. She half-heartedly offers the services of Nora, but I politely decline.

'My master,' say I, 'likes me to wash his small linen for he is very particular about his best holland shirt, and dislikes starch.'

Besides, Nora has more than enough to do already.

In any case, the clincher is the mention of starch. The lady visibly pales. Starch, unlike the meagre nut of soap, clearly doesn't figure in Mrs Fitzgerald's largesse.

So I set about my task and, after an hour's rubbing and scrubbing, rinsing and wringing, my master's linen is laid out upon a hurdle before the kitchen fire to dry.

'Sure it's a fine young man you are,' beams Mrs O'Shaughnessy, the cook, with admiration as she pummels a heap of dough upon the kitchen table. Her sleeves are rolled up and her brawny arms dusted with flour. A smudge of white, like ash, upon the rosy glow of her cheeks. 'There's many an Irishman would think such work beneath them. It'll be a lucky colleen who snares you, it will.'

She glances at skinny Nora. During her frequent but brief trips through the kitchen with trays of cinders and buckets and mops, the poor drudge has gazed open-mouthed at my industry. As I return the empty tub to its accustomed corner, she favours me with a coy, gap-toothed smile, pushing back a lock of greasy hair with her stick-thin arm. I pray she is not the colleen Mrs O'Shaughnessy has in mind!

It is high time to make my escape. I must go to the theatre and learn from Ned if Kitty is returned.

Rehearsal is in full swing when I arrive and Ned is on stage His role as Monsieur Marquis, the comic Frenchman is sizeable, unlike my own dozen lines. Neither Kitty's role of Parley, nor O'Sullivan's of Dicky is as big. They have one fairly lengthy scene together in Act One, but only brief on-off appearances throughout the rest of the play. As a result, Kitty's absence does not so far seem to have been remarked upon.

As I slip into the theatre we are midway through Act Five.

Sir Harry Wildair has been tricked into fighting a duel with the Frenchman.

Being but a rehearsal, Mistress Peg, who plays Sir Harry, is in her normal day dress, not breeches. Anyone unfamiliar with the theatrical device of a woman playing a man's role would have little idea what is going on. And even for me it is not much better.

From the parts of the play I've seen, it seems poor stuff. A hotch-potch of quarrels, confusions and infidelities involving a collection of stock characters that might have been picked from a housewife's pattern book - the bellicose sailor, the affected fop, the ridiculous Frenchman - even a fake ghost! It is certainly not Mr Farquhar's greatest achievement.

Written in haste following the success of Wildair's first appearance in *A Trip to the Jubilee,* it lacks the subtlety of character of the first piece, and of *The Beaux Stratagem.* So at least I gather from overheard conversations between Mr Garrick and his colleagues - for I have seen neither play.

Whatever its want of literary merit, it is a crowd-pleaser and Ned is at the moment creating a great deal of coarse laughter among his fellow players with his prancing Frenchman. I sit back and enjoy his antics, wishing I had but a fraction of his liveliness and originality.

'*Sa, sa, sa,*' he chirrups, flourishing around the stage, '*Feinte a la tete. Sa! Embrasiade - quart sur redouble. Hey!*'

It is dreadful nonsense, but such is Ned's joyful relish that the Frenchman comes to life with every gesture.. When Mistress Peg enters and says '*These French are as great fops in their quarrels as in their amours!*' it is as if she has read my thoughts.

A moment later, O'Sullivan, as Dicky, Sir Harry's servant, runs on and hands a gun to his master while Monsieur Marquis lays down the wager.

'*Dicky,*' says Sir Harry, '*take up the money and carry it home.*'

'*Here it is faith,*' replies O'Sullivan. Then, aside to the invisible audience, '*And if my master be killed, the money is my own.*'

Aye, think I, recalling his conversation with Callaghan in the coffee-house, *you are well cast - you would have your friend Callaghan do the same!*

He scuttles off and a couple of moments later, much to my annoyance, slips into the seat beside me.

'Are you well, Master Archer?' he whispers.

Onstage, Mistress Peg and Ned circle about each other preparing for the duel which neither of them wants.

'I am, sir,' say I curtly.

I do not give him the gratification of my attention. I keep my gaze fixed steadfastly upon the stage.

Rebuffed for the moment, he slouches beside me with a great show of unconcern. Then, when Mr Garrick enters to separate the onstage combatants, he leans over and murmurs, 'You have an air about you this morning, Will, a glow of satisfaction that speaks of amour. You have acted upon my recommendation, perhaps?'

'No, sir,' say I coldly, 'I have no doubt the young ladies are as delectable as you say, but I do not pay for such services.'

I intend it as disapproval, but he takes it as conceit.

'Oho, Will Archer - such confidence!' he says. 'What it is to be young! Fresh-faced and a prick ever ready! Great attractions both to the ladies - especially those who lead sheltered lives. Mayhap you've found such a one?'

His lewdness offends me. I know, after yesterday's overheard conversation between him and Callaghan. whom he means but I don't give him the satisfaction of a reply. Instead I stare in dogged silence at the action onstage where Mistress Peg as Wildair is explaining to Colonel Standard why he and his wife parted.

'Why, then, Colonel, you must know we were a pair of the

189

most happy, toying, foolish people in the world, till she got, I don't know how, a crotchet of jealousy in her head.'

I glance at Ned in the background of the scene. The mask of Monsieur Marquis has temporarily slipped and he looks glum. The words obviously remind him of himself and Kitty.

'We never had an angry word. She only fell a crying overnight. And I went to Italy next morning...'

Beside me, O'Sullivan murmurs appreciatively.

'The captivating Miss Blair has not graced us with her company these last two days - is aught amiss there?' he says, inclining his head in Ned's direction. Whatever his shortcomings, he does not lack perception.

'She is indisposed. A chill.'

I am too abrupt. O'Sullivan smiles disbelievingly.

'To be sure,' says he. 'Our Dublin air is not to everyone's taste.'

Is this a hint that he knows she is no longer in town?

But now the actors are moving on to the next scene. Ned has finished for the day and, jumping nimbly from the stage, heads in my direction.

He stops when he sees O'Sullivan beside me and the words dry on his lips. They acknowledge each other with bare civility.

Then, 'Will,' says he, 'I would have a word with you in private.'

As O'Sullivan shows no sign of accommodating us, I rise and leave the theatre with Ned.

As soon as we are in the open, Ned bursts out, 'She is not returned, Will, and has still sent no word. What am I to do?'

The poor fellow is distraught with worry. His eyes plead for my assistance.

'Be of good cheer, man,' say I. 'I have been thinking of how we may travel to Ballycullen...'

'I cannot,' says Ned despairingly.'I am needed for rehearsal these two days. I cannot absent myself without explanation. And an explanation may do more harm than good. No one has yet commented on Kitty's absence, but there have been looks... If both of us were to miss rehearsal Mr Sheridan may reconsider our contract for the season.'

'Fear not, Ned. I shall find her. And I know someone who may help.'

'Who?'

'The lady who lost her brother - Miss Acres.'

'Are you sure, Will?'

'I can but ask.'

And with that promise, I tell him I shall be about it straight.

Half an hour later I am outside number 56 Great Boater Lane.

Liam, dishevelled as ever, answers the door.

'Is Miss Acres at home? I would see her on an affair of some urgency - a personal matter.'

His look is unreadable but, with a sniff, he lets me in, opens the door to the now familiar servants' parlour and goes off in search of his mistress.

Bridget is in the chair beside the hearth sewing. She nods a greeting but does not get up. Nor does she offer any conversation. The minutes pass in awkward silence, I pacing fretfully, she intent

191

upon her needle.

At last, after what seems an eternity, Eugenie hurries in, with Liam behind her.

'Will,' says she, 'what drama is this that you come a-calling at this hour of the morning? *An affair of some urgency* - *w*hy, you have set me all of a tremble! Bridget, a dish of tea, if you please.'

'Here,' says the jade pertly, 'or upstairs?'

Eugenie turns to me. '*A personal matter* you say? In that case, we should go upstairs to the withdrawing room. Only it is so cheerless...'

'Bridget and me'll make ourselves scarce, miss,' says Liam with some reluctance. 'Then you can hear your gentleman out in private - and in comfort.'

'You're too kind, Liam.'

'Sure, and don't I know it. You see, Master Archer, how we put ourselves out for you?'

The fellow's impudence is unbearable, but I essay a cool smile of gratitude.

While Bridget busies herself with the tea, I enquire after arrangements for her brother's funeral.

'All done,' she says. 'He was buried yesterday morning.'

'And Mr Callaghan attended the service?'

'Together with several from the company. They wished to show their respect.'

There is a derisive huff from Liam who is still in the room. Privacy evidently is not be accorded until the arrival of the tea.

'And Liam attended, on behalf of the household.'

'Only to certify the bastard was under six foot of good Irish soil!' he growls under his breath.

I pretend not to hear, and say, 'I saw Mr Callaghan yesterday. He did not see me. Somewhat to my surprise, he was in company with one of the actors from the Smock Alley Company. Mr Richard O'Sullivan...?'

The name clearly means nothing to her.

'John is a busy man,' she replies. 'He has clients from all walks of life. You should have made yourself known to him, Will. He would have been pleased to see you.'

'I doubt he'd have known me after such a fleeting acquaintance - we only passed on the stairs...'

'But you made an impression, nonetheless,' says she with a laugh. 'He asked about you the following day.'

Another suppressed snigger from Liam. 'Grist to his mill, you'd be, Will Archer,' he sneers. 'A firm pair of buttocks and a pretty face!'

'Liam!' scolds Eugenie. 'Hold your foul tongue - you insult my guest!'

In truth, it is no insult. It is how I earned my living at Mother Ransom's after all!

But I am beginning to tire of his jibes. It is time I repaid him in kind.

'Not at all, Jeannie,' say I easily, 'I am not offended in the least. rather I take it as a compliment.' Then, with a teasing grin at the surly footman, 'You note my personal attributes more closely than I thought, Liam. Mayhap your professed aversion towards me is but feigned?'

He reddens and I see his fist clench. 'Fuck you!' he mutters.

Then, with a guilty glance at his mistress, he storms out of the room.

'Fie,Will,' says Eugenie, her eyes twinkling with mirth, 'I see you give as good as you get.'

'My apologies, Jeannie. I fear I have insulted him, and thwarted my own plans in the process. For my intention in coming here was to ask for his assistance.'

She raises a delicate eyebrow. 'Indeed? You intrigue me. Is this the matter you come about? Here,' she says to Bridget who has brought the tea, 'put it down here and take yourself off to the scullery.'

Once the maid has gone downstairs to the basement I tell Eugenie all about Kitty's disappearance and how we think she has gone to relations in Ballycullen. I explain that, as Ned is required to be at the theatre, I have volunteered to go alone but am not sure how to get there. Also that, as an Englishman, I am wary of what welcome I might receive.

'And that is where you think Liam may be of assistance - to act as guide and bodyguard?'

'I fear that may now be a forlorn hope.'

'Not at all. Liam does not like being bested. But he'll get over it. He'll sulk a while and lick his wounds. But, in the end, he'll come round and like you all the better for standing up to him.'

'You think so?'

'I know so. Besides,' says she, 'Liam will do as I tell him. How do you intend to get there? I do not know Ballycullen itself, but I believe it is some distance away...'

'A hackney - I have seen them for hire...? Ned, I am sure will not begrudge the fare.'

'I have a better idea. My father's gig is stabled at our warehouse. It has not been used for years but I shall send word to Mr Callaghan to have it unearthed this afternoon and made serviceable.'

The idea has clearly caught her imagination for she is as animated as a young girl. She skips to the scullery stairs and calls for Bridget to go fetch Liam. Then turns to me, her face flushed with excitement.

'By your leave, Will, I would accompany you on this adventure.'

'But...'

'Nay,' says she laying a finger on my lips. 'But me no buts, Will Archer. My presence will serve a dual purpose. Not only will it keep Liam in check but also, perhaps, reassure the lady, should we have the good fortune to find her. And in addition,' she says, lowering her eyes, 'it will afford me the pleasure of your company for almost a whole day. You would not deny me that, surely?'

Was Callaghan speaking the truth, then, when he said Eugenie was taken with me? I cannot think it - such a fine lady, and me a penniless player...

All the same, my heart is pounding as I reply, 'I would deny you nothing, Jeannie.'

Fortunately, no more words are necessary for, at this moment, Bridget returns with Liam trailing behind. His face is like thunder and he avoids looking either myself or Eugenie in the eye.

He listens, surly but silent, as his mistress tells him what he must do. She tells him of the journey's destination but not its purpose.

Surprisingly, it is Bridget who objects. 'Begging your pardon, ma'am, but have you lost your wits - traipsing off into those wild parts? Sure the cart will not serve you. I know the area. There be no roads to speak of.'

'Then where we cannot ride, we shall walk,' replies Eugenie undeterred. 'Now, Liam, quit your moping and be about your business. I want all ready for tomorrow morning.'

He slouches off without a word. *Chastened - or brooding?* I distrust his uncharacteristic silence.

'Tomorrow morning?' I say. 'You ask a lot of Mr Callaghan.'

'I have utmost reliance in him - and he has never let me down yet.'

'You are lucky to have found someone who so merits such trust.' I make it sound as innocent as I can. 'You feel he gives as much allegiance to you as to your brother? Theirs was, after all, a closer bond than mere business...'

'Love and loyalty are not always natural bedfellows, Will. If it were so, think you, would there be any unhappy marriages? No, Will, in matters of business, money forges stronger ties than emotion. I am under no illusion, believe me. The reason John guards my fortune well is that I pay him well.'

'So you give him free rein?'

She gives me a quizzical look. 'Are you playing the investigator again, Will Archer? You are angling at something - come, out with it.'

'It is nothing,' I reply offhandedly. 'Only I saw one of your delivery drays outside the inn next to the Music Hall - and one of the men...'

Suddenly I am aware that Bridget is still in the room. She is busy with her sewing and does not appear to be listening to our conversation. But still I would not have her think I was impugning her brother in any way.

'...was - er - someone I - er - didn't expect to see. A fellow I'd thought had another job entirely.'

'Yesterday, was this? The day of my brother's funeral?' She speaks as if to an errant child. 'I am surprised an inquisitor such as yourself has not the answer. With so many at the funeral, John will have hired an extra labourer for the day - business, after all, must go on.'

'Of course,' I say, 'that is the obvious explanation!'

'Any misgivings about propriety should, I suggest be levelled not at John for hiring him, but at your friend for deceiving his other employer - do you not think?'

I laugh in agreement. 'Indeed, I think it was Mr Callaghan who was being deceived - for the fellow carried in but two small kegs, leaving his companion to shoulder the bulk of the work!'

'Well, I shall be sure to tell John next time we meet to take more care to hire diligent workers!'

Then, saying that she must search out appropriate travelling clothes for the morrow, she dismisses me.

I am sure I detect some reluctance in our parting. And at the door she lightly kisses my cheek. No more than a brush of her sweet lips, but enough to make my whole body thrill to the touch.

Leaving Great Boater Lane, I feel my steps lighter, the morning sunlight brighter as I make my way home.

19

....*abiding in the field...*

It is fortunate the weather is fine as we set out for Ballycullen for I have to cling precariously to the rear of a one-horse gig. The small cart has seating room only for two. So, as Liam must drive, he and Eugenie sit in front whilst I fulfil the role of 'tiger' - a boy groom who perches on the back step. I make a somewhat ungainly tiger, however, as I have neither the skill, nor the diminutive stature that such beings possess. I also lack the customary yellow striped waistcoat!

Her father, Eugenie tells me, would, when younger, use the trap to ride out with his wife. It has certainly seen better days. The irons are corroded and the woodwork cracked but, with the axles newly greased it runs tolerably well.

Even from my tricky perch I am able to converse with relative ease. But, for the first part of our journey I am content to watch as the city thins out and gives way to countryside.

Unfortunately, as the buildings grow sparser, so the quality of the road deteriorates. The gig which trundled happily enough over cobbles makes heavy weather of the rutted lanes and I am called upon several times to hop down and put my shoulder to it.

At such times Eugenie, too, will often scramble down to lessen the weight so that much of our journey is passed in light-hearted banter and laughter.

There comes a point, however, when we can go no further.

Our way, Liam informs us, leads off the lane, poor as it is. He points to a grassy track, tussocky and footworn leading into a straggle of trees, impassable for any vehicle.

'It can only be a mile and a half, two at most,' he says.

He unhitches the horse from the shafts and leads it off the road. The beast must accompany us. It would not do to leave it with the trap, only to return and find both stolen.

'Would you care to ride, Miss Eugenie?' he asks. She declines, preferring to walk with us.

While Liam adjusts the harness, replacing driving reins with a leading halter, Eugenie tucks up her skirts and sets off into the wood.

The day is fine. Stray shafts of sunlight pierce the trees, dappling the path. The turf beneath our feet is springy, in places still wet from the morning's dew. Bright drops twinkle on tufts of grass, shattering into myriad rainbows as we pass. At the path's ragged edge the first bluebells are beginning to show, and further in the wood I glimpse small clumps of primula and nodding trumpets of daffodils. The woodland smell of damp earth is spiced with the sour reek of wild garlic and occasional minty burst of pennyroyal. Before long our shoes and hose are darkened with moisture.

'It is strange, is it not,' say I, 'that there is no cart-track into the village. How do they get their goods to market?'

Liam guffaws. 'What goods would they be, Master Archer? These folk grow hardly enough to feed themselves. They have nothing to sell - and cannot afford to buy. A market is no use to them.'

From what I remember of the Yorkshire of my youth, there were always markets. Even countryfolk too poor to have animals or vegetables to sell would forage for mushrooms or wild herbs, cut saplings to make baskets, or make charcoal from fallen wood. Clay pots could be fired or moppets made from rags and sticks. Are these Irish peasants too poor or feckless even to do this?

'How then do they survive?' I ask.

'The best they can. Scrape the soil to grow a few potatoes. Share a scrawny cow or goat with the neighbours for its milk. Ask Bridget when you next see her. She comes from near Knockbyne Castle, not half a mile from here.'

'A castle?'

'A ruin - one of the many sacked by Cromwell and finally razed to the ground during the Williamite wars. Then, what war hadn't destroyed, English landlords sucked dry.'

'Liam...' cautions Eugenie. 'You are upon your hobby-horse again!'

'The Englishman needs to know, ma'am.' All the same, he curbs his treasonable sentiments and we plod on in silence.

After a while we come to a clearing. In the distance I see the ruins of a fine house atop a hill. Liam follows my gaze and says with grim satisfaction.

'And, to be sure, that is what they may expect in return.'

I shake my head, bewildered. 'I do not understand...?'

'That,' says Liam, 'is all that remains of Ballycullen House. The village once stood on the slopes of that hill where the air is healthy and the prospect fine. But then the English landlord decided he would built his House there and the cottages of the poor spoiled his view. These, you understand, were same poor who tended him in his new mansion and from whose labour and rents his income was derived. So he had the old village demolished to make way for his landscaped garden. In his magnanimity he donated the stones for the villagers to carry down to the stinking hollow where the village now stands and let them build their new homes there. Then he upped their rents.'

'But if they'd built them with their own hands, how could he charge them?' I ask in indignation.

'They were built with the landlord's stone on the landlord's land... The same land stolen from their forebears and now leased back to them!' He smiles indulgently. 'You are outraged at the injustice of it all are you, Will Archer? Welcome to Ireland!'

His almost triumphant wallowing in oppression begins to irk me. 'Your country is not unique in this,' I tell him. 'We have unjust landlords in England, too.'

'To be sure, but at least it is your own countrymen who bleed you dry.'

'Boys! Boys!' Eugenie reprimands us. 'Peace! Would you start the war anew between the two of you? Call truce, for my sake. And, Liam, tell us what happened to Ballycullen House.'

'It was burned. Not two months since, so Bridget says.' He shrugs. 'Mysteriously caught fire in the middle of the night.'

Eugenie is shocked. 'And the owner - and his family?'

'Escaped with no more than they stood up in. Then fled back to England.' He gives a satisfied smile. 'The steward, however, who collected the rents, unfortunately perished.'

'How awful!'

'A tragedy, to be sure, ma'am. But here we are at the village. What name do you say we are to enquire after, Master Archer?'

'The lady we seek is called Kitty Blair. I know not whether that be her given name or one adopted for the stage.'

'A good start to be sure!' scoffs Liam. 'Still, it's a fine day for chasing wild geese!'

The 'village' is no more than a cluster of dwellings alongside a widening of the path. To one side, the wood. To the other, an expanse of boggy land leading down to a meandering, peat-coloured stream. There are a few low, stone-built cottages with clay daubed walls and overhanging thatch. Others, deeper into the surrounding woodland are little more than crude huts with a covering of turves.

A scrawny cow snuffles at tussocks of grass at the edge of the wood, its grazing area curtailed by a palisade of rough stakes amidst the undergrowth. Two or three scraggy chickens scatter at our approach, pock-pocking their disapproval.

The disturbance brings out a number of ragged children who stare at us open-mouthed, nudging each other and giggling. They sidle closer, casting wondering glances at the horse which, now we've stopped, is idly champing the grass.

Liam drops into squatting position, eyes on a level with the tallest boy. 'Here,' says he. 'A penny if you'll tend the beast.'

He holds the coin enticingly. The boy approaches, eyes gleaming but just as he reaches out his hand, Liam retracts the coin and palms it. He leaps to his feet, towering above the child.

'It'll be yours when we've concluded our business here. I'd be sore disappointed to pay youse now and return to find money, beast and your good self vanished into thin air!'

The boy utters an aggrieved snort and turns his back on him, muttering something in Irish.

Liam catches his retreating shoulder and spins him around. 'Don't trust me, is it?' says he. 'Tell you what - how if the fine lady vouches for me?'

The boy sullenly raises his eyes to Eugenie, who gives him a beaming smile. 'Look after the horse, boy, and I'll add another two pence to this gentleman's penny.'

The boy needs no further urging. Knuckling his forehead enthusiastically, he takes the halter from Liam. He carefully guides the beast to the choicest patch of grass in the shade of an alder and winds the leash about a convenient branch. Then sits cross-legged beside the grazing horse, reaching out a tentative hand to lightly stroke its mane. Several of his fellows form a group around him, hoping perhaps that he may share his bounty.

'Another tree might be more propitious,' mutters Liam. 'Grass grows rich about an alder, but it is an unlucky tree all the same.'

'Why so?' I ask.

'It bleeds red when cut. You do not pass one on a journey if you can help it.'

Those urchins, too young or too out of favour to be included in the horse fellowship have, like the bedraggled chickens, slowly drifted back. Now they gaze at Eugenie from a distance, open mouthed, awe-struck and expectant.

Eugenie reaches for her purse. The children close in, jostling each other, hands outstretched. Their shrill clamour brings mothers to the doors. The women swoop upon their offspring, gather them up, then stand defiant, arms folded in face of the strangers.

The mistrust in their eyes makes me uncomfortable but before anyone can speak a voice cuts through the sudden silence.

'Will Archer, is that you? What are you doing here?'

At the door of the furthest stone cottage stands a young woman. She is plainly dressed and her hair hangs loose. But it is unmistakably Kitty. And she doesn't sound pleased to see me.

As she strides towards us the neighbours retreat into their own dwellings muttering amongst themselves.

Kitty's eyes sweep over Liam and come to rest on Eugenie. Her sharpness lessens a little - but only a little. 'Miss Acres - I am surprised to see you here.'

It is plain to me that Kitty is not only embarrassed but furious. It is only Eugenie's presence which is holding her back from venting her full spleen upon me for this unexpected intrusion.

While I stand at a loss what to do, Eugenie steps forward and encloses Kitty in a warm embrace. 'Miss Blair,' says she, 'you cannot know how it gratifies me to find you safe. Your friends have been so worried.'

I can see that Kitty is taken aback by this, but it doesn't stop her shooting a venomous glance at me as she replies, 'Worried? But there is no cause for worry. As you see, I am fit and well - and quite capable of arranging my own affairs.'

Behind her, a woman has appeared at the door of the cottage that Kitty came from. She now approaches.

'Kitty my dear, sure you must not keep your friends out in the lane like this. Please, milady,' says she, curtseying to Eugenie, 'do

204

me the honour to step inside. And the gentlemen, too.'

As she ushers us towards her cottage, I hear her chide Kitty under her breath, 'For shame, missy, would you make me a public show!'

The cottage is humble but clean. A bare table and two wooden chairs, one of which is offered to Eugenie. Liam and I stand, heads bowed under the low ceiling, whilst Kitty flounces to the opposite corner and sulks.

Two girls of about fourteen and sixteen scramble up from beside the hearth as we enter and I see that they have been tending a simple wooden cradle in which a baby murmurs. As the woman takes a seat opposite Eugenie, three or four more children creep in. I guess their ages must range from three to ten but all, including the woman, are thin to the point of emaciation, their clothes ragged, their skin sallow. By contrast, Kitty, although without her customary rouge, is the picture of rude health.

'Now, Kitty,' begins the woman, 'will you not introduce me to your friends?'

With an effort, Kitty pulls herself out of her sulk and introduces first Eugenie, then me. Liam she ignores, perhaps because she has forgotten his name or, more likely, because he is only a servant.

'And this,' she concludes, indicating the woman at the table, 'is my aunt Bronagh who, two night's since, sent for me in great distress.'

'Ned thought it must be so,' say I. 'He knew you would not leave without a word else.'

For a fleeting moment, I think I see contrition in her face, but almost immediately her mouth sets in its stubborn line again.

Eugenie takes Aunt Bronagh's hand in hers. 'May I enquire the cause of your distress, ma'am? Illness, was it - or family bereavement?'

Hearing the gentleness in her tone, my admiration for her grows. That she, with all the heartache her brother has caused her, can still feel such sympathy for others - and a stranger at that.

Tears moisten Aunt Bronagh's eyes. 'Oh that it was...' she begins, but is unable to continue.

Kitty comes forward and puts her arm around the woman's shoulders. After comforting her, she tells us the whole story.

'The other night, my landlady, Mrs Bickerstaff, informed me that there was a young man for me at the door. Of course, I thought at first it would be Ned, come to make amends for his ill-humour earlier that day. I had half a mind not to receive him. But Mrs Bickerstaff is not the sort of lady who likes strange men hanging about her door, so I thought it best to go down.'

'I don't blame you, Kitty,' I say. 'I have seen the lady and I would not like to cross her!'

A smile from the old Kitty flickers for a moment, then she resumes her tale. 'To my surprise, the man at the door was my cousin Kenneth, whom I have not seen for years. The last time I saw him, he was a grubby ten-year-old. But now he is a fine, strapping youth of eighteen.'

Kitty notices my glance around the room.

'No, Will, he is not here. He is at present out in the woods foraging for fuel and any wild creature that may fill the pot for tonight's supper. But two night's ago he was at my lodgings, near

206

spent with exhaustion, saying his mother was almost demented with grief and he didn't know what to do. So, hearing that I was at Smock Alley, he had walked and run all the way to Dublin to find me.'

I think of the distance we have come today. 'Surely you did not return all the way here on foot!'

'You know me better than that, Will Archer!' she replies sharply. 'No, I hired a hackney carriage to take us as far as possible, then, like Miss Acres here, I upped the hem of my skirt and plodded the rest of the way on foot. It was fortunate I had thought to don my plain huswife dress and travel light, or I would have arrived as exhausted as Kenneth.'

Aunt Bronagh squeezes her hand. 'She's a good girl, our Kitty, for all her airs and graces. And a great comfort in our present affliction,' she says tearfully.

Kitty pats her Aunt's shoulder.

'You'll have seen the ruins of Ballycullen House on your way here?' continues Kitty. 'Like a lot of fine houses recently, it was burned down. And the authorities are keen to find someone to blame.'

'And who better than the poor Irish peasants...' mutters Liam. He looks Aunt Bronagh in the eye, then glances towards the cradle. 'You have not mentioned a husband, missus, yet your babby cannot be more than a few months old.'

'Indeed, sir. I have a husband - if he is still alive.' Again, tears start to her eyes, but she brushes them angrily aside. 'And a grown son...'

'Kenneth's older brother, Aidan,' says Kitty. 'He's known as a bit of a hot head, careless with his tongue, especially when he's been at the poteen...'

'So the guards came for him?' asks Liam.

'Aunt Bronagh heard the guards were rounding up young men in the area. So Aidan made himself scarce. But the guards weren't prepared to leave empty-handed. They'd have taken Kenneth if Uncle Brendan hadn't put up a fight. So they took him instead. That was two weeks ago. Since then there's been no word of either Aidan or Uncle Brendan.'

'Your Uncle's likely in Kilmainham Gaol,' says Liam, 'along with many another loyal Irishman. But your son, Aidan, he got away, you said?'

It is impressive how Liam seems to have taken control. Both Aunt Bronagh and Kitty are now looking to him as if he might be the solution to their problems.

Aunt Bronagh shakes her head. 'We have family down Kilkenny way, but sure he'd not endanger them. For months before this happened, he said that Ireland was finished. He'd seek his fortune across the sea and join the army fighting the Prussian prince... But that was just his wild talk...'

'Not so wild, missus. There are many of the same mind. And not just against the Prussian prince. There's as many fighting on his side against Austria - for to fight against Austria is to fight against England.'

Eugenie sees that all this talk of war is doing nothing to alleviate the woman's distress.

'Let us be practical here,' says she. 'You have a home to keep and mouths to feed.'

Aunt Bronagh stiffens her shoulders. 'I will not accept charity, madam.'

'I would not offend you by offering it,' replies Eugenie. 'But you have a husband imprisoned, a son gone missing and no income to stand between you and starvation. Now, I have some influence in the town, and you, ma'am have a son of nineteen and,' glancing across to the hearth, 'two daughters of an age to be maidservants. My own maid is a girl from Knockbyne. If Kenneth is as presentable as his two sisters here, I am confident of finding all three positions in good households, if you are willing.'

From the look on her face, it appears that she is anything but willing to lose three more of her children. But Kitty interrupts before she can speak. 'I shall persuade my aunt, Miss Acres. It is excessively generous of you.'

'Not at all, Miss Blair. And now,' says she, turning to me, 'is our business here done, Will?'

'Almost.' I look at Kitty. 'Will you return with us, Kitty?'

'Not today,' she says shortly, avoiding my eye.

'What shall I tell Ned? And Mr Sheridan - he will wonder why you are not at rehearsal...?'

'Tell them as much - or as little - as you please,' she replies petulantly. 'No - on second thoughts, tell Ned nothing but that I am well. And, as for Mr Sheridan, you must say I am indisposed. I shall get Kenneth to bring me back to Dublin tomorrow. I have a little money, and I'm sure he will be able to procure a cart of some sort.'

As we take our leave of Aunt Bronagh and walk across to where the horse is tethered, Kitty pulls my arm. 'I won't forgive you for this, Will,' she hisses. 'You have no business searching me out thus.'

Shocked, I have no time to reply. Kitty shoots me a last vicious look, before turning, all smiles and gratitude, to Eugenie. The two embrace and Kitty, without turning back, disappears into her aunt's cottage.

Liam, having paid the urchins' fees is already leading the horse along the return path and, as Eugenie and I stroll along behind, she links her arm through mine.

'A satisfactory outcome all round,' she says. 'You have found Miss Blair safe and well. And I shall have the satisfaction of doing some good for this poor woman's family. You must be well-contented, Will.'

Yet, despite the linking of our arms, the brush of her body against mine and her gentle chatter as we make our way through the wood, I do not feel as gratified as I should. For Kitty's words still rankle in my mind and I fear that, far from making things better for my friend, Ned, todays's excursion may have made them worse.

20

...any to comfort...

It is mid afternoon when we rattle once more over the city cobbles.

Determined to waste no time, Eugenie will have Liam take her straight to Mr Callaghan's chambers near Christ Church Cathedral. There, she may discuss with the lawyer the possibility of acquiring situations for Kenneth and his two sisters.

Christ Church looks very different in the daylight to when I first saw it on the evening of my visit to the dead-house. Its central tower stands four-square, the ruddy-grey stone warm in the sunlight. But this is the only part of the edifice which can be clearly seen. The rest is hemmed about by the cramped buildings of the Four Courts that so perturbed young Patrick, the boatman's son, who had been sent to fetch me.

That seems an age ago now, so much has happened since. It is with a shock that I remember it is only six days. Six days since I first met the woman who sits in front of me. So close that the breeze wafts stray locks of her hair against my cheeks. So close that her scent has been in my nostrils for the whole of the journey.

We clatter to a halt, and Liam leaps down to help his mistress descend. The scurrying clerks are still about, arms laden with legal documents, looking like black beetles swarming over a dung-heap. John Callaghan's office is somewhere within this maze of narrow lanes, this 'nest of lawyers' as young Patrick called it.

At any rate, the cramped ways are too close packed for the gig to enter. Eugenie tells Liam to return it to its quarters at the wine warehouse, then to wait upon her in an hour and escort her home.

'I could save Liam the trouble,' say I.

'No trouble - just duty,' he says. 'Sure isn't it what I'm paid for?'

'Be not such a crab, Liam,' she scolds him fondly. Then with a smile, she bids me farewell. 'Your chivalry is acknowledged, Will, but you must be impatient to inform your friend of what has passed. We shall see each other again at Mr Handel's concert,' says she. 'Unless, of course, some further pressing *matter of urgency* brings you to my door!' Then, with a swish of skirts, she is gone.

I am still gazing at her retreating form when Liam pulls roughly at my arm. 'Get up,' he grunts.

I turn, annoyed. 'Why?'

'We need to talk.' Then, through gritted teeth, 'I should count it a favour.'

For my part, I cannot see we have anything to talk about, but the request intrigues me, and after his service today I suppose I am indebted to him. So I climb up into the seat that Eugenie has just vacated.

Liam flicks the reins and the horse ambles off in the direction of the river. I wait for him to speak, but he remains silent.

At length I say, 'Where are we headed?'

'To the Acres warehouse hard by Ormond Market. It is where the gig is stabled.'

Another bout of awkward silence ensues.

Then, of a sudden, he bursts out, 'This O'Sullivan, the actor you saw with the petty fogger - what is he?'

'Of what consequence is that to you?'

'None. But it may be of much consequence to my mistress. She puts her faith in Callaghan, but I don't trust him - or those he consorts with. So - O'Sullivan - is he someone you would trust?'

'He has shown me nothing but friendship,' I reply, guardedly. 'He has done me no harm.'

'A mealy-mouthed answer,' scoffs Liam. 'I expected more honesty from you.'

'Very well,' say I, nettled. 'I cannot say I like the fellow. If you must know, I think him a libertine with no respect for anyone's sensibilities but his own.'

'Better - now, what were he and Callaghan talking about?'

'How should I know that?'

'Come, Archer, you call yourself an investigator! You must have heard something.' Then, scorn gives way to impatience. 'Let me be clear - I hold my lady in high regard and would have no harm come to her. I'm a footman, I know my place. Which is more than you do, I think.'

'How so, sir?' I say indignantly.

'She is not for you, Will Archer. You are a poor player- but she is a lady. She is teasing you, can you not see it?'

'What right have you...' I feel my cheeks burning in embarrassment.

Liam shoots me a glance from the corner of his eye. '...a mere footman, would you say?' says he with scornful laugh. 'Well, be that as it may. It is not as an inferior that I give you this advice,

213

but as a friend.'

'A friend!'

'Sure - insufferable prig you may be, but I would not see you hurt for I believe you're a decent fellow at bottom.'

'Much obliged, I'm sure,' I retort stiffly.

'My lady means nothing by it. My advice is enjoy it whilst you may. But when that male-miss lawyer interviews gentlemen such as you say O'Sullivan is, I start to get suspicious. Callaghan may not want her for himself, but who's to say he mayn't put her in the way of one of his friends. He spent enough time with her sodomitical brother to learn his ways...'

'I think Mr Callaghan has respect enough for Miss Jeannie not to treat her as a mere commodity to be disposed of to the highest bidder. He may be mercenary, but I believe he is more principled than your late master. I believe, also, you do your mistress a disservice, Liam, to think she would be deceived by such a one as O'Sullivan. I am sure she has a greater perception than you give her credit for.'

'Perhaps you are right.' He lapses into silence for a few moments. Then he changes the subject completely. 'This man you saw at the Bull's Head - you said you knew him?'

'You weren't in the room...'

'Walls have ears, and so does Bridget! We have Miss Jeannie's interest at heart is all.'

'As do I. But it was not for her sake that I did not name him at the time. It was for fear of offending Bridget, who was still in the room. It was her brother, Sean Kelly.'

'Very wise. She has an excitable nature,' says Liam,

offhandedly. 'Well, well - Sean... Was it so?'

He sinks into a ruminative silence until we arrive at the Acres warehouse a few minutes later. A single storey building of wide doorways between Italianate columns, it has inscribed upon the pediment the same legend as on the dray I saw outside the Bull's Head: *Thos. Acres and Son, Fine wines and spirits.*

Liam jumps down from the seat and motions me to do the same. Then proceeds to ignore me as he leads the horse and gig through an archway adjoining the warehouse and into a cobbled yard. A burly fellow wearing a long leather apron helps him manoeuvre the gig into a ramshackle coach-house and unharness the horse. Then he leads it into one of the stables ranged along the other two sides of the yard.

Several of them are occupied, the upper doors ajar, heads poking through. These must be the horses that pull the delivery drays. As Liam and the drayman complete their task, I go over to one and stroke its muzzle. It bends its head and gently butts my shoulder. The snuffle of its breath, its warm smell of sweat and dung and sweet hay take me back to my childhood in the country.

Those Yorkshire horses, too, were thick-set, muscular beasts, trained to the plough rather than to heavy carts. It was on one of them I first learned to ride - a superannuated, gentle creature that plodded patiently round the paddock with me, an excited six-year-old on her back.

A far cry from the sleek thoroughbred I found myself on last year at the behest of Sir William Hervey, in pursuit of a murderer who would have cast his crime on me. The skin of my inner thighs is still thick from the sores of that chase. And from the so-called

215

balm provide by Mrs Wiggins, my master's London cook, which stank to high heaven, but which was applied so lovingly by Susan.

The memory of Susan's fingers stirs my little soldier. I do miss her - her greasy kirtle, her cheeks ruddy from the kitchen fire, the roughness of her hands. Her down-to-earth enjoyment of our amorous encounters. So different from the feline, streetwise Molly with her laughing eyes and smell of the sea.

And the thought of both of them only reinforces Liam's words about his mistress. It is true, she and her kind are beyond my aspirations. Will Archer, simple Yorkshire tyke, is fit only for pliant wenches, not fine ladies.

His advice, unwelcome as it was, was indeed that of a friend. Perhaps he and I have more in common than I care to admit.

I turn from the horse whose muzzle I have been stroking to offer the footman an apology for my stand-offishness. Only to find him gone.

Since leaving Jeannie at Callaghan's chambers, Liam has interrogated me, berated me, ignored me - and now abandoned me! So much for our budding friendship!

From the Acres warehouse I find my way to the bustling thoroughfare of Capel Street. From here, my route is straightforward. Down to the river at Ormond Quay, across Essex Bridge, passing Custom House Quay on the left, and thence by Fishamble Street and Skinner Row into Lamb Alley.

I have been in Dublin less than a week and already I know parts of it as intimately as the familiar byways of London.

It is but a half-hour's walk, yet the sky is already ruddy with the setting sun as I pass over Essex Bridge. The sails of the barques clustered at the quayside flap black against a fiery sky and gulls swoop and cry, seeking their last booty of the day.

As I walk along Essex Quay to Fishamble Street, the Liffey flows like liquid gold, catching the sunset light, and in the face of such beauty it is almost possible to ignore the refuse stench of the rolling waters.

Ned is waiting for me at my lodgings. He has been entertaining Mrs Fitzgerald with gossip of London society, the latest fashions, and who is in or out of favour with the beau monde of the metropolis. By the time I arrive, she is simpering like a twenty-year old coquette. It is not a pleasant sight.

Fortunately good manners and decorum gain sway over her thirst for further tittle-tattle and she reluctantly leaves us to our private conversation. But not before laying her hand upon Ned's arm and murmuring coyly, 'La, Mr Phillimore, you are a wag and no mistake! You have diverted me mightily. Pray call again soon.'

'Indeed, Madam, it will be my pleasure,' says he, gallantly. He takes her hand and puts it to his lips. 'At your service, Ma'am.'

My landlady retires in a flurry of giggles and blushes.

'You have made a conquest there, Ned,' I grin.

He sinks into a chair and exhales loudly. 'She had me detailing the latest perruques down to their minutest curl. I am exhausted! Wigs are definitely not my forte!'

'I am sure you acquitted yourself bravely.'

'Heroically! But what of you - have you found Kitty?'

I tell him of our journey, the reason for her sudden departure - and of her reaction to my seeking her out.

217

'I fear, Ned, that she will not be in the best of humours when she returns.'

'That I am happy to bear,' says he. 'Tantrums or tenderness, I care not, so long as she is back with me.' He rises and wraps his arm about me. 'You are a true friend, Will. I am eternally in your debt.'

'Aye, well, not eternally perhaps - just until an occasion arises when I may call in the favour!'

It is at this moment that Mistress Peg enters and finds us laughing. 'You are in good spirits, gentlemen.'

Garrick is just behind her.'Will,' says he, 'you have been elusive these last few days. I had need of you - if only to help divert Mistress Peg here from dragging me about the town, spending money on fripperies! What business has kept you from us these last two days?'

'Fie, Davey!' scolds Mistress Peg.'Why must you always play the miser? You would not deny me those little pleasures, surely?' Her tone is bantering, but I sense her annoyance. She has clearly discovered my master's rumoured prudence with money has some basis in fact.

'My dear, I would deny you nothing - but I cannot see how such gewgaws conduce to happiness...'

'To be sure, Will, your master has been in the grumps all day. Would he had some of your good-humour. Have you aught to tell him that may make him more sweet-tempered - for it seems I am incapable of lifting his spirits.'

She sinks tragically on to the settee and pulls such a comically aggrieved face that Mr Garrick cannot forbear breaking into a smile. He seats himself beside her and plants an affectionate kiss on her cheek.

'Nay, Peg, you would try the patience of a saint.' Then, taking her hand in his, he turns to me. 'But tell us, Will, is your inquiry into poor Acres's death concluded? Mr Sheridan informs us it was an unfortunate accident - a robbery gone wrong.'

'That is explanation that has been accepted.'

'But you doubt it?'

'I think there may be more to it - but I have no proof to back up my suspicions.'

'And is it the search for that proof that has kept you from us these last two days?' asks Mistress Peg, her eyes alight with curiosity. 'Pray let us into the mystery. Start by enumerating the players in the drama!'

'Very well,' say I, humouring her. 'There is an ill-used sister, a disreputable lawyer, and a footman with ideas above his station...'

'Already it shows promise,' she laughs delightedly, clapping her hands. 'And is there love and intrigue, too?'

'My love,' says Garrick gravely, 'this is no matter for jesting. These are real people we are talking about, who have suffered a great loss.'

'Yet Will thinks one of them may have done away with the victim,' adds Ned. 'Is that not true, Will?'

I shake my head doubtfully. 'I would not go so far as that. There was undoubtedly personal animosity arising from simmering family resentment. The dead man's treatment of his sister was insupportable. And his attempt to inveigle the family lawyer into his schemes succeeded only in alienating that gentleman. As for the footman, he nursed an inveterate hatred of his master.'

'Motives a-plenty there, I'd say,' says Ned.

'So I thought, but since then I've had intelligence which suggests his death may be part of a bigger picture. It may be that he was somehow caught up in the political unrest which seems rife in this country.'

Mr Garrick's interest is aroused. He has an interest in politics. Not only the theatrical backbiting of London, but also the war between Whigs and Tories in national affairs of state. 'On which side?' he asks 'The English establishment, or the Irish rebels?'

'As yet, that's far from clear,' I reply with a grimace. 'As a member of an old Anglo-Irish family, he would not seem to be a natural friend of either.'

'Sorry,' says Ned, 'but you've lost me - either he's native Irish born or an English settler?'

'Sure, that's not the case at all,' interjects Mistress Peg. The matter of Irish politics brings out her serious side - and simultaneously seems to thicken her Irish accent. She is of native Irish descent and, like the absent Kitty, from a humble background - her success a living proof of O'Sullivan's contention that the stage is blind to social origins.

She proceeds to enlighten Ned on the complexity of Irish society. First, the oppressed Irish population whose country it really is. Then, the first wave of English oppressors who came over last century in Stuart times and have now become almost as patriotically Irish as the Irish themselves. And, finally, the latest influx of English landlords whose sole intention seems to suck the country and its inhabitants dry, and who see little distinction between those inhabitants who were born here and those who were originally English.

It is undoubtedly a partial view of Irish history - but, then, isn't everyone's in this country?

'So Tobias Acres was naturalized Irish?' says Ned.

'Exactly,' say I, 'and thus disliked by the real Irish on one side and the English establishment on the other.'

'So do you think he was an active insurrectionist - or was he caught between factions?' ask Garrick.

'I have not yet discovered. Lord knows, it is easy enough to be caught up unawares, as Charlie and I found last Sunday! Not for any view we might have expressed, but merely for being who we are. And that was between two bands of Irish who were fighting each other!'

'But you were saved by an Irishman...'

'Sean Kelly, yes - who, it turns out, is related to the kitchen maid in the Acres household.'

'There's another suspect, then,' says Ned. 'An embittered Irishman!'

'No more embittered than Liam, the footman,' I remind him.

'Perhaps the two of them were in league with each other!' suggests Mistress Peg excitedly.

'I doubt it. Liam has no great opinion of Sean. *A dunderhead with a cudgel,* he called him. I cannot see them working together.'

'Well,' says Mr Garrick, rising, 'this is all too great a puzzle for my brain. I wish you well in untangling it, Will. But now my stomach is telling me it is dinner time. I have been aware of an

221

enticing odour for these last ten minutes. Let us go and see what our admirable landlady has prepared for us, shall we? Will you join us, Ned?'

The meal turns out to be boiled pig's trotters, which Mistress Peg informs me are called *crubeens* by the Irish. Mrs O'Shaughnessy ladles them out from a cast iron pot in the middle of the table. We eat them with our fingers, accompanied by a mound of cabbage, which seems to be the vegetable of choice in this country. It has appeared at every meal so far and its aroma is ever-present in the lower regions of our lodgings.

Conversation turns inevitably to the forthcoming season.

'Mr Sheridan has persuaded Davey he must do *Hamlet* this season,' says Mistress Peg.

'I am tempted,' says my master. 'It is a role I have not attempted before. But I do not know if I have the maturity for it.'

'Begging your pardon, sir,' says Ned, 'but is not the Dane himself of that age - a student called home from university upon the death of his father?'

'Ye-e-es,' agrees Mr Garrick reluctantly, 'but it is a demanding role - the longest in the canon - and so much of the last act is nonsense, totally unfitting a tragedy. The comic gravedigger, that fop, Osric - the whole contrived duel...'

'Tush, Davey - such trifles can be remedied,' says Mistress Peg. 'The public do not know the play - it has hardly been performed these thirty years. You may edit it as you wish. Besides, I should like to play the mad Ophelia.'

Mr Garrick laughs indulgently. 'Ah, so there we have it! It is not for me, but for yourself, my dear, that you would have me essay the Prince.'

'Nonsense, Davey,' she pouts. 'My thoughts are always for you. The part is made for you - as Ned says, you and the Prince are of an age.'

'Aye - and Betterton, who was the last to make a decent fist of the part, first played it at my age. He, too, was twenty-six. And he later married Mistress Sanderson, the first woman ever to act on the English stage, who played his Ophelia. You are not looking for history to repeat itself, surely...?' He looks up from gnawing his crubeen, a wicked twinkle in his eye.

She takes up her napkin, wipes her fingers and stares at him askance. 'I know nothing of that, sir. You are too bold. For all you may covet the role of husband, I am not ready to dwindle into a wife. And, were I ever to countenance such a prospect, it would not be over a repast of pigs trotters!'

Such is her air of comic disdain that the four of us burst out laughing. And so the meal proceeds in pleasantry until it is time for Ned to leave.

I offer to walk with him part way to his lodging. The evening air will do me good and help dispel the bloated feeling in my stomach resulting from an excess of greasy pork and cabbage.

Released from the restraints of female company, the pair of us laugh, belch and fart our way as far as Bedford Square where his route leads him westwards and I, by rights, should turn back for home.

All day the threatened rain has not come, and now the evening air is close and heavy. I, too, after such an eventful day and

223

convivial evening, am feeling pent-up and restless. So, rather than retrace my steps, I go on towards the river. It is but a hundred yards to Essex Bridge. There I may, by leaning upon the parapet and gazing at the inky waters, hope to still my thoughts.

I am not alone. The furtive travellers of this time of night are already abroad. Few walk openly as I do. Suspicious, they hurry past me or slink under cover of darkness and skulk in shadows. Their business, if not to reach home as quickly as possible, is secret assignations and covert couplings in dark alleys.

The noises of the night are different from those of daylight. Gone is the rumble of wheels, the cries of hawkers and the constant screech of gulls. Now all is the swish of coats round corners, half-heard whispers and muffled cries of pain or pleasure.

I walk with confidence, vigilant for any sudden step or hurried approach. I have no weapon, but I have fists and a physical presence which may deter all but the most desperate. The fists I bunch, my body I spread, squaring my shoulders and holding my arms wide.

In very little time, the increased chill in the air tells me I am at the river. The shadows of the streets give way to the open canvas of sky, dotted with stars and the pale, watery disc of a waning moon.

I go to the very middle of the bridge. Here, the central channel flows clear, a dark ribbon, palely dusted by the weak moon.

Over to my right, at Custom House Quay on the north bank, the hulls of merchant ships creak against each other, lanyards slapping against masts, sails rasping as the night breeze catches them. Faint wafts of spice from their holds mingle with the reek of the river.

The south bank is indiscernible. Somewhere over there is the army of small boats that I saw as Patrick guided me to the deadhouse. Only the faint bump of wood on wood and wisps of putrid stink in the night air bear witness to their presence in the darkness.

Alone in the rustling quiet of the night, I go over and over all the things I've learned. Something inside me tells me that I already have all the pieces of the puzzle and that I am very near solving the riddle of Tobias Acres's murder. If once I can see the vital connection, the rest will all fall into place...

I shiver in sudden apprehension. What is it my mother used to say - *someone's walked over my grave?*

No - it is simply the cool of the night. Gathering myself together, I walk briskly back to the shore.

I need something - or someone - to warm me.

I am on the edge of Custom House Quay. Is it too much to hope that Molly may be here...?

My brain tells me not to be so foolish. But my feet lead me back to the place where we last met.

It is deserted.

What did I expect? That, overwhelmed by my prowess of two night's since, she would wait, like patient Griselda, pining for my return! In my dreams!

Doubtless I was just one of the many...

Disconsolately, I turn towards home. Yet my progress is slow, my steps reluctant.

It is as I am thus lingering that I hear raised voices from an alleyway. In the next moment a ruffian cannons into me, almost

225

knocking me over. With an oath, he pushes me aside.

I call after him in like kind as he stumbles away into the darkness. At the sound of my voice he hesitates, perhaps contemplating a confrontation, but then thinks better of it and blunders on his way.

And then I hear the faint sound of sobbing.

From behind me there is a rustle of skirts and I swing round to see a young woman totter from the alley.

I go to her, catching her as she falls.

I hold her up. She gives a little cry, despairing, no doubt, that she has fallen into the hands of another brute and looks up, frightened, beating her fists feebly against my chest.

Our eyes meet and simultaneously we each utter the other's name.

'Molly?'

'Will?'

'Has he hurt you?'

She draws herself up. 'Not as much as I hurt him, I hope...'

Then, as if the effort has been too much for her, she sags again.

I gather her up in my arms. 'Where do you live, Molly? Let me take you home.'

She points me in the direction I should go, then puts her arms about my neck and leans her head on my chest.

She weighs hardly more than a child, yet even so, after a hundred yards or so, my arms begin to ache.

Fortunately, as come to a narrow archway between two houses, she raises her head and whispers, 'In here.'

Turning sideways, I duck my head and emerge into a cramped court. It cannot be more than twelve feet square and a thick odour arises from the dung-heap in a corner. Walls rise sheer on every side, windows like black holes with here and there the glimmer of solitary candles. Looking up, I see a small square of night sky sprinkled with stars.

I set her down and put my arm around her shoulders for support.

Beside one of the numerous shabby doors stands her cart and it is towards this that she makes her way.

I know what to expect. Such tenement dwellings exist in London, too. Crumbling, decrepit buildings of four or five storeys where sometimes whole families live in single rooms.

Molly, it seems, is more fortunate. She has a room of her own. It is on the third floor and, by the time I have helped her up all those stairs, her strength is almost exhausted.

Her hand trembles as she tries to insert the key into the keyhole. I cover it with mine to still the shaking.

Her room is clean, but sparsely furnished. A bed, a single chair, a wooden press with two drawers. It is very like Sean Kelly's house. And here, too, are feminine touches. A patchwork counterpane upon the bed, a chipped glass containing two or three limp bluebells on the dresser.

As soon as she is safe in her own home, her spirits revive somewhat. I am invited to take a seat upon the solitary chair as she produces a bottle and two glasses from a drawer.

I take a tentative sip and screw my face up as the bitter liquid burns my throat. 'Gin?' I gasp.

'Poteen,' she replies. 'Old Seamus on the ground floor has a still. Drink it down. Sure, won't it put hair on your chest! Sláinte mhaith!' She tips it back in one gulp.

My attempt to do the same leaves me coughing fit to expire.

She slaps my back. 'Oh, my poor little boghdóir,' she laughs.

Cradling my head against her bosom, she rocks me gently, crooning as if to a baby as the fit passes. At length, as I recover, I let myself lean more gratefully against her.

'Why, Master Archer,' she says, pulling away, 'I begin to think you are enjoying this a little too much. You forget the fright I have just had.'

She sits herself down on the bed and draws her legs up under her. For all her laughter at my plight, her face is still pale and there are still traces of fear in her eyes.

I lean forward, 'What happened, Molly? Did the brute offer violence?'

For answer, she shows her ripped dress and bares her arm where livid fingermarks are just starting to show. 'He would have done more,' says she quietly. 'But while he was a-tugging at my skirts, I got my nails upon his face and, when he raised his fist, followed up with my knee in na liathróidí. Then, when he was down, I grabbed a-hold of them and would have wrenched them off completely, but that he dragged me to the floor and punched me hard in the bosom...'

I gasp in shock at such currish behaviour.

'Aye,' says she, putting her hand gingerly to her breast. 'It is sore still. And here, upon my hip, where he delivered one final kick before turning tail like the fecking meatachán he was.'

'Oh, Molly, I'm so sorry... Did you recognise the villain?'

'I've seen him in Ormond market a time or two. One of the butcher boys. I'd caught him a-looking as I wheeled my barrow past his stall...' She gives a sad, almost regretful smile. 'He seemed all right in the daylight...'

She shifts on the bed and grimaces in pain.

I look at her in concern. I lean across and smooth a stray lock of hair from her forehead. 'Is there aught I can do, Molly - anything I can get for you?'

'At this time of night - no - Thank you, Will, I know you mean well. But the thing I most crave is rest.' She gives me a coy grin. 'Your gallantry, sir, is noted. And when I am less sore you shall see how grateful I am.'

'I would just have you well again, Molly - that's all I ask.'

She plants a chaste kiss upon my lips. 'I think you mean it, too, Will Archer. Forgive me,' she says, brushing away a tear, 'I am not used to such kindness.'

I lay her gently down and cover her with the patchwork counterpane. Then, wishing her a good night's sleep, I take my leave.

21

...who can be against us?...

It must be near midnight when I take my leave of Molly. Clouds have covered the pale moon and the few street lamps are now guttering feebly to extinction. The night air is thick, dark as black velvet, so that I have to feel my way along the wall in these narrow streets.

Suddenly, beside me, a door opens and I am momentarily dazzled by the light that cleaves through the blackness. Then dark silhouettes block it out. A man and woman lock in an embrace for a moment before he steps into the lane and the door is closed.

He is close enough to touch me and, though the door has now closed again, cutting off the light, he has clearly recognised me in that brief moment.

'Why, Will, well met! What do you abroad at this hour?'

Richard O'Sullivan is in great good humour. He slaps me upon the back and puts an arm about my shoulders. 'Come,' he says, 'we shall walk together.'

His breath reeks of spirits and his speech, though not exactly slurred, tells me he is intoxicated. He is loud and leans upon me, putting his face too close to mine when he speaks. An evening with his doxy has made him garrulous as he propels me, none too steadily, along the cobbled lanes.

'This chance meeting,' says he, 'is most fortuitous, do you not think? Your being here at this time of night can mean but one thing, surely? You have taken my advice! Was she to your satisfaction, eh Will?' He grinds his fist into my shoulder. 'Did she come up with the goods, eh? Did she melt your little Puritan heart?'

Up till now, I have not attempted to converse with him, just let him ramble drunkenly on whilst we stagger through the night. But now, irked by my lack of response, he comes to a halt and swings me round to face him. Placing his hands upon my shoulders, he half leans, half falls towards me, thrusting his face so close to mine that I am almost stifled by his breath.

'Will- ee - am,' says he, sounding every syllable with drunken tenacity, 'Will, my boy. Come don't be shy. I long to congratulate you on your success - expound, if you please, omitting no salacious detail. I promise I shall not be shocked...'

But shocked he is.

We both are.

For, in concentrating so much upon each other, we have ignored the perils of the night.

A strong grip from behind pinions my arms to my side. My head is wrenched back. My mouth, open to cry out, is stopped with a rag stuffed in so hard I almost choke. From the sound of scuffling beside me, I imagine O'Sullivan is receiving the same treatment.

A cord loops around my wrists, tethering them behind my back. and, for fear I spit out the gag, another is tied around my mouth.

All is conducted in terrifying silence. Our attackers do not speak, only grunt from the exertion of controlling our struggles.

At last, when a loose hobble has been wound, figure-of-eight style round my ankles, I am pushed roughly forward. So roughly that I topple forward, tripped by the restraint. Only just in time I turn my head before my face hits the ground. Grit sears into my cheek but, even as the breath is punched out of my body, I give thanks that my nose remains unbroken.

I am hauled up unceremoniously and thrust forward again. This time, mercifully, my captor's hand keeps hold of my collar.

'March!' he growls.

I have no option but to obey. Half-throttled by his grip, chest heaving as I struggle to breathe only through my nose, I half shuffle, half hop in response to his urging. Blood from my cheek trickles down my neck.

Beside me, as far as I can discern in the darkness, O'Sullivan is faring even less well than I.

He,too, is having difficulty breathing and emits small whimpers of distress as he is propelled along. I feel him lurch against me once or twice, our shoulders buffeting each other. His captor, less tolerant than mine, cuffs him every time he stumbles.

Gradually I become aware that our slow, faltering progress is leading us towards the river.

A chill more icy than the night air grips my spine. *Are O'Sullivan and myself about to suffer the same fate as Tobias Acres? Are these the same men as accosted him?*

Their unnerving reticence persuades me they are no common footpads. They have made no attempt to rob us. It is clear that we are no accidental victims - one of us, at least, is their target. The other has simply had the misfortune of being in the wrong place at the wrong time.

Several times I have tried to catch a glimpse of their faces but both have hats pulled low on their foreheads and scarves obscuring all but their eyes. And these are as good as invisible in the dark, merely darker pools in a band of shadow.

Shoved and jostled as we are, it is difficult to gather my thoughts. Are they bully-boys hired by one of O'Sullivan's creditors? Or is it me they want? Have I got closer than I think to Tobias Acres's murderer?

In any event, I cannot see us escaping this night uninjured.

A beating is the best we may hope for. Both our captors are burly men quite capable of doing us physical harm - but if that is their aim, why did they not do it swiftly and effectively in the shadows of the narrow lanes?

No, the fact that we have been dragged all this way suggests some more fearful purpose...

We come suddenly upon the river. It is a part I do not recognise, where broken-down houses crowd almost to the water's edge. This is no open quayside, only a stinking mudbank sloping down from the noisome warren of dwellings to the ink black river.

In the still night air, I think I catch the distant flapping of sails and descry a few tiny pin-pricks of light away to my right. We must be near a mile from Wood Quay and the area of the city with which I've become familiar.

Here all is dark and unknown. Devoid of people and fraught with danger. A world defined by the ripple of water and the stench of mud. The smell of my captor's sweat - and of my own fear.

233

I am jerked to a halt beside a wall of wood and daub. Beside me I hear O'Sullivan grunt as he is rammed up against the rough plaster. Another fist grabs my collar as the man who has dragged me here releases his hold. O'Sullivan's captor holds us both.

Mine steps towards the river and, cupping his hands round his mouth, gives a soft, owl-like hoot.

Almost immediately it is answered from below and a dim light begins to dance in the gloom.

Slowly it comes closer, wavering erratically through the black night, until it resolves itself as a dark lantern.

Only when it is almost upon us do I discern by its light that there are slabs of stone or rock forming a sort of pathway in the mud bank, up which the lantern bearer is ascending. He remains but a dark shadow swathed in the night.

At last, he comes up level with us. He shines the light upon my face, temporarily blinding me, but says no word.

Then he does the same to O'Sullivan and utters a short guttural laugh.

He signals to his two henchmen, who straightway proceed to bundle us down the rough-hewn path.

This is it, I think, *they are going to drown us!* Visions of Susan flit through my mind. Our secret trysts, the way we laughed... And Charlie - *will he miss his big brother?* I picture them grieving for me - or worse, condemning me for deserting them...!

My eyes mist with tears at the injustice of it all. Tears not of self-pity - rather of anger against my unknown tormentors intent on cutting my life so short.

Behind me I hear a grunt of disgust. 'Fuck me, the dirty sod's be-pissed himself!'

O'Sullivan, it seems, has let his fear get the better of him. His captor shoves him so hard that he stumbles and cannons into me, near knocking me off-balance as well.

My ears are full of his terrified sobs, my nostrils with the stink of urine.

We are at the river's very edge. I prepare myself for the shock of cold water, the fight for breath through my gagged mouth as the current drags my shackled body down...

My heart is thudding so hard that my whole body shakes to its beat.

But nothing happens.

It takes a moment for me to discern that, in the darkness, two skiffs are tied to a post in the muddy bank.

It is into the first of these that O'Sullivan and I are bundled, side by side onto the widest seat athwart the centre of the boat.

Behind us, one of our captors clumsily takes up the oars whilst in front the stranger with the lantern steps unsteadily into the rocking boat. The thought crosses my mind that neither is confident on the water.

Out of the corner of my eye I see the third man untie both vessels from their mooring and get warily into the second boat.

The man with the lantern, meanwhile, has seated himself in the stern facing us. He nods to the fellow behind us who, with a grunt of exertion, ham-fistedly plies the oars.

It takes him several strokes to achieve a rhythm. At first he dips the blades too shallow, showering O'Sullivan and me with spray. Then too deep, making the boat rock precariously. In front of us, the man grabs the side of the boat to maintain his balance. But O'Sullivan and I, with our hands bound, have no such luxury. We bounce like rag-dolls against each other.

At last, our oarsman gains some semblance of competence and we head for the centre of the stream.

No-one has yet uttered a word other than curses. The only noise now is the regular plash of oars, the grunts of exertion from the oarsmen and O'Sullivan's continuous low snivelling.

At last, when the shore has been lost in the darkness and we are, as far as I can judge, in the very middle of the river, the man in the stern signals to his companion.

I feel a shower of drops, cold on my face as he ships the oars.

Then, just as I am preparing to be seized from behind and cast overboard, the man in front of us leans forward and pulls the gags from our mouths.

As the filthy material comes away, O'Sullivan gives a great wail of fear.

I am more thrifty of the cool night air. I heave in a great breath of it. Laden it may be with the stink of the river but, nevertheless, it gives me courage to speak to the man before us.

'So, sir, you have us at your mercy.' My voice, for all I want it to be strong, sounds puny in the vastness of the night. 'If you intend to kill us, it is only fair you tell us why.'

The oarsman behind us gives a mocking grunt.

In front of us, the man with the lantern slowly unwinds the scarf from the lower half of his face and tilts back his battered tricorn.

'Sure, and even now your effrontery doesn't desert you, Will!'

'Sean?'

'The very same.'

'But why?'

Beside me, O'Sullivan gives a gasp and starts shouting, 'Help! Murder!'

I expect Kelly to leap up and silence him. Instead, he leans back in the stern, laughing.

'Shout all you will, you damned turncoat, there's none to hear. Or, in these parts, none that will pay attention.'

And, indeed, his cries are swallowed by the water and the night air. Eventually he desists, his voice hoarse, and falls prey to a bout of coughing and retching. He voids the remains of his evening's excesses over the side. Then he slumps exhausted beside me in a miasma of sour wine, fresh vomit and stale urine.

'I told you last time we met that you should be more particular in your choice of companion, did I not, Will?' Sean Kelly gestures contemptuously at O'Sullivan. 'Do you find he improves on further acquaintance, eh?'

'We met by chance...'

'Chance, you say? Would that be the same chance that led you to that whore, Molly Malone?'

My face, in the lantern light, must express my bewilderment, for Kelly goes on, 'Sure, you didn't recognise our friend Dermot here when you so gallantly rode to her rescue?'

Behind me I hear our oarsman growl, 'Near had my eye out, the bitch!'

'It was you?' I say, twisting round.

'Aye,' says Kelly, calling my attention back to him. 'Going

237

about a man's natural business - a bit too enthusiastically, perhaps,' he scoffs. 'And then don't you come along and interrupt him? Never forgets a face, our Dermot. Which is why, despite the blow to his pride, he comes straight to me. And, bejasus, what do we find? Only you and this turncoat, plotting together...'

'You are mistaken. There is no plot. As I told you, we met by chance. We did not seek each other's company.'

'Sure, that's unfortunate, my friend, because now you'll be enjoying each other's company for eternity. Your only consolation is that Liffey water'll perhaps wash away some of his stink.'

'You mean to drown us?'

'Right you are, to be sure.'

'But why go to all this trouble? Would not a knife or pistol have been quicker?'

'Quicker, perhaps, but a body with holes in it leads to questions being asked, sure it does.'

Beside me, O'Sullivan inhales sharply. I may not like him but I sense his fear. And I do not see why he should suffer because of whatever wrong Kelly suspects me of.

'But, Sean, why will you not listen when I tell you? O'Sullivan and I met totally by chance this evening. Whatever harm you imagine I have done you, he has had no part in it. Your argument, whatever it may be, is with me, not with him.'

'Very eloquent! But don't waste your breath, Will Archer. Whether he's privy to your treachery or not, that snivelling bollox is a disgrace to his country! Now is as good a time as any for him to get what he deserves.'

'And I? What is this treachery you suspect me of? That I am

238

English?' say I heatedly. 'None of us can help where we are born. But, unlike yourself, I do not let my nationality dictate who *I* am. I do not agree with the way my government treats your countrymen. You may choose not to believe me but I sympathise with your cause. And I would help you if it was in my power...'

'*Help*?' retorts Kelly. 'Does it help to spy on me at *The Bull's Head*? And then to go a-telling tales about me? Does it help to make inquiries about me in the place where I was born? What *help* were you in search of at Knockbyne?'

'Knockbyne?' say I, puzzled. 'I have never been there.'

'That's not what I've been told.'

'Then you've been told wrong.'

But suddenly it dawns on me what he is at. I recall a stray remark of Liam's as we trudged through woodland. *Knockbyne Castle, not half a mile from here...* A castle that was destroyed in the Williamite wars, and which gave its name to a village in which Bridget - and presumably Sean also - was born.

'If you mean the journey Miss Acres and I undertook to Ballycullen,' I say, 'then I can tell you it was in aid of one of my friends. It did not concern you in any way. Why should it? What possible reason would I have to make any inquiry about you?'

'That's what I'd like to know. I don't trust you, Will Archer. You may have taken in our Finn - and I must admit you almost convinced me at first. I should have realised my mistake when, only days after seeing me at the Music Hall, you turn up at my door with your story of being caught between rival gangs...'

'But that was pure coincidence...'

'Sure, the same sort of coincidence that took you to the Acres house - where *my sister* works. The same sort of coincidence that finds you in company with this gobshite whenever we meet.' He gestures contemptuously at O'Sullivan. 'We were friends once, did you know that, before he betrayed us all by toadying up to the English!'

His words are becoming impassioned. It is the same fiery anger that I saw at the Music Hall, the same as made him storm away at Merchants Quay.

'*He* will be no loss,' he continues with a wave of the hand towards O'Sullivan, 'but I thought better of you Will Archer - till I discovered my mistake.'

I see there is no use trying to convince him of my innocence in this mood. He is impervious to reason.

And, sure enough, he interprets my silence as proof of guilt.

'You do well to hold your tongue. It has brought you enough trouble already. But you may be sure it will bring you no more. Nor me, neither.'

With that, he reaches into the bottom of the boat and comes up with a marlin spike in his hand.

He shouts over our heads to Dermot behind us. 'Call Ciaran,' he says.

Behind me, the fellow shouts for his companion to bring the second boat alongside.

A few seconds later, he is helping pull in the other skiff.

Its occupant has also removed the scarf that hid his face. Ciaran O'Dowd, the ruffian who was all for beating up Charlie and me last Sunday morning, gives me a rotten-toothed grin.

'Sure and it's grand to see you again, Master Archer. A pity it's for such a short time.'

He steadies the two vessels as Dermot steps from our boat into his.

Sean, meanwhile, is busying himself with the marlin spike, bashing a hole in the side of our skiff. Even as I watch, water begins to slop in through the gap and wash about on the boards around my feet.

Then with much pulling and shoving from the other two which causes both vessels to pitch alarmingly, Sean is hauled into the other boat.

'Think on your betrayal, Will Archer,' he says breathlessly, once he is safely seated, 'while you wait for death.'

Then, with a final coarse laugh, Ciaran applies the oars and their boat skims away into the darkness.

With the lantern gone, it is difficult to see how far the water level is rising. But I took note that Kelly broached the planks high enough for us not to be immediately deluged. He intended our death to be slow. Every time we move, however, the boat rocks and I hear the slosh of water in the bottom.

O'Sullivan, who has not uttered a word since he slumped down beside me after his frantic outburst, will be less than useless if we are to escape a watery death.

But as the sound of oars fades out of earshot I am to be proved wrong.

'Are those bastards gone?' His voice is steady, with none of the weakness and moaning that has characterised him so far.

Has voiding his innards into the river sobered him? Or has he been dissimulating all along?

'Richard?' say I disbelievingly, 'Are you recovered?'

'Aye, Will. Never better. Now, my waistcoat,' he says, 'the left hand pocket - there is a knife.'

I am still having difficulty coming to terms with his transformation.

'You carry a knife?'

'A gentleman cannot be too careful. Especially one like myself who frequents the streets after dark. But we have no time for idle chatter...'

He is seated to my left, so his left hand waistcoat pocket is on the side furthest from me, and my hands are tied behind my back.

As gently as I can, I ease myself around so that my back is towards him. Then I stretch my pinioned hands across his lap.

But I cannot reach, despite him twisting round towards me, and gentle as I have tried to be the boat still rocks alarmingly. Water swashes around my ankles.

The strain on my shoulders becomes painful. I drop my hands.

There is a sharp intake of breath. 'Master Archer, have a care!'

My hands have landed where no gentleman expects another man's hands to be. I apologise, but say, 'I am afraid I must trespass further upon your dignity.'

Edging one buttock up onto his right knee I am at last able to reach the goal. I can feel the hard metal through the padding of his waistcoat. Unfortunately, I can also smell the stale urine from his breeches.

I hold my breath and fumble for the knife. At last my finger ends make contact and I manage to grasp the hilt between my finger and thumb. With utmost care I draw it out, twisting my wrist as best I may the while to let it rest more securely in my palm.

Once I have it firmly, I slide off his lap. Water sloshes in the bottom of the boat

Back to back now I locate the cord about his wrists and carefully start sawing away.

Fortunately, the blade is sharp and it takes hardly a minute for the rope to fray and sever.

He pulls his wrists apart with a cry of relief and kneads the blood back into his hands. Then, taking the knife from me, makes short work of my bonds.

Relief, however, is short lived.

The boat which until now has rocked at our every movement now has a turgid heaviness about it. The water is up to our calves. It cannot be long before it goes down.

Slowly, we bend and untangle the loose halters about our feet. But even as we straighten up, the waterlogged skiff pitches over, flinging us both into the water.

The breath is sucked from my lungs and I go under. Flailing desperately, I surface again, spitting out water. I feel as if an ice-giant has me in his grip. Every muscle and sinew seems to have stiffened with the impact of the freezing water. My face aches with cold.

I exhale with a great gasp of shock - and go under again.

This time is not as bad. The water feels less cold on my numbed skin. I rise with more control to the surface and swing my arms back and forth to keep me there.

O'Sullivan is a little distance from me, puffing and gasping for air.

At a little distance, the boat wallows in the water.

I kick my legs and paddle my hands in an attempt to get towards it. O'Sullivan has the same idea. But as soon as we take hold of the side, the whole thing rolls over, throwing us back into the water.

Yet again we go under and emerge, spluttering.

The hull is like a giant woodlouse on the surface of the river. We struggle towards it and fling our arms over it. Insecure as my grip is, it at least brings some respite from the battle to stay afloat.

I push my sodden hair from my eyes and pant, 'What now?'

O'Sullivan faces me over the slimy keel. 'We paddle. We Shout.'

His voice trembles with the cold that is slowly but surely invading our bodies. We may have secured a brief respite from drowning, but it cannot be many minutes before the cold renders us insensible.

I kick out with my legs below the surface and together we push the upturned boat in what we think may be the direction of the shore. But, with neither sight nor light to guide us, we may, for all we know, merely be drifting down the middle of the stream.

And, as we go, we shout for help until our voices are hoarse.

My fingers are slowly losing sensation. I scrabble desperately to keep my hold upon the slimy planks, but it is like trying to grip ice. I feel myself sinking lower in the water.

O'Sullivan must be suffering the same as I. But soon I cease to think of him. My only thought is my own survival. My whole body is convulsed with uncontrollable shaking as the cold takes hold. I know not if my legs are still kicking for I have ceased to feel them.

My desperate attempts to maintain a purchase on the greasy boards get weaker. I have no more strength to shout. And now the night's all enveloping darkness and silence bring a strange serenity. My body no longer belongs to me. All I crave is peace - and sleep.

How easy, in this velvet dark, to surrender to the water - to lay back and let it take me...

Suddenly the boat lurches.

O'Sullivan has let go and the hull topples in my direction. Feebly I try to regain my hold. But in vain. My numbed hands slip from the wet planks and the boat drifts out of reach.

I cannot see O'Sullivan.

I have no strength left.

Above me stars prick the night sky.

And one has fallen to earth.

It bobs erratically upon the dark waters.

22

...learn of him...

In my dream I hear voices.

'...steady, Patrick...'

'...another, pa...'

'...an Englishman...'

'...hold hard - the tide...'

'...now, sir, a hand if you please...'

Fragments of memory tossed on the waters.

The murky river claims me - rolls me, limp and lifeless...

Let me rest! I want to die - to sleep, perchance to dream...

'Aye, there's the rub,' warns Mr Garrick, 'For in that sleep of death, what dreams may come?'

The first Hamlet in Dublin....

'Two actors side by side, like fish on a slab!'

'... live 'uns, too, there's a novelty...'

Cockles and mussels alive, alive-o!

'...our fee...?'

'...you may be assured...'

Wrapped - ready for despatch.

Oblivion.

I wake in unfamiliar surroundings.

There is a murmur of voices. Somewhere to my left a roaring

fire crackles and spits. Its heat is hot on my cheek.

I am lying on a straw pallet. The ticking is rough against my skin. Sharp ends prick my flesh. I am covered with a coarse wool blanket.

Underneath the blanket I am naked - but I am warm.

And I am ravenously hungry.

Even as the sensation manifests itself, my stomach growls as if in anticipation.

I turn my head to see where the voices are coming from.

Almost immediately they cease, there is a stir and shuffle - and a familiar face looms over me.

'Awake, are you? Sure, you took your time!'

'Liam?' I stretch my neck to see past him. 'Am I at Miss Acres's house?'

'No, indeed you are not.' Another familiar face has joined that of Eugenie's footman. It is Richard Semple.

I fall back on the straw mattress and close my eyes. I must still be dreaming, for how should these two be together?

But Semple is still talking. 'You are at Mr Kennedy's inn. And he has prepared some broth, if you are up to it? No smoked eels, I'm afraid, but best Irish beef...'

My stomach replies for me.

Semple motions to Liam who drags me roughly to my feet while he stoops for the blanket which he wraps around me. Liam dumps me on a settle beside a table where Semple pushes a steaming bowl of broth towards me.

For the moment its savoury aroma and meaty flavour obliterate all else.

Only after I have downed several spoonfuls do I become aware once more of my surroundings.

Liam and Semple are seated opposite me. The footman leans back, arms folded, frowning. But Semple regards me with an enigmatic smile.

'You have an appetite, Master Archer,' he says. 'Only natural, I suppose, after your ordeal. We thought you were dead.'

I pause, the spoon half-way to my lips. 'Richard O'Sullivan,' I say. 'Is he...?'

'Alive? Yes - and being cared for in another room.'

I return to my meal, satisfied with the news of his survival.

Only when I have emptied the bowl and wiped it round with a chunk of bread, does the incongruity of the arrangement strike me. 'Why in another room?' I ask.

It is neither Liam nor Semple who answers.

'Because, Master Archer, our deliberations are not for his ears.'

In my shock, I leap to my feet, sending the empty bowl and spoon flying.

It is the voice of Sir William Hervey. He and his companion have remained seated over by the fire, their backs towards us all the time I have been sating my hunger.

Now he rises and approaches the table where I stand, open-mouthed.

He tuts and waves dismissive fingers towards my midriff and says drily, 'Entertaining as your confusion is, Will my boy, *that* is no sight for this hour of the morning!'

I glance down and realise the blanket has slipped off and I am stark naked! Scarlet, I clap a hand over my little soldier and fumble to retrieve my covering.

Liam pushes me aside and grabs the blanket from the floor. 'A good job my mistress cannot see her prudish Englishman now, eh?' he mutters mockingly as he drapes it around my shoulders.

Clutching it tightly about me, I follow Sir William back to the chairs grouped around the hearth where Semple and, to my surprise, Liam join us.

The remaining member of the party is, as I expected, Nathaniel Grey, Sir William's servile factor. He gives me a curt nod of acknowledgement.

'Now, Semple,' says Sir William, 'if you would request another jug of ale from our host, I think we may begin our business.'

Richard Semple obeys with an alacrity I have not witnessed in him before. And, once the ever discreet Mr Kennedy has replenished the jug and retired, Sir William begins.

'So, Master Archer, can you explain to us your sudden desire to go midnight bathing in the Liffey?'

His jest raises sycophantic laughter from the others. But I know him of old. His smile conceals daggers.

Head of the late Prime Minister Walpole's secret service, Hervey is adept at appearing friendly. But I have witnessed his ruthlessness at first hand and am not fooled by his jocularity. He was not one to be underestimated then, and I fear that Walpole's fall, far from diminishing him, has only enhanced his power.

The knowing smile on his lips - a smile that does not extend to his eyes - reminds me that twice he has saved me from the hangman. Deaths for which I was implicated but not responsible - but what judge would stand upon such niceties?

So he has a hold over me, which is why I must work for him. Thus far, he has been benign, citing our common Yorkshire roots as the reason for his favour. But I am under no illusion that, should I ever forfeit that favour, he would crush me with as little compunction as he would a fly.

Much as the laughter rankles, directed as it is against me, I reply with like cordiality. 'I can assure you, sir, that it was not of my choosing. And the experience has only served to confirm my preference for dry land over water.'

The riposte elicits a curl of the lip from Nathaniel Grey.

Sir William, however, seems mightily pleased by my reply. He slaps his knee and laughs aloud. 'Well said, Will. True Yorkshire grit!' He leans forward, serious now. 'Tell us about this Kelly fellow. Why did he try to kill you?'

I register no surprise at his knowing of Sean Kelly's involvement in the incident. It is Hervey's business to know everything about everyone.

'In truth, Sir William, I do not know. It was, I think, his own suspicions rather than any action of mine that drove him to such a pass. He accused me of spying on him and spreading lies about him. And all based upon his misapprehension of a trip to a small hamlet, Ballycullen, outside the city. A journey undertaken in company with this gentleman,' say I, turning to Liam. 'He will vouch that its purpose was naught to do with Kelly.'

'Well, Donovan?' asks Sir William.

For a moment I am perplexed, until I realise that he refers to

Liam. It is the first time I have heard him graced with a second name.

'He says true, sir. We went in pursuit of some flibbertigibbet actress.'

Sir William asks for details and I tell him the whole tale of Kitty's sudden departure and Ned's distress.

'Had they quarrelled?'

'I cannot say for sure. I think there had been a disagreement.'

'Over what?'

'I am not privy to the exact matter of it, sir. But I suspect it may have had something to do with my advising Ned of an over-familiarity between Kitty and   - another gentleman within the company.'

'Come, sir, be not so punctilious. It is O'Sullivan you mean - the same man as nearly drowned with you last night. Am I right?'

'Indeed, sir. But my suspicions with regard to his relationship with Miss Blair were ill-judged.'

'And his presence with you last night?'

'Unfortunate - he was caught up in a vengeance meant for me alone.'

'It was not a case of you luring him to his death, then, through loyalty to your friend, Ned?'

The suggestion is so preposterous that I am lost for a reply. But then I see Sir William's lip twitch and realise he is in jest. Then he turns to Semple.

'Is anything known of this O'Sullivan?'

Semple gives an admirably succinct account of O'Sullivan's history which matches what the man himself told me the other day

- the loss of his family's business, his coming to Dublin to seek his fortune and his falling in with a company of players.

Then Sir William asks if I have anything to add.

'He and Kelly were acquainted in their youth, sir,' say I. 'There is bad blood between them. Kelly believes he has betrayed the Irish cause - which is why he was quite happy for O'Sullivan to share my fate.'

'Anything else?'

'Only that he is a libertine - he uses women for his pleasure...'

There is a sigh of exasperation. 'Enough of your priggishness, Archer!' Liam rudely interjects. 'Tell Sir William of his dealings with that damned lawyer...'

My patience snaps. 'Sir William,' say I, irritated, 'what is this man doing here? He is naught but a servant!'

Hervey frowns. 'Mind your manners, Will! Servant or no, he is one of my agents just as you are - and it is he you have to thank for your life, sir.'

My mouth drops in confusion and I come near to letting go my blanket again.

'Tell him, Donovan,' says Sir William.

Liam has a look of grim satisfaction at my discomposure. 'Yes, Master Archer, I'm one of Sir William's informers, just like you. And better than you, if truth be told. Like that wretch O'Sullivan, my family was prosperous - and respected - till you English came...'

'To the point, Donovan,' says Sir William sharply.

'Very well, sir.' He proceeds briskly. 'When Master Archer told my mistress he had seen Sean Kelly acting as a drayman, it

252

aroused my suspicions and I decided to keep an eye on him.'

'Good work, Donovan,' says Sir William approvingly. 'Initiative - I like that.'

'Last night I followed Kelly to a tavern where, shortly past eleven, he was joined by one of his ill-favoured cronies. The fellow was walking painfully and had scratches down his cheek.'

'Dermot,' say I. 'I came upon him assaulting - a young woman. I helped her home, where she told me she had given as good as she got...'

'Sure, it seemed so, for he was in a foul temper. Kelly showed scant sympathy - indeed, he seemed to find it funny. Until there was mention that the lady's rescuer was a mutual acquaintance - a certain young man who'd fallen foul of the Ormond Boys last week-end...

'Myself...'

'Sure, as soon as the scuffle was mentioned, your name rose to his lips - and not in a friendly way! I followed them close as they left the inn, close enough to hear talk of row-boats before they parted. Kelly's final command to his companion was to fetch you in. Guessing what he would be at, I went in search of Paddy Rafferty and his son Patrick, the river men who scour the water for corpses - for that is what I thought you'd be before the night's end. As it happened, we found you floating as good as dead, but just in time to revive you. It was young Patrick as pumped the water from O'Sullivan's lungs and breathed his own breath into his mouth and...'

He drops his voice to such a mumble that I scarce catch his last words.

'...and showed me how to do the same for you.'

He can scarce articulate his humiliation - obliged to save one for whom he has such aversion. And, to my shame, one who has shown him so little respect. I feel very humbled. Not to mention ridiculous, sitting here naked under a blanket in front of the man who has saved my life.

I meekly hold out my hand.

'Thank you, Liam,' I say quietly. 'I am sorry I spoke ill of you.'

He clasps my outstretched hand with a curt nod of acknowledgement.

'Very affecting,' says Nathaniel Grey, drily.

'Indeed,' says Sir William. 'But this new-found amicability must go no further, gentlemen. As far as the outside world is concerned, you must appear as you were.'

'The prig of an Englishman,' says Liam casting aside my hand.

'Aye, and the obstreperous servant,' say I.

Grey shifts restlessly. 'Sir William, if I may be so bold - time is getting on...'

'Thank you, Nathaniel' says Sir William, 'As ever, you are keep me up to the mark!'

He addresses Liam, Semple and myself. 'Gentlemen, Kelly and his confederates have gone to ground - sure sign that they are up to no good. I have men looking for them. It is clear that he was driven to the desperate pass of murder because he believed you constituted some sort of threat to him, Will. Remind us what he said.'

254

'He accused me of spying on him and telling tales about him.'

Sir William strokes his chin thoughtfully. 'Spying, eh? On your trip to Ballycullen?'

'Aye, though it was the thought that I may have been to Knockbyne that exercised him.'

'There is talk,' says Semple, hesitantly, 'that the perpetrators of the recent house-burnings hail from Knockbyne, Sir William. It is but a half-mile or so from Ballycullen.'

I turn eagerly to Liam. 'You showed me the burnt-out ruin of Ballycullen House...'

'Sure, and didn't the old woman - the aunt of your fugitive actress - say the Guards had been there after her husband and sons?'

'These men from Ballycullen,' says Sir William, 'they are suspected? Could Kelly have been in league with them...? Where are they now?'

I do not like where this is leading. With the events of the past night I have no way of knowing if Kitty is yet returned, and I would not heap more trouble upon her unfortunate family. 'Aunt Bronagh swore to their innocence, sir...'

'As any wife and mother would,' says Nathaniel Grey silkily.

'The Guards went to the house two weeks ago, sir,' says Liam, unconstrained by my sense of loyalty to my friends. 'The old lady said her son talked of enlisting with the army to fight the Prussian prince - he's long gone, I'd say. As for the husband, they took him. He's likely in Kilmainham Gaol.'

Sir William nods to Grey. 'Check that, Nathaniel. See if the man has aught to say of Kelly.'

Then he turns to me. 'What are these tales Kelly accuses you of?'

I shake my head. 'I can only think he means when I saw him at *The Bull's Head* delivering wine. I said to Miss Acres, Liam's mistress, that he was hardly earning his wage that day!'

'How so?'

'In the time it took the other drayman to unload numerous barrels, Sean only carried in two small kegs...'

Immediately, Sir William is alert. 'Two kegs, you say?'

'Aye, sir.'

'And *The Bull's Head* is next to the Music Hall, is it not?' Sir William slaps his thigh and rises. 'I believe this is it, gentlemen. We have sound intelligence that some outrage is planned for a public event. It is now Friday morning. Mr Handel's oratorio is to be performed on Monday next. Half the notables of Dublin will be there... Those kegs that Kelly delivered, I'll lay my knighthood that they contain not spirits, but gunpowder!'

Within two minutes, we have received our instructions. Semple, under cover of his position at the Customs House, is to seek out any gossip about Kelly from his colleagues. Liam is to keep a close eye on Bridget and the lawyer O'Callaghan to see if either attempts to make contact with him. Meanwhile, Nathaniel Grey will oversee the search for him.

'Mr Semple tells me that a note of any information may be left in the care of the landlord here, Mr Kennedy, whom, he assures me is the soul of discretion,' concludes Sir William. 'Be that as it may, I hardly need remind you that any such letter should be sealed and worded in the discreetest manner. And...,' he says with

256

a chuckle, '...the said missives should be addressed, I think, to a Mr Selby. A nomenclature which I trust Master Archer will appreciate.'

As usual, Hervey's good humour is not without its sting. Selby is a town in Yorkshire,his and my home county - and it is but half a dozen miles from where I was born and raised.It is an unsettling reminder that he knows more about me than I hitherto thought.

But perhaps more unsettling is that I have not yet been charged with any task. Little as I desire one, it is time to face the worst.

'And I, Sir William? Am I to do anything?'

'Oh, yes, Will,' says he with a vulpine smile. 'Yours is perhaps the most vital undertaking of all. But one which I am sure will not be beyond your wit or ingenuity. Your task is to discover by what means these villains intend to make their way from *The Bull's Head* into the Music Hall next door.'

23

...prepare ye the way...

Liam and Semple leave by the back door. Five minutes later our discreet host, Mr Kennedy, bids obsequious farewell to Sir William and Nathaniel Grey at the front entrance.

Once they are gone, he returns to me.

'Now, sir,' says he. His voice is low and deferential, his gaze directed at some point beyond my left ear. *Does his renowned discretion rely on never making eye contact, I wonder.* 'The girl has done her best with your wet clothes and I believe they are just about dry. Mr Semple said to take you into the other gentleman. He is in a similar state to your good self,' says he, indicating the blanket which I'm still clutching about me. 'If you'd care to follow me?'

He takes me up a flight of stairs so gloomy that I must hoist up my covering to avoid tripping over the trailing corners.

Kennedy opens the door of a cramped chamber and steps aside to let me enter. O'Sullivan is lying on the bed. His hair is disheveled, hanging in unruly strands about his face and he too is wrapped in a blanket. As Kennedy withdraws, quietly closing the door, he sits up. His face breaks into a disbelieving smile.

'Will - thank the Lord! I feared...'

He seems genuinely delighted to see me. At a loss for words, he stands and would clasp me to his bosom. But, inadequately covered as we are, it turns into a clumsy dance to preserve our modesty. We desist, laughing.

We sink, side by side, on to the bed. Despite the delicacy of the situation, it is the first time I have felt so at ease with him. Perhaps it is the result of our having stared death in the face together.

As we recount the events of the night it is clear to me that O'Sullivan regards Sean Kelly's fervent nationalism as sufficient reason for the attempt on our lives.

'Firebrands such as he set no value upon human life,' says he. 'Their beliefs blind them. We can only be grateful that the old man and his boy chanced upon us.'

He falters and suddenly starts trembling violently with the realisation of how near death he has come. I know how he is feeling, for I felt the same myself only an hour since. But he has not had the advantage of company and explanation that I have had.

I imagine how he must have regained consciousness in this strange, cramped room. His bewildered gratitude as strangers fed him and tended to his needs. How that gratitude, like mine, turned to relief. A relief redoubled when I appeared. But now the coin has spun - elation has provoked awareness...

I put my arm around his shoulders and wait for him to calm.

It is thus that the girl finds us. She is a plain, slip of a thing in a coarse dress and a mob cap from which escape strands of greasy hair.

She takes in the sight of two men embracing, naked under blankets. She blushes fiery red, hastily deposits a pile of clothes beside us, bobs a curtsey and scurries from the room.

The interruption eases O'Sullivan's black mood. The girl's consternation provokes a half-smile.

'But yesterday I would not have let such an opportunity slip,' he murmurs pensively. He looks straight at me. His eyes still carry the weight of last night's fear. 'I will forswear the company of light women,' he says. 'I have been too much the rake...'

I would not have him fall back into his melancholy. 'Come,' say I, fingering my blanket with distaste, 'let us be out of these, and back to our old selves.'

Quickly we dress and go downstairs to find Mr Kennedy.

'We thank you for your hospitality, sir,' says O'Sullivan. His hand goes to his purse. 'What do we owe you?'

Kennedy looks beyond our ears and holds up a deprecating hand. 'No trouble at all, sirs. I would not take your money.'

No, think I, *for you will already have been well paid.*

So we take our leave.

The day is more advanced that I thought, being already past noon. It must have been mid- morning before I woke after my ordeal - the same, I presume, with O'Sullivan. Yet though it be mid-day the sky is overcast and a thin drizzle of rain further dampens our already sober mood.

'I am not fit company for man nor beast,' says O'Sullivan. 'Pah, my skin crawls with the reek of the river!'

Before we reach Fishamble Street we go our separate ways.

Back at Lamb Lane I sluice my head under the pump in the yard, then go up to my room to change my shirt and breeches which, for all the ministrations of Kennedy's girl, feel stiff and stale. She has not washed them, I guess, merely put them before the fire to dry with the unwholesomeness of the river still ingrained.

Charlie bounces up the stairs just as I am tying back my hair.

'You're back, then? Where've you been? Out all night! Mr Garrick's not pleased, I can tell you.' He draws breath and takes a good look at me. 'Bloody hell! You look a proper fright and no mistake! Someone been having a go at you again?'

'None of your business,' I reply. 'And mind your language.'

But, peering into the scrap of fogged and pitted looking glass, I see that he is right. The fading dirty yellow bruising and scabbed scratches from last Sunday's encounter with Ormond and Liberty Boys have now been augmented by a fresh set of bruises and cuts about my mouth where I was roughly gagged. My eyes, too, are dark and sunken.

'Very well,' say I, as an idea occurs to me how Charlie may be of help, 'I'll tell you - but this must go no further!'

I recount, with some bloodthirsty embellishments and many omissions, the attempt on my life. Vicious footpads figure in my account - but Molly, Richard O'Sullivan and the assembled company at Kennedy's inn are absent. Sean Kelly and his two cronies are obliquely hinted at and I simplify the motive for the assault to delayed revenge. He listens with open-mouthed amazement.

'And just before they left me to die,' I conclude, 'they let slip something about the Music Hall in Fishamble Street. I think Kelly and his mates are up to something. Will you help me find out?'

His eyes light up with excitement. 'Too right I will! I've had naught to do these past few days but twiddle my fingers.' He balls his fist. 'Let's you and me have at these damned bog-trotters, eh Will?'

'Steady! This can be no harum-scarum enterprise. It must be managed quietly.'

As if taking me at my word, he lowers his voice. 'I can keep mum like the next man, don't you fear. What would you have me do, Will? Follow the cove? You know I'm good at that.'

'Yes, Charlie, I know you are. But not this time. Remember when you were at the Music Hall with the choirboys? Did you notice any other ways into the hall? Any doors or hatches?'

'Other than the big front doors, you mean?'

'Aye.'

He frowns with the effort of recall. 'The old witch in black brought the soup tureen from a back room. Some sort of green-room for the musicians. A fireplace, a few chairs and shelves for storing things...'

'You saw in there?'

'Aye. After we'd supped and the old girl had shooed her helpers out the front door, some of the lads needed a piss. There was a back door leading out from that room into a scrub of grass, all walled-in, like.'

'You couldn't get in or out that way?'

'Not unless you was a mountain-goat. Them walls was eight foot if they was an inch. A couple of the boys had a pissing competition up 'em. Managed a yard or so. But I trounced 'em all - four foot at least! Didn't have no cassock hampering me,' he says proudly.

'I'm sure they were all suitably impressed,' say I drily.

'You bet! Showed 'em what an Englishman can do!'

I steer him back to the subject. 'And there were no other doors in the hall?'

'Not as I noticed.'

'And no trapdoors or hatches in the floor?'

'Likewise.'

I picture the Music Hall crammed in the bend of Fishamble Street - *The Bull's Head,* three storeys high, flanking it to the left, the four-storey Kennan factory to the right. No side alleys between it and its neighbours. Only the small, enclosed yard to the rear...

Inside, the Music Hall itself is an elongated horseshoe of a space with, as I recall, tiered seats on three sides, broken only by the corridor from the front entrance, No galleries or balconies and, if Charlie is right, no other door than the one into the back room at the performers' end of the hall. It would seem then the only physical connection with *The Bull's Head* must be below floor level - I must somehow get into the cellar beneath the two buildings.

At some of the newer taverns in London I have seen a type of double doored hatch set into the front pavement down which barrels are rolled. But at *The Bull's Head* the drayman manhandled the barrels in by the front door.

If the only access to the cellar is inside the inn I have a problem...

'Charlie,' I say. 'Can you scout around the Music Hall and the hostelry next door? I want to know of every hatch or window...'

263

'We're going to break in?'

'I didn't say that.'

'No - but that's what you meant, ain't it?'

'That's for me to know and you to be ignorant of - now, off with you, and be careful!'

He needs no more urging, clattering down the stairs two at a time.

In the meantime, I am eager to know if Kitty has kept her word.

Half an hour later, I meet Ned at Kitty's lodging. An ancient farm-cart stands at the door. *The formidable Mrs Bickerstaff will not like that!*

Kitty and a young fellow I take to be her cousin Kenneth are just alighting. One look at Kitty's face tells me she has not enjoyed the journey.

She brushes aside her cousin's helping arm, ignores us all, then tosses her head and marches into the house without a word. Ned and I exchange a wry look.

The grizzled old man on the cart mutters something in Irish to Kenneth, who begins agitatedly to search his pockets. Finding nothing, he looks helplessy after his vanished cousin.

Seeing the problem, Ned finds a coin and presses it into the driver's hand. The old man knuckles his forehead, flicks the reins and the horse shambles off.

As the farm-cart disappears round the corner at the end of the road. Kenneth looks longingly after it, turning his hat in his hands and casting nervous glances at Ned and me.

He is, I remember, but a year my junior, yet he looks much younger. His skinny frame speaks tellingly of his family's hardship, but his face is well proportioned and his eyes bright. He is not unhandsome, but he has not yet the confidence to bring it off.

He starts like a frightened rabbit when I offer my hand. 'I am Will, 'I say. 'It was I who came to your house with the lady the other other day. And you must be Kenneth?'

'Sure that's right,yer honour.' His hands being busy with his hat, he dips an awkward bow.

'You are not returning to Ballycullen tonight?'

'No, yer honour. Cousin Kitty says I must stay.' He looks none too happy about it.

'Here, at her lodgings?'

'No, yer honour.,' he gulps. 'With an acquaintance of hers - a Mr Phil -philli...'

'Kenneth,' I say, laying a reassuring hand upon his arm. 'Pray you, be not so nervous. This is Mr Phillimore. As you see, he is no ogre.'

Another dip, to Ned this time. 'Yer honour.'

'Kenneth,' say I with a sigh, 'there is no need to call us *your honour.* You and I are of an age, and I am but a country boy like yourself.'

His wide-eyed look shows he finds it hard to believe.

Kitty appears at the front door. 'What are you all standing out here for?'says she tartly. 'Come in if you must.'

Ned whispers in my ear as we go in, ' She is pure ice, Will. I fear I am still out of favour.I rely on you to help bring her

265

round...'

Recalling her final words to me as we left Ballycullen, I cannot say I am hopeful of success!

We enter to see the black-clad back of Mrs Bickertsatff hoving out of sight at the end of the passage.

In the parlour, a tea-tray sits on a small table next to Kitty. Ned and I sit as Kitty pours the tea. Then, seeing her cousin hovering uncertainly, she snaps, 'Oh, for pity's sake, Kenneth, sit down.

He drops as if poleaxed on to the nearest chair. His hat rolls from his hands and he stoops to pick it up and clutches it like a drowning man a straw.

I step over, gently prise it from his grasp and lay it beside his chair. 'No need for ceremony, you are among friends,' I say, encouragingly. In the chilly atmosphere, I don't think he believes me!

Kitty pours tea and passes the cups. As she hands me mine, she says, 'I have still not forgiven you, Will Archer.'

I see Kenneth's eyes flick, full of fellow feeling, in my direction. He has doubtless suffered her ill spirits all the way from Ballycullen. It has made him timorous - but I am not so easily cowed.

'I am sorry about that, Kitty,' I say lightly, 'However, as I do not know what I have done to deserve it, your displeasure must be your own affair.' Then, turning to Ned, 'How are rehearsals going, Ned? I have not been able to get to the theatre for several days...'

'Tolerably well, Will. Mr Garrick expresses himself well satisfied.'

'Aye, with the play perhaps, but not with me, it seems.'

266

'Oh, really? Why is that?' asks Ned, interested.

'Oh - just because I nearly got myself killed last night,' I say airily.

Out of the corner of my eye I see curiosity spark in Kitty's face. But she is still in a sulk and bites her tongue.

Ned's face, however, clouds with concern. 'Not again, Will - I thought we had left all that behind in London? This is the Acres affair, I'll wager. I said it would bring you trouble.'

I am about to say that events have moved far beyond Tobias Acres when I realise just how imprudent that would be. The murder of an unremarkable fiddler in a theatre orchestra is one thing. But a potential rebel plot against the highest in the land is something else entirely. Ned, I know, is trustworthy, but can I rely on the excitable Kitty, or even the timorous Kenneth to hold their tongues?

Instead, I make light of it. 'You did indeed warn me, Ned, but trouble seems to dog my footsteps. It follows me willy-nilly! However, pursue me how it will, Dame Fortune must favour me for here I am!' Then, to distract them from further question, I change the subject. 'But how goes your own trouble, Master Kenneth? Have you heard aught of your brother or your father?'

Kitty can hold herself in check no longer. Bursting to be part of the conversation, she answers for him before he has time to open his mouth.

'News reached my aunt this morning that my cousin has taken ship to England. The Earl of Stair is raising an army to fight in the cause of Empress Maria Theresa. Aidan intends to enlist. The talk is it will sail for Flanders within the week.'

Kenneth shoots her an accusing glance. 'The Mammy's fit to die wit' worry, so she is,' he interrupts with feeling. 'And yet cousin Kitty would have me come wit' her and stay here...'

Kitty turns on him. 'Peace, you stupid boy,' she spits. 'Your mammy's woes will disappear the sooner if you get yourself a position. It's money she'll want, not you to wail with her!' She turns to me. 'Your Miss Acres said she would help. Will you take us there tomorrow morning, Will?'

I raise a questioning eyebrow. 'I am forgiven, then? Now you require my services...?'

She holds my gaze boldly, avoiding my question. 'Don't be a tease, Will. Say, will you take us or no?'

'I may - but only if you promise to make your peace with Ned. He has done nothing to deserve your contrariness.'

Her mouth sets firm and I think for a moment she will refuse. But then she relents.'Very well,' says she with a weary sigh. Coyly she offers Ned her cheek to kiss. 'I forgive you, you brute!'

Incredulity shows briefly in Ned's face. He, like me, must wonder how he has come to be the villain of the piece. But kisses her all the same.

The chaste kiss on the cheek is followed by a more passionate caress.

I turn my back on all this fondness. 'And your father,' I ask Kenneth,'have you any news of him?Is he indeed in Kilmainham?'

Grateful for an excuse to avert his eyes from our companions' endearments, he replies, 'We have heard nothing.'

'But you are sure the Guards can have no grounds to keep him, if he is?'

'Sure, sir, the Daddy was always a'telling Aidan not to be so hot-headed. It's true Aidan fell in with a bad crowd...'

'The rebels who burn houses?'

Ned and Kitty are still too busy fondling to heed us.

Nevertheless, Kenneth leans close and lowers his voice. 'It's right you are, sir. Mi Mam and Dad don't know the truth of it. Aidan tried to get me to go along with him once - but I wasn't having none of it.'

'Did he mention any names? Sean Kelly, perhaps, who comes from round those parts? Or Ciaran O'Dowd?'

Kenneth draws back, suspicious. 'I'm not one to blab, so I'm not. Why is it you're askin'?'

'For myself, Kenneth.' I touch the bruises on my face. 'I have them to thank for these. If Kelly and O'Dowd had had their way, I wouldn't be talking to you now.'

I see the shock in his eyes. 'Sure, Aidan did mention Sean Kelly once - it was a long time ago, mind. And I never heard of the other one.'

'No matter,' I say. 'But you're sure your father knew nothing of Aidan's activities?'

'Not a whit, sir. A clampróir - a troublemaker - perhaps. But not a coiriúil - not a criminal.'

The sound of Irish words distracts Kitty from her affectionate toying. 'Come,' she says, 'what are you two whispering about?'

'Only tomorrow's planned visit,' say I. 'I have been asking Kenneth what manner of service he has a fancy for.'

'Nay, don't you go putting ideas into his head,' says Kitty. 'He

269

may start as a boot-catcher and by degrees work himself up. You may be sure he will be grateful for anything Miss Acres can do for him.' But her cousin's affairs cannot detain her long. 'Come, Ned,' she says with a pretty fluttering of lashes, 'I have had an excessively tiring day. And I begin to find company wearisome… You may come again tonight if you wish, my dearest.'

And with this pretty dismissal, we take our leave.

24

...keeping watch...by night...

Leaving Kenneth at Ned's lodgings, I return to Lamb Alley by way of Mr Kennedy's hostelry.

There I beg pen and paper and leave a brief note to 'Mr Selby', couched in what I hope is a suitable ambiguity.

Our fugitive may have had associations with those responsible for the recent burnings. His name is known to Miss B's cousin who, I believe, was among the perpetrators. Having escaped the authorities two weeks since, said cousin is now embarked to fight in King George's War.

Might our man and his accomplices be contemplating a similar course?

I pause for a moment, wondering how far my credit may extend with Sir William. *Nothing ventured, nothing gained,* I tell myself. Then add to my note,

P.S. I am assured the Kilmainham prisoner, of whom we spoke, is innocent. If it be in your power to restore him to his family, they would, I am sure, be eternally grateful.

Sealing it, I hand it to Mr Kennedy who receives it with his customary impassive discretion.

Then I make haste back to my lodgings, where Charlie awaits me, practically hopping with his news.

'Crib's as easy to be cracked as a sparrer's egg, mate!' he informs me with the sang-froid of an experienced house-breaker.

I have never inquired too closely into Charlie's brief life before our paths crossed. But I have met some of his former street friends. Whether his opinion be based upon personal experience or not, I know I can trust it.

The Music Hall, he confirms, has no means of access, other than through the back room.

'I scaled the wall, no trouble,' says he cheekily, 'but a great lump like you...'

I raise a warning finger. 'Have a care, stick shanks! Anyway, the Music Hall is not our prime aim. What of the inn?'

'Leaky as an unstanched wench!' he crows. 'Traps and crannies a-plenty!'

The back of *The Bull's Head,* he informs me, is easily reached. A narrow alley, barely two feet wide, between it and the neighbouring house leads to a private yard at the rear. It caused him no trouble. 'But you,' says he tapping my stomach, 'with your paunch - we-e-e-ll...?'

'I shall squeeze through, jackanapes! But is there no other way in?'

One side of the rear yard, he says, is bounded by the Music Hall wall. Opposite, the windowless side of the neighbouring house extends for five foot or so beyond the back wall of the inn.The remaining perimeter consists of scrubby hedging and a wooden fence that has seen better days.

'There's a gate, of sorts,' says he, 'but it's chained and padlocked. Rusted to buggery, and the wood's all rotten...'

I'd rather not break in. 'What's on the other side of the fence?' I ask.

'A back alley - more a muddy footpath, really - and beyond that the back yards of other houses.'

'So we could get into the yard over the fence easily enough? What about getting into the actual building?'

All along the back wall of the inn, he tells me, there is a ruinous wooden penthouse or lean-to.

'Full of broken barrels, sticks of old furniture and other garbage. At one end there's a dung-heap where they must come out to piss - a proper stink-hole.'

'So there's a back door from the bar?'

'Dunno if it leads from the bar - a back passage more like 'cos there's two small winders, wooden trap things, no glass, set about six feet up. Some sort of storeroom, I'd guess.'

I try to picture it in my mind, remembering my first, and only, visit there to talk to Tobias Acres's fellow musicians.

The street door led straight into the bar-room. The stairs were off to the left, the bar straight ahead. The place was so thick with pipe-smoke and crammed with bodies that I cannot recall any detail else.

But, if Charlie is right, there must be a passageway out to a back door and possibly a store-room, or rooms, behind the bar. It is in that area that the entrance to the cellar is most likely to be found.

Charlie endures my thoughtful silence for no more that a couple of seconds.

'We gonna do the place tonight, eh Will?'

'*I* may - you'll be tucked up in bed.'

'Leave me behind - no way, mate!' He glances slyly up at me.

'What would Mr Garrick say if he knew what you were about - you're in his black books as it is...'

'You'd snitch on me, you tyke!'

'It's for your own good, Will. You'll need me - them traps is awful small. What if you got stuck?'

Loth as I am to put the lad in danger, he has a point.

Reluctantly I concede and, as penance, direct him covertly to obtain one of the dark lanterns I have seen in Mrs Fitzgerald's kitchen. We shall need it for this night's venture.

Supper is an uncomfortable affair. Mr Garrick, as Charlie warned me, is in a crabbed humour. But his displeasure, it transpires, arises not from anger at my overnight absence, but anxiety. An anxiety which is in no way assuaged when he sees the fresh bruises about my mouth. He will have me tell all about my night's adventure.

I do as he requests - again shaping events for the sensibilities of the listeners, just as I did for Charlie. In his case I emphasised the villains' bloodthirstiness - but now I seek to diminish the danger in which I found myself. Instead I draw attention to Richard O'Sullivan's support and the admirable vigilance of Paddy Rafferty and his son, Patrick.

'All the same,' says Garrick when I have done, 'you must have a care of your person. I cannot have a French tailor looking like a prize fighter!'

With that, he retires to his chamber.

Mistress Peg sighs. 'Take no notice, Will. He has been tetchy all day. Nothing I do can please him.'

274

'He is apprehensive, perhaps, of how he will be received here in Dublin?'

'You have hit it, I think. Like all great men, he is the last to recognise his merit. No matter how his last performance is lauded, he is certain the next will be an abject failure.'

'A failure - that can never be!'

'Ah,' says Mistress Peg, rising, ' you and I know that... I wish you good-night, Will. And pray, for all our sakes, keep fast to your bed this night!'

I wake Charlie at two-o'clock and we make our way as quietly as we can downstairs, straddling our legs wide to put our weight only upon each tread's outer extremities to avoid cracking and creaking.

Reaching the ground floor, we make our way through the kitchen. Charlie retrieves the dark lantern from where he concealed it this afternoon when Mrs O'Shaughnessy was serving dinner in the parlour and Nora was emptying slops in the back yard. Those two worthies are now a-bed in the room opposite ours on the top floor. Mrs O'Shaughnessy's snores accompanied our descent.

I retrieve the key from the nail beside the scullery door.. It turns with scarcely a rattle and we are out in the yard.

After the day's rain, the night air is mild. Clouds still obscure the moon, but at least it is dry. Rats scutter in the midden as we pass. Its sharp faecal stink of rot and piss is heavy in the thick night.

Beyond the alley the streets are deserted. We have no need yet of the lantern as our eyes adjust to the dark. Glimmers of moonlight through the rolling clouds light our way.

Only once do we have to retreat into a doorway as a lone watchman does his rounds. He strolls past, unaware of our presence, his reedy whistling fading into the night. Resuming our way, we are at Fishamble Street within minutes.

The Bulls Head is in darkness, its windows blank. Those on the ground floor are protected by wooden shutters, those above uncovered, black and blind.

Once there, Charlie seems to vanish into solid brick. The narrow passageway is no more than a vertical slash of blacker shadow in the dark wall. I have to turn sideways and creep, crab-like, along it. Even so, the rough surface catches at my clothes - scuffing shoulders, knees and buttocks. Before I am half-way along it I am sweating with a fear of the enclosed space - an affliction not heretofore known to me.

On emerging into the rear yard, I sink to my haunches, heaving in great gasps of air.

Charlie bends over me, dismayed. 'What ails thee, Will?'

I saw the air with my arm, unable yet to form a coherent reply.

Eventually the horror subsides.

'It's nothing,' I manage to gasp as I stagger to my feet. My skin is clammy and my head throbs. I fill my lungs with cool night air and exhale slowly. The ache in my skull eases.

'You give me a right turn,' he says. 'Feared of getting stuck, were you?'

'Aye, something like that. But I'm recovered now.'

I look around the yard. It is just as Charlie described it. The unruly hedge scratches a jagged horizon against the night sky. On either side are solid blocks of wall. And, projecting from the back of the inn, the sloping roof of the lean-to shades the area beneath it into a stygian cave of utter blackness.

I extract my tinder box and, after two or three strikes, succeed in igniting the wick in the lantern. It smokes and splutters before settling into a steady glow.

I take it from Charlie and direct its beam under the overhanging canopy. Flickering shadows dance and leap and, on the dung-heap, glowing pricks of red reflected eyes show the ever-present rats.

But our business is not at that end. I swing the lantern beam along the wall until it picks out the two small openings, wooden hatches about two feet square, set at head height.

Treading carefully, for the ground is littered with old chair legs, broken barrel staves and I know not what, I come as close to them as I am able.

Charlie ferrets out an old three-legged stool which seems firm enough. Gingerly I test my weight on it.

It holds.

I hand the lantern to Charlie and climb up. The shutter is old and warped at the edges. I worm my fingers into a crevice between two boards and, after one or two fruitless attempts where splinters of wood crumble or break away, I succeed in gaining a firmer purchase. Inserting both hands I pull hard.

Nothing happens.

Except that I lose my hold, tearing my finger-ends, and fall off the stool.

I curse under my breath as I suck my fingers. Then step up onto my perch once more.

Directing Charlie to shine the light more closely, I examine the edges of the panel for any sign of hinge or clasp.

There is none - only a solid frame of wood.

'Mayhap it don't open, Will,' whispers Charlie. 'Try sliding it - like a sash winder.'

Disinclined to wreak further havoc on my finger-ends, I rummage amongst the debris for something wherewith to prize the panel up.

'We should'a brought a metal crow,' mutters Charlie in disgust. 'First rule in crib-cracking!'

'No matter,' say I, extracting a broken piece of barrel-hoop. 'This will serve the purpose.'

I insert it under the bottom edge and lever it upwards. With a quiver of excitement I feel the shutter give a little.

Soon a narrow gap appears. I cast the metal bar aside and get my both hands into the opening. With a mighty shove I manage to force the panel up another inch or so.

I take a deep breath and put my shoulder to it.

Suddenly it shoots up with a screech and a thump.

Charlie slams shut the cover on the lantern. We stand stock-still, hardly daring to breathe.

I count away ten seconds at least before I relax again. The noise has set the rats a-scurrying and somewhere a dog is barking but, mercifully, it seems not to have alerted any inmates of *The Bull's Head.*

I crane my neck beyond the edge of the wooden roof to glance up at the top storey. The windows are still dark.

Charlie cautiously unshutters the lantern. 'Close shave there, Will. I near shit myself!'

I return to the trap in the wall. It is now a square black hole. Rags of cobweb drift ghostly in the lantern beam. Clearly it has not been opened for some time. As I brush the sticky web aside, a huge black spider scuttles over my hand. Repressing a shudder of revulsion, I fling it away.

'Here, lad,' I say, 'pass me the lantern.'

By its light, I see that the trap opens into a small lime-washed cell. Shelves on one wall are lined with tankards and bottles. In the opposite wall, an open doorway leads out onto a corridor.

I try to get my head and one arm through the gap. It is a tight squeeze. Too tight to risk.

This is where Charlie must come into his own.

I hoist him up and he scrambles easily through the hole feet first. He drops noiselessly to the floor, takes the lantern from me. Then, tapping his finger to the side of his nose and with a conspiratorial wink, he slips through the doorway into the corridor.

A few moments later I hear the muffled rattle of bolts being drawn at the back door. Then the turn of a key and Charlie stands there, grinning.

Closing the door softly behind me, I pause, finger to lips while we pause, listening for any sound within the house. But Mr Neal, the landlord, and any other of his family or staff, must be sound sleepers. I cross my fingers and hope they may continue to be so.

We are in a passage that leads direct from the bar-room at the

279

front of the inn to the back door behind us. Half way along it, and at right angles to it, a second passageway gives access to two small store-rooms. It is through the first of these that Charlie gained access.

There is a draught as we pass the open doorway. It comes from the open window trap. I step into the room and ease it back down. We have no further need of it now the back door is unbolted.

The second room, at the end of the corridor, is like the first except that it contains food, a sort of pantry. There is a sack of potatoes on the floor, and baskets of vegetables - turnips, carrots, cabbage. At waist height a stone shelf holds joints and cuts of meat. Higher shelves bear jars and boxes of herbs and spices. Provisions for events held in the function room on the first floor.

In neither room is there any keg such as I saw Kelly carrying, nor any door or trap that might lead to the cellar.

We retrace our steps to the main passageway. To our left now is the bar-room. Facing us in the opposite wall, is a closed door.

Gently I turn the knob and peer round the edge of the door. A blast of warm air laden with the lingering smell of cooking tells me this must be the kitchen where food is prepared. The lantern reveals a range in the far wall, embers still dully glowing. A scrubbed wooden table occupies most of the room.

Again, no cellar door or trap.

I close the kitchen door and nod Charlie in the direction of the bar-room.

There is no door, only a curtain, its edge greasy from many hands. The air is stale with the residue of the day - flat beer, fusty pipe-smoke, sour sweat.

To our left, the long wooden counter stretches the width of the room. Almost immediately on our right another closed door with bolts top and bottom. This, I judge, must be underneath the staircase that I ascended to the function room.

So, unless this door leads only to an understair closet, it must be the door to the cellar!

I slide the bolts and try the handle. It opens onto the top of a flight of stairs.

Charlie is agog with excitement. Grinning from ear to ear, he silently gives me the thumbs up.

I usher him in first, then close the door behind me. Together we descend into the cellar.

It is a low-roofed cavern with a floor of compacted earth. Thick brick pillars and arches support the joists overhead. The beam of the lantern loses itself in the gloom, but in the shadows I can make out the squat bulk of barrels.

If I judge correctly, the Music Hall must be over to our right.

I swing the lantern in that direction.

Sure enough, there is an archway cut into the wall, wide enough for two men to pass abreast.

More barrels. Most, from their hollow sound when Charlie kicks them, empty.

But it is not empty barrels that have brought me down here. I look about for the two small kegs brought here by Sean Kelly.

And there they are! Just inside the archway between the two cellars. He has made no attempt to conceal them. There they sit, inconspicious, innocuous. Until they are needed...

Until Sean comes back to set them up...

But Charlie has discovered something else. He beckons me.

I go over to where he stands, holding open the lid of a chest filled with bales of cloth.

I recall Sean Kelly telling me of the plight of Irish weavers. Their treatment yet another of the English oppressors' injustices! One from which my landlady's late husband, Fitzgerald, profited - and for which he met his untimely end.

Are these boxes here in the cellar full of Irish-manufactured cloth, destined to be shipped secretly abroad to break the English embargo? Mr Neal, it seems, is not quite the upright citizen he would appear.

If he and Kelly share the same sympathies, is Neal also party to Kelly's plot?

Yet, if so, would he suffer his contraband to be thus endangered?

But while I am pondering these thoughts, Charlie is becoming impatient.

Attempting to replace the lid, he accidentally dislodges it. It falls with a crash against one of the empty barrels, setting up a booming echo that reverberates around the whole cellar.

Frantically, the two of us manoeuvre the lid back into position, then make for the stairs.

But we are not half way up when we hear footsteps on the floor above.

Quickly we scramble back down the steps and squirm our way behind a large barrel in the darkest corner of the cellar. I snap shut the lantern cover.

Only just in time!

The door at the head of the stairs opens and a ray of light pierces the gloom.

'Ralph! Are you down there, you dunderhead? What d'you mean leaving the back door open?' The same voice that directed me to the upper room a week ago. Mr Neal, the landlord.

Two feet appear in the pool of light on the stairs, followed by two bare legs. Then the hem of a nightgown. And eventually the whole man, looking, if anything, stouter and more belligerent than last time. His ruddy face lit like a devil's in the light of a lantern held aloft.

'Speak, you feckin eejit!'

He stands, listening for a moment. From my hiding place, I hear the breath wheezing in his chest and half fear he also might heart my own thumping heart.

At last, after endless seconds, he is satisfied that the errant Ralph is not here. He turns and plods back upstairs, muttering to himself.

'A whoring again, is it, you bollox! I'll learn you, so I will. Play the tom-cat, would you?Sure you may stay out, you whelp, and cool your whirlygigs till morning!'

The shuffle of his slippers recedes - through the bar, down the passage to the back door. The distant rattle of the lock, the clang of bolts. Then the approaching shuffle of his returning feet.

The light wavers briefly at the top of the stairs. I close my eyes , praying that he will but push the door to as he passes. But then, the sound I'm dreading. The door slams shut, the bolts are shot home.

Charlie and I are locked in!

25

...raised incorruptible...

We wait, crouched behind the barrels, until the last creakings of Mr Neal's ascent cease.

Charlie heaves a great sigh.'Bin here afore, ain't we, mate?' he mutters. 'Least we got a glim this time.'

As if to emphasise his point, he slides up the shutter on the lantern. Its feeble light serves only to bring home more forcibly the hopelessness of our situation.

Last Sunday when we awoke in Sean Kelly's cellar, he rescued us, saved us from his loutish confederates. There is a fair chance that he might again be the first person to descend these cellar steps. But this time the outcome will be very different...

On a sudden lunatic whim I contemplate broaching one of Kelly's kegs, laying a trail of powder, lighting it from the wick of the lantern and blowing our way out!

But then reason prevails.

'There must another way out,' I say to Charlie. 'We have an hour before dawn to find it and escape unobserved.'

We set about the task, opening the top of the lantern so that the light shines upwards. For, in the absence of another door, any other egress can only be in the form of a trap-door from the floor above.

Perhaps there is one behind the bar - or even one that Charlie failed to notice in the Music Hall itself?

Accordingly, we first concentrate our search in the cellar beneath the Music Hall. The pillars here are of newer bricks, the floor above our heads of newer wood.

What was it Mr Sheridan said? *Built only last year...*

And built, as Charlie rightly surmised, without a trapdoor in its floor. A fact it takes only a few minutes to confirm. The sole purpose of this cellar is as extra storage space for Mr Neal.

But, as we return through the archway to the older, smaller cellar beneath the hostelry, a thought occurs. If the Music Hall be but recently constructed, what used to be in its place?

It is built, as I recall, at a bend in Fishamble Street, skirted on the one side by *The Bull's Head* and on the other by Kennan's Iron Works. The space it occupies is like a large wedge - narrow at the front but wider at the back. From the street, I remember going through a small fenced yard, the facade of the Hall being set back ten foot or so. But the distance between the corner of *The Bull's Head* to the left and the corner of Kennan's to the right can have been little more than eight feet. Too narrow to construct a suitably impressive facade for a public building - but wide enough for a cart to pass through...

I look up to see Charlie shining the light at the area of the cellar roof which he judges to be just behind the bar. Sure enough, there is the outline of a trap.

He is all for heaving over one of the barrels and climbing up. But I am wary of the noise it may cause. There is no ring on the underside and, once pushed up, it could dislodge anything on top or clatter back onto the wooden floor. Such a clamour is sure to bring Mr Neal upon us once more - and next time he may be armed with more than a lantern.

Instead, I explain my idea of an outside hatchway where goods may once have been delivered to the rear of the premises.

Charlie demurs at first. 'Better to get up behind the bar and leg it,' he protests. 'If there was one in the back yard, we would have seen it.'

'Not necessarily,' I reason. 'Our attention was on the windows in the wall.'

Only with considerable muttering does he agree to switch our search to the back wall. And almost at once we see it. Or, rather, we see among the stacked barrels, two stout wooden stanchions rising at an angle from the earthen floor almost up to the intersection of wall and roof.

Closer investigation shows them continuing upwards and outwards into a darker recess beyond the wall. A recess roofed with a double doored hatch!

Catching my breath with excitement, I drag an empty barrel over and, testing the firmness of its lid, climb up. Stooping almost double, I put my back against the hatch and heave.

It does not move.

Either it is fastened shut or, remembering what must be above it - the trash in the lean-to - it is weighed down with rubbish.

I take a deep breath and give it another shove. This time I think I feel some movement.

Another - and another...

Then, with a dull, tearing sound, one half of the trap collapses inwards. I shield my head with upraised arms as clods and lumps bounce round me me, near knocking me off the barrel.

'Shitting hell!' cries Charlie, backing off and retching.

It is as if the whole of Newgate sewer has engulfed me. And is still dripping - in thick, oily gobbets down my neck, in my hair - coating me in rancid slime.

The trapdoor was underneath the dung heap! A year's worth of rotting vegetables, entrails, the waste of chamber-pots and drunkards' piss has rotted the wood and, with my help, has cascaded into the cellar. And I, curled up, squatting head in arms on top of the barrel, am the first thing in its path!

I hardly dare breathe for fear of what I may inhale. Or open my eyes for fear of what may ooze into them.

Only when something lands on my head and I feel it move and squeak do I leap from the barrel and roll, squirming on the floor.

Then Charlie is beside me. He has grabbed a length of cloth from one of the contraband cases and is scrubbing away at my face and head.

I take it from him and wipe away as much of the foulness as I can, then screw up the material and cast it aside.

'Nay, Will,' he says, retrieving it and bundling it up tight, 'you're not thinking straight. We cannot leave it here, they'll know we've been. Come, now, give me a leg-up.'

I help him through the shattered trap. Then, after passing him the soiled material and lantern, I heave myself up.

Outside it is still dark and - bliss! - raining heavily. I stand drenching myself under a gush of water overflowing from the gutter beneath the eaves.

By the time we run across the yard and scramble over the hedge into the back alley, I am soaked to the skin and shivering

287

with cold - but at least I am smelling less foul.

26

...even the messenger...

It is near ten and Charlie and I are still abed when Kitty comes to call.

In answer to a timid yet persistent knocking on the door, I bid the disturber of my slumbers to enter.

It is Nora, the scullery maid. Her face, fiery red, has the expression of a love-lorn looby as she manages to stutter, 'Misskitty - dow'stairs.' Then she flees.

Her embarrassment is understandable.

Last night - or rather this morning - Charlie and I arrived home just as dawn was tinting the dark night grey.

Coming into the back yard, Charlie caught my arm. 'You can't go in like that, Will - it'll give old Ma Fitzgerald the vapours, smelling her house out! You stink like a week old turd.'

'So - what do you suggest?'

'Nothing else for it, mate...'

His grimace says it all. Stripping naked, I bundled my clothes in a heap outside the back door and spent the next ten minutes sluicing myself under the freezing water of the pump. Charlie, meanwhile, went in search of a towel.

It was while I was thus skipping about, panting against the cold and scrubbing my every crack and crevice that Nora, sleepily embarking upon her morning's tasks, came upon me. In the cold morning light I must have seemed like a pale, prancing devil.

At any rate, her immediate reaction was to drop the can of cinders she was carrying, utter a hoarse cry of terror and, flinging her apron over her face, beat an hysterical retreat into the scullery.

Fortunately, colliding with Charlie in the doorway prevented her waking the whole household with her caterwauling.

Charlie threw me the towel and, holding it before me, dripping and shivering, I scampered, bare-arsed, into the house and up to the attic. Passing Charlie on the way swearing a whimpering Nora to secrecy. He left her fanning herself with her apron in the kitchen rocker.

Lord knows what her simple mind has made of my naked caperings. But, judging by her languishing mooncalf look at me just now, I fear the worst.

Donning my only remaining clean shirt and breeches - regardless of the weather, I must go coatless today! - I wake Charlie. After scribbling a hasty note for 'Mr Selby' I give him directions for Mr Kennedy's establishment and impress upon him that he he must deliver it into the proprietor's hands and his alone.

Then I go downstairs to join Kitty. She has been caught by Mrs Fitzgerald who is at her simpering best. As Mr Garrick, Mistress Peg, Kitty and a bemused Kenneth look on, our landlady holds fawning court. Kenneth, I notice, still has his hat in his hands.

'Oh, la!' says Mrs Fitzgerald. 'My late husband, Mr Fitzgerald, was ardent for a theatrical performance. He had an ear, you know, for a fine turn of phrase. Together, we saw many fine actors. But, on my life, I dare hazard none as accomplished as yourselves...'

'Ah, Will,' cries Mr Garrick, interrupting her, 'you are becoming a positive slug-abed these days. Mistress Kitty here has been attending upon you this half-hour or more. You are to accompany her to poor Miss Acres's house are you not?'

'That is our intention, sir.'

'Well, we must not keep you. Your servant, ma'am,' he says to Mrs Fitzgerald who, with a fulsome smile, recognises a dismissal when she hears one. She curtsies and leaves the room.

I see Mistress Peg eyeing my informal dress.

'Surely, Will, you are not intending to visit a lady in such *deshabille*?'

'I regret that, at the present moment, it is all I have. Both my coat and waistcoat are in no condition...'

'Then you should avoid falling in rivers,' says Mr Garrick testily.

In view of his forbidding further investigations, I do not tell him that it is now more than river water that afflicts them.

Urged by Mistress Peg's prompting, he somewhat reluctantly agrees to lend me one of his own coats.

'But this time I would like it back,' he says. I need no reminding that the last time he lent me his coat it ended up on a dead street boy!

A few minutes later, attired stiffly in my master's bottle green coat - he is of smaller stature than me, so it is rather tight - I set out with Kitty and Kenneth for Eugenie's house in Great Boater Lane.

Liam answers the door. There is nothing in his manner to suggest our altered acquaintance - he is his usual churlish self.

I address him in kind. 'Is your mistress in, fellow?'

'In the house, certainly. But whether she be in to receive company, I cannot say.'

'Perhaps, then, you might enquire?' I say with a thin smile.

He keeps us waiting on the doorstep, much to Kitty's annoyance.

'This,' she hisses to Kenneth, 'is not a manner you should emulate!'

He bows his head and gives his hat a few turns.

From inside the house, I hear Eugenie's voice. 'For shame, Liam - to shut the door on people thus!'

Then she is before us, all apology, and ushering us upstairs. The reception room is as cheerless as ever. She herself, however, is radiant this morning. As she looks at me, her eye seems alight with some secret delight. I feel my heart beat faster.

'So, Miss Blair, this is the young man we spoke of? Come, sir, let me see you.'

She has him stand before the window that she may judge his bearing.

With an exasperated sigh, Kitty snatches his hat from him and prods him between the shoulder blades. 'Stand straight for the lady, you lollpoop. She will think you a crook-back!'

Eugenie is gentler. Lightly, she runs her hand down his upper arm, then tilts up his chin with a delicate finger. 'You are accustomed to hard work?'

'To be sure, ma'am. Aren't I in the forest a-cutting wood most every day?'

'You have a honest mien - a fine regularity of feature. I think

292

you will do.'

'Do you think you may secure him a position with one of your acquaintance, Miss Acres?' asks Kitty.

'I will do better than that,' replies Eugenie. 'I shall take him into my own household. I have been thinking, if I am to be more in society, I shall have need of a carriage. Are you good with animals, Kenneth?'

'Sure I can learn, ma'am...'

'That's the spirit! And, who knows, in time I may promote you to higher duties.'

'Will Liam not object?' I ask.

'Liam has many duties as it is. He cannot do everything. Besides, I am not sure he will be in my service for much longer.'

She sees my brow rise in surprise, but does nothing to satisfy my curiosity.

Instead, she summons refreshments from Bridget and spends the rest of the time in pleasant chatter with Kitty. Kenneth and I are left to exchange mute looks of bewilderment at the inexhaustibility of their interest in the latest peccadilloes of the town.

At length we take our leave. It is arranged that Kenneth will be summoned as soon as arrangements about the new carriage have been made. Room will then be made available for him at Great Boater Lane. In the meantime, he will continue to lodge with Ned.

Kitty is in high spirits as we return towards town. All the way down Aungier Street, she continually draws Kenneth's attention to passing carriages and footmen. 'That,' she tells him of one, 'is the way to comport yourself. But in no way,' she says of another, 'should you imitate that wretch.' The poor lad's head must be spinning!

By the time we reach Dame Street, I have retreated into my own thoughts. What did Eugenie mean about Liam possibly leaving her service? Has she tired of his mutinous behaviour? Or is it of his own volition - has Hervey, perhaps, some other task for him?

It takes a moment, therefore, for me to become aware that someone has addressed me by name. I snap out of my reverie and see that Nathaniel Grey has come up beside us.

Kitty, I see, is all curiosity at this stranger.

He bares his teeth in a smile. 'The celebrated Miss Kitty Blair, I believe. It is an honour, ma'am, to meet you. Pray introduce us, Master Archer.'

Kitty simpers prettily and, with a curtsy, offers him her hand to kiss.

'Kitty,' I say, 'this is Mr Nathaniel Grey...'

I see him regarding me closely, coolly amused at how I shall explain our connection.

'...an old acquaintance - from London.'

'Delighted, sir,' says Kitty. 'Are you also an actor, Mr Grey?'

A dry laugh, 'In a minor way, Miss Blair. But not as much in the public eye as your good self. Might I deprive you of Master Archer's company for a few minutes? I bring news of a mutual friend...'

'Of course, Mr Grey,' she replies hastily. I sense some agitation in her tone, as if she guesses at Grey's identity. 'No need to apologise. My cousin, Kenneth, can escort me back. Keep Will as long as you like - I am sure you have much to catch up on.'

With a commiserating glance at me, she links her arm in Kenneth's and leads him away.

Grey wastes no time in getting down to business. 'We have your letter, Archer. From what you describe, it would seem our friend has yet to set up his *surprise*. A watch has been set on the premises and we hope to apprehend the fellow in the act. Unfortunately, there is a slight problem.'

'The other items in the cellar?'

Grey looks puzzled for a moment, then shakes his head dismissively. 'That does not concern us. Semple will pass the relevant information to the excise as soon as our business is done. No - the problem is that the date of the event has been altered. At the request of certain persons of distinction, it has been moved from Monday to Tuesday.'

'Is that serious?'

'We hope not. But in these matters such a disruption may disconcert the perpetrators. They may act precipitately...'

'We must all be on our guard, then, sir?'

'And you doubly so, Master Archer, for our friend may discover that you are alive still.'

A cold tug of fear clutches my innards. 'Indeed, his sister saw me not an hour ago - I had forgot...'

'It behoves us not to forget anything in our business, Master Archer. I would advise you to lie low between now and next Tuesday.' He tips his hat in farewell, but turns back to say, as if in afterthought. 'Sir William instructs me to say you have done well, sir, and wishes me to convey his congratulations.'

It is clear from his disdainful tone that he sees no reason to endorse his master's compliments.

27

...come unto him all ye that labour...

I spend most of Saturday afternoon up to my elbows in water, soap and lye.

Mrs O'Shaughnessy has taken the graceless Nora to market with her, so I have the back yard to myself. Mrs Fitzgerald is happy to watch me heave out a wooden tub and trail back and forth with hot water from the kitchen range, but she cannot see it in her way to provide for a servant's laundry gratis. She charges me a penny for a half pound of soap and another for a jug of lye. The wood-ash for scrubbing, she says magnanimously, I may have for free.

Thus furnished, and my landlady departed indoors, I retrieve my befouled clothes. Two linen shirts, two sets of stockings, two pairs of breeches, a waistcoat and a greatcoat. Their smell has not improved overnight.

A liberal application of soap and some hearty pummelling is sufficient for the lighter items. But the coats are a different matter. Ideally, they should not be immersed in water. But it is too late for that! I brush them with soap and hot water to get rid of the thickest dirt. Then, taking a fistful of wood-ash, I rub in a little lye and scrub a small area at a time to lift out the remaining stains.

It is a tedious process and by the end the skin on my palms is red-raw. The material of coat and waistcoat has fared little better. In places where the nap was once only scuffed it is now distinctly thin, but at least some colour is restored and the stink just about abated. Before being soaked in the Liffey, deluged in filth and undergoing such scrubbing, these might have lasted me three years. Now I shall be lucky to get three months!

With a sigh of resignation, I hang them out to dry. At least the rain has stopped and, in typical Irish fashion, the sky is now a clear, cloudless blue.

I empty the wash tub into the back alley channel where the murky, soap-scummed water meanders sluggishly among the accumulated debris.

I rinse it under the pump, then lug it back to the scullery. Just in time - for Mrs O'Shaughnessy, red-faced and bothered, hoves into sight, trailing a flustered Nora in her wake.

I take the stairs two at a time up to my room, where I find Charlie spreadeagled on his truckle bed, fast asleep. He is fully clothed and a thin line of dribble edges its way from his slack mouth. He snorts gently and his eyelids twitch.

I suppose I, too, should feel exhausted after my lack of sleep last night. I lay down on my bed. But sleep will not come. Instead I feel strangely restless. The events of the last few days, far from tiring me have animated me. I want to be doing! This enforced inaction irks me.

Disturbed by my tossing and turning, Charlie wakes.

'Wotcher, Will, what time is it?' he enquires sleepily. He rubs his eyes and passes the back of his hand over his mouth.

'Near five, I think.'

'Lord, I'm hungry...'

I realise I have an appetite myself. 'How say you to a meat pie, lad?'

He needs no further urging and, neither of us expecting anything but short commons from Mrs O'Shaughnessy, we set off into town.

Great Ship Street is busier than usual and the reason soon becomes apparent. In the distance we hear the beat of fifes and drums. Sure enough, as we push our way through the throng towards the Castle, we see a small company of soldiers lined up in Bedford Square.

It is clear that we have missed the main part of proceedings for they are marching off towards Essex Bridge as we arrive. They make a splendid sight, their red coats glowing in the late afternoon sun, bayonets glinting.

'Is it a special occasion?' I enquire of a respectable looking gentleman.

'Some bigwig just arrived from England.' He snorts derisively. 'Sure, as if we haven't enough of them already!'

'Mayhap he is some man of refinement arrived for Mr Handel's concert next week?'

'Sure, more like he's another English lordling come to show them Irish who's master!'

His tone is contemptuous. *AnotherAnglo-Irishman,* I think, *caught in the middle, hating both Irish and English alike!*

Charlie and I follow the soldiers as far as Dame Street, where hunger eventually gets the better of him. He pulls at my arm and drags me to a side-street leading down to Custom House Quay. 'Stalls and carts a-plenty down here, Will,' says he.

His nose, as ever, provides a sure guide. Within a couple of minutes we are standing before a pie-cart. The owner, whose girth is sure recommendation for his wares is just about to close for the day. A mere handful of broken pies remain. Seduced by Charlie's spaniel eyes, he sells us four for the price of two.

Once I've paid for them, Charlie perches himself upon a wall and sets to devouring as if he has not eaten for a week. Flakes of pastry fly. Gravy runs unchecked down his chin.

I eat mine with somewhat less speed and   considerably more decorum.

Finishing long before me, Charlie licks his fingers, belches long and loud, then wipes his hands down his breeches.

'Sure,' he says in imitation of the Irish brogue, 'that was grand, so it was!' Then, eyeing mine, 'You sure you can manage all that, Will?'

'Aye, so get your peepers off it!'

But hardly have I put the last bite in my mouth before he digs me in the ribs.

'Say, isn't that the wench as patched us up the other day?'

I follow the direction of his gaze.

Bridget Kelly is hurrying along at the other side of the street. So intent is she on weaving her way through the crowd that she has not noticed us. Soon she is lost amongst the passers-by.

'Seems in a bit of a rush, don't she?' muses Charlie.

Yes, and to what purpose? I wonder. *Is she going to meet her renegade brother?*

Certainly she is headed towards the river.

Both the Custom House and Sean's hovel on the north bank lie in that direction. But Sir William Hervey told us that Kelly has gone to ground. He is unlikely to be found in either of those places...

So what is Bridget's destination? What else lies upon the north bank? The dead-house, the barracks, the hospitals... And, of course, Smithfield Market! His two ruffian associates are butcher boys - they could be harbouring him in the warren of streets around there!

Even as I am about to start after her, I see it is unnecessary. For there, not a hundred yards behind her, taking care not to be seen, is Liam.

And if he is on her trail there is no need for me to interfere. Hervey gave us all our appointed tasks, and mine - to reconnoitre the cellar at *The Bull's Head* - has been completed. The latest instruction, relayed through Nathaniel Grey, is for me to lie low. But lying low does not suit with my present restlessness.

The prospect of an evening moping in my lodgings does not appeal.

I look up to see ominous dark clouds massing in the west as night approaches. If I am to lie low, surely the darkness out here will conceal me as effectively as hiding away in my room...?

I despatch Charlie back to Lamb Alley with instructions to take my washing indoors and to sweetheart Nora into finishing its drying around the kitchen stove.

His full belly makes him compliant and he scurries off without demur.

Left alone, I begin to understand the cause of my restlessness. In part it is anticipation - this enforced inactivity before whatever may happen at the Music Hall.

But also it is the pies.

What made Charlie obedient has stirred another sort of hunger in me.

Without further ado, I hurry towards Custom House Quay where sweet Molly Malone may perhaps help me satisfy it.

By good fortune, she finds me before I find her.

I have spent a fruitless quarter hour prowling the near-deserted quay and its adjacent darkening streets. Her court and tenement room lie somewhere here, I know, but in the dusk all yards seem the same.

I have almost abandoned hope when a pair of hands covers my eyes and a longed-for, familiar voice whispers in my ear.

'Guess who, my brave bow-man!'

I swing round and scoop her up in my arms, planting kisses upon her lips.

'Why, sure, Master Archer,' says she, pulling away and pressing her delightfully sea-scented fingers over my mouth, 'is this any way for a gentleman to behave?' Her lips curve in mock-horror but her eyes are black with desire.

The ordeals of the last two days seem to melt away in those two liquid orbs. 'Oh, Molly...,' I sigh, running my hand through her hair.

Linking her arm through mine, she leads me to the cramped courtyard that has so eluded me. There is the dung-heap in the corner, her cockle-cart inside the narrow archway - and here the stairs that ascend to her room...

The night air is muggy with the impending storm. My shirt

302

clings, clammy, to my warm flesh.

I follow her, meek as a lap-dog, up the confined staircase. A small fire burns in the grate, making the tiny room almost unbearably hot.

And now I am here, it seems a dream. My head is light. I stand, unaccountably enervated, gazing like a loon as, slowly, she unlaces her dress. It falls, rustling to the floor. Her naked body is pale as alabaster in the half-light.

All the time, she has not taken her eyes off mine. It is as if I have been put under a spell, bereft of all will. Her unwavering gaze holds me in thrall.

Now she steps close and with infinite slowness unlaces my breeches, easing them down my thighs. Silently, eyes locked on hers, I raise first one foot, then the other. She kneels in front of me, divesting me of shoes and stockings. Then, rising, she draws my shirt over my head so that I, too, am naked.

Though we can in no way be accounted virgins, nevertheless for breathless seconds we stand here, eyes locked one upon the other. Two innocents, a new Adam and Eve, lost in uncertainty.

Then, with one finger, she traces the line of my parted lips, sliding it past my chin to my shoulders and so down, around my nipples and further, across my belly and into the undergrowth wherein my little soldier quivers erect. But she does not touch him. Instead, she lightly circumvents him, alighting upon the tensed orbs below, scratching gently at their surface.

With her other hand, she takes mine and places it upon her breast, inviting me with her eyes to take the same journey around her body.

Outside, thunder begins to roll as I, too, travel across and down the lineaments of her form, mapping its clefts and contours, the dimpled knolls and furred declivities that lead me at last to the warm, moist crevice between her thighs. Tentatively, I venture in and find it opens up to me, allowing passage for one, two, three questing fingers.

White light flashes momentarily at the window. Her breathing deepens and, territorial survey complete, she seizes my salivating lieutenant and urges him once more into the breach.

A thunderclap rends the night, causing my spellbound lassitude to evaporate. No sooner does my trusty warrior feel the heat of the adversary than I cease to be a lovelorn loon and become a man of vigour.

Clamping my mouth hard to hers, I hoist her up by her buttocks and, ungainly but still interlocked, I carry my enchanting burden to the narrow bed. There, spurred on by the martial accompaniment of the heavens, my little soldier valiantly charges into battle.

I do not know how long the encounter lasts. Only that when, eventually, the final shots are fired, both Molly and I are panting and sweating with exhaustion.

For a long while we lie in each other's arms feeling no need for words, listening to the receding thunder. Until, with the last grumbles of the storm, slumber ambushes us.

I awake to see her tying up her hair. She is fully dressed and the first grey light of dawn is creeping in at the window.

'What time is it?' I murmur.

'Time all god-fearing folk should be up,' she laughs. 'A

quarter to five, and I should be down at the quay-side getting the best of the cockles. Shame on you, Master Archer, for keeping a poor girl from her livelihood so! And shame on you for a-lying there naked as the day you was born tempting a body with your wares!'

I draw the ragged sheet modestly across my stirring manhood. 'Must I go now?'

'Sure you can please yourself. I'm not throwing you out, that's for sure. But I've my living to earn. If you're gone by the time I come back, be sure and leave the key on the nail.'

With that, she flounces out the door. I lay back, smiling, push the sheet aside and, in conversation with my little soldier, relive a little of last night's ecstasy.

28

...the chastisement of our peace...

Later that morning, I return to Lamb Alley to find the place in uproar.

A noisy congregation of neighbours who would be much better occupied at church this Sunday morning stand about, watching Mr Garrick very unhandily nailing boards up at the windows of Mrs Fitzgerald's residence. Charlie holds further lengths of wood and nails and seems to be directing operations.

On catching sight of me, Mr Garrick immediately hails me with a mixture of relief and annoyance. 'Will, at last! Here, you may take over this task.'

He thrusts the hammer into my hands and proceeds, with some asperity, to shoo the onlookers away. 'Now, good people, there is nothing more to see here. Pray, go about your business.'

As my master ushers them away, Charlie takes the opportunity to acquaint me with the morning's events.

'A gang of 'em,' says he with relish. 'Come an hour since a shoutin' and a bawlin' - such language as would set your ears afire! Then they chucks bricks and I know not what else through the winders - every pane smashed to pieces.'

'Come, Will,' says Mr Garrick testily, 'These lower windows must be boarded up securely. Without a ladder there is little can be done for the others for the present. But, wherever you have been gadding this night, you have not time now for idle chatter.'

306

He does not inquire further into my absence. It is a matter he will no doubt return to later. But for now, the street finally empty of spectators, his concerns lie elsewhere. 'I must see how our landlady does,' says he and disappears indoors.

'Is Mrs Fitzgerald hurt?' I ask Charlie.

'Nah,' says he contemptuously. 'More wind and water than anything. A fit of the vapours like you've never seen. Mistress Peg's with her now, the two on'em wailing like graveyard wraiths.'

He chatters on as I finish boarding up the ground floor windows. Inside, as I nail, I catch glimpses of Mrs O'Shaughnessy and Nora busy with dustpan and broom, mop and bucket.

At last I have finished. The upper windows are still open to the weather. As Mr Garrick said, they cannot be secured, from the outside at least, until a ladder can be found. A man to mend the glass will not be found until tomorrow - to work on a Sunday may be frowned upon back in London, but here in Ireland it is near heresy!

Leaving Charlie to stow the tools, I venture into the parlour where Mrs Fitzgerald, red-eyed and bedraggled, her hysterical tempest now abated, is in somewhat calmer mood. Mistress Peg sits facing her, holding her hands as the lady bemoans her misfortune.

It is, she believes, all to do with her late husband, his violent demise at the hands of those ruffian apprentices and the malice they still bear her in the matter of the just execution of several of their number.

'I had thought that business all over,' she complains, damply.

'I cannot think what has stirred it up again...' Then, after another litany of self-pity, she grasps Mr Garrick's hand and mine, saying, 'Oh, but what a comfort it is to have two men such as yourselves in the house. You cannot conceive how helpless we poor women feel.'

For further reassurance, Mr Garrick suggests that Ned might be prevailed upon to spend a night or two here. 'I am confident the villains will not return, ma'am. But it may be as well to be prepared, don't you think?'

Mrs Fitzgerald would have as many trusty men as the house might hold at this time of peril. Her gratitude for my master's consideration is only modified by the spectre of the expense.

'Fear not, ma'am,' says Mr Garrick hastily, 'the gentleman will not expect his keep.'

'Indeed not,' adds Mistress Peg. Then, earning a sour look from my master, she continues. 'Davey will see you are not out of pocket.'

At last our landlady is sufficiently recovered and retires to her room to mend some of the ravages that shock has wrought upon her.

My master takes me aside.

'I shall not ask where you have been all night, Will,' he says disapprovingly. 'But I would know if this outrage upon our landlady's property has aught to do with you?'

I am astonished. 'You think I...?'

'No, no - I do not accuse you,' he protests. 'Only it crossed my mind that it might be the result, not of some historic grudge against the late Mr Fitzgerald, but of enmities you may have more recently incurred?'

'I cannot say, sir. It may be so.'

'Will!' he cries. 'Did I not expressly warn you against further meddling? It was bad enough that you nearly got that fop O'Sullivan killed. But now you put us all in jeopardy!'

'I am sorry, sir,' I reply, mortified. 'Do you wish me to leave?'

He shakes his head impatiently. 'And go where? Don't be so foolish, my boy. Whatever danger you are in, it will be better faced with the support of your friends.'

'You are generous, sir,' I reply gratefully. 'I can only suppose that Kelly has discovered his attempt to murder me has failed and that this unfortunate assault upon Mrs Fitzgerald's property is a sign he still intends me harm. Yet, if all goes well, the threat will be short-lived. I have every hope he will be apprehended within the next two days at most.'

I can see that Mr Garrick wishes to ask how I know this. But he refrains.

I do not know how much he suspects of Sir William Hervey's influence over me. But I do know that his refusal to inquire too closely into my affairs is as much for his own sake as mine. He would not have his faith in me shaken by knowing too much.

'Very well, my boy,' says he, putting his arm about my shoulder. 'In the meantime, whilst I send a note to Ned, you must be an unwilling prisoner here in Lamb Alley - and we your guards!'

For the rest of the day I am never alone. Until the front windows can be repaired, our landlady will have my master and Mistress

Peg remove to her own bedroom at the rear of the house. She will make do with the couch in the late Mr Fitzgerald's dressing room.

'No great sacrifice,' I overhear Mrs O'Shaughnessy mutter to Nora. ''Tis comfortable enough. Lord knows the old master spent most of his nights in there!'

Before embarking upon the business of exchanging bed linen, the same lady dumps two patched and musty smelling bedspreads on the front bedroom floor. Unwilling to countenance nails being driven into the inside window frames, Mrs Fitzgerald will have me and Charlie rig some form of protection from them and a pair of clothes horses.

'Fit only for the rag-bag,' says Mrs O'Shaughnessy with a sniff, 'but still too grand for the likes of us, according to her ladyship - so they must moulder in the bottom of the press while we shiver in our attic!'

The afternoon is well advanced by the time all is done. Ned has been sent for and arrives with Kitty just as tea is served in the parlour.

Our landlady is clearly put out when Mr Garrick insists I join them. She acquiesces with tight-lipped gentility, but it is clear she thinks the latitude allowed her, as hostess and a lady of refinement, should not extend to a mere servant. My relationship with Mr Garrick is a complete mystery to her.

Fortunately, I am spared an awkward half-hour by the arrival of Nora to say a gentleman is asking for me at the front door.

I rise but Mr Garrick stays me. I see the unease in his eye. He will not have me go alone.

'Pray ask the gentleman to step in,' he tells Nora. At the other side of the room Mrs Fitzgerald draws a sharp breath, then smiles obsequiously at Mr Garrick who has casually risen to stand beside me.

The momentary tension is relieved when Nora ushers Liam Donovan into the room.

Mr Garrick regards him suspiciously, but it takes only the merest glance at his untidy livery for Mrs Fitzgerald to know what he is.

'Lawks a'mercy, you stupid girl! What mean you by bringing a footman into polite company?'

Nora descends into red-faced babbling. Seeing Liam's face cloud at the insult, I step forward before he says anything to worsen the situation.

'My apologies, ma'am,' say I. 'I am sure Nora meant no harm. This good fellow is known to me. However, I would not wish to incommode you. So, if you will excuse me, we shall retire.'

Once outside the parlour door, Nora scuttles away. I take firm hold of Liam's arm and guide him upstairs to my room.

The garret being beyond reach of the morning's missiles, the bedroom shared by me and Charlie is unscathed. Hastily I sweep aside the recently laundered clothes that Charlie has left in a heap upon my bed and we sit facing each other.

'Sure the old lady has even more airs than you, Master Archer!' he quips.

'Liam,' say I, 'how many times will you have me apologise for my behaviour towards you?'

'Sure the sound of your contrition is honey to my senses, Will - I cannot have enough of it!' he laughs. 'But enough of that. I

311

come, albeit reluctantly, as the bearer of good tidings. Mistress Eugenie is invited to Mr Handel's concert on Tuesday next and would have you - the Lord knows why! - escort her.'

'But - but that cannot be... The danger...!'

'All who attend will be in danger if we are unable to avert it,' he retorts. 'Do you think I am any happier than yourself with this? I would not have her within a mile of the place if it were in my power! But, as your admirable landlady pointed out, I am but a footman...'

'Aye, just as I am but Mr Garrick's valet...! But we both serve another master.'

'Yes, the same master who has arranged for my mistress to attend the concert,' he says bitterly.

'Sir William...?'

'Indirectly, yes. Through Mr Callaghan the lawyer who, whilst regretting that he himself will not be present, humbly suggests she might like the agreeable young actor of her acquaintance to accompany her... It is Sir William's way of ensuring you are present, in case you may be needed. Indeed, I am to give you orders to keep Sean Kelly's brother under close observation throughout. If at any point he absents himself, it may be proof that he is part of the conspiracy.'

'And you - will you be there?'

'To be sure I will. In wait for Kelly and his confederates in the cellars beneath. In company with Semple. Both of us will be armed. Our task is to apprehend them just before they light the fuse. If they flee, more armed men await them in *The Bull's Head*.'

'Will not the place be crowded with drinkers?'

'Not on Tuesday. Mr Neal, the landlord has closed it for the day. He is, as you know, chief benefactor of the Music Hall, chiefly responsible for its building. He will be among the dignitaries attending. Nothing could be more suitable for our purposes.'

'Is Sir William sure Neal is not part of the plot? Surely he cannot be ignorant of the contraband in his cellar?'

'That is the very reason Sir William thinks he is not involved. If he knew the place was to be blown up, he would have arranged for it to removed. The place has been watched day and night, and no such activity has taken place.'

I look at him, brow furrowed in thought. 'I cannot say I am happy about this business. There is something that doesn't feel right. Do you not think that, Liam?'

'Experience has taught me not to question Sir William's plans, Will,' says he, rising. 'Regardless of whatever feelings you may have, I would advise you to do the same.'

As he goes, I ask if he discovered anything from following Bridget yesterday.

He expresses surprise. 'You saw me?'

'Aye, going towards Custom House Quay. I had half a mind to follow her, too.'

'A pity you didn't - for, not many minutes after, I lost sight of her hard by the Custom House itself. I could not figure where she had gone - there are so many side streets. But then, there she was heading once more for the bridge.'

'Going to her brother?'

'Mayhap - but I did not find out. For at that moment I all but ran into Richard Semple. Of course, we could not acknowledge each other and, by the time we had exchanged apologies as strangers, the little minx had completely disappeared.'

By now we are on the pavement outside the front door. 'I am sure Sean is holed up somewhere with his butcher-boy friends. And Bridget must have told him I brought Kitty and Kenneth to your house after he tried to drown me.' I point to the boarded-up windows. 'I think the damage you see here is by way of a warning.'

Liam puts a hand on my shoulder. 'Then take care, Will Archer. I have saved your life once. I am none too eager to save it again!'

29

Messiah

Tuesday 13th April 1742 - the day of *The Messiah*...

Mr Sheridan arrives mid-morning. 'Upwards of seven hundred are expected,' he tells us breathlessly.

I think of that hall, crammed with so many - and of the conspirators in the cellar beneath. It is difficult to share his excitement.

Mr Garrick attributes my moroseness to the fact that Sean Kelly may still be after me. I have not told him or any of my friends that Kelly is a far greater danger than they can possibly imagine.

My master intends to walk to the Music Hall with Mr Sheridan and Mistress Peg. He suggests I join them but I decline.

'Miss Eugenie Acres has asked me to escort her, sir. I am to meet her there. Ned will accompany me, so you need have no fears for my safety.'

Although Ned is not attending the concert, he has offered to be my bodyguard on the way there. Once I am safely delivered into Eugenie's care, as he puts it, he will go off to meet Kitty.

Shortly after one-o'clock, we set off. The concert is advertised to start at two.

On the way my mind is only half attentive to Ned's banter. My eyes and ears are alert for signs of anything out of the ordinary. Nicholas Street is its usual afternoon self. So is Skinners Row.

Only as we approach the southern end of Fishamble Street do we see anything different from a normal Tuesday. In front of us, along Castle Street and beyond to Bedford Square, the way is blocked with coaches and chairs. More coaches stretch away to our right up Werburgh Street.

The air resounds with the neighing of horses and rough cries of coachmen and chairmen. In several places, fine gentlemen and ladies are alighting from their vehicles, resolved to walk the last few yards rather than stew in the melee.

Progress along Fishamble Street is slow. The few coaches that have found their way here are now at a standstill, unable to advance or retreat. Between them and the buildings on either side is a mass of bodies all making their way at snail's pace towards the Music Hall.

The chaos and confusion has done little, however, to dampen the anticipation of the crowd. The street, vibrant with many-coloured silks and velvets, is alive with excited chatter and laughter,. It seems the whole beau monde of Dublin is gathered in this spot.

I wait with Ned on the corner of Castle Street and Werburgh Street, for it is from this direction that Eugenie will come.

Sure enough, it is not many minutes before she arrives, accompanied by Liam.

'Why, Will,' she cries, 'what confusion is here! Is it not exciting? Come give me your arm. I fear I may be swept away in the flood!'

'Well, ma'am,' growls Liam, 'now you have your beau, I'll be off.'

Giving me a curt nod, he mingles quickly with the crowd, elbowing his way through, towards the Music Hall.

Eugenie shakes her head affectionately. 'Such a cross-patch! I do not know why I put up with him, to be sure.'

After a few civil words Ned also takes his leave, his protective escort role fulfilled. 'Your safety lies in numbers,' he whispers encouragingly. 'He will attempt nothing here.'

The irony of his words does not escape me.

As we draw nearer, I crane my neck to glance towards *The Bull's Head*. The door is firm shut and the windows dark. I can see no sign of Hervey's men. But that, I suppose, is to be expected - for if I were to notice them, so could Kelly and his associates.

And now we are inside the Music Hall and taking our seats. The hall, as I have said, is in the shape of an elongated horseshoe. At its open end, the orchestra is already assembled, the choir of men and choirboys in their best surplices behind them. Mistress Cibber and Madame Avoglio, the two soloists are not yet present. They, I presume will come on with Mr Handel.

Eugenie and I have seats on the left side of the hall on the second tier. Hervey has done his job well, for from here I have an excellent view of Finn Kelly who is busy tuning his violin in the foremost row of musicians.

Surely he could not look so calm if he knows of his brother's desperate plan?

All three tiers of seats along the sides and back of the Hall are now almost full and the murmur of anticipatory chatter has grown to a din over which Eugenie and I have to raise our voices to hear each other.

317

A dozen or so ornate chairs in the centre are as yet unoccupied - seats for the charity benefactors and civic dignitaries I suppose.

Situated, if I am correct, immediately above the spot where Sean Kelly may even now be setting his gunpowder charge...

Roving over the audience, my eye is caught by a black-clad figure seated on the first tier to the right of the entrance.

As if at some secret signal, he raises his head and our eyes lock for a brief moment. With a grim smile, Nathaniel Grey gives the barest of nods and averts his gaze.

Then, of a sudden, a hush descends as various figures make their way to the unoccupied seats. Murmuring flows gently back as people whisper to each other the names and ranks of those assembling and it is with a start of surprise that I see Sir William Hervey among their number. I see him look back over his shoulder to where Grey is sitting. Then he looks straight at me. His expression does not change. Only an eyebrow twitches.

Beside me, Eugenie gives a small shiver. 'What a forbidding-looking man,' she whispers in my ear. 'He does not look charitable in the least!'

'I did not notice,' say I pretending to search. 'Which man do you mean?'

But before she can reply, there is an exclamation of appreciation followed by a smattering of hand-claps.

Mr Sheridan is helping Dr Swift to the seat of honour at the front. The old man shuffles with bent shoulders but, when Mr Sheridan murmurs something in his ear, he turns and raises a frail hand in acknowledgement of the acclaim.

Once he is seated, the applause dies away, only to burst out again with renewed energy as Mr Handel himself appears escorting his two lady soloists.

The maestro waits until they are seated and the audience has quietened. Then, from his seat at the harpsichord he raises a hand and the Overture begins.

My attention is on Finn Kelly in the front row of the orchestra. Like his companions, his body sways with the stately rhythm of the opening bars and his face expresses emotion during the Overture's final plaintive chords. There is nothing to suggest he knows anything of what is being planned below.

Last time I heard this at the rehearsal several days ago, I had not remarked how busy the violinists were. But there they are, now the steady heart-beat accompanying the choir, now entering into a kind of dialogue with the soloists, now hurrying, now hushed...

More than the singers, the strings dictate the pace, the mood, the drama of the oratorio.

I begin to lose myself in this glorious music. A glance at Eugenie tells me she is the same. She sits slightly forward, attentive, her face rapt.

By the time the first of the ladies rises to tell us a virgin shall conceive and bear a son, I have all but forgot that her servant, Liam, is presently beneath our feet ready to apprehend Sean Kelly in the act of setting a charge which could cause havoc amongst the hundreds of people here assembled.

But then the music turns dark and ominous. The Bass soloist begins to sing of darkness covering the earth and I have a sudden vision of broken bodies, severed limbs and the cries of the dying -

all these fine silks and satins stained with the blood of the innocent...

I have an almost overwhelming urge to leap from my seat and run from the Hall - to satisfy myself that the villain is taken. But in this press of people such a notion is futile. I must sit and wait.

I summon reason to still my heart.

Sean cannot be so unnatural to detonate the explosion whilst there is risk of injuring his brother. Surely he will wait until the orchestra retire at the interval - until Finn is away from the main force of the blast?

The Oratorio has now reached familiar ground - the shepherds abiding in the field - and I know that Part One is almost over. But to my anxious mind, the music now seems not noble and stately, but plodding. The joyous announcement of our saviour's birth brings me no solace.

I look around me. Eugenie, still entranced, has almost without my realising it laid her hand on mine. At the front of the audience, the old Dean has apparently nodded off. A few rows behind him, Sir William listens intently, head cocked on one side. *Is he perhaps trying to hear sounds from below?* His minion, Grey, sits , stone-faced, at the back of the Hall.

And Finn Kelly, eyes closed in rapture, strokes his bow across the strings of his instrument, emitting sounds sweet as honey.

'*Come unto him that are heavy laden,*' sing the two ladies, '*and He will give you rest.*'

But rest is far from my thoughts at the moment.

As the chorus jogs its way through *His yoke is easy, and his burden light* and into the finale of Part One, I feel panic rising.

The last chords of *Behold the Lamb of God* die away, signalling the interval. Before Mr Handel, risen from the keyboard, has finished acknowledging the applause, I am pushing my way towards the door.

Approaching the tunnel between the raised tiers at the back of the hall, I see that Grey is already absent from his seat.

Several members of the audience have risen and are making their way out to take the air. They amble slowly, blocking my way. I weave my way as quickly as politeness allows, but still earn censorious remarks.

At last I am out into the small yard that lies between the street and the entrance to the Hall.

As I come into Fishamble Street, I think I see Grey's black coat ten yards or so away. He is in deep conversation with a workman in a leather apron. One of Hervey's men no doubt, set to observe *The Bull's Head*.

A glance along the street shows a lone coachman leaning against his hackney. He chats with a street sweeper. In the other direction, a ribbon-seller undeterred by lack of customers.

How easy it is now to pick out the spies!

But it is not those out here who are my concern. In a few quick strides I am at the door of *The Bull's Head*. The windows are still blank, the interior dark.

Only a written notice stands stark white pinned to the door. *This establishment will be closed on Tuesday 13th April. Business as usual from 14th inst.*

I try the handle.

It turns.

Holding my breath I ease the door open.

Then I am startled by a familiar voice behind me.

'Why, Will, this is very ungentlemanly, to run off so...'

But Eugenie gets no further for suddenly she is propelled forward, knocking me off balance.

I fall into the bar-room of *The Bull's Head.*

In the gloom I trip over a stool and go sprawling with a clatter.

By the time I scramble to my feet, Eugenie is before me, alarm in her eyes.

But it is not my clumsiness that causes her consternation

The man who pushed her in is now behind her, pinioning her throat with his forearm. A stick of some sort dangles from his hand. For the moment I cannot see his face, as he bends to search in his coat pocket.

Then he straightens and mystery of the stick is revealed.

With one deft movement, Finn Kelly uses a small penknife to sever the horsehair on his violin bow. Then stretching the loose threads and winding the ends around the shaft of the bow, he twists it to form a garotte around Eugenie's slender white neck.

Fear spreads icy down my spine.

'Finn,' I plead, 'there is no need for this. The lady is innocent, she has done you no harm. Release her.'

He looks at me, disappointed, as with an errant child. 'What, and have her run squawking 'Murder' out into the street? You jest, Master Archer. No, the lady stays. She chose to follow you. Now, unfortunately, she must share your fate. Move towards the cellar, if you please.'

I plant my feet firm. Apart from the penknife, he has no weapon that I can see.

'I will not - except you let her go.'

'Rash...' he says with a grim smile. He presses the point of the small blade to Eugenie's white throat. A bead of blood blooms ruby red.

I feel anger rising.

In pricking her delicate flesh thus he has let the garotte slacken, but I am still too far away to do anything. My slightest move could prove fatal for Eugenie.

What has frightened me, however, has made her bold.

Wincing from the pull of the horsehair, she twists forward and away from the knife-blade. With one delicate foot, she stamps her sharp heel into his shoe. The shock makes him loosen his hold momentarily. It is a critical error, for she bends forward, breaking his grip entirely, and punches her fists backwards - hard into his groin.

Finn doubles over with a gasp of pain. The violin bow and the knife clatter to the floor.

With admirable speed, Eugenie spins about and with most unladylike precision seizes hold of his privates and, thrusting her other hand under his chin, shoves him backwards and cracks his skull against the wall.

I start forward to her aid. But I am arrested mid-stride for at that very moment the muzzle of a pistol is thrust against my temple.

'Nay, Englishman - stay where you are. And you, madam, release my brother, if you please. Unless you wish to see Master

323

Archer's brains plastered upon the wall...'

For a moment, Eugenie looks defiant, refusing to loose her hold. Finn's face is ashen with pain.

At my ear Sean cocks the pistol.

With a toss of her head and one last twist that causes Finn to yelp, Eugenie releases her grip, letting Finn slump to the floor.

Covering us with the pistol, Sean motions her to join me. He, meanwhile, circles slowly towards his brother. Without taking his eyes off us, he helps Finn to his feet.

Then he bids us move towards the cellar door.

We have no option but to obey.

'The lady first,' growls Sean. 'And no tricks!'

Hitching her skirt above her ankles, Eugenie treads carefully down the narrow stair.

The cellar is lit by a single taper and in its flickering glow the first thing that meets our gaze is Liam.

He is propped unconscious against one of the squat brick pillars, gagged, hands and feet bound. Across his forehead a trickle of blood.

With a small cry, Eugenie rushes to him and kneels beside him.

It is not the injured footman who takes my attention, however.

Looking further into the cellar, into the area beneath the concert hall, I see that the kegs of gunpowder are in position. From the top of each projects a short fuse, perhaps a foot long and, set ready on the ground beside them, flint and tinder.

I look about for sign of Sean Kelly's two cronies, but there is no-one else in the cellar. The glory, it seems, is to belong to the brothers alone!

A brief muttered conversation between the brothers results in Sean handing Finn the pistol.

He then disappears into the shadows and returns with a length of the contraband silk which he proceeds to rip into strips.

'You and the doxy are an unlooked for complication, Master Archer. I had not expected company other than the spy there,' says he with a nod towards the unconscious Liam. Then, with a crooked smile, 'You will not, I hope, object to silken bonds rather than honest hemp?'

As Finn holds the pistol within a foot of my face, Sean binds my hands behind me.

'What do you hope to gain from this?' I ask him. 'Maiming and killing innocent people?'

'Innocent, say you?

Unexpectedly, it is not Sean who replies, but his brother, Finn. 'No, Master Archer, no one in the hall above us is innocent. All have the blood of true Irishmen upon their hands, the murder of women and children upon their consciences. They may not, as Dr Swift jested, have actually eaten our babes in arms, but they have just as surely fed off our land and done their utmost to destroy us.'

Finn speaks calmly with a reasonableness that is more chilling than Sean's passion. There is no anger here - just cold hatred.

'So you would destroy them - and have their deaths upon your conscience? You would see children lose their fathers, see husbands and wives, brothers and sisters rent asunder?'

Finn permits himself a cold smile. 'You are eloquent, Will. But your sympathies are misplaced. Most there are lackeys of the

325

English - the military, the politicians, the overseers. Cut one down today, another will grow tomorrow.'

'And Dr Swift?' I say as Sean pushes me down and starts to tie my ankles. 'He is no English lackey- he has proved himself a friend to the Irish, has he not? But you would snuff out a mind like his? And what of Mr Handel - would you deprive the world of more masterpieces like the *Messiah*?'

'There must be casualties in any war. And make no mistake, this is a war - a struggle for our freedom. Yet I cannot but think the good Dean would appreciate the irony of dying in the cause he has espoused for so long. And as for Herr Handel - can he ever surpass this present work? I have had the privilege of being part of it and know how great a piece it is. Who knows? We may be doing him a favour - cut off at the pinnacle of his achievement, he will never suffer the ignominy of comparison!'

'I doubt he would see it that way,' I say as Sean roughly drags me across to a pillar and props me against it. 'So a week ago - the lucky chance of your being at the rehearsal when a replacement violinist was needed - that was no coincidence? '

'We needed someone in the orchestra - someone to attend rehearsals and ascertain the length of pieces, the loud and soft passages, so that our little surprise could be timed to perfection. And hark...' He lifts his eyes, attentive to the sounds on the floor above. '...the audience reassembles! A moment, whilst the maestro notes the absence of one of his violinists - then, though irritated, decides the performance must continue... And... yes, there is Madame Avoglio...'

Sure enough, from above comes the melancholy opening of

He was despised and rejected of men.

Finn draws his watch from his waistcoat pocket. 'By my reckoning, we have just a little over half an hour.'

Sean has pulled Eugenie away from cradling Liam and stroking his forehead and is now tying her up, too.

She looks at Finn with contempt. 'You are a blackguard, Finn Kelly. You and your brother both. After all we did for you, to repay us thus!'

'Believe me, Miss Acres,' says Finn, 'I am not ungrateful. It pains me that you are here. Not least for the injury to my person that I have sustained from your presence! But none of us, unfortunately, can escape what fate has in store for us.'

'Like murdering my brother?'

Finn inclines his head apologetically. 'Indeed, that was a necessary part of our plan. And one which I make so bold as to suggest was no less beneficial for you than it was for us. His death released you from an unpalatable betrothal. At the same time it gained me access to the orchestra and facilitated our way into this cellar...'

'Of course! You work for Mr Callaghan who manages the wine business for Miss Acres,' I exclaim. 'With Tobias out of the way, and John Callaghan busy with the funeral arrangements, you could arrange for your brother to deliver the explosives along with the liquor supplies to *The Bull's Head* without arousing anyone's suspicions.'

'Apart from yours, it seems,' replies Finn. 'Sean did not expect to be noticed. But then you saw him... And I regret to say, he took matters into his own hands.'

327

'Sure, and if you'd stayed at the bottom of the river like you was supposed to,' interrupts Sean, tying the last knot in Eugenie's bonds, 'then you wouldn't be here now - and nor would Miss Acres. So you've no-one to blame but yourself for the lady's predicament.'

'Now,' says Finn, lowering the pistol, 'I think the time for talking is over. And to dissuade either of you from any further rashness...' He nods to Sean, who uses the last of the silk to gag us with.

Leaving us propped against the pillars, the two brothers walk apart. I can hear little of their muted conversation. But I gather that Finn wants Sean to check upon those watching up above.

I presume he must mean the two Irish ruffians who are Sean's confederates.

But then something that Sean said earlier comes back to me.

He talked of not expecting *other company than the spy...*

They must know, then, that they were being watched. But do they know by whom?

Sean must surely have recognised Liam. Bridget works with him. But does he merely think the guards who want to apprehend him for the attempt on my life have paid Liam to inform on his whereabouts?

Or do they know their whole plot is discovered?

As Sean creeps quietly up the cellar stairs, I wonder if they have any suspicion that Liam is more than he seems?

From the calm way in which Finn perches himself upon a barrel and nods along to the strains of the music that come faintly through the boards above, I cannot think he suspects.

And that gives me hope. I glance across at Eugenie. Her eyes move restlessly around the room. Behind her back, out of Finn's line of sight, I see her wrists surreptitiously scraping against the rough edge of the brickwork.

Suddenly her eyes meet mine and the silent message is clear. By whatever means, we must escape! I, too, start rubbing my bonds along the rough edge of the pillar.

A groan from the other side of the cellar makes us pause momentarily. Liam has awakened from his stupor.

At first he looks blearily about him, but then realisation dawns. He begins to squirm and utter muffled protests through his gag. Then he sees Eugenie. His eyes widen in amazement and his efforts redouble. His muffled cries become frantic.

Finn, shaken from his appreciation of the distant music strides across and strikes him across the face with the back of his hand.

The blow, however, is half-hearted and only makes Liam struggle more.

I can see that Finn, not as naturally violent as his brother, is at a loss what to do. He, after all, is only the originator of the plan. It is Sean and his cronies who have the actual blood on their hands.

He looks desperately towards the staircase, hoping for his brother's return.

This diversion is to my advantage. Gritting my teeth against the tearing of my flesh, I saw my bonds furiously against the rough edge - and feel the silk begin to part...

But just as my hopes rise, there is the sound of feet at the top of the stairs and Sean bursts, half running and half falling into the cellar.

'We are discovered, brother,' he cries. 'Set the charge now, Finn, or we are lost..!'

Finn falls upon the tinder box and scrambles desperately for a spark.

But Sean is before him. Seizing the flaring taper that lights the cellar, he pushes his brother aside and touches it to the two fuses.

Immediately they spark into spluttering life.

Behind her gag, I hear Eugenie's muffled cry. Her eyes are terrified. I arch my back, straining to lift myself from the pillar to get to her.

Meanwhile, Sean grabs Finn's arm and drags him towards the staircase. The sputtering taper in his hand sets up a demonic dance of shadows in the underground chamber.

But before they reach the bottom step, the door at the top is slammed open and the bulky figure of Ciaran O'Dowd, my would-be nemesis, stumbles in.

'Get out of here, boys - the guards...'

He says no more.

A shot rings out and he pitches forward down the staircase, his face a mask of shock. The dead weight of his falling body collides with the brothers, knocking them asunder and extinguishing the taper.

Around me I hear scuffling and panting, interlaced with curses. But I can see nothing save the deceptively innocent twinkling of the two fuses.

Staggering to my feet, I hop and jump towards them, wriggling my hands to free them from the last threads of my silken bonds.

In the dark I collide with a body and the air is punched from my lungs as I am sent sprawling.

Fighting for breath through my gag, I raise my head to see that the fuses are half burnt away. Only a few inches are left - a minute at most.

I struggle to my feet and lurch towards the kegs of powder. Strong hands seize my ankles, bringing me crashing down again. Fortunately my hands are free and break my fall.

I kick out with all my strength and hear the satisfying crunch of bone and a muffled curse in Irish. The grip on my feet slackens and I am able to reach out for the glittering fuses which now are burned nearly to the wood.

With balled fists I thump at the spitting stubs, but they refuse to be extinguished. Ignoring the burning pain, I grasp first one, then the other, wrench them out of the kegs and fling them away.

Like demented fireflies, they wriggle a while on the floor, then expire.

In the pitch dark, a tense blanket of silence descends. before, from the concert hall above, comes a sudden glorious burst of *Hallelujahs!*

30
Coda

For what seems an age I lie panting on the earthen floor of the cellar, the bitter reek of burnt cord in my nostrils. I have not even the strength to remove the gag from my mouth.

Then, of a sudden, the place is filled with light. I screw my eyes against the glare.

When I open them again, I see that the light is not so great. It merely seemed so in contrast to the pitch blackness.

Coming down the staircase, holding a lantern, is Nathaniel Grey. Behind him, Sir William Hervey.

Grey holds the lantern aloft and shines it on the kegs of powder.

'The plot is foiled, Sir William - but the birds, it seems, have flown.'

'Never mind that,' replies Hervey. 'See to these.'

Grey puts the lantern down, goes over to Eugenie and begins untying her restraints.

Meanwhile, Hervey comes to me. 'A pretty pickle, Master Archer, to be sure!'

Kneeling, he works at the knots about my ankles whilst I loosen my gag.

'Miss Acres,' I gasp as soon as I am able, 'is she unharmed?'

'See for yourself,' says Sir William, rising and moving from my line of sight as he frees my ankles.

Sure enough, Eugenie is on her feet, apparently none the worse for her ordeal. I, too, leap to my feet intending, despite of all decorum, to take her into my arms.

But she gives me scarcely a glance, running instead to sink beside Liam. Tenderly she removes his gag and runs her hand through his hair whilst Grey unties the ropes around his hands and feet.

Sir William cannot help but notice the shock on my face. 'Reconcile yourself to disappointment, Will,' he murmurs, not unkindly. 'The lady is not for you.'

He strides across to them. 'Well, Donovan, what transpired here?'

'We were betrayed, milord. Kelly surprised me in the bar above. He was in hiding, waiting for me.'

'Aye,' says Hervey picking up one of the ropes with which Liam was bound, 'he came prepared. And there is but one person who could have apprised him of our intentions.' He turns to me. 'Is that not so, Master Archer?'

I am at a loss for words. 'I...I..but it was not me..!'

I stutter into silence at the accusation in their four faces.

Then Sir William's face creases into a smile. 'Not you, Will, I know that. You are a Yorkshireman, true-bred. You keep your own counsel at times - which is annoying - but you are no traitor. No, the viper in our midst was Semple. He and Sean Kelly, both working at the Custom House, must have been in each other's confidence. It would not surprise me if it were he who was responsible for Kelly's attempt on your life.'

So much now seems clear. Sean's unconvincing denial when I

333

asked him about Semple. His unaccountable change from friendliness to hostility...

'But if you knew he was a traitor, why include him in the discussion of our plans at Mr Kennedy's?' I ask in indignation. 'You deliberately put Liam in peril...'

'Have a care, Master Archer,' warns Grey.

'Nay, Nathaniel, the boy is right. If we *had* known at that point, it would have been truly remiss of me to endanger Donovan. But the fact is, Will, that I did not know. Only now has it become clear,' Sir William replies. 'What is *not* clear is how these two firebrands who were here but a few moments ago have managed to elude us. They did not pass us on the stairs...'

My nose supplies the answer. Now that the smell of the fuses has cleared from my nostrils, another all-too-familiar stink has wormed its way into my senses.

I lead them across to where the ceiling collapsed under the dung-heap. Sure enough, amidst the stinking debris, there is a hole wide enough for a man - or two men - to pass through.

'This leads out into the yard at the rear of the inn,' I tell them. 'They will have escaped over the back fence.'

'No matter. We will catch them soon enough. And Semple, too.'

Through the ceiling of the cellar comes the sound of trumpets, then a deep bass voice, *The trumpet shall sound, and the dead shall be raised...*

'The Oratorio is nearly finished,' says Sir William. 'It is time we were out of here.'

So, with instructions to Grey to see to the removal of

334

O'Dowd's body, we make our way up into *The Bull's Head* and out into the open air.

Two days later *Sir Harry Wildair* opens to universal acclaim. Mistress Peg's return to her home city is accounted a triumph and Mr Garrick's reputation is assured.

After the performance, Eugenie comes backstage to congratulate me upon my small role as Remnant the tailor. She has taken up Mr Garrick's offer of a box for the season and is in company with Liam.

'Sure, Master Archer, it is a hidden talent you have, so,' says Liam with a broad grin.

His attire, I notice sourly, is much improved of late. Gone is the tattered footman's livery. He is now the proper gentleman with velvet coat and embroidered waistcoat.

Eugenie, noting my coolness, regards me in silence for a moment. Her eyes are sad.

'Come, Will,' she says, 'you did not really think that you and I...? It could never be.'

'No, of course,' I reply, finding it hard to keep the bitterness out of my voice, 'it would not do for a fine lady to marry a jobbing actor.'

'Fie, you are jealous!' She takes my hand in hers and holds hard when I attempt to withdraw it. 'Now listen to me, Will Archer, and be not so petulant! Mayhap you think my morals lax to favour Liam so. Indeed I had cause to doubt myself before I knew the truth.'

'The truth?'

'Liam is no footman, no humble servant, but a gentleman born.'

'As I was about to tell you at Mr Kennedy's the other day before Sir William stopped me,' says he. 'My family's lands were stolen by English landlords, our fortune sequestered on trumped-up charges. In seeking to right the wrongs visited upon my family, I became a fugitive and near landed in prison. How Sir William came to hear of my misfortune, I know not. But two years ago he sought me out...'

It is the way Hervey works, I think to myself as Liam continues his story. *He will have those who work for him in his debt through some misdemeanour or misfortune in their past. In my case it is my time at Mother Ransom's and two deaths of which, though innocent, I might still be accused.*

Liam tells how the price of Hervey's intercession with the authorities was to become a servant in the Acres household. His task, to glean what information he could about the mysterious insurrectionist known as *the fiddler* who at the time they suspected to be Tobias Acres.

'I knew nothing of this, you understand,' Eugenie interrupts. My impending forced marriage to John Callaghan consumed my thoughts. Liam provided the only comfort in my distress. It mattered not that he was a mere footman - he was the only one to show me any humanity. And for that he earned my gratitude,' she continues, smiling fondly upon him. 'Despite myself, and wrong though I knew it to be, that gratitude turned to affection - and affection to love.'

'And all this time Liam never revealed himself to you?'

'Never - till now. Having escaped being the pawn in my brother's machinations, I faced the prospect of becoming a social outcast as the mistress who fell in love with her servant. Which is why I voluntarily cast off ladylike behaviour before any might accuse me!' she says with a trill of laughter.

Her high spirits melt my disappointment. 'Certainly your retaliation against Finn Kelly could not be called ladylike,' I say slyly.

'Ah, if my twin Tobias taught me anything in our growing up, it was the vulnerability of male anatomy in the art of underhand fighting! You both do right to be wary of crossing me!'

I turn to Liam raising an eyebrow. 'And you intend to marry this harpy?'

'So she will have me now my fortune is restored,' says he, taking her hand.

And, looking at the pair of them gazing into each other's eyes with such affection, I cannot help but think they are a perfect match.

The day before the last performance of *Sir Harry Wildair* a messenger comes to Lamb Alley with a note from Sir William Hervey.

Mrs Fitzgerald delivers it into my hands herself, all eagerness to know who should be writing to a mere servant and on such fine paper.

I refuse, politely, to satisfy her curiosity and she retires disgruntled.

The note summons me to meet Hervey at Mr Kennedy's.

337

I arrive to find him, Nathaniel Grey and Liam Donovan seated around the fire. Although the afternoon outside is warm with the promise of summer, the dark interior holds a chill all its own.

'Semple is taken,' says Sir William without preliminaries, 'and has confessed all. Including that it was he who stored the contraband silks and linens in Mr Neal's cellar, that worthy gentleman believing all to be legal and above board - as how should he not, being approached by an official from the Custom House itself?'

'He is under arrest, then?' I ask.

Sir William strokes his chin thoughtfully. 'Let us say we have him incarcerated. Though for how long I cannot say. Ideally he should be transferred to London - but the way is perilous...'

Aye, I think, *mayhap there'll be another body for Paddy Rafferty to fish out of the Liffey before long. Semple knows too much to go to trial.*

'And the Kelly brothers?' asks Liam.

'Gone, I'm afraid. These Irish have a way of spiriting away their own.' He nods towards me, 'Like that cousin of your fair colleague, Miss Blair. They are probably aboard ship for Europe to fight in King George's war.'

'For which side, I wonder?' murmurs Grey.

'But on that matter,' continues Sir William more brightly, 'I have put in a word with the Commander of the garrison, Will. The gentleman you mentioned has been released without charge.'

'I thank you, sir. Miss Blair's aunt will be greatly relieved.'

'So, gentlemen,' booms Sir William, slapping his thigh, 'I think we may congratulate ourselves upon a job well done!'

338

'Even though the perpetrators are still abroad, sir?'

'Abroad, but no longer a present danger. Oh, I have no doubt there will be others to take their place, but that is in the nature of things. Swat one fly from the dung-heap and others will land - to be swatted in their turn.'

'Unless Parliament comes up with a more equitable system of government for the Irish,' I suggest.

'Tut, Will, such subversive sentiments are tantamount to treason. It is fortunate that we are the only ones to hear them. But, whatever our view on the shortcomings of our politicians, it is still our job to maintain, in our humble way, the safety of the realm.'

He raises his glass, 'And that, gentlemen, is a sentiment I feel we should drink to.'

Hervey's is not the only note I receive today.

When I return to Lamb Lane, Mr Garrick is waiting for me in the parlour. Amongst letters forwarded to him from England is one addressed to me.

'It was delivered to our old lodgings and was some days in arriving at our new quarters in Bow Street,' he says apologetically. 'I trust it does not contain ill news.'

If it does, I am destined not to discover it yet, for at that very moment Ned and Kitty arrive and she is a-brim with excitement.

So much so that she cannot forbear taking me in her arms and planting a delighted kiss upon my cheek. Ned's face, too, is wreathed in smiles.

'Why, Kitty,' says Mistress Peg, 'are we all to be let in on this cause for celebration?'

339

'Will is an angel!'

'Praise indeed!' laughs Mr Garrick. 'But surely we knew that already?' he adds with a twinkle.

'He has prevailed upon Miss Acres to give permanent employment to Kenneth!' She takes my arm and parades with me around the room. 'You remember that surly dog of a footman? Well, it appears he has given his notice, so Kenneth is to have his place - and here was I expecting him to be a boot-boy only! Such good fortune, and well above his deserts, but he will grow into it in time, I am sure. And that is not all!'

'Yet more angelic intervention?' says Mr Garrick archly.

'Oh, Will!' Another kiss to increase my embarrassment. 'The lady is to be married!'

'Miss Acres - to whom?' I ask, all innocence.

Kitty waggles a dismissive hand, 'Oh, I don't know, that's not important! It seems her downstairs maid - that sad trollop who served us tea - has upped and left without warning. So Miss Acres requires not just one, but *two* new maids on account of her impending marriage.'

'Don't tell me,' I say, 'your two girl cousins..?'

'Cleonagh and Bridie - she asked for them specially. So, Will Archer,' she says, flopping down at last in a rustle of lace and satin, 'what do you think of that!'

'I am very happy for them, Kitty - and you deserve much credit for finding them such good positions.'

Ned claps me upon the back. 'Tush, Will, the credit is all yours, man!' he says. Then, as her lip begins to tremble, 'And Kitty knows it, too. It is because you know Miss Acres that all this has come about.' He bends close and whispers in my ear. 'Be advised, take the praise when you can get it. The minx is so perverse, she'll likely be blaming you for depriving Aunt Bronagh of her children tomorrow!'

'And Aunt Bronagh,' I hazard, 'is she pleased?'

'I know not. I haven't heard from her since Kenneth went off this morning to tell her the news.'

I restrain myself from telling her that Kenneth is likely to return with news that Aunt Bronagh's husband is restored to them. I fear Kitty may kiss me to death!

Once Ned and Kitty have departed, Mr Garrick and Mistress Peg begin their preparations for this evening's performance and I go up to my room to read my letter.

As I break the seal and unfold it, my heart skips a beat. I recognise a hand I have not seen for many a long year. It is my mother's.

She informs me that she is coming to London to see me on a matter of great importance but gives no hint as to what it may be.

Remembering what Mr Garrick said about the delay in forwarding it, I glance in alarm at the date. It is two weeks ago and her journey to London is the day after tomorrow!

I take the stairs two at a time and burst into the parlour.

Mr Garrick looks up, irritated. He always likes a hour of quiet before a performance.

I show him the letter and he agrees that I must take passage at once.

My time in Ireland is over.

341

Historical Notes

The Smock Alley Theatre

The first Smock Alley Theatre was built in 1662. It was the second purpose built theatre in Ireland. However, poor foundations and slapdash building led to a series of collapses in 1670, 1701 and 1734. The following year, it was totally demolished and rebuilt. This is the theatre that figures in this book.

Thomas Sheridan, godson of Jonathon Swift (and later father to Richard Brinsley Sheridan) was the manager. After the triumph of Garrick's *Richard III* in the autumn of 1741 in London, Sheridan invited him and Peg Woffington (with whom he was having an affair at the time) over to Ireland for the 1742 season. It was at Smock Alley that Garrick first played *Hamlet.*

Handel's Messiah

The Messiah was first performed in Dublin on April 13th 1742. In early March Handel began discussions with the appropriate committees for a charity concert and was given permission from St Patrick's and Christ Church cathedrals to use their choirs which amounted to 16 men and 16 boy choristers; several of the men were allocated solo parts. The women soloists were Christina Maria Avoglio and Susannah Cibber, an established stage actress.

The three charities that were to benefit were prisoners' debt relief, the Mercer's Hospital, and the Charitable Infirmary. The performance, in the Fishamble Street hall, was originally announced for 12 April, but was deferred for a day "at the request of persons of Distinction". Seven hundred people attended the premiere on 13 April. So that the largest possible audience could be admitted to the concert, gentlemen were requested to remove their swords, and ladies were asked not to wear hoops in their dresses.

The performance earned unanimous praise and raised around £400, providing about £127 to each of the three nominated charities and securing the release of 142 indebted prisoners.

Fact and Fiction

As in the first Will Archer mystery, *Archer Bows In,* characters are a mixture of real historical figures – Garrick, Peg Woffington, Thomas Sheridan, Jonathon Swift and George Frederick Handel – and those of my own creation. Facts about real-life persons are, to the best of my knowledge, accurate. The rest is, of course made up!

Acknowledgements

James Kelly
The Liberty and Ormond Boys: Factional riot in eighteenth century Dublin
Four Courts Press

- and the young man (whose name I have unfortunately forgotten!) who works at the present-day Smock Alley Theatre and was kind enough to show me round, confirm and add to my knowledge of its history, and show me what remains of the original walls that Will Archer would have been seen in 1742!

16881236R00195

Printed in Poland
by Amazon Fulfillment
Poland Sp. z o.o., Wrocław